Short Stories About Youth & Adolescence

COMING OF AGE

Bruce Emra

National Textbook Company
a division of *NTC Publishing Group* • Lincolnwood, Illinois USA

Bruce Emra teaches English at Northern Highlands Regional High School in Allendale, New Jersey. Like several of the writers in this book, as a high school student he won a Scholastic Writing Award for a short story.

Credits for literary selections: See page 291, which is an extension of the copyright page.

1996 Printing

Published by National Textbook Company, a division of NTC Publishing Group.
© 1994 by NTC Publishing Group, 4255 West Touhy Avenue,
Lincolnwood (Chicago), Illinois 60646-1975 U.S.A.
Library of Congress Catalog Card Number 93–83538
Manufactured in the United States of America.

5 6 7 8 9 0 VP 9 8 7 6 5 4

To the Memory of
Robert S. Berlin

Associate Professor Emeritus, School of Education
New York University

Who taught me to think about my students
as people with feelings
not just intellects

Thanks to the following people for suggestions about and help with this book: Svea Barrett-Tarleton, Anne Bigelow, Zitta Chapman, Faye Conrad, Christopher deVinck, Andy Dunn, Jim Gartenlaub, Pat Riccobene, and Karin Emra.

And thanks to three superb editors: Jane Bachman, John Nolan, and Sue Schumer.

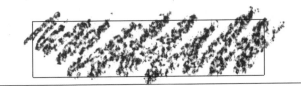

Preface

*Children ten years old wake up and find themselves here, discover
themselves to have been here all along; is this sad? They wake like
sleepwalkers, in full stride; they wake like people brought back from
cardiac arrest or from drowning:* in media res, *surrounded by
familiar people and objects, equipped with a hundred skills. They
know the neighborhood, they can read and write English, they are
old hands at the commonplace mysteries, and yet they feel themselves
to have just stepped off the boat, just converged with their bodies, just
flown down from a trance, to lodge in an eerily familiar life already
well under way.*

*I woke in bits, like all children, piecemeal over the years. I
discovered myself and the world, and forgot them, and discovered
them again. I woke at intervals until, by that September when
Father went down the river, the intervals of waking tipped the scales,
and I was more often awake than not. I noticed this process of
waking, and predicted with terrifying logic that one of these years
not far away I would be awake continuously and never slip back,
and never be free of myself again.*

—Annie Dillard, from *An American Childhood*

Are *you* now "awake" continuously? Are you taking in the world constantly and reacting to the infinite variety of the world constantly?

This book will help you. You will find yourself in many of these
stories, and maybe you will "find yourself" in a larger sense, too. In
ancient Greece "know thyself" was a principal commandment; "know
thyself" should be the personal goal of each of *us,* too.

Every story in this book has been selected because it will help to
further awaken you. There are stories about young people with parents,
with brothers and sisters, with friends, with loves, and out in the world.

In every Part of *Coming of Age* there is an award-winning story written by a young man or woman. These stories in particular might inspire your own writing. After all, Beth Cassavell, Frederick Pollack, Susie Kretschmer, and Amy Boesky all started with a blank piece of paper.

Start reading. You will find yourself—in more ways than one—in these pages.

Bruce Emra

CONTENTS

PART ONE   DO I FIT IN?   1

"Eleven"   3
  Sandra Cisneros

"The Secret Lion"   7
  Alberto Alvaro Ríos

"A Mother in Mannville"   14
  Marjorie Kinnan Rawlings

"Raymond's Run"   23
  Toni Cade Bambara

"Two Kinds"   32
  Amy Tan

"Louisa, Please Come Home"   45
  Shirley Jackson

*"The Man in the Casket"   62
  Beth Cassavell

Responding to Part One   67

PART TWO   FAMILIES AND FRIENDS   69

"Adjö Means Good-bye"   71
  Carrie A. Young

"A Christmas Memory"   76
  Truman Capote

"The Scarlet Ibis"   89
James Hurst

"Sucker"   102
Carson McCullers

"A Private Talk with Holly"   113
Henry Gregor Felsen

"Shaving"   117
Leslie Norris

"Guess What? I Almost Kissed My Father Goodnight"   125
Robert Cormier

"Marigolds"   137
Eugenia Collier

*"Asphalt"   147
Frederick Pollack

Responding to Part Two   155

PART THREE   FALLING IN LOVE   **157**

"Her First Ball"   159
Katherine Mansfield

"The Bass, the River, and Sheila Mant"   167
W. D. Wetherell

"The Osage Orange Tree"   175
William Stafford

"Surprised"   183
Catherine Storr

"I Go Along"   190
Richard Peck

"Broken Chain"   197
Gary Soto

*"And Summer Is Gone"   206
Susie Kretschmer

Responding to Part Three   211

PART FOUR   OUT IN THE WORLD   **213**

"A Visit of Charity"   215
Eudora Welty

*"A Veil of Water"   223
Amy Boesky

"Teenage Wasteland"   228
    Anne Tyler
"Initiation"   239
    Sylvia Plath
"Betty"   250
    Margaret Atwood
"On the Late Bus"   267
    Susan Engberg
"A Walk to the Jetty"   276
    Jamaica Kincaid
Responding to Part Four   289

Index of Authors and Titles   293

*Student-written story

Do I Fit In?

*W*hat adolescent hasn't wondered about his or her place in the classroom, in the grade, in the school—and in the larger world? We are all on a continual search for who we are.

The characters in the seven short stories in this section have varying questions about their places in the world. The narrator in "Two Kinds" and Raymond in "Raymond's Run" may be different ages, different sexes, and from very different backgrounds, but they both are struggling with questions of, "Am I OK? Do I fit in? What will be my place in this world?"

As you read these stories, you will meet various people facing questions of identity. And you will be given a number of chances to create your own writing that deals with these great questions of who we are.

Eleven

Sandra Cisneros

Poet Gwendolyn Brooks called Sandra Cisneros "one of the most brilliant of today's young writers." Cisneros won an American Book Award from the Before Columbus Foundation in 1985 for The House on Mango Street, *a collection of sketches and stories, and a Lannan Literary Award in 1991.*

Her other books include My Wicked, Wicked Ways *(1987), a book of poetry, and* Women Hollering Creek and Other Stories *(1991).*

Cisneros was born in 1954 in Chicago to a Mexican father and a Mexican-American mother. She has been a teacher, poet in the schools, college recruiter, and an arts administrator. She lives in San Antonio, Texas.

What they don't understand about birthdays and what they never tell you is that when you're eleven, you're also ten, and nine, and eight, and seven, and six, and five, and four, and three, and two, and one. And when you wake up on your eleventh birthday you expect to feel eleven, but you don't. You open your eyes and everything's just like yesterday, only it's today. And you don't feel eleven at all. You feel like you're still ten. And you are—underneath the year that makes you eleven.

Like some days you might say something stupid, and that's the part of you that's still ten. Or maybe some days you might need to sit on your mama's lap because you're scared, and that's the part of you that's five. And maybe one day when you're all grown up maybe you will need to cry like if you're three, and that's okay. That's what I tell Mama when she's sad and needs to cry. Maybe she's feeling three.

Because the way you grow old is kind of like an onion or like the rings inside a tree trunk or like my little wooden dolls that fit one inside the other, each year inside the next one. That's how being eleven years old is.

You don't feel eleven. Not right away. It takes a few days, weeks even, sometimes even months before you say Eleven when they ask you. And you don't feel smart eleven, not until you're almost twelve. That's the way it is.

Only today I wish I didn't have only eleven years rattling inside me like pennies in a tin Band-Aid box. Today I wish I was one hundred and two instead of eleven because if I was one hundred and two I'd have known what to say when Mrs. Price put the red sweater on my desk. I would've known how to tell her it wasn't mine instead of just sitting there with that look on my face and nothing coming out of my mouth.

"Whose is this?" Mrs. Price says, and she holds the red sweater up in the air for all the class to see. "Whose? It's been sitting in the coatroom for a month."

"Not mine," says everybody. "Not me."

"It has to belong to somebody," Mrs. Price keeps saying, but nobody can remember. It's an ugly sweater with red plastic buttons and a collar and sleeves all stretched out like you could use it for a jump rope. It's maybe a thousand years old and even if it belonged to me I wouldn't say so.

Maybe because I'm skinny, maybe because she doesn't like me, that stupid Sylvia Saldívar says, "I think it belongs to Rachel." An ugly sweater like that, all raggedy and old, but Mrs. Price believes her. Mrs. Price takes the sweater and puts it right back on my desk, but when I open my mouth nothing comes out.

"That's not, I don't, you're not . . . Not mine," I finally say in a little voice that was maybe me when I was four.

"Of course it's yours," Mrs. Price says. "I remember you wearing it once." Because she's older and the teacher, she's right and I'm not.

Not mine, not mine, not mine, but Mrs. Price is already turning to page thirty-two, and math problem number four. I don't know why but all of a sudden I'm feeling sick inside, like the part of me that's three wants to come out of my eyes, only I squeeze them shut tight and bite down on my teeth real hard and try to remember today I am eleven, eleven. Mama is making a cake for me for tonight, and when Papa comes home everybody will sing Happy birthday, happy birthday to you.

But when the sick feeling goes away and I open my eyes, the red sweater's still sitting there like a big red mountain. I move the red sweater to the corner of my desk with my ruler. I move my pencil and books and eraser as far from it as possible. I even move my chair a little to the right. Not mine, not mine, not mine.

In my head I'm thinking how long till lunchtime, how long till I can take the red sweater and throw it over the schoolyard fence, or leave it hanging on a parking meter, or bunch it up into a little ball and toss it in the alley. Except when math period ends Mrs. Price says loud and in front of everybody, "Now, Rachel, that's enough," because she sees I've shoved the red sweater to the tippy-tip corner of my desk and it's hanging all over the edge like a waterfall, but I don't care.

"Rachel," Mrs. Price says. She says it like she's getting mad. "You put that sweater on right now and no more nonsense."

"But it's not—"

"Now!" Mrs. Price says.

This is when I wish I wasn't eleven, because all the years inside of me—ten, nine, eight, seven, six, five, four, three, two, and one—are pushing at the back of my eyes when I put one arm through one sleeve of the sweater that smells like cottage cheese, and then the other arm through the other and stand there with my arms apart like if the sweater hurts me and it does, all itchy and full of germs that aren't even mine.

That's when everything I've been holding in since this morning, since when Mrs. Price put the sweater on my desk, finally lets go, and all of a sudden I'm crying in front of everybody. I wish I was invisible but I'm not. I'm eleven and it's my birthday today and I'm crying like I'm three in front of everybody. I put my head down on the desk and bury my face in my stupid clown-sweater arms. My face all hot and spit coming out of my mouth because I can't stop the little animal noises from coming out of me, until there aren't any more tears left in my eyes, and it's just my body shaking like when you have the hiccups, and my whole head hurts like when you drink milk too fast.

But the worst part is right before the bell rings for lunch. That stupid Phyllis Lopez, who is even dumber than Sylvia Saldívar, says she remembers the red sweater is hers! I take it off right away and give it to her, only Mrs. Price pretends like everything's okay.

Today I'm eleven. There's a cake Mama's making for tonight, and when Papa comes home from work we'll eat it. There'll be candles and presents and everybody will sing Happy birthday, happy birthday to you, Rachel, only it's too late.

I'm eleven today. I'm eleven, ten, nine, eight, seven, six, five, four, three, two, and one, but I wish I was one hundred and two. I wish I was anything but eleven, because I want today to be far away already, far away like a runaway balloon, like a tiny *o* in the sky, so tiny-tiny you have to close your eyes to see it.

Responding to the Story

1. What does the narrator mean when she says, "When you're eleven, you're also ten, and nine, and eight, and seven, and six, and five, and four, and three, and two, and one"? Do you think her reasoning makes sense? Explain.

2. Why does the narrator wish this day—her birthday, a day that should be happy—would be "far away already"?

3. Are the narrator's feelings this day recognizable to you—believable?

Exploring the Author's Craft

A first-person narrator is a character in a story who can reveal only his or her impressions, feelings, and thoughts. In a story told from the *first-person point of view* ("I"), the narrator is often very compelling; we can be lured into caring about the narrator's concerns and maybe even identify with the narrator.

1. What is the narrator of "Eleven" like? Describe her personality.

2. Is this an accurate portrait of someone turning eleven? Why or why not?

3. In a story told from a first-person point of view, are we likely to know what the other characters are really thinking? Why or why not?

Writing Workshop

Create a first-person narrator and tell about something that happened to that person. Have the character establish his or her age early in your narration of this event. You might begin by jotting down events that you have heard someone in your family tell about.

The Secret Lion

Alberto Alvaro Ríos

Alberto Alvaro Ríos is a professor of English at Arizona State University in Tempe and lives in Chandler, Arizona. He was born in 1952 in Nogales, Arizona, of a Mexican father and an English mother. He has degrees in English and psychology and attended law school at the University of Arizona.

He has written both poetry and short fiction. He won the Walt Whitman Award from the Academy of American Poets for Whispering to Fool the Wind *(1982), and a Western States Book Award for* The Iguana Killer: Twelve Stories of the Heart *(1984). In addition, he has written* Teodoro Luna's Two Kisses *(1990), a book of poetry.*

I was twelve and in junior high school and something happened that we didn't have a name for, but it was there nonetheless like a lion, and roaring, roaring that way the biggest things do. Everything changed. Just like that. Like the rug, the one that gets pulled—or better, like the tablecloth those magicians pull where the stuff on the table stays the same but the gasp! from the audience makes the staying-the-same part not matter. Like that.

What happened was there were teachers now, not just one teacher, teach-erz, and we felt personally abandoned somehow. When a person had all these teachers now, he didn't get taken care of the same way, even though six was more than one. Arithmetic went out the door when we walked in. And we saw girls now, but they weren't the same girls we used to know because we couldn't talk to them anymore, not the same way we used to, certainly not to Sandy, even though she was my neighbor, too. Not even to her. She just played the piano all the time. And there were words, oh there were words in junior high school,

and we wanted to know what they were, and how a person did them—
that's what school was supposed to be for. Only, in junior high school,
school wasn't school, everything was backwardlike. If you went up to
a teacher and said the word to try and find out what it meant you got
in trouble for saying it. So we didn't. And we figured it must have
been that way about other stuff, too, so we never said anything about
anything—we weren't stupid.

But my friend Sergio and I, we solved junior high school. We would
come home from school on the bus, put our books away, change shoes,
and go across the highway to the arroyo.[1] It was the one place we were
not supposed to go. So we did. This was, after all, what junior high had
at least shown us. It was our river, though, our personal Mississippi,
our friend from long back, and it was full of stories and all the branch
forts we had built in it when we were still the Vikings of America, with
our own symbol, which we had carved everywhere, even in the sand,
which let the water take it. That was good, we had decided; whoever
was at the end of this river would know about us.

At the very very top of our growing lungs, what we would do down
there was shout every dirty word we could think of, in every combination
we could come up with, and we would yell about girls, and all the things
we wanted to do with them, as loud as we could—we didn't know what
we wanted to do with them, just things—and we would yell about teachers, and how we loved some of them, like Miss Crevelone, and how we
wanted to dissect some of them, making signs of the cross, like priests,
and we would yell this stuff over and over because it felt good, we
couldn't explain why, it just felt good and for the first time in our lives
there was nobody to tell us we couldn't. So we did.

One Thursday we were walking along shouting this way, and the
railroad, the Southern Pacific, which ran above and along the far side
of the arroyo, had dropped a grinding ball down there, which was, we
found out later, a cannonball thing used in mining. A bunch of them
were put in a big vat which turned around and crushed the ore. One
had been dropped, or thrown—what do caboose men do when they get
bored—but it got down there regardless and as we were walking along
yelling about one girl or another, a particular Claudia, we found it, one
of these things, looked at it, picked it up, and got very very excited, and
held it and passed it back and forth, and we were saying, "Guythisis,
this is, geeGuythis . . .": we had this perception about nature then,

---

1. *arroyo* (ə roi′ō): a small stream or creek. [Spanish]

that nature is imperfect and that round things are perfect: we said, "GuyGodthis is perfect, thisisthis is perfect, it's round, round and heavy, it'sit's the best thing we'veeverseen. Whatisit?" We didn't know. We just knew it was great. We just, whatever, we played with it, held it some more.

And then we had to decide what to do with it. We knew, because of a lot of things, that if we were going to take this and show it to anybody, this discovery, this best thing, was going to be taken away from us. That's the way it works with little kids, like all the polished quartz, the tons of it we had collected piece by piece over the years. Junior high kids too. If we took it home, my mother, we knew, was going to look at it and say, "Throw that dirty thing in the, get rid of it." Simple like, like that. "But ma it's the best thing I" "Getridofit." Simple.

So we didn't. Take it home. Instead, we came up with the answer. We dug a hole and we buried it. And we marked it secretly. Lots of secret signs. And came back the next week to dig it up and, we didn't know, pass it around some more or something, but we didn't find it. We dug up that whole bank, and we never found it again. We tried.

Sergio and I talked about that ball or whatever it was when we couldn't find it. All we used were small words, neat, good. Kid words. What we were really saying, but didn't know the words, was how much that ball was like that place, that whole arroyo: couldn't tell anybody about it, didn't understand what it was, didn't have a name for it. It just felt good. It was just perfect in the way it was that place, that whole going to that place, that whole junior high school lion. It was just iron-heavy, it had no name, it felt good or not, we couldn't take it home to show our mothers, and once we buried it, it was gone forever.

The ball was gone, like the first reasons we had come to that arroyo years earlier, like the first time we had seen the arroyo, it was gone like everything else that had been taken away. This was not our first lesson. We stopped going to the arroyo after not finding the thing, the same way we had stopped going there years earlier and headed for the mountains. Nature seemed to keep pushing us around one way or another, teaching us the same thing every place we ended up. Nature's gang was tough that way, teaching us stuff.

When we were young we moved away from town, me and my family. Sergio's was already out there. Out in the wilds. Or at least the new place seemed like the wilds since everything looks bigger the smaller a man is. I was five, I guess, and we had moved three miles north of

Nogales,[2] where we had lived, three miles north of the Mexican border. We looked across the highway in one direction and there was the arroyo; hills stood up in the other direction. Mountains, for a small man.

When the first summer came the very first place we went to was of course the one place we weren't supposed to go, the arroyo. We went down in there and found water running, summer rainwater mostly, and we went swimming. But every third or fourth or fifth day, the sewage treatment plant that was, we found out, upstream, would release whatever it was that it released, and we would never know exactly what day that was, and a person really couldn't tell right off by looking at the water, not every time, not so a person could get out in time. So, we went swimming that summer and some days we had a lot of fun. Some days we didn't. We found a thousand ways to explain what happened on those other days, constructing elaborate stories about neighborhood dogs, and hadn't she, my mother, miscalculated her step before, too? But she knew something was up because we'd come running into the house those days, wanting to take a shower, even—if this can be imagined—in the middle of the day.

That was the first time we stopped going to the arroyo. It taught us to look the other way. We decided, as the second side of summer came, we wanted to go into the mountains. They were still mountains then. We went running in one summer Thursday morning, my friend Sergio and I, into my mother's kitchen, and said, well, what'zin, what'zin those hills over there—we used her words so she'd understand us—and she said nothingdon'tworryabout it. So we went out, and we weren't dumb, we thought with our eyes to each other, ohhoshe'stryingtokeep somethingfromus. We knew adults.

We had read the books, after all; we knew about bridges and castles and wildtreacherousraging alligatormouth rivers. We wanted them. So we were going to go out and get them. We went back that morning into that kitchen and we said, "We're going out there, we're going into the hills, we're going away for three days, don't worry." She said, "All right."

"You know," I said to Sergio, "if we're going to go away for three days, well, we ought to at least pack a lunch."

But we were two young boys with no patience for what we thought at the time was mom-stuff: making sa-and-wiches. My mother didn't offer. So we got our little kid knapsacks that my mother had sewn

---

2. *Nogales* (nō gal′əs): city in northwest Mexico, across the border from Nogales, Arizona.

for us, and into them we put the jar of mustard. A loaf of bread. Knivesforksplates, bottles of Coke, a can opener. This was lunch for the two of us. And we were weighed down, humped over to be strong enough to carry this stuff. But we started walking, anyway, into the hills. We were going to eat berries and stuff otherwise. "Goodbye." My mom said that.

After the first hill we were dead. But we walked. My mother could still see us. And we kept walking. We walked until we got to where the sun is straight overhead, noon. That place. Where that is doesn't matter; it's time to eat. The truth is we weren't anywhere close to that place. We just agreed that the sun was overhead and that it was time to eat, and by tilting our heads a little we could make that the truth.

"We really ought to start looking for a place to eat."

"Yeah. Let's look for a good place to eat." We went back and forth saying that for fifteen minutes, making it lunch time because that's what we always said back and forth before lunch times at home. "Yeah, I'm hungry all right." I nodded my head. "Yeah, I'm hungry all right too. I'm hungry." He nodded his head. I nodded my head back. After a good deal more nodding, we were ready, just as we came over a little hill. We hadn't found the mountains yet. This was a little hill.

And on the other side of this hill we found heaven.

It was just what we thought it would be.

Perfect. Heaven was green, like nothing else in Arizona. And it wasn't a cemetery or like that because we had seen cemeteries and they had gravestones and stuff and this didn't. This was perfect, had trees, lots of trees, had birds, like we had never seen before. It was like *The Wizard of Oz*, like when they got to Oz and everything was so green, so emerald, they had to wear those glasses, and we ran just like them, laughing, laughing that way we did that moment, and we went running down to this clearing in it all, hitting each other that good way we did.

We got down there, we kept laughing, we kept hitting each other, we unpacked our stuff, and we started acting "rich." We knew all about how to do that, like blowing on our nails, then rubbing them on our chests for the shine. We made our sandwiches, opened our Cokes, got out the rest of the stuff, the salt and pepper shakers. I found this particular hole and I put my Coke right into it, a perfect fit, and I called it my Coke-holder. I got down next to it on my back, because everyone knows that rich people eat lying down, and I got my sandwich in one hand and put my other arm around the Coke in its holder. When I wanted a drink, I lifted my neck a little, put out my lips, and tipped my Coke a little with the crook of my elbow. Ah.

We were there, lying down, eating our sandwiches, laughing,

throwing bread at each other and out for the birds. This was heaven. We were laughing and we couldn't believe it. My mother *was* keeping something from us, ah ha, but we had found her out. We even found water over at the side of the clearing to wash our plates with—we had brought plates. Sergio started washing his plates when he was done, and I was being rich with my Coke, and this day in summer was right.

When suddenly these two men came, from around a corner of trees and the tallest grass we had ever seen. They had bags on their backs, leather bags, bags and sticks.

We didn't know what clubs were, but I learned later, like I learned about the grinding balls. The two men yelled at us. Most specifically, one wanted me to take my Coke out of my Coke-holder so he could sink his golf ball into it.

Something got taken away from us that moment. Heaven. We grew up a little bit, and couldn't go backward. We learned. No one had ever told us about golf. They had told us about heaven. And it went away. We got golf in exchange.

We went back to the arroyo for the rest of that summer, and tried to have fun the best we could. We learned to be ready for finding the grinding ball. We loved it, and when we buried it we knew what would happen. The truth is, we didn't look so hard for it. We were two boys and twelve summers then, and not stupid. Things get taken away.

We buried it because it was perfect. We didn't tell my mother, but together it was all we talked about, till we forgot. It was the lion.

Responding to the Story

1. Why do the narrator and his friend cross the highway and go to the arroyo?

2. How is the missing ball "like that place, that whole arroyo"?

3. What does the sentence "They were still mountains then" mean?

4. In a paragraph, describe the way you think the narrator looks at the age of twelve.

5. Why do you think the story has the title it does?

Exploring the Author's Craft

Tone is an author's attitude about his or her subject. A tone can be humorous or angry, serious or satirical about a topic. What is the tone of "The Secret Lion"? Give examples from the story to back up your answer.

Writing Workshop

Imagine that you are one of the boys who has stumbled on the place that was "green, like nothing else in Arizona." What are your feelings at discovering and existing for a while in this place? What makes this place special? List as many nouns and adjectives as you can to describe the place and the emotions it evokes. Then turn this list into a poem.

Alternate Media Response

1. Draw a map that captures the world these boys live in. Give places a size and importance that is relative to the importance those places play in the boys' lives when they are twelve. Be able to justify everything in your drawing.

2. Write a script for a video dramatization of this story. Do not use a narrator to communicate the author's ideas; everything must be communicated through what is seen or spoken by the characters. Produce this video dramatization of "The Secret Lion."

A Mother in Mannville

Marjorie Kinnan Rawlings

Born in 1896 and raised in Washington, D.C., Marjorie Kinnan Rawlings moved to Madison, Wisconsin, with her mother and brother in 1914, a year after her father died. She received her B.A. degree from the University of Wisconsin in 1918, and in 1919 married Charles A. Rawlings and moved to Rochester, New York, where both worked as journalists.

In an act that was to influence her whole writing career, she and her husband bought an orange grove in Cross Creek, Florida. Her first novel, South Moon Under, *was a story of the Florida scrub country and the people she had come to know there. It was published in 1933, the year of her divorce from Rawlings.*

Encouraged by the success of South Moon Under, *her editor urged her to "do a book about a child in the scrub, which would be designed for what we have come to call younger readers." Rawlings finally got around to writing that book in 1936, and she sent the manuscript of* The Yearling, *a book about a boy and his pet fawn, to Scribner's in December 1937. The book was on the best-seller list for two years and won a Pulitzer Prize. It was made into a movie in 1946 and is still in print.*

In 1941 Rawlings remarried, and in 1942 her autobiography, Cross Creek, *was published. (This too was filmed, in 1983.) Rawlings wrote more novels, but none ever matched the success of* The Yearling.

Tiring of summers in Florida, she bought a house in New York state in 1947 and spent summers there until her death in 1953 in St. Augustine, Florida. She is buried in Island Grove, Florida.

The orphanage is high in the Carolina mountains. Sometimes in winter the snowdrifts are so deep that the institution is cut off from the village below, from all the world. Fog hides the mountain peaks, the snow swirls down the valleys, and a wind blows so bitterly that the orphanage boys who take the milk twice daily to the baby cottage reach the door with fingers stiff in agony of numbness.

"Or when we carry trays from the cookhouse for the ones that are sick," Jerry said, "we get our faces frostbit, because we can't put our hands over them. I have gloves," he added. "Some of the boys don't have any."

He liked the late spring, he said. The rhododendron was in bloom, a carpet of color, across the mountainsides, soft as the May winds that stirred the hemlocks. He called it laurel.

"It's pretty when the laurel blooms," he said. "Some of it's pink and some of it's white."

I was there in the autumn. I wanted quiet, isolation, to do some troublesome writing. I wanted mountain air to blow out the malaria from too long a time in the subtropics. I was homesick, too, for the flaming of maples in October, and for corn shocks and pumpkins and black-walnut trees and the lift of hills. I found them all, living in a cabin that belonged to the orphanage, half a mile beyond the orphanage farm. When I took the cabin, I asked for a boy or man to come and chop wood for the fireplace. The first few days were warm, I found what wood I needed about the cabin, no one came, and I forgot the order.

I looked up from my typewriter one late afternoon, a little startled. A boy stood at the door, and my pointer dog, my companion, was at his side and had not barked to warn me. The boy was probably twelve years old, but undersized. He wore overalls and a torn shirt, and was barefooted.

He said, "I can chop some wood today."

I said, "But I have a boy coming from the orphanage."

"I'm the boy."

"You? But you're small."

"Size don't matter, chopping wood," he said. "Some of the big boys don't chop good. I've been chopping wood at the orphanage a long time."

I visualized mangled and inadequate branches for my fires. I was well into my work and not inclined to conversation. I was a little blunt.

"Very well. There's the ax. Go ahead and see what you can do."

I went back to work, closing the door. At first the sound of the boy dragging brush annoyed me. Then he began to chop. The blows were rhythmic and steady, and shortly I had forgotten him, the sound no more of an interruption than a consistent rain. I suppose an hour and a half passed, for when I stopped and stretched, and heard the boy's steps on the cabin stoop, the sun was dropping behind the farthest mountain, and the valleys were purple with something deeper than the asters.

The boy said, "I have to go to supper now. I can come again tomorrow evening."

I said, "I'll pay you now for what you've done," thinking I should probably have to insist on an older boy. "Ten cents an hour?"[1]

"Anything is all right."

We went together back of the cabin. An astonishing amount of solid wood had been cut. There were cherry logs and heavy roots of rhododendron, and blocks from the waste pine and oak left from the building of the cabin.

"But you've done as much as a man," I said. "This is a splendid pile."

I looked at him, actually, for the first time. His hair was the color of the corn shocks and his eyes, very direct, were like the mountain sky when rain is pending—gray, with a shadowing of that miraculous blue. As I spoke, a light came over him, as though the setting sun had touched him with the same suffused glory with which it touched the mountains. I gave him a quarter.

"You may come tomorrow," I said, "and thank you very much."

He looked at me, and at the coin, and seemed to want to speak, but could not, and turned away.

"I'll split kindling tomorrow," he said over his thin ragged shoulder. "You'll need kindling and medium wood and logs and backlogs."

At daylight I was half wakened by the sound of chopping. Again it was so even in texture that I went back to sleep. When I left my bed in the cool morning, the boy had come and gone, and a stack of kindling was neat against the cabin wall. He came again after school in the afternoon and worked until time to return to the orphanage. His name was Jerry; he was twelve years old, and he had been at the orphanage since he was four. I could picture him at four, with the same grave gray-blue eyes and the same—independence? No, the word that comes to me is "integrity."

The word means something very special to me, and the quality for which I use it is a rare one. My father had it—there is another of whom I am almost sure—but almost no man of my acquaintance possesses it with the clarity, the purity, the simplicity of a mountain stream. But the boy Jerry had it. It is bedded on courage, but it is more than brave.

---

1. *ten cents an hour*: This was a reasonable amount in the 1930s when the cost of things was much less than today.

It is honest, but it is more than honesty. The ax handle broke one day. Jerry said the woodshop at the orphanage would repair it. I brought money to pay for the job and he refused it.

"I'll pay for it," he said. "I broke it. I brought the ax down careless."

"But no one hits accurately every time," I told him. "The fault was in the wood of the handle. I'll see the man from whom I bought it."

It was only then that he would take the money. He was standing back of his own carelessness. He was a free-will agent and he chose to do careful work, and if he failed, he took the responsibility without subterfuge.[2]

And he did for me the unnecessary thing, the gracious thing, that we find done only by the great of heart. Things no training can teach, for they are done on the instant, with no predicated experience.[3] He found a cubbyhole beside the fireplace that I had not noticed. There, of his own accord, he put kindling and "medium" wood, so that I might always have dry fire material ready in case of sudden wet weather. A stone was loose in the rough walk to the cabin. He dug a deeper hole and steadied it, although he came, himself, by a short cut over the bank. I found that when I tried to return his thoughtfulness with such things as candy and apples, he was wordless. "Thank you" was, perhaps, an expression for which he had had no use, for his courtesy was instinctive. He only looked at the gift and at me, and a curtain lifted, so that I saw deep in the clear well of his eyes, and gratitude was there, and affection, soft over the firm granite of his character.

He made simple excuses to come and sit with me. I could no more have turned him away than if he had been physically hungry. I suggested once that the best time for us to visit was just before supper, when I left off my writing. After that, he waited always until my typewriter had been some time quiet. One day I worked until nearly dark. I went outside the cabin, having forgotten him. I saw him going up over the hill in the twilight toward the orphanage. When I sat down on my stoop, a place was warm from his body where he had been sitting.

He became intimate, of course, with my pointer, Pat. There is a strange communion between a boy and a dog. Perhaps they possess the same singleness of spirit, the same kind of wisdom. It is difficult to explain, but it exists. When I went across the state for a week end, I

---

2. *subterfuge* (sub´tėr fyüj): excuse.

3. *with no predicated experience*: That is, his actions were not based on experience.

left the dog in Jerry's charge. I gave him the dog whistle and the key to the cabin, and left sufficient food. He was to come two or three times a day and let out the dog, and feed and exercise him. I should return Sunday night, and Jerry would take out the dog for the last time Sunday afternoon and then leave the key under an agreed hiding place.

My return was belated and fog filled the mountain passes so treacherously that I dared not drive at night. The fog held the next morning, and it was Monday noon before I reached the cabin. The dog had been fed and cared for that morning. Jerry came early in the afternoon, anxious.

"The superintendent said nobody would drive in the fog," he said. "I came just before bedtime last night and you hadn't come. So I brought Pat some of my breakfast this morning. I wouldn't have let anything happen to him."

"I was sure of that. I didn't worry."

"When I heard about the fog, I thought you'd know."

He was needed for work at the orphanage and he had to return at once. I gave him a dollar in payment, and he looked at it and went away. But that night he came in the darkness and knocked at the door.

"Come in, Jerry," I said, "if you're allowed to be away this late."

"I told maybe a story," he said. "I told them I thought you would want to see me."

"That's true," I assured him, and I saw his relief. "I want to hear about how you managed with the dog."

He sat by the fire with me, with no other light, and told me of their two days together. The dog lay close to him, and found a comfort there that I did not have for him. And it seemed to me that being with my dog, and caring for him, had brought the boy and me, too, together, so that he felt that he belonged to me as well as to the animal.

"He stayed right with me," he told me, "except when he ran in the laurel. He likes the laurel. I took him up over the hill and we both ran fast. There was a place where the grass was high and I lay down in it and hid. I could hear Pat hunting for me. He found my trail and he barked. When he found me, he acted crazy, and he ran around and around me, in circles."

We watched the flames.

"That's an apple log," he said. "It burns the prettiest of any wood."

We were very close.

He was suddenly impelled to speak of things he had not spoken of before, nor had I cared to ask him.

"You look a little bit like my mother," he said. "Especially in the dark, by the fire."

"But you were only four, Jerry, when you came here. You have remembered how she looked, all these years?"

"My mother lives in Mannville," he said.

For a moment, finding that he had a mother shocked me as greatly as anything in my life has ever done, and I did not know why it disturbed me. Then I understood my distress. I was filled with a passionate resentment that any woman should go away and leave her son. A fresh anger added itself. A son like this one—The orphanage was a wholesome place, the executives were kind, good people, the food was more than adequate, the boys were healthy, a ragged shirt was no hardship, nor the doing of clean labor. Granted, perhaps, that the boy felt no lack, what blood fed the bowels of a woman who did not yearn over this child's lean body that had come in parturition[4] out of her own? At four he would have looked the same as now. Nothing, I thought, nothing in life could change those eyes. His quality must be apparent to an idiot, a fool. I burned with questions I could not ask. In any, I was afraid, there would be pain.

"Have you seen her, Jerry—lately?"

"I see her every summer. She sends for me."

I wanted to cry out, "Why are you not with her? How can she let you go away again?"

He said, "She comes up here from Mannville whenever she can. She doesn't have a job now."

His face shone in the firelight.

"She wanted to give me a puppy, but they can't let any one boy keep a puppy. You remember the suit I had on last Sunday?" He was plainly proud. "She sent me that for Christmas. The Christmas before that"—he drew a long breath, savoring the memory—"she sent me a pair of skates."

"Roller skates?"

My mind was busy, making pictures of her, trying to understand her. She had not, then, entirely deserted or forgotten him. But why, then—I thought, "I must not condemn her without knowing."

"Roller skates. I let the other boys use them. They're always borrowing them. But they're careful of them."

What circumstance other than poverty—

---

4. *parturition* (pärt ə rish′ ən): process of giving birth to an offspring.

"I'm going to take the dollar you gave me for taking care of Pat," he said, "and buy her a pair of gloves."

I could only say, "That will be nice. Do you know her size?"

"I think it's 8½," he said.

He looked at my hands.

"Do you wear 8½?" he asked.

"No, I wear a smaller size, a 6."

"Oh! Then I guess her hands are bigger than yours."

I hated her. Poverty or no, there was other food than bread, and the soul could starve as quickly as the body. He was taking his dollar to buy gloves for her big stupid hands, and she lived away from him, in Mannville, and contented herself with sending him skates.

"She likes white gloves," he said. "Do you think I can get them for a dollar?"

"I think so," I said.

I decided that I should not leave the mountains without seeing her and knowing for myself why she had done this thing.

The human mind scatters its interests as though made of thistle-down, and every wind stirs and moves it. I finished my work. It did not please me, and I gave my thoughts to another field. I should need some Mexican material.

I made arrangements to close my Florida place. Mexico immediately, and doing the writing there, if conditions were favorable. Then, Alaska with my brother. After that, heaven knew what or where.

I did not take time to go to Mannville to see Jerry's mother, nor even to talk with the orphanage officials about her. I was a trifle abstracted about the boy, because of work and plans. And after my first fury at her—we did not speak of her again—his having a mother, any sort at all, not far away, in Mannville, relieved me of the ache I had had about him. He did not question the anomalous[5] relation. He was not lonely. It was none of my concern.

He came every day and cut my wood and did small helpful favors and stayed to talk. The days had become cold, and often I let him come inside the cabin. He would lie on the floor in front of the fire, with one arm across the pointer, and they would both doze and wait quietly for me. Other days they ran with a common ecstasy through the laurel, and since the asters were now gone, he brought me back vermillion maple leaves, and chestnut boughs dripping with imperial yellow. I was ready to go.

---

5. *anomalous* (ə nom′ə ləs): unusual.

I said to him, "You have been my good friend, Jerry. I shall often think of you and miss you. Pat will miss you too. I am leaving tomorrow."

He did not answer. When he went away, I remember that a new moon hung over the mountains, and I watched him go in silence up the hill. I expected him the next day, but he did not come. The details of packing my personal belongings, loading my car, arranging the bed over the seat, where the dog would ride, occupied me until late in the day. I closed the cabin and started the car, noticing that the sun was in the west and I should do well to be out of the mountains by nightfall. I stopped by the orphanage and left the cabin key and money for my light bill with Miss Clark.

"And will you call Jerry for me to say good-by to him?"

"I don't know where he is," she said. "I'm afraid he's not well. He didn't eat his dinner this noon. One of the other boys saw him going over the hill into the laurel. He was supposed to fire the boiler this afternoon. It's not like him; he's unusually reliable."

I was almost relieved, for I knew I should never see him again, and it would be easier not to say good-by to him.

I said, "I wanted to talk with you about his mother—why he's here—but I'm in more of a hurry than I expected to be. It's out of the question for me to see her now too. But here's some money I'd like to leave with you to buy things for him at Christmas and on his birthday. It will be better than for me to try to send him things. I could so easily duplicate—skates, for instance."

She blinked her honest spinster's eyes.

"There's not much use for skates here," she said.

Her stupidity annoyed me.

"What I mean," I said, "is that I don't want to duplicate things his mother sends him. I might have chosen skates if I didn't know she had already given them to him."

She stared at me.

"I don't understand," she said. "He has no mother. He has no skates."

Responding to the Story

1. List four different things Jerry does that convince the narrator of both his integrity and his thoughtfulness.

2. Where in the story is the first reference to Jerry's not being his usual reliable self? What caused this change in him? How did you react toward Jerry at this moment in the story?

3. What do you think were Jerry's reasons for claiming to have a mother?

4. What did you feel as the story ended, and why do you think you felt this way?

Exploring the Author's Craft

1. The term *irony* refers to the difference between what appears to be and what really is. Situational irony occurs when what is expected in a literary work contrasts with what really happens. What is ironic about this story?

2. Why does the author end with the blunt declarative sentences, "He has no mother. He has no skates"? Why doesn't the author go on to tell what happened next?

Writing Workshop

Think of someone you know or a character you have read about. Put that person in a setting—real or imaginary—and think of what might happen to that person in that setting. Narrate two or three incidents, as Marjorie Kinnan Rawlings did, that reveal the character of that person.

Alternate Media Response

Draw or paint a picture of the narrator's face as you imagine her hearing the last words in the story.

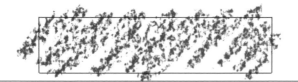

Raymond's Run

Toni Cade Bambara

Todi Cade Bambara has been praised for her ability to capture street talk and for her depiction of the love that exists in African-American families and communities. Born in 1939 in New York City, she was educated at <u>Queens College</u> and studied at the University of Florence and in Paris. Her works include Gorilla, My Love *(1972), a collection of short stories;* The Sea Birds Are Still Alive *(1977);* The Salt Eaters *(1980), a novel; and* If Blessing Comes *(1987). She has also written screenplays, among them "Raymond's Run," produced by PBS in 1985, and "The Bombing of Osage," for which she won the Best Documentary of 1986 Award from the Pennsylvania Association of Broadcasters and the Documentary Award from the National Black Programming Consortium. Ms. Bambara lives in Philadelphia.*

I don't have much work to do around the house like some girls. My mother does that. And I don't have to earn my pocket money by hustling; George runs errands for the big boys and sells Christmas cards. And anything else that's got to get done, my father does. All I have to do in life is mind my brother Raymond, which is enough.

Sometimes I slip and say my little brother Raymond. But as any fool can see he's much bigger and he's older too. But a lot of people call him my little brother cause he needs looking after cause he's not quite right. And a lot of smart mouths got lots to say about that too, especially when George was minding him. But now, if anybody has anything to say to Raymond, anything to say about his big head, they have to come by me. And I don't play the dozens[1] or believe in standing around with somebody in my face doing a lot of talking. I much rather just knock you down and take my chances even if I am a little girl with skinny arms and a squeaky voice, which is how I got the name Squeaky. And if things get too rough, I run. And as anybody can tell you, I'm the fastest thing on two feet.

There is no track meet that I don't win the first place medal. I used to win the twenty-yard dash when I was a little kid in kindergarten. Nowadays, it's the fifty-yard dash. And tomorrow I'm subject to run the quarter-meter relay all by myself and come in first, second, and third. The big kids call me Mercury[2] cause I'm the swiftest thing in the neighborhood. Everybody knows that—except two people who know better, my father and me. He can beat me to Amsterdam Avenue with me having a two fire-hydrant headstart and him running with his hands in his pockets and whistling. But that's private information. Cause can you imagine some thirty-five-year-old man stuffing himself into PAL shorts to race little kids? So as far as everyone's concerned, I'm the fastest and that goes for Gretchen, too, who has put out the tale that she is going to win the first-place medal this year. Ridiculous. In the second place, she's got short legs. In the third place, she's got freckles. In the first place, no one can beat me and that's all there is to it.

I'm standing on the corner admiring the weather and about to take a stroll down Broadway so I can practice my breathing exercises, and I've got Raymond walking on the inside close to the buildings, cause he's subject to fits of fantasy and starts thinking he's a circus performer and that the curb is a tightrope strung high in the air. And sometimes after a rain he likes to step down off his tightrope right into the gutter and slosh around getting his shoes and cuffs wet. Then I get hit when I get home. Or sometimes if you don't watch him he'll dash across traffic to the island in the middle of Broadway and give the pigeons a fit. Then I have to go behind him apologizing to all the old people sitting around trying to get some sun and getting all upset with the pigeons fluttering around them, scattering their newspapers and upsetting the waxpaper lunches in their laps. So I keep Raymond on the inside of me, and he plays like he's driving a stage coach which is O.K. by me so long as he doesn't run me over or interrupt my breathing

---

1. *play the dozens*: a game in which each of two persons tries to outdo the other in insults directed against members of the other's family.

2. *Mercury*: in Roman myth, the messenger of the gods, often pictured with a winged helmet.

exercises, which I have to do on account of I'm serious about my running, and I don't care who knows it.

Now some people like to act like things come easy to them, won't let on that they practice. Not me. I'll high-prance down 34th Street like a rodeo pony to keep my knees strong even if it does get my mother uptight so that she walks ahead like she's not with me, don't know me, is all by herself on a shopping trip, and I am somebody else's crazy child. Now you take Cynthia Procter for instance. She's just the opposite. If there's a test tomorrow, she'll say something like, "Oh, I guess I'll play handball this afternoon and watch television tonight," just to let you know she ain't thinking about the test. Or like last week when she won the spelling bee for the millionth time, "A good thing you got 'receive,' Squeaky, cause I would have got it wrong. I completely forgot about the spelling bee." And she'll clutch the lace on her blouse like it was a narrow escape. Oh, brother. But of course when I pass her house on my early morning trots around the block, she is practicing the scales on the piano over and over and over and over. Then in music class she always lets herself get bumped around so she falls accidently on purpose onto the piano stool and is so surprised to find herself sitting there that she decides just for fun to try out the ole keys. And what do you know— Chopin's[3] waltzes just spring out of her fingertips and she's the most surprised thing in the world. A regular prodigy.[4] I could kill people like that. I stay up all night studying the words for the spelling bee. And you can see me any time of day practicing running. I never walk if I can trot, and shame on Raymond if he can't keep up. But of course he does, cause if he hangs back someone's liable to walk up to him and get smart, or take his allowance from him, or ask him where he got that great big pumpkin head. People are so stupid sometimes.

So I'm strolling down Broadway breathing out and breathing in on counts of seven, which is my lucky number, and here comes Gretchen and her sidekicks: Mary Louise, who used to be a friend of mine when she first moved to Harlem from Baltimore and got beat up by everybody till I took up for her on account of her mother and my mother used to sing in the same choir when they were young girls, but people ain't grateful, so now she hangs out with the new girl Gretchen and talks about me like a dog; and Rosie, who is as fat as I am skinny and has a big mouth where Raymond is concerned and is too stupid to know that there is not a big deal of difference between herself and Raymond and

---

3. *Chopin* (shō′pan): Frédéric François (1810–1849): Polish composer and pianist.

4. *prodigy* (prod′ə jē): person, especially a child, who is remarkably talented.

that she can't afford to throw stones.[5] So they are steady coming up Broadway and I see right away that it's going to be one of those Dodge City scenes cause the street ain't that big and they're close to the buildings just as we are. First I think I'll step into the candy store and look over the new comics and let them pass. But that's chicken and I've got a reputation to consider. So then I think I'll just walk straight on through them or even over them if necessary. But as they get to me, they slow down. I'm ready to fight, cause like I said I don't feature a whole lot of chitchat, I much prefer to just knock you down right from the jump and save everybody a lotta precious time.

"You signing up for the May Day races?" smiles Mary Louise, only it's not a smile at all. A dumb question like that doesn't deserve an answer. Besides, there's just me and Gretchen standing there really, so no use wasting my breath talking to shadows.

"I don't think you're going to win this time," says Rosie, trying to signify with her hands on her hips all salty, completely forgetting that I have whupped her behind many times for less salt than that.

"I always win cause I'm the best," I say straight at Gretchen who is, as far as I'm concerned, the only one talking in this ventriloquist-dummy routine. Gretchen smiles, but it's not a smile, and I'm thinking that girls never really smile at each other because they don't know how and don't want to know how and there's probably no one to teach us how, cause grown-up girls don't know either. Then they all look at Raymond who has just brought his mule team to a standstill. And they're about to see what trouble they can get into through him.

"What grade you in now, Raymond?"

"You got anything to say to my brother, you say it to me, Mary Louise Williams of Raggedy Town, Baltimore."

"What are you, his mother?" sasses Rosie.

"That's right, Fatso. And the next word out of anybody and I'll be *their* mother too." So they just stand there and Gretchen shifts from one leg to the other and so do they. Then Gretchen puts her hands on her hips and is about to say something with her freckle-face self but doesn't. Then she walks around me looking me up and down but keeps walking up Broadway, and her sidekicks follow her. So me and Raymond smile at each other and he says, "Gidyap" to his team and I continue with my breathing exercises, strolling down Broadway toward the ice

---

5. *can't afford to throw stones*: An allusion to the expression "People who live in glass houses shouldn't throw stones," meaning that one can't afford to criticize another for a fault that one also has.

man on 145th with not a care in the world cause I am Miss Quicksilver herself.

I take my time getting to the park on May Day because the track meet is the last thing on the program. The biggest thing on the program is the May Pole dancing, which I can do without, thank you, even if my mother thinks it's a shame I don't take part and act like a girl for a change. You'd think my mother'd be grateful not to have to make me a white organdy dress with a big satin sash and buy me new white baby-doll shoes that can't be taken out of the box till the big day. You'd think she'd be glad her daughter ain't out there prancing around a May Pole getting the new clothes all dirty and sweaty and trying to act like a fairy or a flower or whatever you're supposed to be when you should be trying to be yourself, whatever that is, which is, as far as I am concerned, a poor Black girl who really can't afford to buy shoes and a new dress you only wear once a lifetime cause it won't fit next year.

I was once a strawberry in a Hansel and Gretel pageant when I was in nursery school and didn't have no better sense than to dance on tiptoe with my arms in a circle over my head doing umbrella steps and being a perfect fool just so my mother and father could come dressed up and clap. You'd think they'd know better than to encourage that kind of nonsense. I am not a strawberry. I do not dance on my toes. I run. That is what I am all about. So I always come late to the May Day program, just in time to get my number pinned on and lay in the grass till they announce the fifty-yard dash.

I put Raymond in the little swings, which is a tight squeeze this year and will be impossible next year. Then I look around for Mr. Pearson, who pins the numbers on. I'm really looking for Gretchen if you want to know the truth, but she's not around. The park is jam-packed. Parents in hats and corsages and breast-pocket handkerchiefs peeking up. Kids in white dresses and light-blue suits. The parkees unfolding chairs and chasing the rowdy kids from Lenox as if they had no right to be there. The big guys with their caps on backwards, leaning against the fence swirling the basketballs on the tips of their fingers, waiting for all these crazy people to clear out the park so they can play. Most of the kids in my class are carrying bass drums and glockenspiels and flutes. You'd think they'd put in a few bongos or something for real like that.

Then here comes Mr. Pearson with his clipboard and his cards and pencils and whistles and safety pins and fifty million other things he's always dropping all over the place with his clumsy self. He sticks out in a crowd because he's on stilts. We used to call him Jack and the Beanstalk to get him mad. But I'm the only one that can outrun him and get away, and I'm too grown for that silliness now.

"Well, Squeaky," he says, checking my name off the list and handing me number seven and two pins. And I'm thinking he's got no right to call me Squeaky, if I can't call him Beanstalk.

"Hazel Elizabeth Deborah Parker," I correct him and tell him to write it down on his board.

"Well, Hazel Elizabeth Deborah Parker, going to give someone else a break this year?" I squint at him real hard to see if he is seriously thinking I should lose the race on purpose just to give someone else a break. "Only six girls running this time," he continues, shaking his head sadly like it's my fault all of New York didn't turn out in sneakers. "That new girl should give you a run for your money." He looks around the park for Gretchen like a periscope in a submarine movie. "Wouldn't it be a nice gesture if you were . . . to ahhh . . ."

I give him such a look he couldn't finish putting that idea into words. Grownups got a lot of nerve sometimes. I pin number seven to myself and stomp away, I'm so burnt. And I go straight for the track and stretch out on the grass while the band winds up with "Oh, the Monkey Wrapped His Tail Around the Flag Pole," which my teacher calls by some other name. The man on the loudspeaker is calling everyone over to the track and I'm on my back looking at the sky, trying to pretend I'm in the country, but I can't, because even grass in the city feels hard as sidewalk, and there's just no pretending you are anywhere but in a "concrete jungle" as my grandfather says.

The twenty-yard dash takes all of two minutes cause most of the little kids don't know no better than to run off the track or run the wrong way or run smack into the fence and fall down and cry. One little kid, though, has got the good sense to run straight for the white ribbon up ahead so he wins. Then the second-graders line up for the thirty-yard dash and I don't even bother to turn my head to watch cause Raphael Perez always wins. He wins before he even begins by psyching the runners, telling them they're going to trip on their shoelaces and fall on their faces or lose their shorts or something, which he doesn't really have to do since he is very fast, almost as fast as I am. After that is the forty-yard dash which I use to run when I was in first grade. Raymond is hollering from the swings cause he knows I'm bout to do my thing cause the man on the loudspeaker has just announced the fifty-yard dash, although he might just as well be giving a recipe for angel food cake cause you can hardly make out what he's saying for the static. I get up and slip off my sweat pants and then I see Gretchen standing at the starting line, kicking her legs out like a pro. Then as I get into place I see that ole Raymond is on line on the other side of the fence, bending down with his fingers on the ground just like he knew what he was doing. I was going to yell at him but then I didn't. It burns up your energy to holler.

Every time, just before I take off in a race, I always feel like I'm in a dream, the kind of dream you have when you're sick with fever and feel all hot and weightless. I dream I'm flying over a sandy beach in the early morning sun, kissing the leaves of the trees as I fly by. And there's always the smell of apples, just like in the country when I was little and used to think I was a choo-choo train, running through the fields of corn and chugging up the hill to the orchard. And all the time I'm dreaming this, I get lighter and lighter until I'm flying over the beach again, getting blown through the sky like a feather that weighs nothing at all. But once I spread my fingers in the dirt and crouch over the Get on Your Mark, the dream goes and I am solid again and am telling myself, Squeaky you must win, you must win, you are the fastest thing in the world, you can even beat your father up Amsterdam if you really try. And then I feel my weight coming back just behind my knees then down to my feet then into the earth and the pistol shot explodes in my blood and I am off and weightless again, flying past the other runners, my arms pumping up and down and the whole world is quiet except for the crunch as I zoom over the gravel in the track. I glance to my left and there is no one. To the right, a blurred Gretchen, who's got her chin jutting out as if it would win the race all by itself. And on the other side of the fence is Raymond with his arms down to his side and the palms tucked up behind him, running in his very own style, and it's the first time I ever saw that and I almost stop to watch my brother Raymond on his first run. But the white ribbon is bouncing toward me and I tear past it, racing into the distance till my feet with a mind of their own start digging up footfuls of dirt and brake me short. Then all the kids standing on the side pile on me, banging me on the back and slapping my head with their May Day programs, for I have won again and everybody on 151st Street can walk tall for another year.

"In first place . . ." the man on the loudspeaker is clear as a bell now. But then he pauses and the loudspeaker starts to whine. Then static. And I lean down to catch my breath and here comes Gretchen walking back, for she's overshot the finish line too, huffing and puffing with her hands on her hips taking it slow, breathing in steady time like a real pro and I sort of like her a little for the first time. "In first place . . ." and then three or four voices get all mixed up on the loudspeaker and I dig my sneaker into the grass and stare at Gretchen who's staring back, we both wondering just who did win.

I can hear old Beanstalk arguing with the man on the loudspeaker and then a few others running their mouths about what the stop-watches say. Then I hear Raymond, yanking at the fence to call me and I wave to shush him, but he keeps rattling the fence like a gorilla in a cage like in them gorilla movies, but then like a dancer or something he starts climbing up nice and easy but very fast. And it occurs to me, watching how smoothly he climbs hand over hand and remembering how he looked running with his arms down to his side and with the wind pulling his mouth back and his teeth showing and all, it occurred to me that Raymond would make a very fine runner. Doesn't he always keep up with me on my trots? And he surely knows how to breathe in counts of seven cause he's always doing it at the dinner table, which drives my brother George up the wall. And I'm smiling to beat the band cause if I've lost this race, or if me and Gretchen tied, or even if I've won, I can always retire as a runner and begin a whole new career as a coach with Raymond as my champion. After all, with a little more study I can beat Cynthia and her phony self at the spelling bee. And if I bugged my mother, I could get piano lessons and become a star. And I have a big rep as the baddest thing around. And I've got a roomful of ribbons and medals and awards. But what has Raymond got to call his own?

So I stand there with my new plans, laughing out loud by this time as Raymond jumps down from the fence and runs over with his teeth showing and his arms down to the side, which no one before him has quite mastered as a running style. And by the time he comes over I'm jumping up and down so glad to see him—my brother Raymond, a great runner in the family tradition. But of course everyone thinks I'm jumping up and down because the men on the loudspeaker have finally gotten themselves together and compared notes and are announcing "In first place—Miss Hazel Elizabeth Deborah Parker." (Dig that.) "In second place—Miss Gretchen P. Lewis." And I look over at Gretchen wondering what the "P" stands for. And I smile. Cause she's good, no doubt about it. Maybe she'd like to help me coach Raymond; she obviously is serious about running, as any fool can see. And she nods to congratulate me and then she smiles. And I smile. We stand there with this big smile of respect between us. It's about as real a smile as girls can do for each other, considering we don't practice real smiling every day, you know, cause maybe we too busy being flowers or fairies or strawberries instead of something honest and worthy of respect . . . you know . . . like being people.

Responding to the Story

1. This story could have been placed in the "Families and Friends" unit, but instead we find it in "Do I Fit In?" Does Squeaky fit in her neighborhood? Explain. If she *does* fit in, why does she?

2. Do you think the author was able to create a believable first-person female voice? Explain. Would this story have been different if the main character were a boy? If so, how?

3. Do you agree with Hazel Elizabeth Deborah Parker that "girls never really smile at each other because they don't know how and don't want to know how and there's probably no one to teach us how, cause grown-up girls don't know either"? Do you agree with her explanation—found in the last paragraph—of why this happens? Explain her reasoning and then give your reaction.

Exploring the Author's Craft

Authors use a variety of techniques to define a *character*. In this story, we learn about Squeaky through what she tells us about herself. Therefore, despite its title, this story is not really about Raymond. Nevertheless, Raymond is essential to the story. Explain how his presence helps to characterize Squeaky.

Writing Workshop

Listen carefully to the way various people around you speak. Notice the words they use, their tone of voice, and whether they speak slowly or quickly. Then create a fictional first-person narrator based on someone you have observed. Tell about a happening the way that person would tell it.

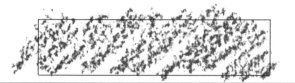

Two Kinds

Amy Tan

Amy Tan was born in Oakland in 1952 of Chinese descent. Her first novel, The Joy Luck Club *(1989), is a series of related stories about four Chinese women and their California-born daughters. Writer Alice Walker observed that "Amy Tan shows us . . . the mystery of the mother-daughter bond in ways that we have not experienced before."*

Tan received her B.A. degree from San Jose State in 1973 and her M.A. degree in 1974; she did postgraduate study at the University of California at Berkeley. She worked for several years as a consultant to programs for disabled children. Her second book, The Kitchen God's Wife, *was published in 1992. She was married in 1974 and lives in San Francisco.*

My mother believed you could be anything you wanted to be in America. You could open a restaurant. You could work for the government and get good retirement. You could buy a house with almost no money down. You could become rich. You could become instantly famous.

"Of course, you can be prodigy, too," my mother told me when I was nine. "You can be best anything. What does Auntie Lindo know? Her daughter, she is only best tricky."

America was where all my mother's hopes lay. She had come to San Francisco in 1949 after losing everything in China: her mother and father, her family home, her first husband, and two daughters, twin baby girls. But she never looked back with regret. There were so many ways for things to get better.

We didn't immediately pick the right kind of prodigy. At first my mother thought I could be a Chinese Shirley Temple.[1] We'd watch Shirley's old movies on TV as though they were training films. My mother would poke my arm and say, "*Ni kan*"—You watch. And I would see Shirley tapping her feet, or singing a sailor song, or pursing her lips into a very round O while saying, "Oh my goodness."

"*Ni kan*," said my mother as Shirley's eyes flooded with tears. "You already know how. Don't need talent for crying!"

Soon after my mother got this idea about Shirley Temple, she took me to a beauty training school in the Mission district and put me in the hands of a student who could barely hold the scissors without shaking. Instead of getting big fat curls, I emerged with an uneven mass of crinkly black fuzz. My mother dragged me off to the bathroom and tried to wet down my hair.

"You look like Negro Chinese," she lamented, as if I had done this on purpose.

The instructor of the beauty training school had to lop off these soggy clumps to make my hair even again. "Peter Pan is very popular these days," the instructor assured my mother. I now had hair the length of a boy's, with straight-across bangs that hung at a slant two inches above my eyebrows. I liked the haircut and it made me actually look forward to my future fame.

In fact, in the beginning, I was just as excited as my mother, maybe even more so. I pictured this prodigy part of me as many different images, trying each one on for size. I was a dainty ballerina girl standing by the curtains, waiting to hear the right music that would send me floating on my tiptoes. I was like the Christ child lifted out of the straw manger, crying with holy indignity. I was Cinderella stepping from her pumpkin carriage with sparkly cartoon music filling the air.

In all of my imaginings, I was filled with a sense that I would soon become *perfect*. My mother and father would adore me. I would be beyond reproach. I would never feel the need to sulk for anything.

But sometimes the prodigy in me became impatient. "If you don't hurry up and get me out of here, I'm disappearing for good," it warned. "And then you'll always be nothing."

Every night after dinner, my mother and I would sit at the Formica kitchen table. She would present new tests, taking her examples from stories of amazing children she had read in *Ripley's Believe It or Not*, or *Good Housekeeping*, *Reader's Digest*, and a dozen other magazines she kept

---

1. *Shirley Temple*: a child movie star of the 1930s.

in a pile in our bathroom. My mother got these magazines from people whose houses she cleaned. And since she cleaned many houses each week, we had a great assortment. She would look through them all, searching for stories about remarkable children.

The first night she brought out a story about a three-year-old boy who knew the capitals of all the states and even most of the European countries. A teacher was quoted as saying the little boy could also pronounce the names of the foreign cities correctly.

"What's the capital of Finland?" my mother asked me, looking at the magazine story.

All I knew was the capital of California, because Sacramento was the name of the street we lived on in Chinatown. "Nairobi!" I guessed, saying the most foreign word I could think of. She checked to see if that was possibly one way to pronounce "Helsinki" before showing me the answer.

The tests got harder—multiplying numbers in my head, finding the queen of hearts in a deck of cards, trying to stand on my head without using my hands, predicting the daily temperatures in Los Angeles, New York, and London.

One night I had to look at a page from the Bible for three minutes and then report everything I could remember. "Now Jehoshaphat had riches and honor in abundance and . . . that's all I remember, Ma," I said.

And after seeing my mother's disappointed face once again, something inside of me began to die. I hated the tests, the raised hopes and failed expectations. Before going to bed that night, I looked in the mirror above the bathroom sink and when I saw only my face staring back—and that it would always be this ordinary face—I began to cry. Such a sad, ugly girl! I made high-pitched noises like a crazed animal, trying to scratch out the face in the mirror.

And then I saw what seemed to be the prodigy side of me—because I had never seen that face before. I looked at my reflection, blinking so I could see more clearly. The girl staring back at me was angry, powerful. This girl and I were the same. I had new thoughts, willful thoughts, or rather thoughts filled with lots of won'ts. I won't let her change me, I promised myself. I won't be what I'm not.

So now on nights when my mother presented her tests, I performed listlessly, my head propped on one arm. I pretended to be bored. And I was. I got so bored I started counting the bellows of the foghorns out on the bay while my mother drilled me in other areas. The sound was comforting and reminded me of the cow jumping over the moon. And the next day, I played a game with myself, seeing if my mother would give up on me before eight bellows. After a while I usually counted only one, maybe two bellows at most. At last she was beginning to give up hope.

Two or three months had gone by without any mention of my being a prodigy again. And then one day my mother was watching *The Ed Sullivan Show*[2] on TV. The TV was old and the sound kept shorting out. Every time my mother got halfway up from the sofa to adjust the set, the sound would go back on and Ed would be talking. As soon as she sat down, Ed would go silent again. She got up, the TV broke into loud piano music. She sat down. Silence. Up and down, back and forth, quiet and loud. It was like a stiff embraceless dance between her and the TV set. Finally she stood by the set with her hand on the sound dial.

She seemed entranced by the music, a little frenzied piano piece with this mesmerizing quality, sort of quick passages and then teasing lilting ones before it returned to the quick playful parts.

"*Ni kan*," my mother said, calling me over with hurried hand gestures, "Look here."

I could see why my mother was fascinated by the music. It was being pounded out by a little Chinese girl, about nine years old, with a Peter Pan haircut. The girl had the sauciness of a Shirley Temple. She was proudly modest like a proper Chinese child. And she also did this fancy sweep of a curtsy, so that the fluffy skirt of her white dress cascaded slowly to the floor like the petals of a large carnation.

In spite of these warning signs, I wasn't worried. Our family had no piano and we couldn't afford to buy one, let alone reams of sheet music and piano lessons. So I could be generous in my comments when my mother badmouthed the little girl on TV.

"Play note right, but doesn't sound good! No singing sound," complained my mother.

"What are you picking on her for?" I said carelessly. "She's pretty good. Maybe she's not the best, but she's trying hard." I knew almost immediately I would be sorry I said that.

"Just like you," she said. "Not the best. Because you not trying." She gave a little huff as she let go of the sound dial and sat down on the sofa.

The little Chinese girl sat down also to play an encore of "Anitra's

2. *The Ed Sullivan Show*: a weekly television show of the 1950s and 1960s that featured various kinds of performers.

Dance'' by Grieg. I remember the song, because later on I had to learn how to play it.

Three days after watching *The Ed Sullivan Show*, my mother told me what my schedule would be for piano lessons and piano practice. She had talked to Mr. Chong, who lived on the first floor of our apartment building. Mr. Chong was a retired piano teacher and my mother had traded housecleaning services for weekly lessons and a piano for me to practice on every day, two hours a day, from four until six.

When my mother told me this, I felt as though I had been sent to hell. I whined and then kicked my foot a little when I couldn't stand it anymore.

"Why don't you like me the way I am? I'm *not* a genius! I can't play the piano. And even if I could, I wouldn't go on TV if you paid me a million dollars!" I cried.

My mother slapped me. "Who ask you be genius?" she shouted. "Only ask you be your best. For you sake. You think I want you be genius? Hnnh! What for! Who ask you!"

"So ungrateful," I heard her mutter in Chinese. "If she had as much talent as she has temper, she would be famous now."

Mr. Chong, whom I secretly nicknamed Old Chong, was very strange, always tapping his fingers to the silent music of an invisible orchestra. He looked ancient in my eyes. He had lost most of the hair on top of his head and he wore thick glasses and had eyes that always looked tired and sleepy. But he must have been younger than I thought, since he lived with his mother and was not yet married.

I met Old Lady Chong once and that was enough. She had this peculiar smell like a baby that had done something in its pants. And her fingers felt like a dead person's, like an old peach I once found in the back of the refrigerator; the skin just slid off the meat when I picked it up.

I soon found out why Old Chong had retired from teaching piano. He was deaf. "Like Beethoven!"[3] he shouted to me. "We're both listening only in our head!" And he would start to conduct his frantic silent sonatas.

Our lessons went like this. He would open the book and point to

---

3. *Beethoven* (bā′ tō vən), *Ludvig van* (1770–1827): German composer who, when he became deaf, was unable to hear his own compositions.

different things, explaining their purpose: "Key! Treble! Bass! No sharps or flats! So this is C major! Listen now and play after me."

And then he would play the C scale a few times, a simple chord, and then, as if inspired by an old, unreachable itch, he gradually added more notes and running trills and a pounding bass until the music was really something quite grand.

I would play after him, the simple scale, the simple chord, and then I just played some nonsense that sounded like a cat running up and down on top of garbage cans. Old Chong smiled and applauded and then said, "Very good! But now you must learn to keep time!"

So that's how I discovered that Old Chong's eyes were too slow to keep up with the wrong notes I was playing. He went through the motions in half-time. To help me keep rhythm, he stood behind me, pushing down on my right shoulder for every beat. He balanced pennies on top of my wrists so I would keep them still as I slowly played scales and arpeggios. He had me curve my hand around an apple and keep that shape when playing chords. He marched stiffly to show me how to make each finger dance up and down, staccato like an obedient little soldier.

He taught me all these things, and that was how I also learned I could be lazy and get away with mistakes, lots of mistakes. If I hit the wrong notes because I hadn't practiced enough, I never corrected myself. I just kept playing in rhythm. And Old Chong kept conducting his own private reverie.

So maybe I never really gave myself a fair chance. I did pick up the basics pretty quickly, and I might have become a good pianist at that young age. But I was so determined not to try, not to be anybody different that I learned to play only the most ear-splitting preludes, the most discordant[4] hymns.

Over the next year, I practiced like this, dutifully in my own way. And then one day I heard my mother and her friend Lindo Jong both talking in a loud bragging tone of voice so others could hear. It was after church, and I was leaning against the brick wall wearing a dress with stiff white petticoats. Auntie Lindo's daughter, Waverly, who was about my age, was standing farther down the wall about five feet away. We had grown up together and shared all the closeness of two sisters squabbling over crayons and dolls. In other words, for the most part, we hated each other. I thought she was snotty. Waverly Jong had

---

4. *discordant* (dis kôrd'nt): not in harmony; harsh.

gained a certain amount of fame as "Chinatown's Littlest Chinese Chess Champion."

"She bring home too many trophy," lamented Auntie Lindo that Sunday. "All day she play chess. All day I have no time to do nothing but dust off her winnings." She threw a scolding look at Waverly, who pretended not to see her.

"You lucky you don't have this problem," said Auntie Lindo with a sigh to my mother.

And my mother squared her shoulders and bragged: "Our problem worser than yours. If we ask Jing-mei wash dish, she hear nothing but music. It's like you can't stop this natural talent."

And right then, I was determined to put a stop to her foolish pride.

A few weeks later, Old Chong and my mother conspired to have me play in a talent show which would be held in the church hall. By then, my parents had saved up enough to buy me a secondhand piano, a black Wurlitzer spinet with a scarred bench. It was the showpiece of our living room.

For the talent show, I was to play a piece called "Pleading Child" from Schumann's[5] *Scenes from Childhood*. It was a simple, moody piece that sounded more difficult than it was. I was supposed to memorize the whole thing, playing the repeat parts twice to make the piece sound longer. But I dawdled over it, playing a few bars and then cheating, looking up to see what notes followed. I never really listened to what I was playing. I daydreamed about being somewhere else, about being someone else.

The part I liked to practice best was the fancy curtsy: right foot out, touch the rose on the carpet with a pointed foot, sweep to the side, left leg bends, look up and smile.

My parents invited all the couples from the Joy Luck Club[6] to witness my debut. Auntie Lindo and Uncle Tin were there. Waverly and her two older brothers had also come. The first two rows were filled with children both younger and older than I was. The littlest ones got to go first. They recited simple nursery rhymes, squawked out tunes on miniature violins, twirled Hula Hoops, pranced in pink ballet tutus, and when they bowed or curtsied, the audience would sigh in unison, "Awww," and then clap enthusiastically.

When my turn came, I was very confident. I remember my childish

---

5. *Schumann, Robert* (1810–1856): German composer.

6. *Joy Luck Club*: social group to which the family belongs.

excitement. It was as if I knew, without a doubt, that the prodigy side of me really did exist. I had no fear whatsoever, no nervousness. I remember thinking to myself, This is it! This is it! I looked out over the audience, at my mother's blank face, my father's yawn, Auntie Lindo's stiff-lipped smile, Waverly's sulky expression. I had on a white dress layered with sheets of lace, and a pink bow in my Peter Pan haircut. As I sat down I envisioned people jumping to their feet and Ed Sullivan rushing up to introduce me to everyone on TV.

And I started to play. It was so beautiful. I was so caught up in how lovely I looked that at first I didn't worry how I would sound. So it was a surprise to me when I hit the first wrong note and I realized something didn't sound quite right. And then I hit another and another followed that. A chill started at the top of my head and began to trickle down. Yet I couldn't stop playing, as though my hands were bewitched. I kept thinking my fingers would adjust themselves back, like a train switching to the right track. I played this strange jumble through two repeats, the sour notes staying with me all the way to the end.

When I stood up, I discovered my legs were shaking. Maybe I had just been nervous and the audience, like Old Chong, had seen me go through the right motions and had not heard anything wrong at all. I swept my right foot out, went down on my knee, looked up and smiled. The room was quiet, except for Old Chong, who was beaming and shouting, "Bravo! Bravo! Well done!" But then I saw my mother's face, her stricken face. The audience clapped weakly, and as I walked back to my chair, with my whole face quivering as I tried not to cry, I heard a little boy whisper loudly to his mother, "That was awful," and the mother whispered back, "Well, she certainly tried."

And now I realized how many people were in the audience, the whole world it seemed. I was aware of eyes burning into my back. I felt the shame of my mother and father as they sat stiffly throughout the rest of the show.

We could have escaped during intermission. Pride and some strange sense of honor must have anchored my parents to their chairs. And so we watched it all: the eighteen-year-old boy with a fake mustache who did a magic show and juggled flaming hoops while riding a unicycle. The girl with white makeup who sang from *Madama Butterfly* and got honorable mention. And the eleven-year-old boy who won first prize playing a tricky violin song that sounded like a busy bee.

After the show, the Hsus, the Jongs, and the St. Clairs from the Joy Luck Club came up to my mother and father.

"Lots of talented kids," Auntie Lindo said vaguely, smiling broadly.

"That was somethin' else," said my father, and I wondered if he was referring to me in humorous way, or whether he even remembered what I had done.

Waverly looked at me and shrugged her shoulders. "You aren't a genius like me," she said matter-of-factly. And if I hadn't felt so bad, I would have pulled her braids and punched her stomach.

But my mother's expression was what devastated me: a quiet, blank look that said she had lost everything. I felt the same way, and it seemed as if everybody were now coming up, like gawkers at the scene of an accident, to see what parts were actually missing. When we got on the bus to go home, my father was humming the busy-bee tune and my mother was silent. I kept thinking she wanted to wait until we got home before shouting at me. But when my father unlocked the door to our apartment, my mother walked in and then went to the back, into the bedroom. No accusations. No blame. And in a way, I felt disappointed. I had been waiting for her to start shouting, so I could shout back and cry and blame her for all my misery.

I assumed my talent-show fiasco[7] meant I never had to play the piano again. But two days later, after school, my mother came out of the kitchen and saw me watching TV.

"Four clock," she reminded me as if it were any other day. I was stunned, as though she were asking me to go through the talent-show torture again. I wedged myself more tightly in front of the TV.

"Turn off TV," she called from the kitchen five minutes later.

I didn't budge. And then I decided. I didn't have to do what my mother said anymore. I wasn't her slave. This wasn't China. I had listened to her before and look what happened. She was the stupid one.

She came out from the kitchen and stood in the arched entryway of the living room. "Four clock," she said once again, louder.

"I'm not going to play anymore," I said nonchalantly. "Why should I? I'm not a genius."

She walked over and stood in front of the TV. I saw her chest was heaving up and down in an angry way.

"No!" I said, and I now felt stronger, as if my true self had finally emerged. So this was what had been inside me all along.

"No! I won't!" I screamed.

She yanked me by the arm, pulled me off the floor, snapped off the TV. She was frighteningly strong, half pulling, half carrying me toward the piano as I kicked the throw rugs under my feet. She lifted me up

---

7. *fiasco* (fē''as'kō): complete failure.

and onto the hard bench. I was sobbing by now, looking at her bitterly. Her chest was heaving even more and her mouth was open, smiling crazily as if she were pleased I was crying.

"You want me to be someone that I'm not!" I sobbed. "I'll never be the kind of daughter you want me to be!"

"Only two kinds of daughters," she shouted in Chinese. "Those who are obedient and those who follow their own mind! Only one kind of daughter can live in this house. Obedient daughter!"

"Then I wish I wasn't your daughter. I wish you weren't my mother," I shouted. As I said these things I got scared. It felt like worms and toads and slimy things crawling out of my chest, but it also felt good, as if this awful side of me had surfaced at last.

"Too late change this," said my mother shrilly.

And I could sense her anger rising to its breaking point. I wanted to see it spill over. And that's when I remembered the babies she had lost in China, the ones we never talked about. "Then I wish I'd never been born!" I shouted. "I wish I were dead! Like them."

It was as if I had said the magic words. Alakazam!—and her face went blank, her mouth closed, her arms went slack, and she backed out of the room, stunned, as if she were blowing away like a small brown leaf, thin, brittle, lifeless.

It was not the only disappointment my mother felt in me. In the years that followed, I failed her so many times, each time asserting my own will, my right to fall short of expectations. I didn't get straight As. I didn't become class president. I didn't get into Stanford.[8] I dropped out of college.

For unlike my mother, I did not believe I could be anything I wanted to be. I could only be me.

And for all those years, we never talked about the disaster at the recital or my terrible accusations afterward at the piano bench. All that remained unchecked, like a betrayal that was now unspeakable. So I never found a way to ask her why she had hoped for something so large that failure was inevitable.

And even worse, I never asked her what frightened me the most: Why had she given up hope?

For after our struggle at the piano, she never mentioned my playing again. The lessons stopped. The lid to the piano was closed, shutting out the dust, my misery, and her dreams.

---

8. *Stanford*: university in California.

So she surprised me. A few years ago, she offered to give me the piano, for my thirtieth birthday. I had not played in all those years. I saw the offer as a sign of forgiveness, a tremendous burden removed.

"Are you sure?" I asked shyly. "I mean, won't you and Dad miss it?"

"No, this is your piano," she said firmly. "Always your piano. You only one can play."

"Well, I probably can't play anymore," I said. "It's been years."

"You pick up fast," said my mother, as if she knew this was certain. "You have natural talent. You could been genius if you want to."

"No I couldn't."

"You just not trying," said my mother. And she was neither angry nor sad. She said it as if to announce a fact that could never be disproved. "Take it," she said.

But I didn't at first. It was enough that she had offered it to me. And after that, every time I saw it in my parents' living room, standing in front of the bay windows, it made me feel proud, as if it were a shiny trophy I had won back.

Last week I sent a tuner over to my parents' apartment and had the piano reconditioned, for purely sentimental reasons. My mother had died a few months before and I had been getting things in order for my father, a little bit at a time. I put the jewelry in special silk pouches. The sweaters she had knitted in yellow, pink, bright orange—all the colors I hated—I put those in moth-proof boxes. I found some old Chinese silk dresses, the kind with little slits up the sides. I rubbed the old silk against my skin, then wrapped them in tissue and decided to take them home with me.

After I had the piano tuned, I opened the lid and touched the keys. It sounded even richer than I remembered. Really, it was a very good piano. Inside the bench were the same exercise notes with handwritten scales, the same secondhand music books with their covers held together with yellow tape.

I opened up the Schumann book to the dark little piece I had played at the recital. It was on the left-hand side of the page, "Pleading Child." It looked more difficult than I remembered. I played a few bars, surprised at how easily the notes came back to me.

And for the first time, or so it seemed, I noticed the piece on the right-hand side. It was called "Perfectly Contented." I tried to play this one as well. It had a lighter melody but the same flowing rhythm and turned out to be quite easy. "Pleading Child" was shorter but slower; "Perfectly Contented" was longer, but faster. And after I played them both a few times, I realized they were two halves of the same song.

Responding to the Story

1. Why do you think the narrator started performing "listlessly" and decided "I won't let her [the girl's mother] change me"?

2. What does the mother say is her reason for pushing her daughter to take piano lessons? Do you think the mother is right to do this? Explain your answer in at least one paragraph.

3. Why does the mother say to Auntie Lindo, "Our problem worser than yours. If we ask Jing-mei wash dish, she hear nothing but music. It's like you can't stop this natural talent"?

4. What are the final outrageous "magic" words the narrator says to her mother? Why does she choose these words?

5. How do "Pleading Child" and "Perfectly Contented" have a double meaning in the story? What does the last sentence of the story mean?

Exploring the Author's Craft

A *simile* compares two things that have common characteristics but are essentially unlike each other. The words *like* or *as* are usually used in similes. When Amy Tan describes Old Lady Chong, she writes, ". . .her fingers felt like a dead person's, like an old peach I once found in the back of the refrigerator; the skin just slid off the meat when I picked it up." What are the similarities when the two dissimilar things are compared?

Later the narrator describes playing "some nonsense that sounded like a cat running up and down on top of garbage cans." Recognizing that similes can make characters and events more vivid, try writing several.

1. Write a word portrait of a person you know. Limit yourself to two paragraphs, and in your description, create an appropriate simile.

2. Describe an action. Include a simile for comic effect as the narrator of "Two Kinds" did when she described her piano playing.

Writing Workshop

Tell about an incident of your own growing up that deals with parental expectations and your reactions. Did you rise to your parents' hopes and perform beautifully, or did you resist? Use dialogue to create scenes that show the incident; don't just sum up the event.

Alternate Media Response

1. Write and perform a piece of music that captures the tension between mother and daughter in this story. There may be several sections to your creation, sections that parallel parts of the story.

2. Create and perform a dance that tells the story of mother and daughter in "Two Kinds."

3. With others in your class, dramatize a segment of this story and record it on videotape. Your scene should stand on its own without a need for viewers to read the short story.

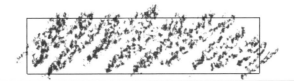

Louisa, Please Come Home

Shirley Jackson

Shirley Jackson (1919–1965) is known for her stories and novels that contain bizarre situations and terrifying characters, but she also wrote about life in a family of four children.

When she was fourteen, she moved with her family from San Francisco to New York. After a year at the University of Rochester, she spent a year at home writing. She then attended Syracuse University, where she met the literary critic Stanley Edgar Hyman. They were married in 1940 and moved to New York City. Her amusing story, "My Life with R. H. Macy," was based on a job she held there.

In 1945, they moved to North Bennington, Vermont, where The Road Through the Wall *was published in 1948. That same year the* New Yorker *published "The Lottery," Jackson's most famous story. It provoked shock, outrage, and praise. It was included in* Prize Stories in 1949: The O. Henry Awards *and is a classic example of Jackson's ability to turn seemingly ordinary events into shocking tales.*

Her novel Hangasman *appeared in 1951. Then she wrote* Life Among the Savages *(1953), a deft account of living with four children under the age of ten, and* Raising Demons *(1957), also autobiographical.* The Sundial *appeared in 1958,* The Haunting of Hill House *in 1959, and* We Have Always Lived in the Castle *in 1962. Two collections of her works appeared after her death:* The Magic of Shirley Jackson *(1966) and* Come Along with Me *(1968).*

"Louisa," my mother's voice came over the radio; it frightened me badly for a minute, "Louisa," she said, "please come home. It's been three long long years since we saw you last; Louisa, I promise you that everything will be all right. We all miss you so. We want you back again. Louisa, please come home.''

Once a year. On the anniversary of the day I ran away. Each time I heard it I was frightened again, because between one year and the next I would forget what my mother's voice sounded like, so soft and yet strange with that pleading note. I listened every year. I read the stories in the newspapers—"Louise Tether vanished one year ago"—or two years ago, or three; I used to wait for the twentieth of June as though it were my birthday. I kept all the clippings at first, but secretly; with my picture on all the front pages I would have looked kind of strange if anyone had seen me cutting it out. Chandler, where I was hiding, was close enough to my old home so that the papers made a big fuss about all of it, but of course the reason I picked Chandler in the first place was because it was a big enough city for me to hide in.

I didn't just up and leave on the spur of the moment, you know. I always knew that I was going to run away sooner or later, and I had made plans ahead of time, for whenever I decided to go. Everything had to go right the first time, because they don't usually give you a second chance on that kind of thing and anyway if it had gone wrong I would have looked like an awful fool, and my sister Carol was never one for letting people forget it when they made fools of themselves. I admit I planned it for the day before Carol's wedding on purpose, and for a long time afterward I used to try and imagine Carol's face when she finally realized that my running away was going to leave her one bridesmaid short. The papers said that the wedding went ahead as scheduled, though, and Carol told one newspaper reporter that her sister Louisa would have wanted it that way; "She would never have meant to spoil my wedding," Carol said, knowing perfectly well that that would be exactly what I'd meant. I'm pretty sure that the first thing Carol did when they knew I was missing was go and count the wedding presents to see what I'd taken with me.

Anyway, Carol's wedding may have been fouled up, but *my* plans went fine—better, as a matter of fact, than I had ever expected. Everyone was hurrying around the house putting up flowers and asking each other if the wedding gown had been delivered, and opening up cases of champagne and wondering what they were going to do if it rained and they couldn't use the garden, and I just closed the front door behind me and started off. There was only one bad minute when Paul saw me; Paul has always lived next door and Carol hates him worse than she does me. My mother always used to say that every time I did something to make the family ashamed of me Paul was sure to be in it somewhere.

For a long time they thought he had something to do with my running away, even though he told over and over again how hard I tried to duck away from him that afternoon when he met me going down the driveway. The papers kept calling him "a close friend of the family," which must have overjoyed my mother, and saying that he was being questioned about possible clues to my whereabouts. Of course he never even knew that I was running away; I told him just what I told my mother before I left—that I was going to get away from all the confusion and excitement for a while; I was going downtown and would probably have a sandwich somewhere for supper and go to a movie. He bothered me for a minute there, because of course he wanted to come too. I hadn't meant to take the bus right there on the corner but with Paul tagging after me and wanting me to wait while he got the car so we could drive out and have dinner at the Inn, I had to get away fast on the first thing that came along, so I just ran for the bus and left Paul standing there; that was the only part of my plan I had to change.

I took the bus all the way downtown, although my first plan had been to walk. It turned out much better, actually, since it didn't matter at all if anyone saw me on the bus going downtown in my own home town, and I managed to get an earlier train out. I bought a round-trip ticket; that was important, because it would make them think I was coming back; that was always the way they thought about things. If you did something you had to have a reason for it, because my mother and my father and Carol never did anything unless *they* had a reason for it, so if I bought a round-trip ticket the only possible reason would be that I was coming back. Besides, if they thought I was coming back they would not be frightened so quickly and I might have more time to hide before they came looking for me. As it happened, Carol found out I was gone that same night when she couldn't sleep and came into my room for some aspirin, so all the time I had less of a head start than I thought.

I knew that they would find out about my buying the ticket; I was not silly enough to suppose that I could steal off and not leave any traces. All my plans were based on the fact that the people who get caught are the ones who attract attention by doing something strange or noticeable, and what I intended all along was to fade into some background where they would never see me. I knew they would find out about the round-trip ticket, because it was an odd thing to do in a town where you've lived all your life, but it was the last unusual thing I did. I thought when I bought it that knowing about that round-trip ticket would be some consolation to my mother and father. They would know that no matter how long I stayed away at least I always had a ticket home. I did keep the return-trip ticket quite a while, as a matter of fact. I used to carry it in my wallet as a kind of lucky charm.

I followed everything in the papers. Mrs. Peacock and I used to read them at the breakfast table over our second cup of coffee before I went off to work.

"What do you think about this girl disappeared over in Rockville?" Mrs. Peacock would say to me, and I'd shake my head sorrowfully and say that a girl must be really crazy to leave a handsome, luxurious home like that, or that I had kind of a notion that maybe she didn't leave at all—maybe the family had her locked up somewhere because she was a homicidal maniac. Mrs. Peacock always loved anything about homicidal maniacs.

Once I picked up the paper and looked hard at the picture. "Do you think she looks something like me?" I asked Mrs. Peacock, and Mrs. Peacock leaned back and looked at me and then at the picture and then at me again and finally she shook her head and said, "No. If you wore your hair longer, and curlier, and your face was maybe a little fuller, there might be a little resemblance, but then if you looked like a homicidal maniac I wouldn't ever of let you in my house."

"I think she kind of looks like me," I said.

"You get along to work and stop being vain," Mrs. Peacock told me.

Of course when I got on the train with my round-trip ticket I had no idea how soon they'd be following me, and I suppose it was just as well, because it might have made me nervous and I might have done something wrong and spoiled everything. I knew that as soon as they gave up the notion that I was coming back to Rockville with my round-trip ticket they would think of Crain, which is the largest city that train went to, so I only stayed in Crain part of one day. I went to a big department store where they were having a store-wide sale; I figured that would land me in a crowd of shoppers and I was right; for a while there was a good chance that I'd never get any farther away from home than the ground floor of that department store in Crain. I had to fight my way through the crowd until I found the counter where they were having a sale of raincoats, and then I had to push and elbow down the counter and finally grab the raincoat I wanted right out of the hands of some old monster who couldn't have used it anyway because she was much too fat. You would have thought she had already paid for it, the way she howled. I was smart enough to have the exact change, all six dollars and eighty-nine cents, right in my hand, and I gave it to the salesgirl, grabbed the raincoat and the bag she wanted to put it in, and fought my way out again before I got crushed to death.

That raincoat was worth every cent of the six dollars and eighty-nine cents; I wore it right through until winter that year and not even a button ever came off it. I finally lost it the next spring when I left it somewhere and never got it back. It was tan, and the minute I put it on in the ladies' room of the store I began thinking of it as my "old" raincoat; that was good. I had never before owned a raincoat like that and my mother would have fainted dead away. One thing I did that I thought was kind of clever. I had left home wearing a light short coat; almost a jacket, and when I put on the raincoat of course I took off my light coat. Then all I had to do was empty the pockets of the light coat into the raincoat and carry the light coat casually over to a counter where they were having a sale of jackets and drop it on the counter as though I'd taken it off a little way to look at it and had decided against it. As far as I ever knew no one paid the slightest attention to me, and before I left the counter I saw a woman pick up my jacket and look it over; I could have told her she was getting a bargain for three ninety-eight.

It made me feel good to know that I had gotten rid of the light coat. My mother picked it out for me and even though I liked it and it was expensive it was also recognizable and I had to change it somehow. I was sure that if I put it in a bag and dropped it into a river or into a garbage truck or something like that sooner or later it would be found and even if no one saw me doing it, it would almost certainly be found, and then they would know I had changed my clothes in Crain.

That light coat never turned up. The last they ever found of me was someone in Rockville who caught a glimpse of me in the train station in Crain, and she recognized me by the light coat. They never found out where I went after that; it was partly luck and partly my clever planning. Two or three days later the papers were still reporting that I was in Crain; people thought they saw me on the streets and one girl who went into a store to buy a dress was picked up by the police and held until she could get someone to identify her. They were really looking, but they were looking for Louisa Tether, and I had stopped being Louisa Tether the minute I got rid of that light coat my mother bought me.

One thing I was relying on: there must be thousands of girls in the country on any given day who are nineteen years old, fair-haired, five feet four inches tall, and weighing one hundred and twenty-six pounds. And if there are thousands of girls like that, there must be, among those thousands, a good number who are wearing shapeless tan raincoats; I started counting tan raincoats in Crain after I left the department store and I passed four in one block, so I felt well hidden. After that I made myself even more invisible by doing just what I told my mother I was going to—I stopped in and had a sandwich in a little coffee shop, and then I went to a movie. I wasn't in any hurry at all, and rather than try to find a place to sleep that night I thought I would sleep on the train.

It's funny how no one pays any attention to you at all. There were hundreds of people who saw me that day, and even a sailor who tried to pick me up in the movie, and yet no one really *saw* me. If I had tried to check into a hotel the desk clerk might have noticed me, or if I had tried to get dinner in some fancy restaurant in that cheap raincoat I would have been conspicuous, but I was doing what any other girl looking like me and dressed like me might be doing that day. The only person who might be apt to remember me would be the man selling tickets in the railroad station, because girls looking like me in old raincoats didn't buy train tickets, usually, at eleven at night, but I had thought of that, too, of course; I bought a ticket to Amityville, sixty miles away, and what made Amityville a perfectly reasonable disguise is that at Amityville there is a college, not a little fancy place like the one I had left so recently with nobody's blessing, but a big sprawling friendly affair, where my raincoat would look perfectly at home. I told myself I was a student coming back to the college after a week end at home. We got to Amityville after midnight, but it still didn't look odd when I left the train and went into the station, because while I was in the station, having a cup of coffee and killing time, seven other girls— I counted—wearing raincoats like mine came in or went out, not seeming to think it the least bit odd to be getting on or off trains at that hour of the night. Some of them had suitcases, and I wished that I had had some way of getting a suitcase in Crain, but it would have made me noticeable in the movie, and college girls going home for week ends often don't bother; they have pajamas and an extra pair of stockings at home, and they drop a toothbrush into one of the pockets of those invaluable raincoats. So I didn't worry about the suitcase then, although I knew I would need one soon. While I was having my coffee I made my own mind change from the idea that I was a college girl coming back after a week end at home to the idea that I was a college girl who was on her way home for a few days; all the time I tried to think as much as possible like what I was pretending to be, and after all, I *had* been a college girl for a while. I was thinking that even now the letter was in the mail, traveling as fast as the U.S. Government could make it go, right to my father to tell him why I wasn't a college student any more;

I suppose that was what finally decided me to run away, the thought of what my father would think and say and do when he got that letter from the college.

That was in the paper, too. They decided that the college business was the reason for my running away, but if that had been all, I don't think I would have left. No, I had been wanting to leave for so long, ever since I can remember, making plans till I was sure they were fool-proof, and that's the way they turned out to be.

Sitting there in the station at Amityville, I tried to think myself into a good reason why I was leaving college to go home on a Monday night late, when I would hardly be going home for the week end. As I say, I always tried to think as hard as I could the way that suited whatever I wanted to be, and I liked to have a good reason for what I was doing. Nobody ever asked me, but it was good to know that I could answer them if they did. I finally decided that my sister was getting married the next day and I was going home at the beginning of the week to be one of her bridesmaids. I thought that was funny. I didn't want to be going home for any sad or frightening reason, like my mother being sick, or my father being hurt in a car accident, because I would have to look sad, and that might attract attention. So I was going home for my sister's wedding. I wandered around the station as though I had nothing to do, and just happened to pass the door when another girl was going out; she had on a raincoat just like mine and anyone who happened to notice would have thought that it was me who went out. Before I bought my ticket I went into the ladies' room and got another twenty dollars out of my shoe. I had nearly three hundred dollars left of the money I had taken from my father's desk and I had most of it in my shoes because I honestly couldn't think of another safe place to carry it. All I kept in my pocketbook was just enough for whatever I had to spend next. It's uncomfortable walking around all day on a wad of bills in your shoe, but they were good solid shoes, the kind of comfortable old shoes you wear whenever you don't really care how you look, and I had put new shoelaces in them before I left home so I could tie them good and tight. You can see, I planned pretty carefully, and no little detail got left out. If they had let me plan my sister's wedding there would have been a lot less of that running around and screaming and hysterics.

I bought a ticket to Chandler, which is the biggest city in this part of the state, and the place I'd been heading for all along. It was a good place to hide because people from Rockville tended to bypass it unless they had some special reason for going there—if they couldn't find the doctors or orthodontists or psychoanalysts or dress material they wanted in Rockville or Crain, they went directly to one of the really big cities, like the state capital; Chandler was big enough to hide in, but not big enough to look like a metropolis to people from Rockville. The ticket seller in the Amityville station must have seen a good many college girls buying tickets for Chandler at all hours of the day or night because he took my money and shoved the ticket at me without even looking up.

Funny. They must have come looking for me in Chandler at some time or other, because it's not likely they would have neglected any possible place I might be, but maybe Rockville people never seriously believed that anyone would go to Chandler from choice, because I never felt for a minute that anyone was looking for me there. My picture was in the Chandler papers, of course, but as far as I ever knew no one ever looked at me twice, and I got up every morning and went to work and went shopping in the stores and went to movies with Mrs. Peacock and went out to the beach all that summer without ever being afraid of being recognized. I behaved just like everyone else, and dressed just like everyone else, and even *thought* just like everyone else, and the only person I ever saw from Rockville in three years was a friend of my mother's and I knew *she* only came to Chandler to get her poodle bred at the kennels there. She didn't look as if she was in a state to recognize anybody but another poodle fancier, anyway, and all I had to do was step into a doorway as she went by, and she never looked at me.

Two other college girls got on the train to Chandler when I did; maybe both of them were going home for their sisters' weddings. Neither of them was wearing a tan raincoat, but one of them had on an old blue jacket that gave the same general effect. I fell asleep as soon as the train started, and once I woke up and for a minute I wondered where I was and then I realized that I was doing it, I was actually carrying out my careful plan and had gotten better than halfway with it, and I almost laughed, there in the train with everyone asleep around me. Then I went back to sleep and didn't wake up until we got into Chandler about seven in the morning.

So there I was. I had left home just after lunch the day before, and now at seven in the morning of my sister's wedding day I was so far away, in every sense, that I *knew* they would never find me. I had all day to get myself settled in Chandler, so I started off by having breakfast in a restaurant near the station, and then went off to find a place to live, and a job. The first thing I did was buy a suitcase, and it's funny how people don't really notice you if you're buying a suitcase near a railroad station. Suitcases look *natural* near railroad stations, and I picked out one of those stores that sell a little bit of everything and bought a cheap suitcase and a pair of stockings and some handkerchiefs and a little traveling clock, and I put everything into the suitcase and carried that. Nothing is hard to do unless you get upset or excited about it.

Later on, when Mrs. Peacock and I used to read in the papers about my disappearing, I asked her once if she thought that Louisa Tether had gotten as far as Chandler and she didn't.

"They're saying now she was kidnapped," Mrs. Peacock told me, "and that's what *I* think happened. Kidnapped, and murdered, and they do *terrible* things to young girls they kidnap."

"But the papers say there wasn't any ransom note."

"That's what they *say*." Mrs. Peacock shook her head at me. "How do we know what the family is keeping secret? Or if she was kidnapped by a homicidal maniac, why should *he* send a ransom note? Young girls like you don't know a lot of the things that go on. *I* can tell you."

"I feel kind of sorry for the girl," I said.

"You can't ever tell," Mrs. Peacock said. "Maybe she went with him willingly."

I didn't know, that first morning in Chandler, that Mrs. Peacock was going to turn up that first day, the luckiest thing that ever happened to me. I decided while I was having breakfast that I was going to be a nineteen-year-old girl from upstate with a nice family and a good background who had been saving money to come to Chandler and take a secretarial course in the business school there. I was going to have to find some kind of a job to keep on earning money while I went to school; courses at the business school wouldn't start until fall, so I would have the summer to work and save money and decide if I really wanted to take secretarial training. If I decided not to stay in Chandler I could easily go somewhere else after the fuss about my running away had died down. The raincoat looked wrong for the kind of conscientious young girl I was going to be, so I took it off and carried it over my arm. I think I did a pretty good job on my clothes, altogether. Before I left home I decided that I would have to wear a suit, as quiet and unobtrusive as I could find, and I picked out a gray suit, with a white blouse, so with just one or two small changes like a different blouse or some kind of a pin on the lapel, I could look like whoever I decided to be. Now the suit looked absolutely right for a young girl planning to take a secretarial course, and I looked like a thousand other people when I walked down the street carrying my suitcase and my raincoat over my arm; people get off trains every minute looking just like that. I bought a morning paper and stopped in a drugstore for a cup of coffee and a look to see the rooms for rent. It was all so usual—suitcase, coat, rooms for rent—that when I asked the soda clerk how to get to Primrose Street he never even looked at me. He certainly didn't care whether I ever got to Primrose Street or not, but he told me very politely where it was and what bus to take. I didn't really need to take the bus for economy, but it would have looked funny for a girl who was saving money to arrive in a taxi.

"I'll never forget how you looked that first morning," Mrs. Peacock told me once, much later. "I knew right away you were the kind of girl I like to rent rooms to—quiet, and well-mannered. But you looked almighty scared of the big city."

"I wasn't scared," I said. "I was worried about finding a nice room. My mother told me so many things to be careful about I was afraid I'd never find anything to suit her."

"*Any*body's mother could come into my house at any time and know that her daughter was in good hands," Mrs. Peacock said, a little huffy.

But it was true. When I walked into Mrs. Peacock's rooming house on Primrose Street, and met Mrs. Peacock, I knew that I couldn't have done this part better if I'd been able to plan it. The house was old, and comfortable, and my room was nice, and Mrs. Peacock and I hit it off right away. She was very pleased with me when she heard that my mother had told me to be sure the room I found was clean and that the neighborhood was good, with no chance of rowdies following a girl if she came home after dark, and she was even more pleased when she heard that I wanted to save money and take a secretarial course so I could get a really good job and earn enough to be able to send a little home every week; Mrs. Peacock believed that children owed it to their parents to pay back some of what had been spent on them while they were growing up. By the time I had been in the house an hour, Mrs. Peacock knew all about my imaginary family upstate: my mother, who was a widow; and my sister, who had just gotten married and still lived at my mother's home with her husband, and my young brother Paul, who worried my mother a good deal because he didn't seem to want to settle down. My name was Lois Taylor, I told her. By that time, I think I could have told her my real name and she would never have connected it with the girl in the paper, because by then she was feeling that she almost knew my family, and she wanted me to be sure and tell my mother when I wrote home that Mrs. Peacock would make herself personally responsible for me while I was in the city and take as good care of me as my own mother would. On top of everything else, she told me that a stationery store in the neighborhood was looking for a girl assistant, and there I was. Before I had been away from home for twenty-four hours I was an entirely new person. I was a girl named Lois

Taylor who lived on Primrose Street and worked down at the stationery store.

I read in the papers one day about how a famous fortuneteller wrote to my father offering to find me and said that astral signs had convinced him that I would be found near flowers. That gave me a jolt, because of Primrose Street, but my father and Mrs. Peacock and the rest of the world thought that it meant that my body was buried somewhere. They dug up a vacant lot near the railroad station where I was last seen, and Mrs. Peacock was very disappointed when nothing turned up. Mrs. Peacock and I could not decide whether I had run away with a gangster to be a gun moll, or whether my body had been cut up and sent somewhere in a trunk. After a while they stopped looking for me, except for an occasional false clue that would turn up in a small story on the back pages of the paper, and Mrs. Peacock and I got interested in the stories about a daring daylight bank robbery in Chicago. When the anniversary of my running away came around, and I realized that I had really been gone for a year, I treated myself to a new hat and dinner downtown, and came home just in time for the evening news broadcast and my mother's voice over the radio.

"Louisa," she was saying, "please come home."

"That poor poor woman," Mrs. Peacock said. "Imagine how she must feel. They say she's never given up hope of finding her little girl alive someday."

"Do you like my new hat?" I asked her.

I had given up all idea of the secretarial course because the stationery store had decided to expand and include a lending library and a gift shop, and I was now the manager of the gift shop and if things kept on well would someday be running the whole thing; Mrs. Peacock and I talked it over, just as if she had been my mother, and we decided that I would be foolish to leave a good job to start over somewhere else. The money that I had been saving was in the bank, and Mrs. Peacock and I thought that one of these days we might pool our savings and buy a little car, or go on a trip somewhere, or even a cruise.

What I am saying is that I was free, and getting along fine, with never a thought that I knew about ever going back. It was just plain rotten bad luck that I had to meet Paul. I had gotten so I hardly ever thought about any of them any more, and never wondered what they were doing unless I happened to see some item in the papers, but there must have been something in the back of my mind remembering them all the time because I never even stopped to think; I just stood there on the street with my mouth open, and said, "*Paul!*" He turned around and then of course I realized what I had done, but it was too late. He stared at me for a minute, and then frowned, and then looked puzzled; I could see him first trying to remember, and then trying to believe what he remembered; at last he said, "Is it possible?"

He said I had to go back. He said if I didn't go back he would tell them where to come and get me. He also patted me on the head and told me that there was still a reward waiting there in the bank for anyone who turned up with conclusive news of me, and he said that after he had collected the reward I was perfectly welcome to run away again, as far and as often as I liked.

Maybe I did want to go home. Maybe all that time I had been secretly waiting for a chance to get back; maybe that's why I recognized Paul on the street, in a coincidence that wouldn't have happened once in a million years—he had never even *been* to Chandler before, and was only there for a few minutes between trains; he had stepped out of the station for a minute, and found me. If I had not been passing at that minute, if he had stayed in the station where he belonged, I would never have gone back. I told Mrs. Peacock I was going home to visit my family upstate. I thought that was funny.

Paul sent a telegram to my mother and father, saying that he had found me, and we took a plane back; Paul said he was still afraid that I'd try to get away again and the safest place for me was high up in the air where he knew I couldn't get off and run.

I began to get nervous, looking out the taxi window on the way from the Rockville airport; I would have sworn that for three years I hadn't given a thought to that town, to those streets and stores and houses I used to know so well, but here I found that I remembered it all, as though I hadn't ever seen Chandler and *its* houses and streets; it was almost as though I had never been away at all. When the taxi finally turned the corner into my own street, and I saw the big old white house again, I almost cried.

"Of course I wanted to come back," I said, and Paul laughed. I thought of the return-trip ticket I had kept as a lucky charm for so long, and how I had thrown it away one day when I was emptying my pocketbook; I wondered when I threw it away whether I would ever want to go back and regret throwing away my ticket. "Everything looks just the same," I said. "I caught the bus right there on the corner; I came down the driveway that day and met you."

"If I had managed to stop you that day," Paul said, "you would probably never have tried again."

Then the taxi stopped in front of the house and my knees were shaking when I got out. I grabbed Paul's arm and said, "Paul . . . wait a minute," and he gave me a look I used to know very well, a look that said "If you back out on me now I'll see that you never forget it," and put his arm around me because I was shivering and we went up the walk to the front door.

I wondered if they were watching us from the window. It was hard for me to imagine how my mother and father would behave in a situation like this, because they always made such a point of being quiet and dignified and proper; I thought that Mrs. Peacock would have been halfway down the walk to meet us, but here the front door ahead was still tight shut. I wondered if we would have to ring the doorbell; I never had to ring this doorbell before. I was still wondering when Carol opened the door for us. "Carol!" I said. I was shocked because she looked so old, and then I thought that of course it had been three years since I had seen her and she probably thought that *I* looked older, too. "Carol," I said, "Oh, Carol!" I was honestly glad to see her.

She looked at me hard and then stepped back and my mother and father were standing there, waiting for me to come in. If I had not stopped to think I would have run to them, but I hesitated, not quite sure what to do, or whether they were angry with me, or hurt, or only just happy that I was back, and of course once I stopped to think about it all I could find to do was just stand there and say "Mother?" kind of uncertainly.

She came over to me and put her hands on my shoulders and looked into my face for a long time. There were tears running down her cheeks and I thought that before, when it didn't matter, I had been ready enough to cry, but now, when crying would make me look better, all I wanted to do was giggle. She looked old, and sad, and I felt simply foolish. Then she turned to Paul and said, "Oh, *Paul*—how can you do this to me again?"

Paul was frightened; I could see it. "Mrs. Tether—" he said.

"What is your name, dear?" my mother asked me.

"Louisa Tether," I said stupidly.

"No, dear," she said, very gently, "your *real* name?"

Now I could cry, but now I did not think it was going to help matters any. "Louisa Tether," I said. "That's my name."

"Why don't you people leave us alone?" Carol said; she was white, and shaking, and almost screaming because she was so angry. "We've spent years and years trying to find my lost sister and all people like you see in it is a chance to cheat us out of the reward—doesn't it mean *anything* to you that *you* may think you have a chance for some easy money, but *we* just get hurt and heartbroken all over again? Why don't you leave us *alone*?"

"Carol," my father said, "you're frightening the poor child. Young lady," he said to me, "I honestly believe that you did not realize the cruelty of what you tried to do. You look like a nice girl: try to imagine your own mother—"

I tried to imagine my own mother; I looked straight at her.

"—if someone took advantage of her like this. I am sure you were not told that twice before, this young man—" I stopped looking at my mother and looked at Paul—"has brought us young girls who pretended to be our lost daughter; each time he protested that he had been genuinely deceived and had no thought of profit, and each time we hoped desperately that it would be the right girl. The first time we were taken in for several days. The girl *looked* like our Louisa, she *acted* like our Louisa, she knew all kinds of small family jokes and happenings it seemed impossible that anyone *but* Louisa could know, and yet she was an imposter. And the girl's mother—my wife—has suffered more each time her hopes have been raised." He put his arm around my mother—his wife—and with Carol they stood all together looking at me.

"Look," Paul said wildly, "give her a *chance*—she *knows* she's Louisa. At least give her a chance to *prove* it."

"How?" Carol asked. "I'm sure if I asked her something like—well—like what was the color of the dress she was supposed to wear at my wedding—"

"It was pink," I said. "I wanted blue but you said it had to be pink."

"I'm sure she'd know the answer," Carol went on as though I hadn't said anything. "The other girls you brought here, Paul—*they* both knew."

It wasn't going to be any good. I ought to have known it. Maybe they were so used to looking for me by now that they would rather keep on looking than have me home; maybe once my mother had looked in my face and seen there nothing of Louisa, but only the long careful concentration I had put into being Lois Taylor, there was never any chance of my looking like Louisa again.

I felt kind of sorry for Paul; he had never understood them as well as I did and he clearly felt there was still some chance of talking them into opening their arms and crying out, "Louisa! Our long-lost daughter!" and then turning around and handing him the reward; after that, we could all live happily ever after. While Paul was still trying to argue with my father I walked over a little way and looked into the living room again; I figured I wasn't going to have much time to look around and I wanted one last glimpse to take away with me; sister Carol kept a good eye on me all the time, too. I wondered what the two girls before me had tried to steal, and I wanted to tell her that if I ever planned to steal anything from that house I was three years too late; I could have taken whatever I wanted when I left the first time. There was nothing there I could take now, any more than there had been before. I realized that all I wanted was to stay—I wanted to stay so much that I felt like hanging onto the stair rail and screaming, but even though a temper tantrum might bring them some fleeting recollection of their dear lost Louisa I hardly thought it would persuade them to invite me to stay. I could just picture myself being dragged kicking and screaming out of my own house.

"Such a lovely old house," I said politely to my sister Carol, who was hovering around me.

"Our family has lived here for generations," she said, just as politely.

"Such beautiful furniture," I said.

"My mother is fond of antiques."

"Fingerprints," Paul was shouting. We were going to get a lawyer, I gathered, or at least Paul thought we were going to get a lawyer and I wondered how he was going to feel when he found out that we weren't. I couldn't imagine any lawyer in the world who could get my mother and my father and my sister Carol to take me back when they had made up their minds that I was not Louisa; could the law make my mother look into my face and recognize me?

I thought that there ought to be some way I could make Paul see that there was nothing we could do, and I came over and stood next to him. "Paul," I said, "can't you see that you're only making Mr. Tether angry?"

"Correct, young woman," my father said, and nodded at me to show that he thought I was being a sensible creature. "He's not doing himself any good by threatening me."

"Paul," I said, "these people don't want us here."

Paul started to say something and then for the first time in his life thought better of it and stamped off toward the door. When I turned to follow him—thinking that we'd never gotten past the front hall in my great homecoming—my father—excuse me, Mr. Tether—came up behind me and took my hand. "My daughter was younger than you are," he said to me very kindly, "but I'm sure you have a family somewhere who love you and want you to be happy. Go back to them, young lady. Let me advise you as though I were really your father—stay away from that fellow, he's wicked and he's worthless. Go back home where you belong."

"We know what it's like for a family to worry and wonder about a daughter," my mother said. "Go back to the people who love you."

That meant Mrs. Peacock, I guess.

"Just to make sure you get there," my father said, "let us help toward your fare." I tried to take my hand away, but he put a folded bill into it and I had to take it. "I hope someday," he said, "that someone will do as much for our Louisa."

"Good-bye, my dear," my mother said, and she reached up and patted my cheek. "Very good luck to you."

"I hope your daughter comes back someday," I told them. "Good-bye."

The bill was a twenty, and I gave it to Paul. It seemed little enough for all the trouble he had taken and, after all, I could go back to my job in the stationery store. My mother still talks to me on the radio, once a year, on the anniversary of the day I ran away.

"Louisa," she says, "please come home. We all want our dear girl back, and we need you and miss you so much. Your mother and father love you and will never forget you. Louisa, please come home."

Responding to the Story

1. How did you feel while you were reading this story?
2. Did you like Louisa/Lois? Did you hate her? Did you feel sympathetic when she reveals near the story's end, "I realized that all I wanted was to stay . . ."?
3. Give your reactions to Louisa's parents, her sister, and Paul.
4. Why do you think Carol was at the house when Louisa returned, three years after Louisa's disappearance? Remember that Carol was married the day after Louisa left. Is she just visiting her parents? Is she back home because the marriage didn't work out? Does she frequently stay with her parents because they are upset over Louisa's continuing absence? Justify your answer with evidence from the text, if you can.
5. Does the author provide a *motivation* for Louisa's leaving home? If so, what is it?

Exploring the Author's Craft

Discuss what makes this story different from the first five stories in Part One. Consider *plot* (especially the ending), characterization, tone, and what you think might have been the *author's purpose* in writing the story.

Sometimes the names of characters are revealing. Does the family's name tell you anything about the meaning of the story?

Writing Workshop

Here's your chance for some unconventionality. Working with a small group, create a story with a teenager as its main character. The plot should be believable, but not commonplace or expected.

The Man in the Casket

Beth Cassavell

Student-written story

Beth Cassavell hopes to attend law school and pursue a career in foreign relations with the newly formed Commonwealth of Independent States. She has studied Russian as a student at Dartmouth and at the University of St. Petersburg in Russia. She has this to say about her story:

"I wrote 'The Man in the Casket' at age sixteen, at a time in my life when I was trying to figure out who I was. The events that inspired it showed me that much of who I was at the time was inspired by isolated childhood events. Certain memories were painful and perhaps distorted somewhat, due to my emotions at the time. Whether clear or clouded, these memories make for a good story."

I reached into my mom's pocketbook for a tissue. I wasn't the only one who was teary-eyed and sniffling but for me it was because of the pollenating flowers. They cluttered every corner of the cold and grey room. The threatening walls ugly with ornate trimming and the Corinthian columns added to the inelegance.

That day is engraved into my memory not because of depression but because of boredom. I stared at a brown stain on the worn carpet hoping somebody would see how bored I was and take me home. I scratched my neck; the black woolen dress my mother had vested me in felt like steel wool. I looked at my gawky knees. The dress used to cover them when it was new but my nine-year-old body was too big for it now.

Not to mention that this rambunctious nine-year-old didn't want to be attired in a Stone Age dress, confined in a room with a hundred little Italian ladies in orthopedic shoes weeping into their hand-embroidered handkerchiefs. Clinging to their Rosary beads as if they were the essence of life itself, they bewailed and bemoaned the contents of the cold marble casket. I sat in the last row of folding chairs and longed to frolic in the freshly fallen February snow.

I had no choice. My grandfather loved to inconvenience me. He had had his first heart attack in the middle of our annual February Florida vacation almost exactly a year before his death. We had to fly home. After his first stroke my mom forced me into teaching him how to read. He had lost most of his memory due to the stroke.

His lips would tremble as he tried to conquer each syllable. He had thin pale lips exactly like my dad has.

"The ra . . . ra . . ."

"Rain."

"Don't tell me what rain is. I've lived through hurricanes and downpours you could only imagine!" he snapped at me. "The rain gently fa . . ."

"Falling," I interjected impatiently. As far as patience goes, well, I have never had any. I watched in frustration as my grandfather ran his hands deliberately through his white hair. He was stalling. He didn't want to be there as much as I didn't want to be there but we both had an obligation. I've never been quite sure what mine was.

"I don't know why I have to read. My eyes are bad anyway."

"Dad, it's your duty as a responsible adult to be able to read." My mother was so good to him. He was only her father-in-law but she treated him as her own father. He was my own grandfather and I treated him like gum on the bottom of my shoe. Then again, I was his own grandchild.

Whenever my parents would leave on vacation my grandfather would babysit for me. I resented every minute of his presence in my house. After all, I was eight years old and knew everything.

"It's eight o'clock," he informed me. I hated go-to-bed inferences. "Shouldn't you be in bed?"

"I don't have to be in bed until nine, after 'The Dukes of Hazard.' I don't have to listen to you anyway." I sure told him.

"I've had just about enough from you. You know, you can be so unpleasant and downright obnoxious sometimes?" my grandfather said. "You're a spoiled brat." Bluntness was always an annoying quality of his. "You never smile. You should try to be more like your cousin, Rebecca. She doesn't have half as much as you have and she's always smiling and laughing."

The ultimate insult! A comparison to your "perfect" cousin. "I don't want to hear it!" I screamed. I wanted to erupt into a fit of anger—

bite, scratch, kick. I could feel the animosity pounding through every artery and vein in my eight-year-old body. My skin was taking on a shade of crimson. "I can't wait 'til Mommy and Daddy come home. I hate it when you watch me."

"Who the hell do you think you are speaking to me like that? Do you think I enjoy babysitting for a brat like you?"

I was running up the stairs as he spoke, hoping he didn't think I was listening to him. I despised it when he got the last word in. He always did.

The memories came flooding back to me. I had blocked them out completely during this wake-funeral ordeal but the emotional dam was breaking. I swore to myself I would not cry. Why should I cry over him?

I looked up from the stained carpet and the first thing that caught my attention was my dad. I never really thought about my dad losing his own father. He seemed to be dealing with the situation calmly. I watched as he talked with anyone and everyone. My dad is a born talker. I suppose talking and socializing helped him to block out his emotions. The only emotions my dad usually displays are anger and happiness. My mother always says he's exactly like his father. She's wrong. Although I hate to admit it, my grandfather did have other emotions.

One day when my grandfather was struggling over a Sunday newspaper, I witnessed something I never thought I ever would. My grandfather was crying. Actually, it was more like a whimpering or sulking. And for that one short moment, as I was diverted from "The Dukes of Hazard," I actually felt something for my grandfather. It wasn't love; I never knew enough of him to love him, but the feeling was still there. It was almost a feeling of curiosity. I never knew anything about the person my grandfather was. I had never bothered to ask him and he never bothered to tell me.

I never told anyone about it. It was the kind of incident that just got lost in the shuffle of events. He died the next day and things got intensely hectic in my house—the funeral, the wake, the relatives living in our house. I resented his death more than anything he ever did to me when he was alive. Not only had I been ignored since his death but he also got the last word in. How could I outdo death? And what about the wondering and regretting this put me through?

"What are you, deaf?" my brother yelled at me. "You have to go up there and pay last respects to grandpa."

"Huh?" For a moment I forgot this whole damn thing was a tribute to him. "What are you supposed to do?" I asked. I had never been to a funeral before.

"I don't know, go pray or something." My brother made things so religious.

"Do I have to?"

My brother glared at me. "Go!"

I had been sitting in one of those folding chairs for so long that my legs had fallen asleep. Shooting pains ran through my calves as I walked up to the marble coffin. That coffin must have cost at least eight hundred dollars. The bike I wanted only cost two hundred dollars. There was actually a line of people waiting to pay last respects to my grandfather. I got in line.

I watched as my great aunt Sophie bent over into the coffin and briskly kissed him again and again, wailing and crying. This was going to take all day! I hoped I wasn't supposed to kiss it. All it was was the vapid flesh and bones of someone I barely knew. I might as well kiss a rock.

After my great aunt Sophie, my famed cousin Rebecca was on line. She cried also and her tears dripped into the casket like there was some kind of drought in there. I watched as her lips mumbled some prerehearsed prayer. She bent over and kissed him. I was next on line. Suddenly I felt the great disadvantage I had in my humanness. I looked down at the man in the casket. I couldn't do it; I couldn't pray.

"Why do you always do this to me? Why? Why did you have to be so stubborn and unfriendly, so impatient and unloving? Why couldn't you love me? Why?" I stopped. I realized. I cried.

Responding to the Story

1. Is this reaction of a granddaughter to her grandfather's death believable? Justify your response with your own observations or experiences.

2. Explain how you interpret the last paragraph of the story.

Exploring the Author's Craft

1. *Diction* is an author's choice of words or phrases. This choice has a direct effect on the tone of a work. Describe the overall

tone (the author's attitude toward her subject) of this work. Support your opinion with words and phrases from the story.

2. Many young people write sincerely and frankly, yet the work fails to have emotional power for the reader. Beth Cassavell's story does have the power to move most readers. Is the emotional effect of the story created in spite of the tone or because of the tone?

Writing Workshop

Write a poem, essay, or story about a grandparent-grandchild relationship.

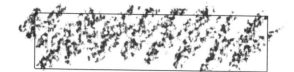

Responding to

Part One

1. All but one of these stories is told from the point of view of a person looking back to a time before he or she was age twenty. Discuss whether the one exception, "A Mother in Mannville," seems to belong in a section called "Do I Fit In?"

2. A first-person story is compelling when the narrator has unusual experiences or fresh insights into common experiences. Which stories in Part One were the most interesting to you? Explain why.

Families and Friends

L *ike it or not, we are born into families and we must, for the most part, manage with whom we've been placed. Our friends we can choose. However these various relationships work out, our interactions with family members and with friends have profound influences throughout our lives.*

In this section you will meet brothers, sisters, parents, and friends. You might have a relationship right now like one of these. Probably you'll have your own variation. The stories will help you reflect on your own life and the people you've been closest to in the years of your life. Use the questions and activities to help you think about the stories and about your own life, and also to help you create literature that is distinctly yours.

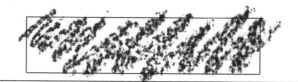

Adjö Means Good-bye

Carrie A. Young

Carrie A. Young was born in Lynchburg, Virginia, and currently lives in Florida. She was formerly employed as a social worker with a foster care agency in New York City. Adjö Means Good-bye *was her first published story.*

It has been a long time since I knew Marget Swenson. How the years have rushed by! I was a child when I knew her, and now I myself have children. The circle keeps turning, keeps coming full.

The mind loses many things as it matures, but I never lost Marget; she has remained with me, like the first love and the first hurt. The mind does not lose what is meaningful to one's existence. Marget was both my first love and first hurt. I met her when she joined our sixth-grade class.

She stood before the class holding tightly to the teacher's hand, her blue, frightened eyes sweeping back and forth across the room until they came to rest on my face. From that very first day we become friends. Marget, just fresh from Sweden, and me, a sixth-generation American. We were both rather shy and quiet and perhaps even lonely, and that's why we took to each other. She spoke very little English, but somehow we managed to understand each other. We visited one another at home practically every day. My young life had suddenly become deliciously complete. I had a dear friend.

Sometimes we talked and laughed on the top of the big, dazzling green hill close to the school. We had so much to talk about; so many things were new to her. She asked a thousand questions and I—I, filled to bursting with pride that it was from me that she wished to learn, responded eagerly and with excesses of superlatives.[1]

---

1. *superlatives* (sə pėr′lə tiv): the highest degree of comparisons of adjectives or adverbs, such as *finest, best, greatest.*

Now, sometimes, when I drive my children to school and watch them race up the walks to the doors, I wonder what lies ahead in the momentary darkness of the hall corridors, and think of Marget once more. I think of how she came out of a dark corridor one day, the day she really looked at my brother when she was visiting me. I saw her following him with new eyes, puzzled eyes, and a strange fear gripped me. "Your brother," she whispered to me, "is African?"

I was a little surprised and a little hurt. Didn't we cheer for Tarzan when we went to the movies? Were not the Africans always frightened and cowardly? But I answered, "No silly," and I continued to wait.

"He looks different from you."

"He should," I said, managing to laugh. My brother was darker than anyone else in the family. "He's a boy and I'm a girl. But we're both Negro, of course."

She opened her mouth to say something else, then closed it and the fear slipped away.

Marget lived up on the hill. That was the place where there were many large and pretty houses. I suppose it was only in passing that I knew only white people lived there. Whenever I visited, Marget's mother put up a table in their garden, and Marget and I had milk and *kaka,* a kind of cake. Mrs. Swenson loved to see me eat. She was a large, round woman, with deep blue eyes and very red cheeks. Marget, though much smaller, of course, looked quite like her. We did our homework after we had the cake and milk, compositions or story reading. When we finished, Mrs. Swenson hugged me close and I knew I was loved in that home. A child knows when it is loved or only tolerated. But I was loved. Mrs. Swenson thanked me with a thick, Swedish accent for helping Marget.

Marget and I had so much fun with words, and there were times when we sat for hours in my garden or hers, or on the hilltop, surrounded by grass and perhaps the smell of the suppers being prepared for our fathers still at work downtown. Her words were Swedish, mine, English. We were surprised how much alike many of them sounded, and we laughed at the way each of us slid our tongues over the unfamiliar words. I learned the Swedish equivalents of mother, father, house, hello, friend, and good-bye.

One day Marget and I raced out of school as soon as the ringing bell released us. We sped down the hill, flashed over gray concrete walks and green lawns dotted with dandelions and scattered daisies, our patent leather buckled shoes slapping a merry tattoo[2] as we went, our long

---

2. *tattoo:* series of taps.

stockings tumbling down our legs. We were going to Marget's to plan her birthday party. Such important business for ten-year-olds!

Eventually, after much planning and waiting, the day of the party came. I put on my pink organdy dress with the big bertha collar,[3] and a new pair of patent leather shoes that tortured my feet unbearably. Skipping up the hill to Marget's I stopped at a lawn which looked deserted. I set down my gift and began to pick the wild flowers that were growing there. Suddenly, from out of nowhere, an old man appeared. "What do you think you're doing, pulling up my flowers?" he shouted. Once again I held myself tightly against the fear, awaiting that awful thing that I felt must come. "I wanted to take them to my friend," I explained. "She's having a birthday today."

The old man's eyes began to twinkle. "She is, is she? Well, you just wait a minute, young lady." He went away and came back with garden shears and cut a handful and then an armful of flowers, and with a smile sent me on my way. My childish fears had been ambushed by a kindness.

I arrived at the party early and Marget and I whizzed around, putting the finishing touches on the decorations. There were hardly enough vases for all the flowers the old man had given me. Some fifteen minutes later the doorbell rang and Marget ran around to the front, saying, "Oh, here they come!"

But it was Mary Ann, another girl in our class, and she was alone. She put her present for Marget on the table and the three of us talked. Occasionally, Marget got up and went around to the front to see who had come unheralded[4] by the doorbell. No one.

"I wonder what's taking them so long?" Mary Ann asked.

Growing more upset by the minute, Marget answered, "Maybe they didn't remember what time the party was."

How does a child of ten describe a sense of foreboding, the feeling that the bad things have happened because of herself? I sat silently, waiting.

When it got to be after five, Mrs. Swenson called Marget inside; she was there for a long time, and when she came out, she looked very, very sad. "My mother does not think they are coming," she said.

"Why not?" Mary Ann blurted.

"Betty Hatcher's mother was here last night and she talked a long

---

3. *big bertha collar:* wide collar that covers the shoulders.
4. *unheralded:* unannounced.

time with my mother. I thought it was about the party. Mother kept saying, 'Yes, yes, she is coming.' "

I took Marget's hand. "Maybe they were talking about me," I said. Oh! I remember so painfully today how I wanted her quick and positive denial to that thrust of mine into darkness where I knew something alive was lurking. Although she did it quite casually, I was aware that Marget was trying to slip her hand from mine, as though she might have had the same thought I had voiced aloud. I opened my hand and let her go. "Don't be silly," she said.

No one came. The three of us sat in the middle rows and rows of flowers and ate our ice cream and cake. Our pretty dresses, ribbons, and shoes were dejected blobs of color. It was as if the world had swung out around us and gone past, leaving us whole, but in some way indelibly stamped forever.

It was different between Marget and me after her birthday. She stopped coming to my house, and when at school I asked her when she would, she looked as though she would cry. She had to do something for her mother, was her unvarying excuse. So, one day, I went to her house, climbed up the hill where the old man had picked the flowers, and a brooding, restless thing grew within me at every step, almost a *knowing*. I had not, after all, been invited to Marget's. My throat grew dry and I thought about turning back, and for the first time the hill and all the homes looked alien, even threatening to me.

Marget almost jumped when she opened the door. She stared at me in shock. Then, quickly, in a voice I'd never heard before, she said, "My mother says you can't come to my house anymore."

I opened my mouth, and closed it without speaking. The awful thing had come; the knowing was confirmed. Marget, crying, closed the door in my face. When I turned to go down the stairs and back down the hill to my house, my eyes, too, were filled with tears. No one had to tell me that the awful thing had come because Marget was white and I was not. I just *knew it* deep within myself. I guess I expected it to happen. It was only a question of when.

June. School was coming to a close. Those days brimmed with strange, uncomfortable moments when Marget and I looked at each other and our eyes darted quickly away. We were little pawns,[5] one white, one colored, in a game over which we had no control then. We did not speak to each other at all.

---

5. *pawns:* in chess, the pieces of lowest value; here, an unimportant person who is used to gain some advantage.

On the last day of school, I screwed up a strange and reckless courage and took my autograph book to where Marget was sitting. I handed it to her. She hesitated, then took it, and without looking up, wrote words I don't remember now; they were quite common words, the kind everyone was writing in everyone else's book. I waited. Slowly, she passed her book to me and in it I wrote with a slow, firm hand some of the words she had taught me. I wrote *Adjö min vän*. Good-bye, my friend. I released her, let her go, told her not to worry; told her that I no longer needed her. *Adjö*.

Whenever I think of Marget now, and I do at the most surprising times, I wonder if she ever thinks of me, if she is married and has children, and I wonder if she has become a queen by now, instead of a pawn.

Responding to the Story

1. Explain why Marget was the narrator's "first love and first hurt."

2. What does the author mean when she says of Marget, "I wonder if she ever thinks of me . . . and I wonder if she has become a queen by now, instead of a pawn"?

Exploring the Author's Craft

The narrator implies from the beginning that this story will have an unhappy ending. Trace the steps that move this story from happiness to sadness. The technique of providing clues to future action is called *foreshadowing*. Does the foreshadowing in this story spoil the ending? Why or why not?

Writing Workshop

1. Does prejudice still exist in our society today? Write an essay in which you explain your opinion; support your position with anecdotes of personal experience if possible.

2. Write a diary entry from Marget's point of view after she tells the narrator that she can't come to Marget's house anymore.

A Christmas Memory

Truman Capote

When Truman Capote died in 1984, he left an unfinished novel,
Answered Prayers, *which, when excerpts appeared in* Esquire,
*caused a sensation among his friends. Real persons appeared as some
characters in the book, and other characters were thinly disguised
portraits of Capote's many famous and wealthy friends.*

*Capote was born Truman Persons in New Orleans in 1924.
After his parents divorced when he was four, he lived with various
relatives in the South until his mother remarried a man whose
last name was Capote. He attended Trinity School and St. John's
Academy in New York, as well as public schools in Greenwich,
Connecticut.*

After his short story "Miriam" appeared in Mademoiselle
*in 1945 and won the O. Henry Memorial Award in 1946, Capote
was launched as a writer. His first novel* Other Voices, Other
Rooms *appeared in 1948, followed by* A Tree of Night and Other
Stories *in 1949. Capote lived in Europe for many years, where he
wrote richly evocative travel articles, as well as* The Grass Harp
(1951), which was written in Sicily.

Two of his most famous novels are Breakfast at Tiffany's
(1958) and In Cold Blood *(1966), which he called a "nonfic-
tional novel." Capote took six years to write the work about a
Kansas farmer and three members of his family who were murdered,
apparently for no reason.* Breakfast at Tiffany's *was made into a
film in 1961 starring Audrey Hepburn, and* In Cold Blood *appeared as a film in 1967. A television version of "A Christmas
Memory" was produced in 1967 and is frequently rerun in December.*

I imagine a morning in late November. A coming of winter morning more than twenty years ago. Consider the kitchen of a spreading old house in a country town. A great black stove is its main feature; but there is also a big round table and a fireplace with two rocking chairs placed in front of it. Just today the fireplace commenced its seasonal roar.

A woman with shorn[1] white hair is standing at the kitchen window. She is wearing tennis shoes and a shapeless gray sweater over a summery calico dress. She is small and sprightly, like a bantam hen; but, due to a long youthful illness, her shoulders are pitifully hunched. Her face is remarkable—not unlike Lincoln's, craggy like that, and tinted by sun and wind; but it is delicate too, finely boned, and her eyes are sherry-colored and timid. "Oh my," she exclaims, her breath smoking the windowpane, "it's fruitcake weather!"

The person to whom she is speaking is myself. I am seven; she is sixty-something. We are cousins, very distant ones, and we have lived together—well, as long as I can remember. Other people inhabit the house, relatives; and though they have power over us, and frequently make us cry, we are not, on the whole, too much aware of them. We are each other's best friend. She calls me Buddy, in memory of a boy who was formerly her best friend. The other Buddy died in the 1880s, when she was still a child. She is still a child.

"I knew it before I got out of bed," she says, turning away from the window with a purposeful excitement in her eyes. "The courthouse bell sounded so cold and clear. And there were no birds singing; they've gone to warmer country, yes indeed. Oh, Buddy, stop stuffing biscuit and fetch our buggy. Help me find my hat. We've thirty cakes to bake."

It's always the same: a morning arrives in November, and my friend, as though officially inaugurating the Christmas time of year that exhilarates her imagination and fuels the blaze of her heart, announces: "It's fruitcake weather! Fetch our buggy. Help me find my hat."

The hat is found, a straw cartwheel corsaged with velvet roses out-of-doors has faded: it once belonged to a more fashionable relative. Together, we guide our buggy, a dilapidated baby carriage, out to the garden and into a grove of pecan trees. The buggy is mine; that is, it was bought for me when I was born. It is made of wicker, rather unraveled, and the wheels wobble like a drunkard's legs. But it is a faithful object; springtimes, we take it to the woods and fill it with flowers, herbs, wild fern for our porch pots; in the summer, we pile it with picnic

---

1. *shorn:* cut close.

paraphernalia and sugar-cane fishing poles and roll it down to the edge of a creek; it has its winter uses, too: as a truck for hauling firewood from the yard to the kitchen, as a warm bed for Queenie, our tough little orange and white rat terrier who has survived distemper and two rattlesnake bites. Queenie is trotting beside it now.

Three hours later we are back in the kitchen hulling a heaping buggyload of windfall pecans. Our backs hurt from gathering them: how hard they were to find (the main crop having been shaken off the trees and sold by the orchard's owners, who are not us) among the concealing leaves, the frosted, deceiving grass. Caarackle! A cheery crunch, scraps of miniature thunder sound as the shells collapse and the golden mound of sweet oily ivory meat mounts in the milk-glass bowl. Queenie begs to taste, and now and again my friend sneaks her a mite, though insisting we deprive ourselves. "We mustn't, Buddy. If we start, we won't stop. And there's scarcely enough as there is. For thirty cakes." The kitchen is growing dark. Dusk turns the window into a mirror: our reflections mingle with the rising moon as we work by the fireside in the firelight. At last, when the moon is quite high, we toss the final hull into the fire and, with joined sighs, watch it catch flame. The buggy is empty, the bowl is brimful.

We eat our supper (cold biscuits, bacon, blackberry jam) and discuss tomorrow. Tomorrow the kind of work I like best begins: buying. Cherries and citron, ginger and vanilla and canned Hawaiian pineapple, rinds and raisins and walnuts and whiskey and oh, so much flour, butter, so many eggs, spices, flavorings: why, we'll need a pony to pull the buggy home.

But before these purchases can be made, there is the question of money. Neither of us has any. Except for skinflint sums[2] persons in the house occasionally provide (a dime is considered very big money); or what we earn ourselves from various activities: holding rummage sales, selling buckets of hand-picked blackberries, jars of homemade jam and apply jelly and peach preserves, rounding up flowers for funerals and weddings. Once we won seventy-ninth prize, five dollars, in a national football contest. Not that we know a fool thing about football. It's just that we enter any contest we hear about: at the moment our hopes are centered on the fifty-thousand-dollar Grand Prize being offered to name a new brand of coffee (we suggested "A.M."; and, after some hesitation, for my friend thought it perhaps sacrilegious, the slogan "A.M.! Amen!"). To tell the truth, our only *really* profitable enterprise was the

---

2. *skinflint sums:* small amounts; a skinflint is a stingy person.

Fun and Freak Museum we conducted in a back-yard woodshed two summers ago. The Fun was a stereopticon[3] with slide views of Washington and New York lent us by a relative who had been to those places (she was furious when she discovered why we'd borrowed it); the Freak was a three-legged biddy chicken hatched by one of our own hens. Everybody hereabouts wanted to see that biddy: we charged grownups a nickel, kids two cents. And took in a good twenty dollars before the museum shut down due to the decrease of the main attraction.

But one way and another we do each year accumulate Christmas savings, a Fruitcake Fund. These moneys we keep hidden in an ancient bead purse under a loose board under the floor under a chamber pot under my friend's bed. The purse is seldom removed from this safe location except to make a deposit, or, as happens every Saturday, a withdrawal; for on Saturdays I am allowed ten cents to go to the picture show. My friend has never been to a picture show, nor does she intend to: "I'd rather hear you tell the story, Buddy. That way I can imagine it more. Besides, a person my age shouldn't squander their eyes. When the Lord comes, let me see Him clear." In addition to never having seen a movie, she has never: eaten in a restaurant, traveled more than five miles from home, received or sent a telegram, read anything except funny papers and the Bible, worn cosmetics, cursed, wished someone harm, told a lie on purpose, let a hungry dog go hungry. Here are a few things she has done, does do: killed with a hoe the biggest rattlesnake ever seen in this county (sixteen rattles), dip snuff (secretly), tame hummingbirds (just try it) till they balance on her finger, tell ghost stories (we both believe in ghosts) so tingling they chill you in July, talk to herself, take walks in the rain, grow the prettiest japonicas[4] in town, know the recipe for every sort of old-time Indian cure, including a magical wart-remover.

Now, with supper finished, we retire to the room in a faraway part of the house where my friend sleeps in a scrap-quilt-covered iron bed painted rose pink, her favorite color. Silently, wallowing in the pleasures of conspiracy, we take the bead purse from its secret place and spill its contents on the scrap quilt. Dollar bills, tightly rolled and green as May buds. Somber fifty-cent pieces, heavy enough to weight a dead man's eyes. Lovely dimes, the liveliest coin, the one that really jingles. Nickels and quarters, worn smooth as creek pebbles. But mostly a hateful heap

---

3. *stereopticon* (ster'' ē op' tə kən): a projector designed to combine two images on a screen into one three-dimensional image.

4. *japonicas* (jə pon' ə kə): a shrub with white, pink, or red flowers.

of bitter-odored pennies. Last summer others in the house contracted to pay us a penny for every twenty-five flies we killed. Oh, the carnage of August: the flies that flew to heaven! Yet it was not work in which we took pride. And, as we sit counting pennies, it is as though we were back tabulating dead flies. Neither of us has a head for figures; we count slowly, lose track, start again. According to her calculations, we have $12.73. According to mine, exactly $13. "I do hope you're wrong, Buddy. We can't mess around with thirteen. The cakes will fall. Or put somebody in the cemetery. Why, I wouldn't dream of getting out of bed on the thirteenth." This is true: she always spends thirteenths in bed. So, to be on the safe side, we subtract a penny and toss it out the window.

Of the ingredients that go into our fruitcakes, whiskey is the most expensive, as well as the hardest to obtain: State laws forbid its sale. But everybody knows you can buy a bottle from Mr. Haha Jones. And the next day, having completed our more prosaic shopping, we set out for Mr. Haha's business address, a "sinful" (to quote public opinion) fish-fry and dancing café down by the river. We've been there before, and on the same errand; but in previous years our dealings have been with Haha's wife, an iodine-dark Indian woman with brassy peroxided hair and a dead-tired disposition. Actually, we've never laid eyes on her husband, though we've heard that he's an Indian too. A giant with razor scars across his cheeks. They call him Haha because he's so gloomy, a man who never laughs. As we approach his café (a large log cabin festooned inside and out with chains of garish-gay naked light bulbs and standing by the river's muddy edge under the shade of river trees where moss drifts though the branches like gray mist) our steps slow down. Even Queenie stops prancing and sticks close by. People have been murdered in Haha's café. Cut to pieces. Hit on the head. There's a case coming up in court next month. Naturally these goings-on happen at night when the colored lights cast crazy patterns and the victrola wails. In the daytime Haha's is shabby and deserted. I knock at the door, Queenie barks, my friend calls: "Mrs. Haha, ma'am? Anyone to home?"

Footsteps. The door opens. Our hearts overturn. It's Mr. Haha Jones himself! And he *is* a giant; he *does* have scars; he *doesn't* smile. No, he glowers at us through Satan-tilted eyes and demands to know: "What you want with Haha?"

For a moment we are too paralyzed to tell. Presently my friend half-finds her voice, a whispery voice at best: "If you please, Mr. Haha, we'd like a quart of your finest whiskey."

His eyes tilt more. Would you believe it? Haha is smiling! Laughing, too. "Which one of you is a drinkin' man?"

"It's for making fruitcakes, Mr. Haha. Cooking."

This sobers him. He frowns. "That's no way to waste good whiskey." Nevertheless, he retreats into the shadowed café and seconds later appears carrying a bottle of daisy-yellow unlabeled liquor. He demonstrates its sparkle in the sunlight and says: "Two dollars."

We pay him with nickels and dimes and pennies. Suddenly, as he jangles the coins in his hand like a fistful of dice, his face softens. "Tell you what," he proposes, pouring the money back into our bead purse, "just send me one of them fruitcakes instead."

"Well," my friend remarks on our way home, "there's a lovely man. We'll put an extra cup of raisins in *his* cake."

The black stove, stoked with coal and firewood, glows like a lighted pumpkin. Eggbeaters whirl, spoons spin round in bowls of butter and sugar, vanilla sweetens the air, ginger spices it; melting, nose-tingling odors saturate the kitchen, suffuse the house, drift out to the world on puffs of chimney smoke. In four days our work is done. Thirty-one cakes, dampened with whiskey, bask on window sills and shelves.

Who are they for?

Friends. Not necessarily neighbor friends: indeed, the larger share is intended for persons we've met maybe once, perhaps not at all. People who've struck our fancy. Like President Roosevelt. Like the Reverend and Mrs. J. C. Lucey, Baptist missionaries to Borneo who lectured here last winter. Or the little knife grinder who comes through town twice a year. Or Abner Packer, the driver of the six o'clock bus from Mobile, who exchanges waves with us every day as he passes in a dust-cloud whoosh. Or the young Wistons, a California couple whose car one afternoon broke down outside the house and who spent a pleasant hour chatting with us on the porch (young Mr. Wiston snapped our picture, the only one we've ever had taken). Is it because my friend is shy with everyone *except* strangers that these strangers, and merest acquaintances, seem to us our truest friends? I think yes. Also, the scrapbooks we keep of thank-you's on White House stationery, time-to-time communications from California and Borneo, the knife grinder's penny post cards, make us feel connected to eventful worlds beyond the kitchen with its view of a sky that stops.

Now a nude December fig branch grates against the window. The kitchen is empty, the cakes are gone; yesterday we carted the last of them to the post office, where the cost of stamps turned our purse inside out. We're broke. That rather depresses me, but my friend insists on celebrating—with two inches of whiskey left in Haha's bottle. Queenie has a spoonful in a bowl of coffee (she likes her coffee chicory-flavored and strong). The rest we divide between a pair of jelly glasses. We're both quite awed at the prospect of drinking straight whiskey; the taste of it brings screwed-up expressions and sour shudders. But by and by we begin to sing, the two of us singing different songs simultaneously. I don't know the words to mine, just: *Come on along, come on along, to the dark-town strutters' ball.* But I can dance: that's what I mean to be, a tapdancer in the movies. My dancing shadow rollicks on the walls; our voices rock the chinaware; we giggle: as if unseen hands were tickling us. Queenie rolls on her back, her paws plow the air, something like a grin stretches her black lips. Inside myself, I feel warm and sparky as those crumbling logs, carefree as the wind in the chimney. My friend waltzes round the stove, the hem of her poor calico skirt pinched between her fingers as though it were a party dress: *Show me the way to go home,* she sings, her tennis shoes squeaking on the floor. *Show me the way to go home.*

Enter: two relatives. Very angry. Potent with eyes that scold, tongues that scald. Listen to what they have to say, the words tumbling together into a wrathful tune: "A child of seven! whiskey on his breath! are you out of your mind? feeding a child of seven! must be loony! road to ruination! remember Cousin Kate? Uncle Charlie? Uncle Charlie's brother-in-law? shame! scandal! humiliation! kneel, pray, beg the Lord!"

Queenie sneaks under the stove. My friend gazes at her shoes, her chin quivers, she lifts her skirt and blows her nose and runs to her room. Long after the town has gone to sleep and the house is silent except for the chimings of clocks and the sputter of fading fires, she is weeping into a pillow already as wet as a widow's handkerchief.

"Don't cry," I say, sitting at the bottom of her bed and shivering despite my flannel nightgown that smells of last winter's cough syrup, "don't cry," I beg, teasing her toes, tickling her feet, "you're too old for that."

"It's because," she hiccups, "I *am* too old. Old and funny."

"Not funny. Fun. More fun than anybody. Listen. If you don't stop crying you'll be so tired tomorrow we can't go cut a tree."

She straightens up. Queenie jumps on the bed (where Queenie is not allowed) to lick her cheeks. "I know where we'll find real pretty trees, Buddy. And holly, too. With berries big as your eyes. It's way off in the woods. Farther than we've ever been. Papa used to bring us Christmas trees from there: carry them on his shoulder. That's fifty years ago. Well, now: I can't wait for morning."

Morning. Frozen rime[5] lusters the grass; the sun, round as an orange and orange as hot-weather moons, balances on the horizon, burnishes the silvered winter woods. A wild turkey calls. A renegade hog grunts in the undergrowth. Soon, by the edge of knee-deep, rapid-running water, we have to abandon the buggy. Queenie wades the stream first, paddles across barking complaints at the swiftness of the current, the pneumonia-making coldness of it. We follow, holding our shoes and equipment (a hatchet, a burlap sack) above our heads. A mile more: of chastising thorns, burrs and briers that catch at our clothes; of rusty pine needles brilliant with gaudy fungus and molted feathers. Here, there, a flash, a flutter, an ecstasy of shrillings remind us that not all the birds have flown south. Always, the path unwinds through lemony sun pools and pitch-black vine tunnels. Another creek to cross: a disturbed armada of speckled trout froths the water round us, and frogs the size of plates practice belly flops; beaver workmen are building a dam. On the farther shore, Queenie shakes herself and trembles. My friend shivers, too: not with cold but enthusiasm. One of her hat's ragged roses sheds a petal as she lifts her head and inhales the pine-heavy air. "We're almost there; can you smell it, Buddy?" she says, as though we were approaching an ocean.

And, indeed, it is a kind of ocean. Scented acres of holiday trees, prickly-leafed holly. Red berries shiny as Chinese bells: black crows swoop upon them screaming. Having stuffed our burlap sacks with enough greenery and crimson to garland a dozen windows, we set about choosing a tree. "It should be," muses my friend, "twice as tall as a boy. So a boy can't steal the star." The one we pick is twice as tall as me. A brave handsome brute that survives thirty hatchet strokes before it keels with a creaking rending cry. Lugging it like a kill, we commence the long trek out. Every few yards we abandon the struggle, sit down and pant. But we have the strength of triumphant huntsmen; that and the tree's virile, icy perfume revive us, goad us on. Many compliments accompany our sunset return along the red clay road to town; but my friend is sly and noncommital when passers-by praise the treasure perched in our buggy: what a fine tree and where did it come from? "Yonderways," she murmurs vaguely. Once a car stops and the rich mill owner's lazy wife leans out and whines: "Give ya two-bits cash for that ol tree." Ordinarily my friend is afraid of saying no; but on this occasion she promptly shakes her head: "We wouldn't take a dollar."

---

5. *rime:* frost.

The mill owner's wife persists. "A dollar, my foot! Fifty cents. That's my last offer. Goodness, woman, you can get another one." In answer, my friend gently reflects: "I doubt it. There's never two of anything."

Home: Queenie slumps by the fire and sleeps till tomorrow, snoring loud as a human.

A trunk in the attic contains: a shoebox of ermine tails (off the opera cape of a curious lady who once rented a room in the house), coils of frazzled tinsel gone gold with age, one silver star, a brief rope of dilapidated, undoubtedly dangerous candy-like light bulbs. Excellent decorations, as far as they go, which isn't far enough: my friend wants our tree to blaze "like a Baptist window," droop with weighty snows of ornament. But we can't afford the made-in-Japan splendors at the five-and-dime. So we do what we've always done: sit for days at the kitchen table with scissors and crayons and stacks of colored paper. I make sketches and my friend cuts them out: lots of cats, fish too (because they're easy to draw), some apples, some watermelons, a few winged angels devised from saved-up sheets of Hershey-bar tin foil. We use safety pins to attach these creations to the tree; as a final touch, we sprinkle the branches with shredded cotton (picked in August for this purpose). My friend, surveying the effect, clasps her hands together. "Now honest, Buddy. Doesn't it look good enough to eat?" Queenie tries to eat an angel.

After weaving and ribboning holly wreaths for all the front windows, our next project is the fashioning of family gifts. Tie-dye scarves for the ladies, for the men a homebrewed lemon and licorice and aspirin syrup to be taken "at the first Symptoms of a Cold and after Hunting." But when it comes time for making each other's gift, my friend and I separate to work secretly. I would like to buy her a pearl-handled knife, a radio, a whole pound of chocolate-covered cherries (we tasted some once, and she always swears: "I could live on them, Buddy, Lord yes I could— and that's not taking His name in vain"). Instead, I am building her a kite. She would like to give me a bicycle (she's said so on several million occasions: "If only I could, Buddy. It's bad enough in life to do without something *you* want; but confound it, what gets my goat is not being able to give somebody something you want *them* to have. Only one of these days I will, Buddy. Locate you a bike. Don't ask how. Steal it, maybe"). Instead, I'm fairly certain that she is building me a kite—the same as last year, and the year before: the year before that we exchanged slingshots. All of which is fine by me. For we are champion kite-fliers who study the wind like sailors; my friend, more accomplished than I, can get a kite aloft when there isn't enough breeze to carry clouds.

Christmas Eve afternoon we scrape together a nickel and go to the butcher's to buy Queenie's traditional gift, a good gnawable beef bone. The bone, wrapped in funny paper, is placed high in the tree near the silver star. Queenie knows it's there. She squats at the foot of the tree staring up in a trance of greed: when bedtime arrives she refuses to budge. Her excitement is equaled by my own. I kick the covers and turn my pillow as though it were a scorching summer's night. Somewhere a rooster crows: falsely, for the sun is still on the other side of the world.

"Buddy, are you awake?" It is my friend, calling from her room, which is next to mine; and an instant later she is sitting on my bed holding a candle. "Well, I can't sleep a hoot," she declares. "My mind's jumping like a jack rabbit. Buddy, do you think Mrs. Roosevelt will serve our cake at dinner?" We huddle in the bed, and she squeezes my hand I-love-you. "Seems like your hand used to be so much smaller. I guess I hate to see you grow up. When you're grown up, will we still be friends?" I say always. "But I feel so bad, Buddy. I wanted so bad to give you a bike. I tried to sell my cameo Papa gave me. Buddy"— she hesitates, as though embarrassed—"I made you another kite." Then I confess that I made her one, too; and we laugh. The candle burns too short to hold. Out it goes, exposing the starlight, the stars spinning at the window like a visible caroling that slowly, slowly daybreak silences. Possibly we doze; but the beginnings of dawn splash us like cold water: we're up, wide-eyed and wandering while we wait for others to waken. Quite deliberately my friend drops a kettle on the kitchen floor. I tap-dance in front of closed doors. One by one the household emerges, looking as though they'd like to kill us both; but it's Christmas, so they can't. First, a gorgeous breakfast: just everything you can imagine— from flapjacks and fried squirrel to hominy grits and honey-in-the-comb. Which puts everyone in a good humor except my friend and me. Frankly, we're so impatient to get at the presents we can't eat a mouthful.

Well, I'm disappointed. Who wouldn't be? With socks, a Sunday school shirt, some handkerchiefs, a hand-me-down sweater and a year's subscription to a religious magazine for children. *The Little Shepherd*. It makes me boil. It really does.

My friend has a better haul. A sack of Satsumas,[6] that's her best present. She is proudest, however, of a white wool shawl knitted by her married sister. But she *says* her favorite gift is the kite I built her. And it *is* very beautiful; though not as beautiful as the one she made me,

---

6. *Satsumas:* mandarin oranges.

which is blue and scattered with gold and green Good Conduct stars; moreover, my name is painted on it, "Buddy."

"Buddy, the wind is blowing."

The wind is blowing, and nothing will do till we've run to a pasture below the house where Queenie has scooted to bury her bone (and where, a winter hence, Queenie will be buried, too). There, plunging through the healthy waist-high grass, we unreel our kites, feel them twitching at the string like sky fish as they swim into the wind. Satisfied, sun-warmed, we sprawl in the grass and peel Satsumas and watch our kites cavort. Soon I forget the socks and hand-me-down sweater. I'm as happy as if we'd already won the fifty-thousand-dollar Grand Prize in that coffee-naming contest.

"My, how foolish I am!" my friend cries, suddenly alert, like a woman remembering too late she has biscuits in the oven. "You know what I've always thought?" she asks in a tone of discovery, and not smiling at me but a point beyond. "I've always thought a body would have to be sick and dying before they saw the Lord. And I imagined that when He came it would be like looking at the Baptist window: pretty as colored glass with the sun pouring through, such a shine you don't know it's getting dark. And it's been a comfort: to think of that shine taking away all the spooky feeling. But I'll wager it never happens. I'll wager at the very end a body realizes the Lord has already shown Himself. That things as they are"—her hand circles in a gesture that gathers clouds and kites and grass and Queenie pawing earth over her bone—"just what they've always seen, was seeing Him. As for me, I could leave the world with today in my eyes."

This is our last Christmas together.

Life separates us. Those who Know Best decide that I belong in a military school. And so follows a miserable succession of bugle-blowing prisons, grim reveille-ridden[7] summer camps. I have a new home too. But it doesn't count. Home is where my friend is, and there I never go.

And there she remains, puttering around the kitchen. Alone with Queenie. Then alone. ("Buddy dear," she writes in her wild hard-to-read script, "yesterday Jim Macy's horse kicked Queenie bad. Be thankful she didn't feel much. I wrapped her in a Fine Linen sheet and rode her in the buggy down to Simpson's pasture where she can be with all

---

7. *reveille-ridden* (rev ′ ə lē): controlled by the sound of a bugle blown to awaken the campers in the morning.

her Bones . . ."). For a few Novembers she continues to bake her fruitcakes single-handed; not as many, but some: and, of course, she always sends me "the best of the batch." Also, in every letter she encloses a dime wadded in toilet paper: "See a picture show and write me the story." But gradually in her letters she tends to confuse me with her other friend, the Buddy who died in the 1880's; more and more thirteenths are not the only days she stays in bed: a morning arrives in November, a leafless birdless coming of winter morning, when she cannot rouse herself to exclaim: "Oh my, it's fruitcake weather!"

And when that happens, I know it. A message saying so merely confirms a piece of news some secret vein had already received, severing from me an irreplaceable part of myself, letting it loose like a kite on a broken string. That is why, walking across a school campus on this particular December morning, I keep searching the sky. As if I expected to see, rather like hearts, a lost pair of kites hurrying toward heaven.

Responding to the Story

1. The narrator says of his "sixty-something" cousin and friend: "She is still a child." What does he mean? Give evidence to support your answer.

2. Considering the things the narrator's friend has never done and what she has done, do you feel she is advantaged or disadvantaged? Explain.

3. The narrator's friend tells him, "I've always thought that a body would have to be sick and dying before they saw the Lord." But her view changes. What is her conclusion about what it is to see "Him"?

4. Why do you think the narrator included more happy events than sad ones in the story?

Exploring the Author's Craft

The narrator's memory serves him well, for he is able to describe events using concrete descriptions of objects, surroundings, and emotions. Another writer might have noted that the fruitcakes contained nuts; recall Capote's precise description of finding, gathering, and cracking pecans, and the feelings connected with these tasks. What effect do the *concrete details* throughout have on the story?

Writing Workshop

Capture in two- or three-hundred words some moment that brought you happiness in childhood. Use concrete details to bring alive the joyous experience.

Alternate Media Response

Find or take a series of photographs that tell this story. Should the photos be in black-and-white or color? You decide.

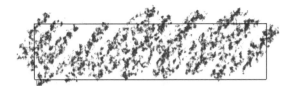

The Scarlet Ibis

James Hurst

James Hurst has the unusual distinction of being known for one story, the one in this anthology, although he published a few other stories in the 1960s and 1970s. Hurst has had a varied career. Born in 1922, he trained as a chemical engineer, studied voice at the Juilliard School of Music in New York and in Rome, and spent thirty-four years in banking at a New York City bank. He retired in 1985 and lives in North Carolina, the state in which he was born.

I t was in the clove of seasons,[1] summer was dead but autumn had not yet been born, that the ibis lit in the bleeding tree. The flower garden was stained with rotting brown magnolia petals and ironweeds grew rank amid the purple phlox. The five o'clocks by the chimney still marked time, but the oriole nest in the elm was untenanted and rocked back and forth like an empty cradle. The last graveyard flowers were blooming, and their smell drifted across the cotton field and through every room of our house, speaking softly the names of our dead.

It's strange that all this is still so clear to me, now that that summer has long since fled and time has had its way. A grindstone stands where the bleeding tree stood, just outside the kitchen door, and now if an oriole sings in the elm, its song seems to die up in the leaves, a silvery dust. The flower garden is prim, the house a gleaming white, and the pale fence across the yard stands straight and spruce. But sometimes (like right now), as I sit in the cool, green-draped parlor, the grindstone

---

1. *clove of seasons:* the division between seasons.

begins to turn, and time with all its changes is ground away—and I remember Doodle.

Doodle was just about the craziest brother a boy ever had. Of course, he wasn't a crazy crazy like old Miss Leedie, who was in love with President Wilson and wrote him a letter every day, but was a nice crazy, like someone you meet in your dreams. He was born when I was six and was, from the outset, a disappointment. He seemed all head, with a tiny body which was red and shriveled like an old man's. Everybody thought he was going to die—everybody except Aunt Nicey, who had delivered him. She said he would live because he was born in a caul[2] and cauls were made from Jesus' nightgown. Daddy had Mr. Heath, the carpenter, build a little mahogany coffin for him. But he didn't die, and when he was three months old Mama and Daddy decided they might as well name him. They named him William Armstrong, which was like tying a big tail on a small kite. Such a name sounds good only on a tombstone.

I thought myself pretty smart at many things, like holding my breath, running, jumping, or climbing the vines in Old Woman Swamp, and I wanted more than anything else someone to race to Horsehead Landing, someone to box with, and someone to perch with in the top fork of the great pine behind the barn, where across the fields and swamps you could see the sea. I wanted a brother. But Mama, crying, told me that even if William Armstrong lived, he would never do these things with me. He might not, she sobbed, even be "all there." He might, as long as he lived, lie on the rubber sheet in the center of the bed in the front bedroom where the white marquisette curtains billowed out in the afternoon sea breeze, rustling like palmetto fronds.

It was bad enough having an invalid brother, but having one who possibly was not all there was unbearable, so I began to make plans to kill him by smothering him with a pillow. However, one afternoon as I watched him, my head poked between the iron posts of the foot of the bed, he looked straight at me and grinned. I skipped through the rooms, down the echoing halls, shouting, "Mama, he smiled. He's all there! He's all there!" and he was.

When he was two, if you laid him on his stomach, he began to try to move himself, straining terribly. The doctor said that with his weak heart this strain would probably kill him, but it didn't. Trembling, he'd push himself up, turning first red, then a soft purple, and finally collapse

---

2. *caul:* membrane that sometimes covers the head of a newborn.

back onto the bed like an old worn-out doll. I can still see Mama watching him, her hand pressed tight across her mouth, her eyes wide and unblinking. But he learned to crawl (it was his third winter), and we brought him out of the front bedroom, putting him on the rug before the fireplace. For the first time he became one of us.

As long as he lay all the time in bed, we called him William Armstrong, even though it was formal and sounded as if we were referring to one of our ancestors, but with his creeping around on the deerskin rug and beginning to talk, something had to be done about his name. It was I who renamed him. When he crawled, he crawled backwards, as if he were in reverse and couldn't change gears. If you called him, he'd turn around as if he were going in the other direction, then he'd back right up to you to be picked up. Crawling backward made him look like a doodlebug, so I began to call him Doodle, and in time even Mama and Daddy thought it was a better name than William Armstrong. Only Aunt Nicey disagreed. She said caul babies should be treated with special respect since they might turn out to be saints. Renaming my brother was perhaps the kindest thing I ever did for him, because nobody expects much from someone called Doodle.

Although Doodle learned to crawl, he showed no signs of walking, but he wasn't idle. He talked so much that we all quit listening to what he said. It was about this time that Daddy built him a go-cart and I had to pull him around. At first I just paraded him up and down the piazza, but then he started crying to be taken out into the yard and it ended up by my having to lug him wherever I went. If I so much as picked up my cap, he'd start crying to go with me and Mama would call from wherever she was, "Take Doodle with you."

He was a burden in many ways. The doctor had said that he mustn't get too excited, too hot, too cold, or too tired and that he must always be treated gently. A long list of don'ts went with him, all of which I ignored once we got out of the house. To discourage his coming with me, I'd run with him across the ends of the cotton rows and careen him around corners on two wheels. Sometimes I accidentally turned him over, but he never told Mama. His skin was very sensitive, and he had to wear a big straw hat whenever he went out. When the going got rough and he had to cling to the sides of the go-cart, the hat slipped all the way down over his ears. He was a sight. Finally, I could see I was licked. Doodle was my brother and he was going to cling to me forever, no matter what I did, so I dragged him across the burning cotton field to share with him the only beauty I knew, Old Woman Swamp. I pulled the go-cart through the saw-tooth fern, down into the green dimness where the palmetto fronds whispered by the stream. I lifted him out and set him down in the soft rubber grass beside a tall pine. His eyes were round with wonder as he gazed about him, and his little hands began to stroke the rubber grass. Then he began to cry.

"For heaven's sake, what's the matter?" I asked, annoyed.

"It's so pretty," he said. "So pretty, pretty, pretty."

After that day Doodle and I often went down into Old Woman Swamp. I would gather wildflowers, wild violets, honeysuckle, yellow jasmine, snakeflowers, and water lilies, and with wire grass we'd weave them into necklaces and crowns. We'd bedeck ourselves with our handiwork and loll about thus beautified, beyond the touch of the everyday world. Then when the slanted rays of the sun burned orange in the tops of the pines, we'd drop our jewels into the stream and watch them float away toward the sea.

There is within me (and with sadness I have watched it in others) a knot of cruelty borne by the stream of love, much as our blood sometimes bears the seed of our destruction, and at times I was mean to Doodle. One day I took him up to the barn loft and showed him his casket, telling him how we all had believed he would die. It was covered with a film of Paris green sprinkled to kill the rats, and screech owls had built a nest inside it.

Doodle studied the mahogany box for a long time, then said, "It's not mine."

"It is," I said. "And before I'll help you down from the loft, you're going to have to touch it."

"I won't touch it," he said sullenly.

"Then I'll leave you here by yourself," I threatened, and made as if I were going down.

Doodle was frightened of being left. "Don't go leave me, Brother," he cried, and he leaned toward the coffin. His hand, trembling, reached out, and when he touched the casket he screamed. A screech owl flapped out of the box into our faces, scaring us and covering us with Paris green. Doodle was paralyzed, so I put him on my shoulder and carried him down the ladder, and even when we were outside in the bright sunshine, he clung to me, crying, "Don't leave me. Don't leave me."

When Doodle was five years old, I was embarrassed at having a brother of that age who couldn't walk, so I set out to teach him. We were down in Old Woman Swamp and it was spring and the sick-sweet smell of bay flowers hung everywhere like a mournful song. "I'm going to teach you to walk, Doodle," I said.

He was sitting comfortably on the soft grass, leaning back against the pine. "Why?" he asked.

I hadn't expected such an answer. "So I won't have to haul you around all the time."

"I can't walk, Brother," he said.

"Who says so?" I demanded.

"Mama, the doctor—everybody."

"Oh, you can walk," I said, and I took him by the arms and stood him up. He collapsed onto the grass like a half-empty flour sack. It was as if he had no bones in his little legs.

"Don't hurt me, Brother," he warned.

"Shut up. I'm not going to hurt you. I'm going to teach you to walk." I heaved him up again, and again he collapsed.

This time he did not lift his face up out of the rubber grass. "I just can't do it. Let's make honeysuckle wreaths."

"Oh yes you can, Doodle," I said. "All you got to do is try. Now come on," and I hauled him up once more.

It seemed so hopeless from the beginning that it's a miracle I didn't give up. But all of us must have something or someone to be proud of, and Doodle had become mine. I did not know then that pride is a wonderful, terrible thing, a seed that bears two vines, life and death. Every day that summer we went to the pine beside the stream of Old Woman Swamp, and I put him on his feet at least a hundred times each afternoon. Occasionally I too became discouraged because it didn't seem as if he was trying, and I would say, "Doodle, don't you *want* to learn to walk?"

He'd nod his head, and I'd say, "Well, if you don't keep trying, you'll never learn." Then I'd paint for him a picture of us as old men, white-haired, him with a long white beard and me still pulling him around in the go-cart. This never failed to make him try again.

Finally one day, after many weeks of practicing, he stood alone for a few seconds. When he fell, I grabbed him in my arms and hugged him, our laughter pealing through the swamp like a ringing bell. Now we knew it could be done. Hope no longer hid in the dark palmetto thicket but perched like a cardinal in the lacy toothbrush tree, brilliantly visible. "Yes, yes," I cried, and he cried it too, and the grass beneath us was soft and the smell of the swamp was sweet.

With success so imminent, we decided not to tell anyone until he could actually walk. Each day, barring rain, we sneaked into Old Woman Swamp, and by cotton-picking time Doodle was ready to show what he could do. He still wasn't able to walk far, but we could wait no longer. Keeping a nice secret is very hard to do, like holding your breath. We chose to reveal all on October eighth, Doodle's sixth birthday, and for weeks ahead we mooned around the house, promising everybody a most spectacular surprise. Aunt Nicey said that, after so much talk, if we produced anything less tremendous than the Resurrection, she was going to be disappointed.

At breakfast on our chosen day, when Mama, Daddy, and Aunt Nicey were in the dining room, I brought Doodle to the door in the go-cart just as usual and had them turn their backs, making them cross their hearts and hope to die if they peeked. I helped Doodle up, and when he was standing alone I let them look. There wasn't a sound as Doodle walked slowly across the room and sat down at his place at the table. Then Mama began to cry and ran over to him, hugging him and kissing him. Daddy hugged him too, so I went to Aunt Nicey, who was thanks praying in the doorway, and began to waltz her around. We danced together quite well until she came down on my big toe with her brogans, hurting me so badly I thought I was crippled for life.

Doodle told them it was I who had taught him to walk, so everyone wanted to hug me, and I began to cry.

"What are you crying for?" asked Daddy, but I couldn't answer. They did not know that I did it for myself; that pride, whose slave I was, spoke to me louder than all their voices, and that Doodle walked only because I was ashamed of having a crippled brother.

Within a few months Doodle had learned to walk well and his go-cart was put up in the barn loft (it's still there) beside his little mahogany coffin. Now, when we roamed off together, resting often, we never turned back until our destination had been reached, and to help pass the time, we took up lying. From the beginning Doodle was a terrible liar and he got me in the habit. Had anyone stopped to listen to us, we would have been sent off to Dix Hill.

My lies were scary, involved, and usually pointless, but Doodle's were twice as crazy. People in his stories all had wings and flew wherever they wanted to go. His favorite lie was about a boy named Peter who had a pet peacock with a ten-foot tail. Peter wore a golden robe that glittered so brightly that when he walked through the sunflowers they turned away from the sun to face him. When Peter was ready to go to sleep, the peacock spread his magnificent tail, enfolding the boy gently like a closing go-to-sleep flower, burying him in the gloriously iridescent, rustling vortex. Yes, I must admit it. Doodle could beat me lying.

Doodle and I spent lots of time thinking about our future. We decided that when we were grown we'd live in Old Woman Swamp and pick dog-tongue[3] for a living. Beside the stream, he planned, we'd build us a house of whispering leaves and the swamp birds would be our chickens. All day long (when we weren't gathering dog-tongue) we'd swing through the cypresses on the rope vines, and if it rained we'd huddle beneath an umbrella tree and play stickfrog. Mama and Daddy could come and live with us if they wanted to. He even came up with the idea that he could marry Mama and I could marry Daddy. Of course, I was old enough to know this wouldn't work out, but the picture he painted was so beautiful and serene that all I could do was whisper Yes, yes.

Once I had succeeded in teaching Doodle to walk, I begin to believe in my own infallibility[4] and I prepared a terrific development program for him, unknown to Mama and Daddy, of course. I would teach him to run, to swim, to climb trees, and to fight. He, too, now believed in my infallibility, so we set the deadline for these accomplishments less than a year away, when, it had been decided, Doodle could start to school.

That winter we didn't make much progress, for I was in school and Doodle suffered from one bad cold after another. But when spring came, rich and warm, we raised our sights again. Success lay at the end of summer like a pot of gold, and our campaign got off to a good start. On hot days, Doodle and I went down to Horsehead Landing and I gave him swimming lessons or showed him how to row a boat. Sometimes we descended into the cool greenness of Old Woman Swamp and climbed the rope vines or boxed scientifically beneath the pine where he had learned to walk. Promise hung about us like the leaves, and wherever we looked, ferns unfurled and birds broke into song.

That summer, the summer of 1918, was blighted. In May and June there was no rain and the crops withered, curled up, then died under the thirsty sun. One morning in July a hurricane came out of the east, tipping over the oaks in the yard and splitting the limbs of the elm trees. That afternoon it roared back out of the west, blew the fallen oaks around, snapping their roots and tearing them out of the earth like a hawk at the entrails of a chicken. Cotton bolls were wrenched from the stalks and lay like green walnuts in the valleys between the rows, while

---

3. *dog-tongue:* a plant having tonguelike leaves and red flowers, usually known as hound's tongue.

4. *infallibility:* the quality of being incapable of making mistakes.

the cornfield leaned over uniformly so that the tassels touched the ground. Doodle and I followed Daddy out into the cotton field, where he stood, shoulders sagging, surveying the ruin. When his chin sank down onto his chest, we were frightened, and Doodle slipped his hand into mine. Suddenly Daddy straightened his shoulders, raised a giant knuckly fist, and with a voice that seemed to rumble out of the earth itself began cursing heaven, hell, the weather, and the Republican Party. Doodle and I, prodding each other and giggling, went back to the house, knowing that everything would be all right.

And during that summer, strange names were heard through the house: Château Thierry, Amiens, Soissons, and in her blessing at the supper table, Mama once said, "And bless the Pearsons, whose boy Joe was lost at Belleau Wood."[5]

So we came to that clove of seasons. School was only a few weeks away, and Doodle was far behind schedule. He could barely clear the ground when climbing up the rope vines and his swimming was certainly not passable. We decided to double our efforts, to make that last drive and reach our pot of gold. I made him swim until he turned blue and row until he couldn't lift an oar. Wherever we went, I purposely walked fast, and although he kept up, his face turned red and his eyes became glazed. Once, he could go no further, so he collapsed on the ground and began to cry.

"Aw, come on, Doodle," I urged. "You can do it. Do you want to be different from everybody else when you start school?"

"Does it make any difference?"

"It certainly does," I said. "Now, come on," and I helped him up.

As we slipped through dog days, Doodle began to look feverish, and Mama felt his forehead, asking him if he felt ill. At night he didn't sleep well, and sometimes he had nightmares, crying out until I touched him and said, "Wake up, Doodle. Wake up."

It was Saturday noon, just a few days before school was to start. I should have already admitted defeat, but my pride wouldn't let me. The excitement of our program had now been gone for weeks, but still we kept on with a tired doggedness. It was too late to turn back, for we had both wandered too far into a net of expectations and had left no crumbs behind.

Daddy, Mama, Doodle, and I were seated at the dining-room table

---

5. *Château Thierry . . . Belleau Wood:* places in France where famous battles were fought during World War I.

having lunch. It was a hot day, with all the windows and doors open in case a breeze should come. In the kitchen Aunt Nicey was humming softly. After a long silence, Daddy spoke. "It's so calm, I wouldn't be surprised if we had a storm this afternoon."

"I haven't heard a rain frog," said Mama, who believed in signs, as she served the bread around the table.

"I did," declared Doodle. "Down in the swamp."

"He didn't," I said contrarily.

"You did, eh?" said Daddy, ignoring my denial.

"I certainly did," Doodle reiterated, scowling at me over the top of his iced-tea glass, and we were quiet again.

Suddenly, from out in the yard, came a strange croaking noise. Doodle stopped eating, with a piece of bread poised ready for his mouth, his eyes popped round like two blue buttons. "What's that?" he whispered.

I jumped up, knocking over my chair, and had reached the door when Mama called, "Pick up the chair, sit down again, and say excuse me."

By the time I had done this, Doodle had excused himself and had slipped out into the yard. He was looking up into the bleeding tree. "It's a great big red bird!" he called.

The bird croaked loudly again, and Mama and Daddy came out into the yard. We shaded our eyes with our hands against the hazy glare of the sun and peered up through the still leaves. On the topmost branch a bird the size of a chicken, with scarlet feathers and long legs, was perched precariously. Its wings hung down loosely, and as we watched, a feather dropped away and floated slowly down through the green leaves.

"It's not even frightened of us," Mama said.

"It looks tired," Daddy added. "Or maybe sick."

Doodle's hands were clasped at his throat, and I had never seen him stand still so long. "What is it?" he asked.

Daddy shook his head. "I don't know, maybe it's —"

At that moment the bird began to flutter, but the wings were uncoordinated, and amid much flapping and a spray of flying feathers, it tumbled down, bumping through the limbs of the bleeding tree and landing at our feet with a thud. Its long, graceful neck jerked twice into an S, then straightened out, and the bird was still. A white veil came over the eyes and the long white beak unhinged. Its legs were crossed and its clawlike feet were delicately curved at rest. Even death did not mar its grace, for it lay on the earth like a broken vase of red flowers, and we stood around it, awed by its exotic beauty.

"It's dead," Mama said.

"What is it?" Doodle repeated.

"Go bring me the bird book," said Daddy.

I ran into the house and brought back the bird book. As we watched, Daddy thumbed through its pages. "It's a scarlet ibis," he said, pointing to a picture. "It lives in the tropics—South America to Florida. A storm must have brought it here."

Sadly, we all looked back at the bird. A scarlet ibis! How many miles it had traveled to die like this, in *our* yard, beneath the bleeding tree.

"Let's finish lunch," Mama said, nudging us back toward the dining room.

"I'm not hungry," said Doodle, and he knelt down beside the ibis.

"We've got peach cobbler for dessert," Mama tempted from the doorway.

Doodle remained kneeling. "I'm going to bury him."

"Don't you dare touch him," Mama warned. "There's no telling what disease he might have had."

"All right," said Doodle. "I won't."

Daddy, Mama, and I went back to the dining-room table, but we watched Doodle through the open door. He took out a piece of string from his pocket and, without touching the ibis, looped one end around its neck. Slowly, while singing softly *Shall We Gather at the River,* he carried the bird around to the front yard and dug a hole in the flower garden, next to the petunia bed. Now we were watching him through the front window, but he didn't know it. His awkwardness at digging the hole with a shovel whose handle was twice as long as he was made us laugh, and we covered our mouths with our hands so he wouldn't hear.

When Doodle came into the dining room, he found us seriously eating our cobbler. He was pale and lingered just inside the screen door. "Did you get the scarlet ibis buried?" asked Daddy.

Doodle didn't speak but nodded his head.

"Go wash your hands, and then you can have some peach cobbler," said Mama.

"I'm not hungry," he said.

"Dead birds is bad luck," said Aunt Nicey, poking her head from the kitchen door. "Specially *red* dead birds!"

As soon as I had finished eating, Doodle and I hurried off to Horsehead Landing. Time was short, and Doodle still had a long way to go if he was going to keep up with the other boys when he started school. The sun, gilded with the yellow cast of autumn, still burned fiercely, but the dark green woods through which we passed were shady and cool. When we reached the landing, Doodle said he was too tired to swim, so we got into a skiff and floated down the creek with the tide. Far off in the marsh a rail was scolding, and over on the beach locusts were singing in the myrtle trees. Doodle did not speak and kept his head turned away, letting one hand trail limply in the water.

After we had drifted a long way, I put the oars in place and made Doodle row back against the tide. Black clouds began to gather in the southwest, and he kept watching them, trying to pull the oars a little faster. When we reached Horsehead Landing, lightning was playing across half the sky and thunder roared out, hiding even the sound of the sea. The sun disappeared and darkness descended, almost like night. Flocks of marsh crows flew by, heading inland to their roosting trees, and two egrets, squawking, arose from the oyster-rock shallows and careened away.

Doodle was both tired and frightened, and when he stepped from the skiff he collapsed onto the mud, sending an armada of fiddler crabs rustling off into the marsh grass. I helped him up, and as he wiped the mud off his trousers, he smiled at me ashamedly. He had failed and we both knew it, so we started back home, racing the storm. We never spoke (What are the words that can solder cracked pride?), but I knew he was watching me, watching for a sign of mercy. The lightning was near now, and from fear he walked so close behind me he kept stepping on my heels. The faster I walked, the faster he walked, so I began to run. The rain was coming, roaring through the pines, and then, like a bursting Roman candle, a gum tree ahead of us was shattered by a bolt of lightning. When the deafening peal of thunder had died, and in the moment before the rain arrived, I heard Doodle, who had fallen behind, cry out, "Brother, Brother, don't leave me! Don't leave me!"

The knowledge that Doodle's and my plans had come to naught was bitter, and that streak of cruelty within me awakened. I ran as fast as I could, leaving him far behind with a wall of rain dividing us. The drops stung my face like nettles, and the wind flared the wet glistening leaves of the bordering trees. Soon I could hear his voice no more.

I hadn't run too far before I became tired, and the flood of childish spite evanesced[6] as well. I stopped and waited for Doodle. The sound of rain was everywhere, but the wind had died and it fell straight down in parallel paths like ropes hanging from the sky. As I waited, I peered through the downpour, but no one came. Finally I went back and found him huddled beneath a red nightshade bush beside the road. He

---

6. *evanesced* (ev˝ə nesd´): disappeared.

was sitting on the ground, his face buried in his arms, which were resting on his drawn-up knees. "Let's go, Doodle," I said.

He didn't answer, so I placed my hand on his forehead and lifted his head. Limply, he fell backwards onto the earth. He had been bleeding from the mouth, and his neck and the front of his shirt were stained a brilliant red.

"Doodle! Doodle!" I cried, shaking him, but there was no answer but the ropy rain. He lay very awkwardly, with his head thrown far back, making his vermilion neck appear unusually long and slim. His little legs, bent sharply at the knees, had never before seemed so fragile, so thin.

I began to weep, and the tear-blurred vision in red before me looked very familiar. "Doodle!" I screamed above the pounding storm and threw my body to the earth above his. For a long long time, it seemed forever, I lay there crying, sheltering my fallen scarlet ibis from the heresy of rain.

Responding to the Story

1. Explain the role of the narrator's pride in this story. Do you believe that pride can affect behavior as much as the narrator's pride affected his behavior?

2. James Hurst created a sympathetic character in Doodle. Compile a list of all the specific references to Doodle that help endear him to the reader.

3. How is Doodle's death foreshadowed?

Exploring the Author's Craft

1. The *climax* or climactic moment is the turning point in a story. It often occurs near the end of a short story and is the point at which the main conflict must be resolved. What is the climactic moment in "The Scarlet Ibis"? Are the narrator's actions at this moment believable?

2. A *symbol* is something that represents something else. For example, a heart represents or stands for love. Is the scarlet ibis an appropriate symbol for Doodle? Why or why not?

Writing Workshop

Perceptive readers may have noticed the frequent references to the color red in this story. Can a color be a symbol? Is it a symbol in this story, or are the references to red just chance? If red is a symbol here, what does it symbolize? Write a short paper in which you discuss the use of red in this story.

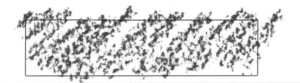

Sucker

Carson McCullers

Carson McCullers (born Lulu Carson Smith in 1917 in Columbus, Georgia) went to New York City at the age of seventeen where she took courses in creative writing at Columbia and New York University. She was married in 1937 to Reeves McCullers. They were divorced but remarried in 1945.

Her most notable works include The Heart Is a Lonely Hunter *(1940),* Reflections in a Golden Eye *(1941), and* A Member of the Wedding *(1946), which was adapted for the stage and won a Drama Critics Circle Award. It ran for over five hundred performances and starred Julie Harris, Ethel Waters, and Brandon de Wilde, all of whom starred in the film version as well. It tells of Frankie, a thirteen-year-old, who wants to accompany her brother and his wife on their honeymoon.*

Her later works include The Ballad of the Sad Cafe: The Novels and Stories of Carson McCullers *(1951);* The Square Root of Wonderful *(1958); and* The Mortgaged Heart *(1971), a posthumous collection of her work.* The Ballad of the Sad Cafe, *a novella, was dramatized in 1963 by Edward Albee. She died in 1967.*

McCullers is frequently allied with other Southern writers, Eudora Welty, Flannery O'Connor, and William Faulkner, whose works also are often about lonely misfits. McCullers wrote "Sucker" when she was seventeen years old.

It was always like I had a room to myself. Sucker slept in my bed with me but that didn't interfere with anything. The room was mine and I used it as I wanted to. Once I remember sawing a trap door in the floor. Last year when I was a sophomore in high school I tacked on my wall some pictures of girls from magazines and one of them was just in her underwear. My mother never bothered me because she had the younger kids to look after. And Sucker thought anything I did was always swell.

Whenever I would bring any of my friends back to my room all I had to do was just glance at Sucker and he would get up from whatever he was busy with and maybe half smile at me, and leave without saying a word. He never brought kids back there. He's twelve, four years younger than I am, and he always knew without me even telling him that I didn't want kids that age meddling with my things.

Half the time I used to forget that Sucker isn't my brother. He's my first cousin but practically ever since I remember he's been in our family. You see his folks were killed in a wreck when he was a baby. To me and my kid sisters he was like our brother.

Sucker used to always remember and believe every word I said. That's how he got his nickname. Once a couple of years ago I told him that if he'd jump off our garage with an umbrella it would act as a parachute and he wouldn't fall hard. He did it and busted his knee. That's just one instance. And the funny thing was that no matter how many times he got fooled he would still believe me. Not that he was dumb in other ways—it was just the way he acted with me. He would look at everything I did and quietly take it in.

There is one thing I have learned, but it makes me feel guilty and is hard to figure out. If a person admires you a lot you despise him and don't care—and it is the person who doesn't notice you that you are apt to admire. This is not easy to realize. Maybelle Watts, this senior at school, acted like she was the Queen of Sheba[1] and even humiliated me. Yet at this same time I would have done anything in the world to get her attentions. All I could think about day and night was Maybelle until I was nearly crazy. When Sucker was a little kid and on up until the time he was twelve I guess I treated him as bad as Maybelle did me.

Now that Sucker has changed so much it is a little hard to remember him as he used to be. I never imagined anything would suddenly happen that would make us both very different. I never knew that in order to get what has happened straight in my mind I would want to think back on him as he used to be and compare and try to get things settled. If I could have seen ahead maybe I would have acted different.

I never noticed him much or thought about him and when you consider how long we have had the same room together it is funny the

---

1. *Queen of Sheba:* queen who visited King Solomon; the account is in the Bible in I Kings.

few things I remember. He used to talk to himself a lot when he'd think he was alone—all about him fighting gangsters and being on ranches and that sort of kids' stuff. He'd get in the bathroom and stay as long as an hour and sometimes his voice would go up high and excited and you could hear him all over the house. Usually, though, he was very quiet. He didn't have many boys in the neighborhood to buddy with and his face had the look of a kid who is watching a game and waiting to be asked to play. He didn't mind wearing the sweaters and coats that I outgrew, even if the sleeves did flop down too big and make his wrists look as thin and white as a little girl's. That is how I remember him— getting a little bigger every year but still being the same. That was Sucker up until a few months ago when all this trouble began.

Maybelle was somehow mixed up in what happened so I guess I ought to start with her. Until I knew her I hadn't given much time to girls. Last fall she sat next to me in General Science class and that was when I first began to notice her. Her hair is the brightest yellow I ever saw and occasionally she will wear it set into curls with some sort of gluey stuff. Her fingernails are pointed and manicured and painted a shiny red. All during class I used to watch Maybelle, nearly all the time except when I thought she was going to look my way or when the teacher called on me. I couldn't keep my eyes off her hands, for one thing. They are very little and white except for that red stuff, and when she would turn the pages of her book she always licked her thumb and held out her little finger and turned very slowly. It is impossible to describe Maybelle. All the boys are crazy about her but she didn't even notice me. For one thing she's almost two years older than I am. Between periods I used to try and pass very close to her in the halls but she would hardly ever smile at me. All I could do was sit and look at her in class— and sometimes it was like the whole room could hear my heart beating and I wanted to holler or light out and run for hell.

At night, in bed, I would imagine about Maybelle. Often this would keep me from sleeping until as late as one or two o'clock. Sometimes Sucker would wake up and ask me why I couldn't get settled and I'd tell him to hush his mouth. I suppose I was mean to him lots of times. I guess I wanted to ignore somebody like Maybelle did me. You could always tell by Sucker's face when his feelings were hurt. I don't remember all the ugly remarks I must have made because even when I was saying them my mind was on Maybelle.

That went on for nearly three months and then somehow she began to change. In the halls she would speak to me and every morning she copied my homework. At lunch time once I danced with her in the gym. One afternoon I got up nerve and went around to her house with a carton of cigarettes. I knew she smoked in the girls' basement and sometimes outside of school—and I didn't want to take her candy because I think that's been run into the ground. She was very nice and it seemed to me everything was going to change.

It was that night when this trouble really started. I had come into my room late and Sucker was already asleep. I felt too happy and keyed up to get in a comfortable position and was awake thinking about Maybelle a long time. Then I dreamed about her and it seemed I kissed her. It was a surprise to wake up and see the dark. I lay still and a little while passed before I could come to and understand where I was. The house was quiet and it was a very dark night.

Sucker's voice was a shock to me. "Pete? . . ."

I didn't answer anything or even move.

"You do like me as much as if I was your own brother, don't you, Pete?"

I couldn't get over the surprise of everything and it was like this was the real dream instead of the other.

"You have liked me all the time like I was your own brother, haven't you?"

"Sure," I said.

Then I got up for a few minutes. It was cold and I was glad to come back to bed. Sucker hung on to my back. He felt little and warm and I could feel his warm breathing on my shoulder.

"No matter what you did I always knew you liked me."

I was wide awake and my mind seemed mixed up in a strange way. There was this happiness about Maybelle and all that—but at the same time something about Sucker and his voice when he said these things made me take notice. Anyway I guess you understand people better when you are happy than when something is worrying you. It was like I had never really thought about Sucker until then. I felt I had always been mean to him. One night a few weeks before I had heard him crying in the dark. He said he had lost a boy's beebee gun and was scared to let anybody know. He wanted me to tell him what to do. I was sleepy and tried to make him hush and when he wouldn't I kicked at him. That was just one of the things I remembered. It seemed to me he had always been a lonesome kid. I felt bad.

There is something about a dark cold night that makes you feel close to someone you're sleeping with. When you talk together it is like you are the only people awake in the town.

"You're a swell kid, Sucker," I said.

It seemed to me suddenly that I did like him more than anybody else I knew—more than any other boy, more than my sisters, more in a certain way even than Maybelle. I felt good all over and it was like when they play sad music in the movies. I wanted to show Sucker how much I really thought of him and make up for the way I had always treated him.

We talked for a good while that night. His voice was fast and it was like he had been saving up these things to tell me for a long time. He mentioned that he was going to try to build a canoe and that the kids down the block wouldn't let him in on their football team and I don't know what all. I talked some too and it was a good feeling to think of him taking in everything I said so seriously. I even spoke of Maybelle a little, only I made out like it was her who had been running after me all this time. He asked questions about high school and so forth. His voice was excited and he kept on talking fast like he could never get the words out in time. When I went to sleep he was still talking and I could still feel his breathing on my shoulder, warm and close.

During the next couple of weeks I saw a lot of Maybelle. She acted as though she really cared for me a little. Half the time I felt so good I hardly knew what to do with myself.

But I didn't forget about Sucker. There were a lot of old things in my bureau drawer I'd been saving—boxing gloves and Tom Swift books and second rate fishing tackle. All this I turned over to him. We had some more talks together and it was really like I was knowing him for the first time. When there was a long cut on his cheek I knew he had been monkeying around with this new first razor set of mine, but I didn't say anything. His face seemed different now. He used to look timid and sort of like he was afraid of a whack over the head. That expression was gone. His face, with those wide-open eyes and his ears sticking out and his mouth never quite shut, had the look of a person who is surprised and expecting something swell.

Once I started to point him out to Maybelle and tell her he was my kid brother. It was an afternoon when a murder mystery was on at the movie. I had earned a dollar working for my Dad and I gave Sucker a quarter to go and get candy and so forth. With the rest I took Maybelle. We were sitting near the back and I saw Sucker come in. He began to stare at the screen the minute he stepped past the ticket man and he stumbled down the aisle without noticing where he was going. I started to punch Maybelle but couldn't quite make up my mind. Sucker looked a little silly—walking like a drunk with his eyes glued to the movie. He was wiping his reading glasses on his shirt tail and his knickers flopped down. He went on until he got to the first few rows where the kids usually sit. I never did punch Maybelle. But I got to thinking it was good to have both of them at the movie with the money I earned.

I guess things went on like this for about a month or six weeks. I felt so good I couldn't settle down to study or put my mind on anything. I wanted to be friendly with everybody. There were times when I just had to talk to some person. And usually that would be Sucker. He felt as good as I did. Once he said: "Pete, I am gladder that you are like my brother than anything else in the world."

Then something happened between Maybelle and me. I never have figured out just what it was. Girls like her are hard to understand. She began to act different toward me. At first I wouldn't let myself believe this and tried to think it was just my imagination. She didn't act glad to see me anymore. Often she went out riding with this fellow on the football team who owns this yellow roadster.[2] The car was the color of her hair and after school she would ride off with him, laughing and looking into his face. I couldn't think of anything to do about it and she was on my mind all day and night. When I did get a chance to go out with her she was snippy and didn't seem to notice me. This made me feel like something was the matter—I would worry about my shoes clopping too loud on the floor, or the fly of my pants, or the bumps on my chin. Sometimes when Maybelle was around, a devil would get into me and I'd hold my face stiff and call grown men by their last names without the Mister and say rough things. In the night I would wonder what made me do all this until I was too tired for sleep.

At first I was so worried I just forgot about Sucker. Then later he began to get on my nerves. He was always hanging around until I would get back from high school, always looking like he had something to say to me or wanted me to tell him. He made me a magazine rack in his Manual Training class[3] and one week he saved his lunch money and bought me three packs of cigarettes. He couldn't seem to take it in that I had things on my mind and didn't want to fool with him. Every afternoon it would be the same—him in my room with this waiting expression on his face. Then I wouldn't say anything or I'd maybe answer him rough-like and he would finally go on out.

I can't divide that time up and say this happened one day and that

---

2. *roadster:* a small automobile with a fabric top that seats two people.
3. *Manual Training class:* class in which boys were trained in various crafts, such as woodworking.

the next. For one thing I was so mixed up the weeks just slid along into each other and I felt like hell and didn't care. Nothing definite was said or done. Maybelle still rode around with this fellow in his yellow roadster and sometimes she would smile at me and sometimes not. Every afternoon I went from one place to another where I thought she would be. Either she would act almost nice and I would begin thinking how nice things would finally clear up and she would care for me—or else she'd behave so that if she hadn't been a girl I'd have wanted to grab her by that white little neck and choke her. The more ashamed I felt for making a fool of myself the more I ran after her.

Sucker kept getting on my nerves more and more. He would look at me as though he sort of blamed me for something, but at the same time knew that it wouldn't last long. He was growing fast and for some reason began to stutter when he talked. Sometimes he had nightmares or would throw up his breakfast. Mom got him a bottle of cod liver oil.

Then the finish came between Maybelle and me. I met her going to the drug store and asked for a date. When she said no I remarked something sarcastic. She told me she was sick and tired of my being around and that she had never cared a rap about me. She said all that. I just stood there and didn't answer anything. I walked home very slowly.

For several afternoons I stayed in my room by myself. I didn't want to go anywhere or talk to anyone. When Sucker would come in and look at me sort of funny I'd yell at him to get out. I didn't want to think of Maybelle and I sat at my desk reading *Popular Mechanics* or whittling at a toothbrush rack I was making. It seemed to me I was putting that girl out of my mind pretty well.

But you can't help what happens to you at night. This is what made things how they are now.

You see a few nights after Maybelle said those words to me I dreamed about her again. It was like that first time and I was squeezing Sucker's arm so tight I woke him up. He reached for my hand.

"Pete, what's the matter with you?"

All of a sudden I felt so mad my throat choked—at myself and the dream of Maybelle and Sucker and every single person I knew. I remembered all the times Maybelle had humiliated me and everything bad that had ever happened. It seemed to me for a second that nobody would ever like me but a sap like Sucker.

"Why is it we aren't buddies like we were before? Why—?"

"Shut your trap!" I threw off the cover and got up and turned on the light. He sat in the middle of the bed, his eyes blinking and scared.

There was something in me and I couldn't help myself. I don't think anybody ever gets that mad but once. Words came without me knowing what they would be. It was only afterward that I could remember each thing I said and see it all in a clear way.

"Why aren't we buddies? Because you're the dumbest slob I ever saw! Nobody cares anything about you! And just because I felt sorry for you sometimes and tried to act decent don't think I give a darn about a dumb-bunny like you!"

If I'd talked loud or hit him it wouldn't have been so bad. But my voice was slow and like I was very calm. Sucker's mouth was part way open and he looked as though he'd knocked his funny bone. His face was white and sweat came out on his forehead. He wiped it away with the back of his hand and for a minute his arm stayed raised that way as though he was holding something away from him.

"Don't you know a single thing? Haven't you ever been around at all? Why don't you get a girl friend instead of me? What kind of a sissy do you want to grow up to be anyway?"

I didn't know what was coming next. I couldn't help myself or think.

Sucker didn't move. He had on one of my pajama jackets and his neck stuck out skinny and small. His hair was damp on his forehead.

"Why do you always hang around me? Don't you know when you're not wanted?"

Afterward I could remember the change in Sucker's face. Slowly the blank look went away and he closed his mouth. His eyes got narrow and his fists shut. There had never been such a look on him before. It was like every second he was getting older. There was a hard look to his eyes you don't see usually in a kid. A drop of sweat rolled down his chin and he didn't notice. He just sat there with those eyes on me and he didn't speak and his face was hard and didn't move.

"No you don't know when you're not wanted. You're too dumb. Just like your name—a dumb Sucker."

It was like something had busted inside me. I turned off the light and sat down in the chair by the window. My legs were shaking and I was so tired I could have bawled. The room was cold and dark. I sat there for a long time and smoked a squashed cigarette I had saved. Outside the yard was black and quiet. After a while I heard Sucker lie down.

I wasn't mad anymore, only tired. It seemed awful to me that I had talked like that to a kid only twelve. I couldn't take it all in. I told myself I would go over to him and try to make it up. But I just sat there in the cold until a long time had passed. I planned how I could straighten it out in the morning. Then, trying not to squeak the springs, I got back in bed.

Sucker was gone when I woke up the next day. And later when I wanted to apologize as I had planned he looked at me in this new hard way so that I couldn't say a word.

All of that was two or three months ago. Since then Sucker has grown faster than any boy I ever saw. He's almost as tall as I am and his bones have gotten heavier and bigger. He won't wear any of my old clothes any more and has bought his first pair of long pants[4]—with some leather suspenders to hold them up. Those are just the changes that are easy to see and put into words.

Our room isn't mine at all any more. He's gotten up this gang of kids and they have a club. When they aren't digging trenches in some vacant lot and fighting they are always in my room. On the door there is some foolishness written in Mercurochrome saying "Woe to the Outsider who Enters" and signed with crossed bones and their secret initials. They have rigged up a radio and every afternoon it blares out music. Once as I was coming in I heard a boy telling something in a loud voice about what he saw in the back of his brother's automobile. I could guess what I didn't hear. *That's what her and my brother do. It's the truth—parked in the car.* For a minute Sucker looked surprised and his face was almost like it used to be. Then he got hard and tough again. "Sure, dumbbell. We know all that." They didn't notice me. Sucker began telling them how in two years he was planning to be a trapper in Alaska.

But most of the time Sucker stays by himself. It is worse when we are alone together in the room. He sprawls across the bed in those long corduroy pants with the suspenders and just stares at me with that hard, half-sneering look. I fiddle around my desk and can't get settled because of those eyes of his. And the thing is I just have to study because I've gotten three bad cards this term already. If I flunk English I can't graduate next year. I don't want to be a bum and I just have to get my mind on it. I don't care a flip for Maybelle or any particular girl any more and it's only this thing between Sucker and me that is the trouble now. We never speak except when we have to before the family. I don't even want to call him Sucker any more and unless I forget I call him

---

4. *long pants:* At the time this story takes place, boys wore either short pants or knickers (pants that came just below the knee) with long socks until they reached a certain age, usually twelve or thirteen.

by his real name, Richard. At night I can't study with him in the room and I have to hang around the drug store, smoking and doing nothing, with the fellows who loaf there.

More than anything I want to be easy in my mind again. And I miss the way Sucker and I were for a while in a funny, sad way that before this I never would have believed. But everything is so different that there seems to be nothing I can do to get it right. I've sometimes thought if we could have it out in a big fight that would help. But I can't fight him because he's four years younger. And another thing— sometimes this look in his eyes makes me almost believe that if Sucker could he would kill me.

Responding to the Story

1. How did you feel about Sucker when the story ended? In several paragraphs explain why you think you came to feel the way you did. (Think about the ways the author described Sucker throughout the story.)

2. "If a person admires you a lot you despise him and don't care—and it is the person who doesn't notice you that you are apt to admire."

   a. Explain what the narrator means by these words. How are these words relevant to the story?

   b. Write a short paper in which you support or refute the idea in this quotation. Base your paper on your own experiences.

3. Do you see any similarities between the narrator of "Sucker" and the narrator of "The Scarlet Ibis"? Are there some differences between the two? Explain.

Exploring the Author's Craft

This story was carefully structured. Explain how the stories of the narrator and Maybelle and the narrator and Sucker parallel each other.

Writing Workshop

In any form you wish—story, essay, poem, or short script—create a written work that explores a relationship between two siblings. If you are writing prose, write about two or three different incidents that show the changing nature of the relationship between the two.

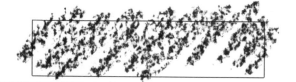

A Private Talk with Holly

Henry Gregor Felsen

Henry Gregor Felsen's book Hot Rod, *published in 1949, was one of the first young adult books to deal with realistic themes, and it was immensely popular with young people.* Two and the Town *(1952) was about teenage pregnancy, a topic not widely dealt with in the 1950s, and although read avidly by teenagers, it caused considerable controversy.*

Felsen's other books about cars included Crash Club, Fever Heat, Road Rocket, Street Rod, *and* Rag Top.

He was born in Brooklyn in 1916 and attended the State University of Iowa for two years. He and his wife had two children, Daniel and Holly. He now lives in Michigan.

I t was a summertime Saturday morning, and I was up before dawn to go fishing. I tiptoed out of the house so I wouldn't disturb anyone, but when I reached my car, someone was already up and waiting for me—my seventeen-year-old daughter, Holly. She was dressed in jeans, a blue denim shirt, and a khaki fishing vest, and she was checking out her tackle box. I knew that she had something important on her mind.

Holly first became my fishing buddy when she was about six years old. For years, I couldn't go fishing without taking her along, but when she reached her teens, she began to develop other interests. After a while, the only time she'd go with me was when she needed to have a private talk; the most private place we had was our little boat on a remote lake at dawn.

We reached the lake, near West Des Moines, Iowa, before the sun was up, unloaded our boat, and slid it into the water. Holly took her usual place in the bow while I pushed off. I switched on the electric motor, and it propelled us quietly across the calm water. The night mist was just beginning to lift, slowly unveiling the pines and birches that lined the shore. A beaver, irritated by our intrusion, slapped the water with his strong, broad tail to show his displeasure.

"The usual starting place?" Holly asked.

"The usual."

I steered the boat to a quiet inlet dotted with tree stumps and came to a stop. Bass country.

"The usual bet?" Holly asked. She smiled, but her dark-brown eyes were serious, almost sad.

"The usual," I said. That was a dollar for the first fish and a dollar for the largest.

Silently, with studied care, she attached a plug to her line. Then, with a delicate but sure hand, she cast the plug alongside one of the stumps and began a slow retrieve, twitching the plug along to put it in lifelike motion. I picked out two stumps set fairly close together and cast an imitation minnow between them.

We fished around the stumps for several minutes without getting a bite. I couldn't help wondering what was on Holly's mind, but I knew she would talk to me when *she* was ready—it would only hurt to try to hurry her. At times, being a parent demands as much patience as fishing.

"Let's try drifting the bottom," my daughter said. "I have a feeling they're swimming very deep this morning."

I steered the boat out into open water, and we rigged our lures to run deep. I switched off the motor and let the boat drift very slowly, our lines trailing behind us. Now the sun was rising, and the lake and woods were bathed in the pure, clear light of dawn. Holly put on an old, battered fishing hat to shade her eyes. I looked around. There were no other boats on the lake. It was as though we were the only human beings on earth.

"Dad . . ."

I knew from her tone that the moment had come. "Yes?"

"You know my plans for college—to go to junior college in town this fall, then transfer after two years to the state university . . ."

"They're good plans," I said. "Among other benefits, we'll be able to do this for another two years."

She looked away, and I looked at the long, brown hair that curled out from under the old fishing hat. She looked so little—so fragile. Two short years, and she would be gone.

"Dad, would you be mad if I changed my plans?"

My throat seemed to close. My words had to be forced out. "Don't tell me you don't want to go to college . . ."

"I do, Dad. It's just . . . well, I don't want you to think I'm unhappy at home or anything, but I want to go away to the university this fall."

"Well," I said, grasping at straws, "I suppose we'd still have our summers to do a little fishing."

She turned to look at me. "I wouldn't be home in the summer. I'd like to stay in school all year long and finish in three years. That way, I'll have my education and be ready for a job a year earlier."

And that was it. All of a sudden, good-bye forever to my big little girl. My feelings must have shown in my face, because she gave me an out. "It's up to you, Dad. I know it will cost more, and I'll be away most of the time. If you don't want me to go, I'll stay here."

Before I could answer, the fishing rod jerked almost out of my hands as the tip plunged into the water. I could tell by the strength of the pull that I had a big one hooked. Holly forgot everything in the excitement of pulling in the big fish. She grabbed the net and dipped it into the water so she could get it under him when he neared the boat. Slowly, with the line taut almost to the breaking point, I worked the fish in. Holly netted him and used both hands to hoist him into the boat. What we had was the most beautiful bass I'd ever tangled with.

"Oh, Dad," Holly said, "this is one you have to take home and have mounted for your study wall. It's the biggest bass I've ever seen!"

Her words sank in, and I took a long, hard look at that bass, considering. Finally, I unhooked him carefully, lifted him, and, as Holly stared in disbelief, put him gently back into the lake. In an instant, he was gone.

"Honey," I said, "I've always dreamed of having a fish like that mounted on my wall, where I could look at him whenever I wanted to. But a fish on a wall is a lifeless thing, no matter how much you prize it. That fish was so full of life and fought so hard for his freedom that I had to let him go back where he belonged, to live his own life."

Our lines went back into the water again, and we resumed our drifting and fishing. Holly's back was toward me. "Thanks, Dad," she said, without turning around. "I knew you'd understand."

But she didn't know. And she couldn't know. And she won't know until some day in the future, when her own child—with or without a word of warning—turns a back on home and walks out into the grown-up world forever.

Responding to the Story

Explain what each character felt during this talk out on the water. Then tell whose feelings you most related to and explain why.

Exploring the Author's Craft

Every story must have a *conflict,* a struggle between two opposing forces. The opposing forces may be within a character, someone who is trying to make a decision, for example. A character may be in conflict with some outside force—nature, society, or another character. Many stories have more than one conflict. What are the conflicts in this story?

Writing Workshop

A parent might understand this story more than a teenager does. Can teenagers empathize with the poignancy of a child's growing up and leaving? Here's a writing challenge: Write a poem or story that captures the point of view of a parent in relationship to his or her child. Explore the child's point of view, as the author of "A Private Talk with Holly" did, but be sure to get inside the feelings of the parent.

Alternate Media Response

1. Draw a picture of any scene of this story.
2. Create a fifteen-minute film or video that tells this story. Include both the peaceful fishing setting and the quiet conversation that occurs.

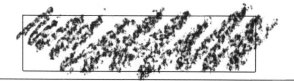

Shaving

Leslie Norris

Leslie Norris was born in Merthyr Tydfil, Glamorganshire, Wales, in 1921. He attended Training College in Coventry from 1947–49 and the University of Southhampton Institute of Education from 1955–58. He has been assistant teacher, deputy head teacher, and head teacher in schools in Yeovil, Bath, and Chichester. He was a resident poet at Eton College in 1977 and is currently affiliated with Brigham Young University in Utah.

In addition to poetry, Norris has written stories, collected in Sliding and Other Stories *(1976) and* The Girl from Cardigan: Sixteen Stories *(1988), and short radio plays. He has published in the* New Yorker, *the* Atlantic, Esquire, *and* Audubon *magazines.*

Earlier, when Barry had left the house to go to the game, an overnight frost had still been thick on the roads. But the brisk April sun had soon dispersed it, and now he could feel the spring warmth on his back through the thick tweed of his coat. His left arm was beginning to stiffen up where he'd jarred it in a tackle, but it was nothing serious. He flexed his shoulders against the tightness of his jacket and was surprised again by the unexpected weight of his muscles, the thickening strength of his body. A few years back, he thought, he had been a small, unimportant boy, one of a swarming gang laughing and jostling to school, hardly aware that he possessed an identity. But time had transformed him. He walked solidly now, and often alone. He was tall, strongly made, his hands and feet were adult and heavy, the rooms in which all his life he'd moved had grown too small for him. Sometimes a devouring restlessness drove him from the house to walk long distances in the dark. He hardly understood how it had happened. Amused and quiet, he walked the High Street among the morning shoppers.

He saw Jackie Bevan across the road and remembered how, when they were both six years old, Jackie had swallowed a pin. The flustered teachers had clucked about Jackie as he stood there, bawling, cheeks awash with tears, his nose wet. But now Jackie was tall and suave, his thick, pale hair sleekly tailored, his gray suit enviable. He was talking to a girl as golden as a daffodil.

"Hey, hey!" called Jackie. "How's the athlete, how's Barry boy?"

He waved a graceful hand at Barry.

"Come and talk to Sue," he said.

Barry shifted his bag to his left hand and walked over, forming in his mind the answers he'd make to Jackie's questions.

"Did we win?" Jackie asked. "Was the old Barry Stanford magic in glittering evidence yet once more this morning? Were the invaders sent hunched and silent back to their hovels in the hills? What was the score? Give us an epic account, Barry, without modesty or delay. This is Sue, by the way."

"I've seen you about," the girl said.

"You could hardly miss him," said Jackie. "Four men, roped together, spent a week climbing him—they thought he was Everest. He ought to carry a warning beacon, he's a danger to aircraft."

"Silly," said the girl, smiling at Jackie. "He's not much taller than you are."

She had a nice voice too.

"We won," Barry said. "Seventeen points to three, and it was a good game. The ground was hard, though."

He could think of nothing else to say.

"Let's all go for a frivolous cup of coffee," Jackie said. "Let's celebrate your safe return from the rough fields of victory. We could pour libations[1] all over the floor for you."

"I don't think so," Barry said. "Thanks. I'll go straight home."

"Okay," said Jackie, rocking on his heels so that the sun could shine on his smile. "How's your father?"

"No better," Barry said. "He's not going to get better."

"Yes, well," said Jackie, serious and uncomfortable, "tell him my mother and father ask about him."

"I will," Barry promised. "He'll be pleased."

---

1. *libations:* liquid, often wine, poured in celebration of something.

Barry dropped the bag in the front hall and moved into the room which had been the dining room until his father's illness. His father lay in the white bed, his long body gaunt, his still head scarcely denting the pillow. He seemed asleep, thin blue lids covering his eyes, but when Barry turned away he spoke.

"Hullo, son," he said. "Did you win?"

His voice was a dry, light rustling, hardly louder than the breath which carried it. Its sound moved Barry to a compassion that almost unmanned him, but he stepped close to the bed and looked down at the dying man.

"Yes," he said. "We won fairly easily. It was a good game."

His father lay with his eyes closed, inert,[2] his breath irregular and shallow.

"Did you score?" he asked.

"Twice," Barry said. "I had a try in each half."

He thought of the easy certainty with which he'd caught the ball before his second try; casually, almost arrogantly he had taken it on the tips of his fingers, on his full burst for the line, breaking the fullback's tackle. Nobody could have stopped him. But watching his father's weakness he felt humble and ashamed, as if the morning's game, its urgency and effort, was not worth talking about. His father's face, fine-skinned and pallid, carried a dark stubble of beard, almost a week's growth, and his obstinate, strong hair stuck out over his brow.

"Good," said his father, after a long pause. "I'm glad it was a good game."

Barry's mother bustled about the kitchen, a tempest of orderly energy.

"Your father's not well," she said. "He's down today, feels depressed. He's a particular man, your father. He feels dirty with all that beard on him."

She slammed shut the stove door.

"Mr. Cleaver was supposed to come up and shave him," she said, "and that was three days ago. Little things have always worried your father, every detail must be perfect for him."

Barry filled a glass with milk from the refrigerator. He was very thirsty.

"I'll shave him," he said.

His mother stopped, her head on one side.

---

2. *inert:* not moving.

"Do you think you can?" she asked. "He'd like it if you can."

"I can do it," Barry said.

He washed his hands as carefully as a surgeon. His father's razor was in a blue leather case, hinged at the broad edge and with one hinge broken. Barry unfastened the clasp and took out the razor. It had not been properly cleaned after its last use and lather had stiffened into hard yellow rectangles between the teeth of the guard. There were water-shaped rust stains, brown as chocolate, on the surface of the blade. Barry removed it, throwing it in the wastebin. He washed the razor until it glistened, and dried it on a soft towel, polishing the thin handle, rubbing its metal head to a glittering shine. He took a new blade from its waxed envelope, the paper clinging to the thin metal. The blade was smooth and flexible to the touch, the little angles of its cutting clearly defined. Barry slotted it into the grip of the razor, making it snug and tight in the head.

The shaving soap, hard, white, richly aromatic, was kept in a wooden bowl. Its scent was immediately evocative and Barry could almost see his father in the days of his health, standing before his mirror, thick white lather on his face and neck. As a little boy Barry had loved the generous perfume of the soap, had waited for his father to lift the razor to his face, for one careful stroke to take away the white suds in a clean revelation of the skin. Then his father would renew the lather with a few sweeps of his brush, one with an ivory handle and the bristles worn, which he still used.

His father's shaving mug was a thick cup, plain and serviceable. A gold line ran outside the rim of the cup, another inside, just below the lip. Its handle was large and sturdy, and the face of the mug carried a portrait of the young Queen Elizabeth II, circled by a wreath of leaves, oak perhaps, or laurel. A lion and unicorn balanced precariously on a scroll above her crowned head, and the Union Jack, the Royal Standard, and other flags were furled each side of the portrait. And beneath it all, in small black letters, ran the legend: "Coronation June 2nd 1953." The cup was much older than Barry. A pattern of faint translucent cracks, fine as a web, had worked itself haphazardly, invisibly almost, through the white glaze. Inside, on the bottom, a few dark bristles were lying, loose and dry. Barry shook them out, then held the cup in his hand, feeling its solidness. Then he washed it ferociously, until it was clinically clean.

Methodically he set everything on a tray, razor, soap, brush, towels. Testing the hot water with a finger, he filled the mug and put that, too, on the tray. His care was absorbed, ritualistic. Satisfied that his preparations were complete, he went downstairs, carrying the tray with one hand.

His father was waiting for him. Barry set the tray on a bedside table and bent over his father, sliding an arm under the man's thin shoulders, lifting him without effort so that he sat against the high pillows.

"You're strong . . ." his father said. He was as breathless as if he'd been running.

"So are you," said Barry.

"I was," his father said. "I used to be strong once."

He sat exhausted against the pillows.

"We'll wait a bit," Barry said.

"You could have used your electric razor," his father said. "I expected that."

"You wouldn't like it," Barry said. "You'll get a closer shave this way."

He placed the large towel about his father's shoulders.

"Now," he said, smiling down.

The water was hot in the thick cup. Barry wet the brush and worked up the lather. Gently he built up a covering of soft foam on the man's chin, on his cheeks and his stark cheekbones.

"You're using a lot of soap," his father said.

"Not too much," Barry said. "You've got a lot of beard."

His father lay there quietly, his wasted arms at his sides.

"It's comforting," he said. "You'd be surprised how comforting it is."

Barry took up the razor, weighing it in his hand, rehearsing the angle at which he'd use it. He felt confident.

"If you have prayers to say, . . ." he said.

"I've said a lot of prayers," his father answered.

Barry leaned over and placed the razor delicately against his father's face, setting the head accurately on the clean line near the ear where the long hair ended. He held the razor in the tips of his fingers and drew the blade sweetly through the lather. The new edge moved light as a touch over the hardness of the upper jaw and down to the angle of the chin, sliding away the bristles so easily that Barry could not feel their release. He sighed as he shook the razor in the hot water, washing away the soap.

"How's it going?" his father asked.

"No problem," Barry said. "You needn't worry."

It was as if he had never known what his father really looked like. He was discovering under his hands the clear bones of the face and head; they became sharp and recognizable under his fingers. When he moved his father's face a gentle inch to one side, he touched with his fingers the frail temples, the blue veins of his father's life. With infinite and meticulous care he took away the hair from his father's face.

"Now for your neck," he said. "We might as well do the job properly."

"You've got good hands," his father said. "You can trust those hands, they won't let you down."

Barry cradled his father's head in the crook of his left arm, so that the man could tilt back his head, exposing the throat. He brushed fresh lather under the chin and into the hollows alongside the stretched tendons. His father's throat was fleshless and vulnerable, his head was a hard weight on the boy's arm. Barry was filled with unreasoning protective love. He lifted the razor and began to shave.

"You don't have to worry," he said. "Not at all. Not about anything."

He held his father in the bend of his strong arm and they looked at each other. Their heads were very close.

"How old are you?" his father said.

"Seventeen," Barry said. "Near enough seventeen."

"You're young," his father said, "to have this happen."

"Not too young," Barry said. "I'm bigger than most men."

"I think you are," his father said.

He leaned his head tiredly against the boy's shoulder. He was without strength, his face was cold and smooth. He had let go all his authority, handed it over. He lay back on his pillow, knowing his weakness and his mortality, and looked at his son with wonder, with a curious humble pride.

"I won't worry then," he said. "About anything."

"There's no need," Barry said. "Why should you worry?"

He wiped his father's face clean of all soap with a damp towel. The smell of illness was everywhere, overpowering even the perfumed lather. Barry settled his father down and took away the shaving tools, putting them by with the same ceremonial precision with which he'd prepared them: the cleaned and glittering razor in its broken case; the soap, its bowl wiped and dried, on the shelf between the brush and the coronation mug; all free of taint.[3] He washed his hands and scrubbed his nails. His hands were firm and broad, pink after their scrubbing. The fingers were short and strong, the little fingers slightly crooked, and soft dark hair grew on the backs of his hands and his fingers just above the knuckles. Not long ago they had been small bare hands, not very long ago.

---

3. *taint:* trace of something harmful or bad.

Barry opened wide the bathroom window. Already, although it was not yet two o'clock, the sun was retreating and people were moving briskly, wrapped in their heavy coats against the cold that was to come. But now the window was full in the beam of the dying sunlight, and Barry stood there, illuminated in its golden warmth for a whole minute, knowing it would soon be gone.

Responding to the Story

1. How does the shaving bowl represent two different parts of Barry's relationship with his father over the years?

2. The author describes the preparing and putting away of the shaving tools as "ritualistic" and "ceremonial." Are these words appropriate to these simple acts? Explain.

3. What prompts the father to "let go all his authority" and hand it over to his son?

Exploring the Author's Craft

1. Writers often imply more than they say directly. Explain what is implied in each of the following lines or passages.

    a. "It's comforting," he said. "You'd be surprised how comforting it is."

    b. "You're young," his father said, "to have this happen." "Not too young," Barry said. "I'm bigger than most men." "I think you are," his father said.

    c. "But now the window was full in the beam of the dying sunlight, and Barry stood there, illuminated in its golden warmth for a whole minute, knowing it would soon be gone."

2. Diction is an author's choice of words or phrases, and those words intrinsically contribute to the *mood* or atmosphere of a story. In "Shaving" a tender, delicate, and warm mood is conveyed by words such as *cradled* as the boy holds his father's head. Identify five more single words that contribute to the

mood you think the story portrays. (A story may have more than one mood.)

Writing Workshop

This extraordinary story is centered on one seemingly simple activity: a boy shaving his sick father. The story's richness far transcends a simple activity, of course, but the writer first captured, in minute detail, all the actions of the one shave.

1. Observe someone performing an extended action, either in your own home, or in a classroom, gym, restaurant, store, or office. Record in as much detail as you can how that action is performed.

2. Write a prose selection in which you tell about a parent and child involved in an activity together. Guide the reader through the action so that the reader feels that she or he is there with the parent and child.

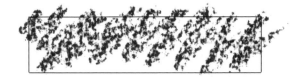

Guess What? I Almost Kissed My Father Goodnight

Robert Cormier

Robert Cormier worked as a reporter in Worcester and Fitchburg, Massachusetts, before turning to fiction. He was born in 1925 in Leominster, Massachusetts, where he continues to live. He was married in 1948, and he and his wife have four children.

The Chocolate War *(1974),* I Am the Cheese *(1977), and* After the First Death *(1979) all won Outstanding Book of the Year awards from* The New York Times *and Best Book for Young Adults awards from the American Library Association.* The Bumblebee Flies Anyway *(1983) also won the ALA award. Cormier's other works include* Beyond the Chocolate War *(1985),* Fade *(1988),* Take Me Where the Good Times Are *(1991), and* Tunes for Bears to Dance To *(1992). His short stories are collected in* Eight Plus One *(1980).*

Cormier has said that he writes books with young adult characters, not young adult books. The many letters he receives from his readers attest to the wide popularity of his books, which deal with serious subjects in a way that appeals to adults and younger readers alike.

I've got to get to the bottom of it all somehow and maybe this is the best way. It's about my father. For instance, I found out recently that my father is actually forty-five years old. I knew that he was forty-something but it never meant anything to me. I mean, trying to

125

imagine someone over forty and what it's like to be that old is the same as trying to imagine what the world would be like in, say, 1999. Anyway, he's forty-five, and he has the kind of terrible job that fathers have; in his case, he's office manager for a computer equipment concern. Nine-to-five stuff. Four weeks vacation every year but two weeks must be taken between January and May so he usually ends up painting the house or building a patio or something like that in April, and then we travel the other two weeks in July. See America First. He reads a couple of newspapers every day and never misses the seven o'clock news on television.

Here are some other vital statistics my research turned up: He's five ten, weighs 160 pounds, has a tendency toward high blood pressure, enjoys a glass of beer or two while he's watching the Red Sox on television, sips one martini and never two before dinner, likes his steak medium rare and has a habit of saying that "tonight, by God, I'm going to stay up and watch Johnny Carson," but always gropes his way to bed after the eleven o'clock news, which he watches only to learn the next day's weather forecast. He has a pretty good sense of humor but a weakness for awful puns which he inflicts on us at the dinner table: "Do you carrot all for me? I'm in a stew over you." We humor him. By we, I mean my sisters. Annie, who is nineteen and away at college, and Debbie, who is fourteen and spends her life on the telephone. And me: I'm Mike, almost sixteen and a sophomore in high school. My mother's name is Ellen—Dad calls her Ellie—and she's a standard mother: "Clean up your room! Is your homework done?"

Now that you've gotten the basic details, I'll tell you about that day last month when I walked downtown from school to connect with the North Side bus which deposits me in front of my house. It was one of those terrific days in spring and the air smelled like vacation, and it made you ache with all the things you wanted to do and all the places you wanted to see and all the girls you wanted to meet. Like the girl at the bus stop that I've been trying to summon up the nerve to approach for weeks: so beautiful she turns my knees liquid. Anyway, I barreled through Bryant Park, a shortcut, the turf spring-soft and spongy under my feet and the weeping willows hazy with blossom. Suddenly I screeched to a halt, like Bugs Bunny in one of those crazy television cartoons. There's a car parked near the Civil War cannon. Ours. I recognize the dent in the right front fender Annie put there last month when she was home from college. And there are also those decals on the side window that give the geography of our boring vacation trips, *Windy Chasms,* places like that.

The car is unoccupied. Did somebody steal it and abandon it here?

Wow, great! I walk past the splashing fountain that displays one of those embarrassing naked cherubs and stop short again. There he is: my father. Sitting on a park bench. Gazing out over a small pond that used to have goldfish swimming around until kids started stealing them. My father was deep in thought, like a statue in a museum. I looked at my watch. Two-thirty in the afternoon, for crying out loud. What was he doing there at this time of day? I was about to approach him but hesitated, held back for some reason—I don't know why. Although he looked perfectly normal, I felt as though I had somehow caught him naked, had trespassed on forbidden territory, the way I'm afraid to have my mother come barging into my bedroom at certain moments. I drew back, studying him as if he were a sudden stranger. I saw the familiar thinning short hair, the white of his scalp showing through. The way the flesh in his neck has begun to pucker like turkey skin. Now, he sighed. I saw his shoulders heave, and the rest of his body shudder like the chain reaction of freight cars. He lifted his face to the sun, eyes closed. He seemed to be reveling in the moment, all his pores open. I tiptoed away. People talk about tiptoeing but I don't think I ever really tiptoed before in my life. Anyway, I leave him there, still basking on that park bench, because I've got something more important to do at the bus stop. Today, I have vowed to approach the girl, talk to her, say something, *anything*. After all, I'm not exactly Frankenstein and some girls actually think I'm fun to be with. Anyway, she isn't at the bus stop. I stall around and miss the two-forty-five deliberately. She never shows up. At three-thirty, I thumb home and pick up a ride in a green MG, which kind of compensates for a rotten afternoon.

At dinner that evening, I'm uncommunicative, thinking of the girl and all the science homework waiting in my room. Dinner at our house is a kind of ritual that alternates between bedlam and boredom with no sense of direction whatever. Actually, I don't enjoy table talk. I have this truly tremendous appetite and I eat too fast, like my mother says. The trouble is that I'm always being asked a question or expected to laugh at some corny joke when my mouth is full, which it usually is. But that evening I stopped eating altogether when my mother asked my father about his day at the office.

"Routine," he said.

I thought of that scene in the park.

"Did you have to wait around all day for that Harper contract?" my mother asked.

"Didn't even have time for a coffee break," he said, reaching for more potatoes.

I almost choked on the roast beef. He lied: my father actually lied.

I sat there, terrified, caught in some kind of terrible no-man's-land. It was as if the lie itself had thrust me into panic. Didn't I fake my way through life most of the time—telling half-truths to keep everybody happy, either my parents or my teachers or even my friends? What would happen if everybody started telling the truth all of a sudden? But I was bothered by his motive. I mean—why did he have to pretend that he *wasn't* in the park that afternoon? And the first question came back to haunt me worse than before—what was he doing there, anyway, in the first place?

I found myself studying him across the table, scrutinizing him with the eyes of a stranger. But it didn't work. He was simply my father. Looked exactly as he always did. He was his usual dull unruffled self, getting ready to take his evening nap prior to the television news. Stifling a yawn after desert. Forget it, I told myself. There's a simple explanation for everything.

Let's skip some time now until the night of the telephone call. And let me explain about the telephone setup at our house. First of all, my father never answers the phone. He lets it ring nine or ten or eleven times and merely keeps on reading the paper and watching television because he claims—and he's right—that most of the calls are for Debbie or me. Anyway, a few nights after that happening at the park, the phone rang about ten-thirty and I barreled out of my room because he and my mother get positively explosive about calls after nine on school nights.

When I lifted the receiver, I found that my father had already picked up the downstairs extension. There was a pause and then he said: "I've got it, Mike."

"Yes, sir," I said. And hung up.

I stood there in the upstairs hallway, not breathing. His voice was a murmur and even at that distance I detected some kind of intimacy. Or did the distance itself contribute that hushed, secretive quality? I returned to my room and put a Blood, Sweat and Tears on the stereo. I remembered that my mother was out for the evening, a meeting of the Ladies' Auxiliary. I got up and looked in the mirror. Another lousy pimple, on the right side of my nose to balance the one on the left. Who had called him on the telephone at that hour of the night? And why had he answered the call in record time? Was it the same person he'd been waiting for in Bryant Park? Don't be ridiculous, Mike, I told myself; think of real stuff, like pimples. Later, I went downstairs and my father was slumped in his chair, newspaper like a fragile tent covering his face. His snores capsized the tent and it slid to the floor. He needed a shave, his beard like small slivers of ice. His feet were fragile, something I had never noticed before; they were mackerel white, half in and half out of his slippers. I went back upstairs without checking the refrigerator, my hunger suddenly annihilated by guilt. He wasn't mysterious: he was my father. And he snored with his mouth open.

The next day I learned the identity of the girl at the bus stop: like a bomb detonating. Sally Bettencourt. There's a Sally Bettencourt in every high school in the world—the girl friend of football heroes, the queen of the prom, Miss Apple Blossom Time. That's Sally Bettencourt of Monument High. And I'm not a football hero, although I scored three points in the intramural basketball tournament last winter. And she *did* smile at me a few weeks ago while waiting for the bus. Just for the record, let me put down here how I found out her name. She was standing a few feet from me, chatting with some girls and fellows, and I drifted toward her and saw her name written on the cover of one of her books. Detective work.

The same kind of detective work sent me investigating my father's desk the next day. He keeps all his private correspondence and office papers in an old battered roll-top my mother found at an auction and sandpapered and refinished. No one was at home. The desk was unlocked. I opened drawers and checked some diarylike type notebooks. Nothing but business stuff. All kinds of receipts. Stubs of cancelled checks. Dull. But a bottom drawer revealed the kind of box that contains correspondence paper and envelopes. Inside, I found envelopes of different shapes and sizes and colors. Father's Day cards he had saved through the years. I found one with a scrawled "Mikey" painstakingly written when I was four or five probably. His secret love letters—from Annie and Debbie and me.

"Looking for something?"

His shadow fell across the desk. I mumbled something, letting irritation show in my voice. I have found that you can fake adults out by muttering and grumbling as if you're using some foreign language that they couldn't possibly understand. And they feel intimidated or confused. Anyway, they decide not to challenge you or make an issue of it. That's what happened at that moment. There I was snooping in my father's desk and because I muttered unintelligibly when he interrupted me, *he* looked embarrassed while I stalked from the room as if I was the injured party, ready to bring suit in court.

Three things happened in the next week and they had nothing to do with my father: First, I called Sally Bettencourt. The reason why I called her is that I could have sworn she smiled again at me at the bus stop one afternoon. I mean, not a polite smile but a smile for *me*, as if she recognized me as a person, an individual. Actually I called her three times in four days. She was (*a*) not at home and the person on the line (her mother? her sister?) had no idea when she'd arrive; (*b*) she was taking a shower—"Any message?" "No"; (*c*) the line was busy. What would I have said to her, if she'd answered? I've always had the feeling that I'm a real killer on the phone when I don't have to worry about what to do with my hands or how bad my posture is. The second thing that happened was a terrible history test which I almost flunked: a low *C* that could possibly keep me off the Honor Roll, which would send my mother into hysterics. Number 3: I received my assignment from the Municipal Park Department for my summer job—lifeguard at Pool Number 38. Translation: Pool Number 38 is for children twelve years old and younger, not the most romantic pool in the city.

Bugged by history, I talked Mister Rogers, the teacher, into allowing me some extra work to rescue my mark and I stayed up late one night, my stereo earphones clamped on my head so that I wouldn't disturb anyone as the cool sounds of the Tinted Orange poured into my ears. Suddenly, I awoke—shot out of a cannon. My watch said one-twenty. One-twenty in the morning. I yawned. My mouth felt rotten, as if the French Foreign Legion had marched through it barefoot (one of my father's old jokes that I'd heard about a million times). I went downstairs for a glass of orange juice. A light spilled from the den. I sloshed orange juice on my shirt as I stumbled toward the room. He's there: my father. Slumped in his chair. Like death. And I almost drop dead myself. But his lips flutter and he produces an enormous snore. One arm dangles to the floor, limp as a draped towel. His fingers are almost touching a book that had evidently fallen from his hand. I pick it up. Poetry. A poet I never heard of. Kenneth Fearing. Riffling the pages, I find that the poems are mostly about the Depression. In the front of the book there's an inscription. Delicate handwriting, faded lavender ink. "To Jimmy, I'll never forget you. Muriel." Jimmy? My father's name is James and my mother and his friends call him Jim. But Jimmy? I notice a date at the bottom of the page, meticulously recorded in that same fragile handwriting—November 2, 1942—when he was young enough to be called Jimmy. By some girl whose name was Muriel, who gave him a book of poems that he takes out and reads in the dead of night even if they are poems about the Depression. He stirs, grunting, clearing his throat, his hand like a big white spider searching the floor for the book. I replace the book on the floor and glide out of the room and back upstairs.

The next day I began my investigation in earnest and overlooked no details. That's when I found out what size shoes, socks, shirts, etc., that he wears. I looked in closets and bureaus, his workbench in the cellar, not knowing what I was searching for but the search itself important. There was one compensation: at least, it kept my mind off Sally Bettencourt. I had finally managed to talk to her on the telephone. We spoke mostly in monosyllables. It took me about ten minutes to identify myself ("The fellow at *what* bus stop?") because apparently all those smiles sent in my direction had been meaningless and my face was as impersonal as a label on a can of soup. The conversation proceeded downward from that point and reached bottom when she said: "Well, thanks for calling, Mark." I didn't bother to correct her. She was so sweet about it all. All the Sally Bettencourts of the world are that way: that's why you keep on being in love with them when you know it's entirely useless. Even when you hang up and see your face in the hallway mirror—what a terrible place to hang a mirror—your face all crumpled up like a paper bag. And the following day, she wasn't at the bus stop, of course. But then neither was I.

What I mean about the bus stop is this: I stationed myself across the street to get a glimpse of her, to see if she really was as beautiful as I remembered or if the phone call had diminished her loveliness. When she didn't arrive, I wandered through the business district. Fellows and girls lingered in doorways. Couples held hands crossing the street. A record store blared out "Purple Evenings" by the Tinted Orange. I spotted my father. He was crossing the street, dodging traffic, as if he was dribbling an invisible ball down a basketball court. I checked my watch: two fifty-five. Stepping into a doorway, I observed him hurrying past the Merchants Bank and Appleton's Department Store and the Army-Navy Surplus Supply Agency. He paused in front of the Monument Public Library. And disappeared inside. My father—visiting the library? He didn't even have a library card, for crying out loud.

I'm not exactly crazy about libraries, either. Everybody whispers or talks low as if the building has a giant volume knob turned down to practically zero. As I stood here, I saw Laura Kincaid drive up in her new LeMans. A quiet, dark green LeMans. Class. "If I had to describe Laura Kincaid in one word, it would be 'class,' " I'd heard my father say once. The car drew into a parking space, as if the space had been waiting all day for her arrival. She stepped out of the door. She is blond, her hair the color of lemonade as it's being poured on a hot day. I stood there, paralyzed. A scene leaped in my mind: Laura Kincaid at a New Year's Party at our house, blowing a toy horn just before midnight while I watched in awe from the kitchen, amazed at how a few glasses of booze could convert all these bankers and Rotary Club members and Chamber of Commerce officials into the terrible kind of people you see dancing to Guy Lombardo on television while the camera keeps cutting back to Times Square where thousands of other people, most of them closer to my age, were also acting desperately happy. I stood there thinking of that stuff because I was doing some kind of juggling act in my mind— trying to figure out why was she at this moment walking across the street, heading for the library, her hair a lemon halo in the sun, her nylons flashing as she hurried. What was her hurry? There was barely any traffic. Was she on her way to a rendezvous? Stop it, you nut, I told myself, even as I made my way to the side entrance.

The library is three stories high, all the stacks and bookshelves built around an interior courtyard. I halted near the circulation desk with no books in my arms to check out. Feeling ridiculous, I made my way to the bubbler. The spray of water was stronger than I expected: my nostrils were engulfed by water. For some reason, I thought of Sally Bettencourt and how these ridiculous events kept happening to me and I ached with longing for her, a terrible emptiness inside of me that needed to be filled. I climbed the stairs to the third floor, my eyes flying all over the place, trying to spot my father. And Laura Kincaid. And knowing all the time that it was merely a game, impossible, ridiculous.

And then I saw them. Together. Standing at the entrance to the alcove that was marked 818 to 897. Two books were cradled in her arms like babies. My father wasn't looking at the books or the shelves or the walls or the ceilings or the floor or anything. He was looking at her. Then, they laughed. It was like a silent movie. I mean—I saw their eyes light up and their lips moving but didn't hear anything. My father shook his head, slowly, a smile lingering tenderly on his face. I drew back into the alcove labeled 453 to 521, across from them, apprehensive, afraid that suddenly they might see me spying on them. His hand reached up and touched her shoulder. They laughed again, still merrily. She indicated the books in her arms. He nodded, an eagerness in his manner. He didn't look as if he had ever snored in his life or taken a nap after dinner. They looked around. She glanced at her watch. He gestured vaguely.

Pressed against the metal bookshelf, I felt conspicuous, vulnerable, as if they would suddenly whirl and see me, and point accusing fingers. But nothing like that happened. She finally left, simply walked away, the books still in her arm. My father watched her go, his face in shadow. She walked along the balcony, then down the spiral stairs, the nylons still flashing, her hair a lemon waterfall. My father watched until she disappeared from view. I squinted, trying to discern his features, to see whether he was still my father, searching for the familiar landmarks of his face and body, needing some kind of verification. I watched him for a minute or two as he stood there looking down, his eyes tracing the path of her departure as if she were still visible. I studied his face: was this my father? And then this terrible numbness invaded my body, like a Novocain of the spirit, killing all my emotions. And the numbness even pervaded my mind, slowing down my thoughts. For which I was grateful. All the way home on the bus, I stared out the window, looking at the landscapes and the buildings and the people but not really seeing them, as if I was storing them in my mind like film to develop them later when they'd have meaning for me.

At dinner, the food lay unappetizingly on my plate. I had to fake my way through the meal, lifting the fork mechanically. I found it difficult not to look at my father. What I mean is—I didn't want to look at him. And because I didn't, I kept doing it. Like when they tell you not to think of a certain subject and you can't help thinking of it.

"Aren't you feeling well, Mike?" my mother asked.

I leaped about five feet off my chair. I hadn't realized how obvious I must have appeared: the human eating machine suddenly toying with his food—steak, at that, which requires special concentration.

"He's probably in love," Debbie said.

And that word *love*. I found it difficult to keep my eyes away from my father.

"I met Laura Kincaid at the library today," I heard my father say.

"Was she able to get a copy of the play?" my mother asked.

"Two of them," he said, munching. "I still think *Streetcar Named Desire* is pretty ambitious for you girls to put on."

"The Women's Auxiliary knows no fear of Tennessee Williams," my mother said in that exaggerated voice she uses when she's kidding around.

"You know, that's funny, Dad," I heard myself saying. "I saw you in the library this afternoon and was wondering what you were doing there."

"Oh? I didn't see you, Mike."

"He was supposed to pick up the play on my library card. But then Laura Kincaid came by . . ." That was my mother explaining it all, although I barely made out the words.

I won't go into the rest of the scene and I won't say that my appetite suddenly came back and that I devoured the steak. Because I didn't. That was two days ago and I still feel funny about it all. Strange I mean. That's why I'm writing this, putting it all down, all the evidence I gathered. That first time in the park when he was sitting there. The telephone call. That book of poetry he reads late at night, "To Jimmy, I'll never forget you. Muriel." Laura Kincaid in the library. Not much evidence, really. Especially when I look at him and see how he's my father all right.

Last night, I came downstairs after finishing my homework and he had just turned off the television set. "Cloudy tomorrow, possible showers," he said, putting out the lights in the den.

We stood there in the half-darkness.

"Homework done, Mike?"

"Yes."

"Hey, Dad."

"Yes, Mike?" Yawning.

I didn't plan to ask him. But it popped out. "I was looking through a book of yours the other day. Poetry by some guy named Fearing or Nearing or something." I couldn't see his face in the half dark. Keeping my voice light, I said: "Who's this Muriel who gave you the book, anyway?"

His laugh was a playful bark. "Boy, that was a long time ago. Muriel Stanton." He closed the kitchen window. "I asked her to go to the Senior Prom but she went with someone else. We were friends. I mean— I thought we were more than friends until she went to the Prom with someone else. And so she gave me a gift—of friendship—at graduation." We walked into the kitchen together. "That's a lousy swap, Mike. A book instead of a date with a girl you're crazy about." He smiled ruefully. "Hadn't thought of good old Muriel for years."

You see? Simple explanations for everything. And if I exposed myself as a madman and asked him about the other stuff, the park and the telephone call, I knew there would be perfectly logical reasons. And yet. And yet. I remember that day in the library, when Laura Kincaid walked away from him. I said that I couldn't see his face, not clearly anyway, but I could see a bit of his expression. And it looked familiar but I couldn't pin it down. And now I realized why it was familiar: it reminded me of my own face when I looked into the mirror the day I hung up the phone after talking to Sally Bettencourt. All kind of crumpled up. Or was that my imagination? Hadn't my father been all the way across the library courtyard, too far away for me to tell what kind of expression was on his face?

Last night, standing in the kitchen, as I poured a glass of milk and he said: "Doesn't your stomach ever get enough?" I asked him: "Hey, Dad. You get lonesome sometimes? I mean: that's a crazy question, maybe. But I figure grownups, like fathers and mothers—you get to feeling *down* sometimes, don't you?"

I could have sworn his eyes narrowed and something leaped in them, some spark, some secret thing that had suddenly come out of hiding.

"Sure, Mike. Everybody gets the blues now and then. Even fathers are people. Sometimes, I can't sleep and get up and sit in the dark in the middle of the night. And it gets lonesome because you think of . . ."

"What do you think of, Dad?"

He yawned. "Oh, a lot of things."

That's all. And here I am sitting up in the middle of the night writing this, feeling lonesome, thinking of Sally Bettencourt, and how I haven't a chance with her and thinking, too, of Muriel Stanton who wouldn't go to the Senior Prom with my father. How he gets lonesome sometimes. And sits up in the night, reading poetry. I think of his anguished face at the library and the afternoon at Bryant Park, and all the mysteries of his life that show he's a person. Human.

Earlier tonight, I saw him in his chair, reading the paper, and I said, "Goodnight, Dad," and he looked up and smiled, but an absent kind of smile, as if he was thinking of something else, long ago and far away, and, for some ridiculous feeling, I felt like kissing him goodnight. But didn't, of course. Who kisses his father at sixteen?

Responding to the Story

1. Why is the narrator surprised at seeing his father sitting on a park bench? Do you understand how Mike felt at that moment? Explain.

2. "Didn't I fake my way through life most of the time—telling half-truths to keep everybody happy, either my parents or my teachers or even my friends?" Do these words ring true to life as you know it? Explain.

3. "Even fathers are people." What does Mike's father mean by these words? What evidence do you have that these words are or aren't true about all fathers, not just Mike's?

Exploring the Author's Craft

Figurative language is language that makes use of comparisons to bring a picture to the reader's mind. *Similes* make comparisons using *like* or *as,* and *metaphors* simply say one thing is another. Note some of the similes and metaphors in this story:

"His beard like small slivers of ice . . ."

"His feet were mackerel white . . ."

"My face was as impersonal as a label on a can of soup."

"Your face all crumpled up like a paper bag . . ."

"He was crossing the street, dodging traffic, as if he was dribbling an invisible ball down a basketball court."

"Her hair the color of lemonade . . ."

"Her hair a lemon waterfall . . ."

Find and list several other examples of figurative language in this story.

Writing Workshop

Think of someone whom you know well and whose physical characteristics are clear to you. Now describe that person in two or three paragraphs; use at least three *original* similes and/or metaphors.

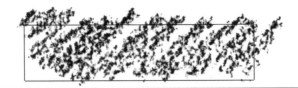

Marigolds

Eugenia Collier

Eugenia Collier won the Gwendolyn Brooks Award for Fiction from
Negro Digest *for "Marigolds" in 1969. Since then, the story has
been widely reprinted.*

Born in Baltimore in 1928, Collier graduated magna cum
laude *from Howard University in 1948 and received an M.A.
degree from Columbia University in 1950. She was a case worker
in Baltimore for five years and then became an assistant instructor
at Morgan State College in 1955. She became a professor at the
Community College of Baltimore in 1970. She and her former
husband, whom she married in 1948, have three sons.*

When I think of the home town of my youth, all that I seem to
remember is dust—the brown, crumbly dust of late summer—
arid, sterile dust that gets into the eyes and makes them water, gets into
the throat and between the toes of bare brown feet. I don't know why
I should remember only the dust. Surely there must have been lush
green lawns and paved streets under leafy shade trees somewhere in
town; but memory is an abstract painting—it does not present things
as they are, but rather as they *feel.* And so, when I think of that time
and that place, I remember only the dry September of the dirt roads
and grassless yards of the shanty-town where I lived. And one other
thing I remember, another incongruency of memory—a brilliant splash
of sunny yellow against the dust—Miss Lottie's marigolds.

Whenever the memory of those marigolds flashes across my mind,
a strange nostalgia comes with it and remains long after the picture has
faded. I feel again the chaotic emotions of adolescence, illusive as smoke,
yet as real as the potted geranium before me now. Joy and rage and wild
animal gladness and shame become tangled together in the multi-

colored skein of fourteen-going-on-fifteen as I recall that devastating moment when I was suddenly more woman than child, years ago in Miss Lottie's yard. I think of those marigolds at the strangest times; I remember them vividly now as I desperately pass away the time waiting for you, who will not come.

I suppose that futile waiting was the sorrowful background music of our impoverished little community when I was young. The Depression that gripped the nation was no new thing to us, for the black workers of rural Maryland had always been depressed. I don't know what it was that we were waiting for; certainly not for the prosperity that was "just around the corner," for those were white folks' words, which we never believed. Nor did we wait for hard work and thrift to pay off in shining success as the American Dream promised, for we knew better than that, too. Perhaps we waited for a miracle, amorphous in concept but necessary if one were to have the grit to rise before dawn each day and labor in the white man's vineyard until after dark, or to wander about in the September dust offering one's sweat in return for some meager share of bread. But God was chary[1] with miracles in those days, and so we waited—and waited.

We children, of course, were only vaguely aware of the extent of our poverty. Having no radios, few newspapers, and no magazines, we were somewhat unaware of the world outside our community. Nowadays we would be called "culturally deprived" and people would write books and hold conferences about us. In those days everybody we knew was just as hungry and ill-clad as we were. Poverty was the cage in which we all were trapped, and our hatred of it was still the vague, undirected restlessness of the zoo-bred flamingo who knows that nature created him to fly free.

As I think of those days I feel most poignantly the tag end of summer, the bright dry times when we began to have a sense of shortening days and the imminence of the cold.

By the time I was fourteen my brother Joey and I were the only children left at our house, the older ones having left home for early marriage or the lure of the city, and the two babies having been sent to relatives who might care for them better than we. Joey was three years younger than I, and a boy, and therefore vastly inferior. Each morning our mother and father trudged wearily down the dirt road and around the bend, she to her domestic job, he to his daily unsuccessful

---

1. *chary:* (char´ē): careful.

quest for work. After our few chores around the tumbledown shanty, Joey and I were free to run wild in the sun with other children similarly situated.

For the most part, those days are ill-defined in my memory, running together, combining like a fresh watercolor painting left out in the rain. I remember squatting in the road drawing a picture in the dust, a picture which Joey gleefully erased with one sweep of his dirty foot. I remember fishing for minnows in a muddy creek and watching sadly as they eluded my cupped hands, while Joey laughed uproariously. And I remember, that year, a strange restlessness of body and of spirit, a feeling that something old and familiar was ending, and something unknown and therefore terrifying was beginning.

One day returns to me with special clarity for some reason, perhaps because it was the beginning of the experience that in some inexplicable way marked the end of innocence. I was loafing under the great oak tree in our yard, deep in some reverie which I have now forgotten except that it involved some secret, secret thoughts of one of the Harris boys across the yard. Joey and a bunch of kids were bored now with the old tire suspended from an oak limb which had kept them entertained for awhile.

"Hey, Lizabeth," Joey yelled. He never talked when he could yell. "Hey, Lizabeth, let's us go somewhere."

I came reluctantly from my private world. "Where at, Joey?"

The truth was that we were becoming tired of the formlessness of our summer days. The idleness whose prospect had seemed so beautiful during the busy days of spring now had degenerated to an almost desperate effort to fill up the empty midday hours.

"Let's go see can we find us some locusts on the hill," someone suggested.

Joey was scornful. "Ain't no more locusts there. Y'all got 'em all while they was still green."

The argument that followed was brief and not really worth the effort. Hunting locust trees wasn't fun any more by now.

"Tell you what," said Joey finally, his eyes sparkling. "Let's us go over to Miss Lottie's."

The idea caught on at once, for annoying Miss Lottie was always fun. I was still child enough to scamper along with the group over rickety fences and through bushes that tore our already raggedy clothes, back to where Miss Lottie lived. I think now that we must have made a tragicomic spectacle, five or six kids of different ages, each of us clad in only one garment—the girls in faded dresses that were too long or too short, the boys in patchy pants, their sweaty brown chests gleaming in the hot sun. A little cloud of dust followed our thin legs and bare feet as we tramped over the barren land.

When Miss Lottie's house came into view we stopped, ostensibly to plan our strategy, but actually to reinforce our courage. Miss Lottie's house was the most ramshackle of all our ramshackle homes. The sun and rain had long since faded its rickety frame siding from white to a sullen gray. The boards themselves seemed to remain upright not from being nailed together but rather from leaning together like a house that a child might have constructed from cards. A brisk wind might have blown it down, and the fact that it was still standing implied a kind of enchantment that was stronger than the elements. There it stood, and as far as I know is standing yet—a gray rotting thing with no porch, no shutters, no steps, set on a cramped lot with no grass, not even any weeds—a monument to decay.

In front of the house in a squeaky rocking chair sat Miss Lottie's son, John Burke, completing the impression of decay. John Burke was what was known as "queer-headed." Black and ageless, he sat, rocking day in and day out in a mindless stupor, lulled by the monotonous squeak-squawk of the chair. A battered hat atop his shaggy head shaded him from the sun. Usually John Burke was totally unaware of everything outside his quiet dream world. But if you disturbed him, if you intruded upon his fantasies, he would become enraged, strike out at you, and curse at you in some strange enchanted language which only he could understand. We children made a game of thinking of ways to disturb John Burke and then to elude his violent retribution.

But our real fun and our real fear lay in Miss Lottie herself. Miss Lottie seemed to be at least a hundred years old. Her big frame still held traces of the tall, powerful woman she must have been in youth, although it was now bent and drawn. Her smooth skin was a dark reddish-brown, and her face had Indianlike features and the stern stoicism that one associates with Indian faces. Miss Lottie didn't like intruders either, especially children. She never left her yard, and nobody ever visited her. We never knew how she managed those necessities which depend on human interaction—how she ate, for example, or even whether she ate. When we were tiny children, we thought Miss Lottie was a witch and we made up tales, that we half believed ourselves, about her exploits. We were far too sophisticated now, of course, to believe the witch nonsense. But old fears have a way of clinging like cobwebs, and so when we sighted the tumbledown shack, we had to stop to reinforce our nerves.

"Look, there she is," I whispered, forgetting that Miss Lottie could not possibly have heard me from that distance. "She's fooling with them crazy flowers."

"Yeh, look at 'er."

Miss Lottie's marigolds were perhaps the strangest part of the picture. Certainly they did not fit in with the crumbling decay of the rest of her yard. Beyond the dusty brown yard, in front of the sorry gray house, rose suddenly and shockingly a dazzling strip of bright blossoms, clumped together in enormous mounds, warm and passionate and sungolden. The old black witch-woman worked on them all summer, every summer, down on her creaky knees, weeding and cultivating and arranging, while the house crumbled and John Burke rocked. For some perverse reason, we children hated those marigolds. They interfered with the perfect ugliness of the place; they were too beautiful; they said too much that we could not understand; they did not make sense. There was something in the vigor with which the old woman destroyed the weeds that intimidated us. It should have been a comical sight—the old woman with the man's hat on her cropped white head, leaning over the bright mounds, her big backside in the air—but it wasn't comical, it was something we could not name. We had to annoy her by whizzing a pebble into her flowers or by yelling a dirty word, then dancing away from her rage, reveling in our youth and mocking her age. Actually, I think it was the flowers we wanted to destroy, but nobody had the nerve to try it, not even Joey, who was usually fool enough to try anything.

"Y'all git some stones," commanded Joey now, and was met with instant giggling obedience as everyone except me began to gather pebbles from the dusty ground. "Come on, Lizabeth."

I just stood there peering through the bushes, torn between wanting to join the fun and feeling that it was all a bit silly.

"You scared, Lizabeth?"

I cursed and spat on the ground—my favorite gesture of phony bravado. "Y'all children get the stones, I'll show you how to use 'em."

I said before that we children were not consciously aware of how thick were the bars of our cage. I wonder now, though, whether we were not more aware of it than I thought. Perhaps we had some dim notion of what we were, and how little chance we had of being anything else. Otherwise, why would we have been so preoccupied with destruction? Anyway, the pebbles were collected quickly, and everybody looked at me to begin the fun.

"Come on, y'all."

We crept to the edge of the bushes that bordered the narrow road in front of Miss Lottie's place. She was working placidly, kneeling over the flowers, her dark hand plunged into the golden mound. Suddenly *zing*—an expertly aimed stone cut the head off one of the blossoms.

"Who out there?" Miss Lottie's backside came down and her head came up as her sharp eyes searched the bushes.

"You better git!"

We had crouched down out of sight in the bushes, where we stifled the giggles that insisted on coming. Miss Lottie gazed warily across the road for a moment, then cautiously returned to her weeding. *Zing*—Joey sent a pebble into the blooms, and another marigold was beheaded.

Miss Lottie was enraged now. She began struggling to her feet, leaning on a rickety cane and shouting. "Y'all git! Go on home!" Then the rest of the kids let loose with their pebbles, storming the flowers and laughing wildly and senselessly at Miss Lottie's impotent rage. She shook her stick at us and started shakily toward the road crying, "John Burke! John Burke, come help!"

Then I lost my head entirely, mad with the power of inciting such rage, and ran out of the bushes in the storm of pebbles, straight toward Miss Lottie chanting madly, "Old witch, fell in a ditch, picked up a penny and thought she was rich!" The children screamed with delight, dropped their pebbles and joined the crazy dance, swarming around Miss Lottie like bees and chanting, "Old lady witch!" while she screamed curses at us. The madness lasted only a moment, for John Burke, startled at last, lurched out of his chair, and we dashed for the bushes just as Miss Lottie's cane went whizzing at my head.

I did not join the merriment when the kids gathered again under the oak in our bare yard. Suddenly I was ashamed, and I did not like being ashamed. The child in me sulked and said it was all in fun, but the woman in me flinched at the thought of the malicious attack that I had led. The mood lasted all afternoon. When we ate the beans and rice that was supper that night, I did not notice my father's silence, for he was always silent these days, nor did I notice my mother's absence, for she always worked until well into evening. Joey and I had a particularly bitter argument after supper; his exuberance got on my nerves. Finally I stretched out upon the pallet in the room we shared and fell into a fitful doze.

When I awoke, somewhere in the middle of the night, my mother had returned, and I vaguely listened to the conversation that was audible through the thin walls that separated our rooms. At first I heard no words, only voices. My mother's voice was like a cool, dark room in summer—peaceful, soothing, quiet. I loved to listen to it; it made things seem all right somehow. But my father's voice cut through hers, shattering the peace.

"Twenty-two years, Maybelle, twenty-two years," he was saying, "and I got nothing for you, nothing, nothing."

"It's all right, honey, you'll get something. Everybody out of work now, you know that."

"It ain't right. Ain't no man ought to eat his woman's food year in and year out, and see his children running wild. Ain't nothing right about that."

"Honey, you took good care of us when you had it. Ain't nobody got nothing nowadays."

"I ain't talking about nobody else, I'm talking about *me*. God knows I try." My mother said something I could not hear, and my father cried out louder, "What must a man do, tell me that?"

"Look, we ain't starving. I git paid every week, and Mrs. Ellis is real nice about giving me things. She gonna let me have Mr. Ellis's old coat for you this winter——"

"Damn Mr. Ellis's coat! And damn his money! You think I want white folks' leavings? Damn. Maybelle"—and suddenly he sobbed, loudly and painfully, and cried helplessly and hopelessly in the dark night. I had never heard a man cry before. I did not know men ever cried. I covered my ears with my hands but could not cut off the sound of my father's harsh, painful, despairing sobs. My father was a strong man who could whisk a child upon his shoulders and go singing through the house. My father whittled toys for us and laughed so loud that the great oak seemed to laugh with him, and taught us how to fish and hunt rabbits. How could it be that my father was crying? But the sobs went on, unstifled, finally quieting until I could hear my mother's voice, deep and rich, humming softly as she used to hum to a frightened child.

The world had lost its boundary lines. My mother, who was small and soft, was now the strength of the family; my father, who was the rock on which the family had been built, was sobbing like the tiniest child. Everything was suddenly out of tune, like a broken accordion. Where did I fit into this crazy picture? I do not now remember my thoughts, only a feeling of great bewilderment and fear.

Long after the sobbing and the humming had stopped, I lay on the pallet, still as stone with my hands over my ears, wishing that I too could cry and be comforted. The night was silent now except for the sound of the crickets and of Joey's soft breathing. But the room was too crowded with fear to allow me to sleep, and finally, feeling the terrible aloneness of 4 A.M., I decided to awaken Joey.

"Ouch! What's the matter with you? What you want?" he demanded disagreeably when I had pinched and slapped him awake.

"Come on, wake up."

"What for? Go 'way."

I was lost for a reasonable reply. I could not say, "I'm scared and I don't want to be alone," so I merely said, "I'm going out. If you want to come, come on."

The promise of adventure awoke him. "Going out now? Where at, Lizabeth? What you going to do?"

I was pulling my dress over my head. Until now I had not thought of going out. "Just come on," I replied tersely.

I was out the window and halfway down the road before Joey caught up with me.

"Wait, Lizabeth, where you going?"

I was running as if the Furies[2] were after me, as perhaps they were—running silently and furiously until I came to where I had half-known I was headed: to Miss Lottie's yard.

The half-dawn light was more eerie than complete darkness, and in it the old house was like the ruin that my world had become—foul and crumbling, a grotesque caricature. It looked haunted, but I was not afraid because I was haunted too.

"Lizabeth, you lost your mind?" panted Joey.

I had indeed lost my mind, for all the smoldering emotions of that summer swelled in me and burst—the great need for my mother who was never there, the hopelessness of our poverty and degradation, the bewilderment of being neither child nor woman and yet both at once, the fear unleashed by my father's tears. And these feelings combined in one great impulse toward destruction.

"Lizabeth!"

I leaped furiously into the mounds of marigolds and pulled madly, trampling and pulling and destroying the perfect yellow blooms. The fresh smell of early morning and of dew-soaked marigolds spurred me on as I went tearing and mangling and sobbing while Joey tugged my dress or my waist crying, "Lizabeth, stop, please stop!"

And then I was sitting in the ruined little garden among the uprooted and ruined flowers, crying and crying, and it was too late to undo what I had done. Joey was sitting beside me, silent and frightened, not knowing what to say. Then, "Lizabeth, look."

I opened my swollen eyes and saw in front of me a pair of large

---

2. *Furies:* three spirits of revenge in Greek and Roman myth.

calloused feet; my gaze lifted to the swollen legs, the age-distorted body clad in a tight cotton night dress, and then the shadowed Indian face surrounded by stubby white hair. And there was no rage in the face now, now that the garden was destroyed and there was nothing any longer to be protected.

"M-miss Lottie!" I scrambled to my feet and just stood there and stared at her, and that was the moment when childhood faded and womanhood began. That violent, crazy act was the last act of childhood. For as I gazed at the immobile face with the sad, weary eyes, I gazed upon a kind of reality which is hidden to childhood. The witch was no longer a witch but only a broken old woman who had dared to create beauty in the midst of ugliness and sterility. She had been born in squalor and lived in it all her life. Now at the end of that life she had nothing except a falling-down hut, a wrecked body, and John Burke, the mindless son of her passion. Whatever verve there was left in her, whatever was of love and beauty and joy that had not been squeezed out by life, had been there in the marigolds she had so tenderly cared for.

Of course I could not express the things that I knew about Miss Lottie as I stood there awkward and ashamed. The years have put words to the things I knew in that moment, and as I look back upon it, I know that the moment marked the end of innocence. Innocence involves an unseeing acceptance of things at face value, an ignorance of the area below the surface. In that humiliating moment I looked beyond myself and into the depths of another person. This was the beginning of compassion, and one cannot have both compassion and innocence.

The years have taken me worlds away from that time and that place, from the dust and squalor of our lives and from the bright thing that I destroyed in a blind childish striking out. Miss Lottie died long ago and many years have passed since I last saw her hut, completely barren at last, for despite my wild contrition she never planted marigolds again. Yet, there are times when the image of those passionate yellow mounds returns with a painful poignancy. For one does not have to be ignorant and poor to find that his life is barren as the dusty yards of our town. And I too have planted marigolds.

Responding to the Story

1. Why do you think the narrator "leaped furiously into the mounds of marigolds and pulled madly, trampling and pulling

and destroying the perfect yellow blooms"? How did you feel when you read these words and others describing that scene?

2. Why does the narrator describe "that violent, crazy act" as "the moment when childhood faded and womanhood began"?

3. Do you believe that whole phases of lives can change in moments, or are changes gradual? Explain.

4. "Memory is an abstract painting—it does not present things as they are but rather as they *feel*." Tell a story of a vivid incident that you recall because of how it felt, even if you can't recall exactly every detail of how it was.

Exploring the Author's Craft

One cannot read this story without feeling as if one has been in this poor, fading town. How does the author achieve this? Look over the story and list all the physical aspects of the town that Eugenia Collier describes. Note how repetition of details helps reinforce the reader's impression of the *setting*. How important is setting in this story?

Writing Workshop

Capture in words a place you know as vividly as Eugenia Collier knew her setting. Take your time and include all the details and references to the various senses that characterize this place.

Asphalt

Frederick Pollack

Student-written story

Frederick Pollack's story won first prize for the short story in the 1963 Scholastic Writing Awards. He was a senior at Palo Alto California Senior High School at the time.

> "We neither love nor hurt because we do not try to reach each other."
> Edward Albee, The Zoo Story

Kroch's and Brentano's in Chicago advertises itself as the Largest Bookstore in the World but apparently can't afford air conditioning. Luckily, the paperbacks—all the books I usually have enough money to buy casually—are in the basement, where it is damp and relatively cool. The New Arrivals rack is right at the bottom of the stairwell, and I was standing there, engrossed in the new Ballantine edition of H. G. Wells' stories, when my father came up behind me and tapped me on the shoulder.

I'd told him over the phone that I'd meet him in Kroch's, but hadn't said exactly where—and Kroch's is a big place. I suppose I should have stayed near the entrance waiting for him. But I wanted to browse, and all that's near the entrance is the Psychiatry section, with Freud's eyes staring unblinkingly at me from the covers of his *Collected Works* spread across the top shelf. I always tell myself I should read more in that field, but somehow I can never become interested. At any rate, I'd drifted away from the entrance, and when Pop came in at noon I was downstairs. He'd been looking for me for ten minutes.

He was angry, of course. I knew that as soon as he tapped me on the shoulder and growled my name—even before I'd turned around and

147

glanced at his flushed, heavy face. "Hi, Pop," I said and then kept trying to make him be quiet. I've always hated being embarrassed, especially in public, and having people stare at me. Fortunately, there weren't many people downstairs in Kroch's that day. Eventually he ground to a halt, told me to come along, and started up the stairs. I followed about three steps behind. It was the first time I'd seen him in five months.

He had the use of his brother's massive Oldsmobile for the day, and had parked it illegally right in front of the bookstore. He never worries about cops, especially not those of his home town. We got in. He gunned the motor with less anger than I'd expected, and we drove off. I watched the marble front of Kroch's recede into the surrounding cityscape, reflecting that his brief tirade had at least served some purpose: we'd in effect said hello already . . . I didn't have to kiss him. Not that I mind kissing him, mind you, it's just that I feel a bit self-conscious about it. I suppose it would seem too cold if we just shook hands.

There was nothing I especially needed to tell him; he'd ask later how school was, and how things were at home, and I'd tell him that my grades so far this year were mediocre but I hoped to make a comeback with a few big tests and reports, that the teachers were especially bad this year, and the other kids were as usual, that Mom was feeling okay, that Sis was sick with a virus. So there was silence as we drove down Wabash and across the river into the Near North Side, silence like someone sprawled across us in the front seat. I looked out the window at the baking city.

Abruptly he began to talk—about his job, his contacts, the vagaries of his friends, the difficulties posed by certain of his relationships, the Kandinsky retrospective at the Guggenheim.[1] I wanted to hear more about the Kandinsky show, but he didn't have much to say about it. I chuckled or grunted at appropriate intervals and eventually he attained such a peak of good humor that I asked him how his flight in from New York had been and how was Uncle Max with whom he was staying. Fine, and fine.

I asked him where we were going. Usually his response to that question is "Keep quiet and follow me," but today was different for some reason. He said he thought we might go see his friend Jacobson. I'd expected that might be it—Pop doesn't have too many friends on the North Side and Jake's the one he usually visits when he comes back to Chicago.

---

1. *Kandinsky . . . Guggenheim:* Wassily Kandinsky (1866–1944): Russian painter whose works were being shown at the Guggenheim Museum in New York City.

But was there any place I'd rather go first? he asked. Surprised, I turned and looked at him. He was staring at me with his gray eyes (mine are black, like my mother's). "Why, no," I said, ". . . we usually go visiting and I like your friends. Whatever you want to do." He grunted, and very shortly we parked.

Jacobson is a short man of about fifty with large eyes and a scraggly beard. He is a moderately successful painter who belongs to no school, certainly not abstract expressionism.[2] His style and subject matter have changed often in the years I've known him. I saw him the last time Pop visited Chicago; at that time Jake was painting harsh, angular semiabstractions of cities. Pop said they had little subtlety and less variation, but I liked the bright harsh surface they presented to my mind. As we climbed to his studio I hoped to see more of these paintings.

We knocked; he opened the door, and as Pop and he embraced I wandered into the cool, whitewashed cavern where his easel stood and his new paintings hung. It was immediately evident that he had ended his "City" series.

The two men stood somewhere behind me, discussing the new development. Pop was praising it warmly; Jake was expressing his great hopes. I stared disconsolately at his newest work braced on his easel, a picture for which the new pictures hanging on the walls were obviously prototypes. They were all landscapes, many with skeletal trees which writhed like those of van Gogh,[3] but painted in misty pastels. There were people in the pictures, many of them girls . . . their sad eyes begged companionship, and something about them made one want to be beside them. But of course one could not . . . I don't think I'll ever like this new tack of Jacobson's; these pictures confuse me, make me feel uneasy.

We ate lunch. I was grateful to Jacobson when he asked me how school was; my ambiguous, vaguely confident generalities satisfied him, and Pop too. I wouldn't have to talk to him about it later, to *explain* the situation, to *analyze* things. I sat by an open window overlooking the small garden court for some hours while they talked. Jacobson has a large library which includes a good selection of science fiction. I started Bester's *The Demolished Man*. A cool wind trickled occasionally over my face. I was annoyed by the chirping of birds and the thick smell of warm grass rising from the garden, but the window was the coolest place in the studio.

---

2. *abstract expressionism:* style of painting that conveys emotions and feelings through nonrepresentational images.

3. *van Gogh* (van gō'), Vincent (1853–1890): Dutch painter.

Around three-thirty Pop sat down next to me; Jacobson was, I think, on the phone. He asked me hesitantly whether I was enjoying myself. Sure, I said. He said he hadn't seen Jake in some time and wouldn't have a chance tomorrow, but that he felt guilty seeing him on my time. Was I angry? Not a bit, I said. It must be pretty boring for you, he said. No, I muttered, I'm reading. What book? he asked. You wouldn't like it, I said. It's escapist. He moved away and I returned to the book.

We left about ten minutes later. The sun was lower in the sky and appeared larger. The air was like dishwater; the city stank of heat and settling soot. Pop asked me if there was a film I wanted to see. No, I said, the only one in the area was that Italian film *L'Avventura*, which I'd already seen. Albee's *The Zoo Story* was playing on the same bill as Beckett's *Krapp's Last Tape* in a theatre downtown. He hadn't seen them, but I'd read the reviews and they sounded depressing, so that was out.

We went down to Twelfth Street where goods are sold through customer peddling. Pop wanted to buy me something; I now have a beautiful pair of Italian shoes. I'll only be able to wear them for dress-up because I need arch supports, but still they're nice to have. I thanked him.

I knew where we were going next, although he'd said nothing. We go there whenever he comes back to Chicago. I never argue, you know. I don't like to "thrash things out" with him because there's nothing I want to "thrash out," nothing I think really *has* to be "thrashed out," but if I *had* to discuss something with him I'd tell him I don't like going south of Twelfth. I pity the underprivileged wretches down there as much as the next liberal, but I get no charge out of looking at them and their sordid surroundings. But he goes back there every time and takes me with him. He used to live in that area when he was a boy.

Things are at their worst three blocks south of Twelfth. This is Maxwell Street. Maxwell Street used to be the melting pot of Chicago in the early part of this century, but the Poles and the Irish bubbled away, and the Jews—including my parents—made the grade and rose like steam into the middle class, into West Rogers Park, Evanston, and the suburbs. Maxwell Street is a slum, the property of a few odd men out of the great ethnic migrations to the other parts of the city, and of the Negroes and Puerto Ricans who are trapped here. Today the streets and sidewalks were crowded with stands and pushcarts, dispensing goods of every description—wormy cabbages, picture frames, mink stoles made from synthetic fibers, old mattresses, damaged boxes of cereals, hot dogs, hamburgers 60 per cent pork. From a loudspeaker, over a plate-glass window bearing the legend *BODEGA,* flowed *"Que bonita bandera"* like mellifluous, brightly colored oil-slick. Pop, rummaging through one of the displays, said that you can save hundreds here if you know *how* to buy. I grunted and sucked air through my teeth. The smell was like melting sulphur. *"Que bonita bandera, que bonita bandera. . . ."*

Pop said my name; I turned and looked at him. He had found a box of spectacles, the nineteenth century kind: two glass octagons and thin brown wires. He had placed a pair on the bridge of his nose and was staring at me. I laughed dutifully but felt uneasy; they gave his face an unwonted benignity.[4] I told him to take them off; he'd never look like Benjamin Franklin. He chuckled at this.

We wandered through the neighborhood. There is a department store on the corner of Halsted Street, one of those institutions which makes it so expensive to be poor. Like Field's and Sears, its rich cousins uptown, it had been built in the last century. Unlike them, it had been allowed to deteriorate. Pop stood on the corner for an interminable time, staring at the building.

"I used to work here during the Depression," he said.

"I know," I said. "You told me about it last time we were here."

I suppose he didn't hear me, for he began to tell me about his employer, the owner of the store when he had worked there, a German who admired Hitler and made life tough for Pop in accordance with the historical traditions of the Fatherland. We walked north; there was a boarded-up building, sooty and rotting.

"That was once the best restaurant on the South Side," he said. "You and Mom ate there sometimes in the old days."

"Yes. When I was taking her out, in the old days."

A streetcar clanged past us as we walked, one of the last of its kind in the city. He told me about Kelly, the conductor, who had become one of his fellow officers in the E.T.O.[5] Every building and street corner in this neighborhood spurred him on to more reminiscences of his childhood and young manhood. I had never known him to be so garrulous about the subject. We turned on some street whose name I've forgotten and passed the bar, still in operation, where the big-time gangsters had hung out once. We turned north again and walked several blocks into an area which was undergoing considerable alteration. And then, on a deserted middle-of-nowhere street corner, he stopped.

---

4. *unwonted benignity:* unusual kindly feeling.
5. *E.T.O.:* in World War II, European Theater of Operations.

"That brown building over there was my school," he said, and stopped. He looked at me. I was trying to stifle a yawn.

"Sorry," I said.

"Tired?" he asked angrily.

"Not a bit," I said. "I bet you were the only one in your class who made good."

"Yes, but that's not the point," he said vaguely.

"Point of what?" I asked, rather irritated now.

He said nothing, but turned and walked a few feet away from me at a diagonal. Half the block was nothing but a flat field of black asphalt, a parking lot. Across from it was an electrical powerhouse and, incredibly enough, a few trees.

"I used to live here."

"On this asphalt?" I asked with what I thought was great good humor.

"There used to be a house here. I lived here with my mother and father, three brothers and three sisters. It was crowded and hot and wretched. We all had a certain affection for each other. Three blocks from here is where I first met your mother. I could show you the place."

"What's the point?" I said firmly. Suddenly I was tired. All the discomfort of this hot day was clinging to me like grease, like loathsome grease. I was irritated with his unfathomable talk, with his stare, with the obvious depression which was twisting his eyebrows and lips. I wanted to leave, and I made him know it. I think I told him I was getting a bit hungry. He nodded, and muttered something, I think it was "I guess there is no point." We went back to the car and drove quickly out of the South Side.

We ate at the Red Star Inn, a *gemütlich*[6] German restaurant on the Near North Side. He told me he was leaving tomorrow, sometime around ten P.M. I wouldn't be able to see him, of course; I had homework and he had plenty of people he had to see. He told me to give his regards to Mom and to Sis, who had been in bed for a week with a virus. I said I would. He asked me how school was. "Fine," I said. I told him it had been a pleasure seeing him, that this Wienerschnitzel was delicious and thanks for the Italian shoes. We finished simultaneously and he drove me home.

It was dusk now, a humid summer twilight in Chicago. We drove north on the Outer Drive, which borders Lake Michigan. There were still many people on the beaches—teenage boys and girls, mostly, lying

---

6. *gemütlich* (gə müt′ lik): pleasant, congenial [German].

unashamedly in each other's arms, sweating on each other. I turned and looked past my father's head at the beautiful apartment houses of the Gold Coast. The hum of the air conditioners was almost audible above the whoosh of the cars. Lights were going on in the windows of the sumptuous apartments, yellow lights, warm and inviting. Pop turned on the radio and twisted the station-selector knob with increasing irritation, searching for a symphony, finding only the harsh, bright whine of rock 'n' roll. I rested my arm on the ledge of the open window and looked out at the lake. The breeze dried the sweat on my forehead, whipped through my hair. It was cooler here.

Responding to the Story

1. "What is the point?" the narrator asked his father at one moment. What do you see as the point of this story?

2. How did you feel about this father and son and their relationship?

3. Why do you think Frederick Pollack entitled his story "Asphalt"?

Exploring the Author's Craft

This writer showed extraordinary skill in making a relationship come alive, and he did the same with various parts of a city. Without looking at the story again, recall and write down as many aspects of the Chicago setting at the time the story was written as you can.

Writing Workshop

A comparison and contrast essay touches upon similarities (comparisons) and differences (contrasts) between whatever two things are being discussed. Write a comparison and contrast essay about "Asphalt" and either "Shaving" or "Guess What? I Almost Kissed My Father Goodnight."

You might want to structure your essay by first writing about similarities between the two stories and then writing about the differences. Before you begin, jot down in two lists the similarities and differences.

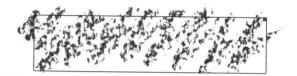

Responding to
Part Two

1. In this section, titled "Families and Friends," there are three stories about the relationships of sons and fathers but no stories about the relationships of daughters and mothers. Are the relationships between daughters and mothers different from those of sons and fathers? Do daughters and mothers understand each other more, or less, easily than fathers and sons do? Explain.

2. In most stories in Part Two, setting plays an active role in the narrative. As you look back on the stories, which setting stands out most strongly in your mind and why?

3. Analyze the beginnings of the stories in this part. Which beginnings seem the most compelling to you?

Falling in Love

A fourteen-year-old boy is entranced with Sheila Mant, "at seventeen, all but out of reach," but our hero likes to fish for bass, too. Can romance blossom in a canoe that has a fishing line trailing out the back?

In another story Tossie says about someone whom she has met, "I sort of can't help liking him. You know. I like him being around. I feel sort of . . ."

"Sort of what?" her sister asks.

"Comfortable. When he's there." The sister wonders if this is a part of love.

In Gary Soto's "Broken Chain" we read of Alfonso who "didn't want to be the handsomest kid at school, but he was determined to be better looking than average." He meets Sandra and tells us "it felt like love."

Most collections of stories for students don't even acknowledge the essential part of coming-of-age that involves romance and all its manifestations. Enjoy this section of the book, which deals with infatuations and the various hesitant steps along the path called love.

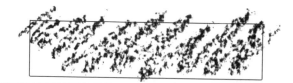

Her First Ball

Katherine Mansfield

Katherine Mansfield's influence on the development of the short story is widely recognized, and several of her stories, notably "The Garden Party," "Prelude," "Miss Brill," and "The Doll's House," are famous as examples of her art.

Born Kathleen Mansfield Beauchamp in 1888 in Wellington, New Zealand, the third of six children, she published her work under a pseudonym.

She studied the cello at Queen's College in London from 1903– 06 and continued her musical studies in New Zealand in 1906– 07. She returned to London in 1908 and was married in 1909 but left her husband almost immediately.

Her first collection of stories, In a German Pension, *was published in 1911, the year she met John Middleton Murry, whom she married in 1918. Murry, an editor, critic, and essayist, published several of her early stories in a succession of magazines he edited. Increasingly ill with tuberculosis, she spent much of her time in southern France and died in 1923 at Fontainebleau.*

Bliss, and Other Stories *appeared in 1920,* The Garden Party, and Other Stories *in 1922, and* The Doves' Nest, and Other Stories *and* Something Childish *were published after her death.*

Exactly when the ball began Leila would have found it hard to say. Perhaps her first real partner was the cab. It did not matter that she shared the cab with the Sheridan girls and their brother. She sat back in her own little corner of it, and the bolster on which her hand rested felt like the sleeve of an unknown young man's dress suit; and away they bowled, past waltzing lampposts and houses and fences and trees.

"Have you really never been to a ball before, Leila? But, my child, how too weird—" cried the Sheridan girls.

"Our nearest neighbor was fifteen miles," said Leila softly, gently opening and shutting her fan.

Oh, dear, how hard it was to be indifferent like the others! She tried not to smile too much; she tried not to care. But every single thing was so new and exciting . . . Meg's tuberoses[1], Jose's long loop of amber, Laura's little dark head, pushing above her white fur like a flower through snow. She would remember forever. It even gave her a pang to see her cousin Laurie throw away the wisps of tissue paper he pulled from the fastenings of his new gloves. She would like to have kept those wisps as a keepsake, as a remembrance. Laurie leaned forward and put his hand on Laura's knee.

"Look here, darling," he said. "The third and the ninth[2] as usual. Twig?"[3]

Oh, how marvelous to have a brother! In her excitement Leila felt that if there had been time, if it hadn't been impossible, she couldn't have helped crying because she was an only child, and no brother had ever said "Twig?" to her; no sister would ever say, as Meg said to Jose that moment, "I've never known your hair go up more successfully than it has tonight!"

But of course, there was no time. They were at the drill hall already; there were cabs in front of them and cabs behind. The road was bright on either side with moving fanlike lights, and on the pavement happy couples seemed to float through the air; little satin shoes chased each other like birds.

"Hold on to me, Leila; you'll get lost," said Laura.

"Come on, girls, let's make a dash for it," said Laurie.

Leila put two fingers on Laura's pink velvet cloak, and they were somehow lifted past the big golden lantern, carried along the passage, and pushed into the little room marked "Ladies." Here the crowd was so great there was hardly space to take off their things; the noise was deafening. Two benches on either side were stacked high with wraps. Two old women in white aprons ran up and down tossing fresh armfuls. And everybody was pressing forward trying to get at the little dressing table and mirror at the far end.

A great quivering jet of gas lighted the ladies' room. It couldn't

---

1. *tuberoses* (tüb´rōz): white, lilylike flowers.

2. *third and the ninth:* Laurie wants his sister Laura to reserve the third and the ninth dance for him.

3. *Twig:* slang term popular in the 1920s meaning "to understand."

wait; it was dancing already. When the door opened again and there came a burst of tuning from the drill hall, it leaped almost to the ceiling.

Dark girls, fair girls were patting their hair, tying ribbons again, tucking handkerchiefs down the fronts of their bodices, smoothing marble-white gloves. And because they were all laughing it seemed to Leila that they were all lovely.

"Aren't there any invisible hairpins?" cried a voice. "How most extraordinary! I can't see a single invisible hairpin."

"Powder my back, there's a darling," cried someone else.

"But I must have a needle and cotton. I've torn simply miles and miles of the frill," wailed a third.

Then, "Pass them along, pass them along!" The straw basket of programs was tossed from arm to arm. Darling little pink-and-silver programs,[4] with pink pencils and fluffy tassels. Leila's fingers shook as she took one out of the basket. She wanted to ask someone, "Am I meant to have one too?" but she had just time to read: "Waltz 3. *Two, Two in a Canoe.* Polka 4. *Making the Feathers Fly,*" when Meg cried, "Ready, Leila?" and they pressed their way through the crush in the passage towards the big double doors of the drill hall.

Dancing had not begun yet, but the band had stopped tuning, and the noise was so great it seemed that when it did begin to play it would never be heard. Leila, pressing close to Meg, looking over Meg's shoulder, felt that even the little quivering colored flags strung across the ceiling were talking. She quite forgot to be shy; she forgot how in the middle of dressing she had sat down on the bed with one shoe off and one shoe on and begged her mother to ring up her cousins and say she couldn't go after all. And the rush of longing she had had to be sitting on the veranda of their forsaken up-country home, listening to the baby owls crying "More pork" in the moonlight, was changed to a rush of joy so sweet that it was hard to bear alone. She clutched her fan, and gazing at the gleaming, golden floor, the azaleas, the lanterns, the stage at one end with its red carpet and gilt chairs and the band in a corner, she thought breathlessly, "How heavenly; how simply heavenly!"

All the girls stood grouped together at one side of the doors, the men at the other, and the chaperones in dark dresses, smiling rather foolishly, walked with little careful steps over the polished floor towards the stage.

---

4. *programs:* At one time dancers at formal balls carried small programs that not only contained a printed list of the dances but provided space to write the names of one's partners for those dances.

"This is my little country cousin Leila. Be nice to her. Find her partners; she's under my wing," said Meg, going up to one girl after another.

Strange faces smiled at Leila—sweetly, vaguely. Strange voices answered, "Of course, my dear." But Leila felt the girls didn't really see her. They were looking towards the men. Why didn't the men begin? What were they waiting for? There they stood, smoothing their gloves, patting their glossy hair and smiling among themselves. Then, quite suddenly, as if they had only just made up their minds that that was what they had to do, the men came gliding over the parquet. There was a joyful flutter among the girls. A tall, fair man flew up to Meg, seized her program, scribbled something; Meg passed him on to Leila. "May I have the pleasure?" He ducked and smiled. There came a dark man wearing an eyeglass, then cousin Laurie with a friend, and Laura with a little freckled fellow whose tie was crooked. Then quite an old man—fat, with a big bald patch on his head—took her program, and murmured, "Let me see, let me see!" And he was a long time comparing his program, which looked black with names, with hers. It seemed to give him so much trouble that Leila was ashamed. "Oh, please don't bother," she said eagerly. But instead of replying the fat man wrote something, glanced at her again. "Do I remember this bright little face?" he said softly. "Is it known to me of yore?" At that moment the band began playing; the fat man disappeared. He was tossed away on a great wave of music that came flying over the gleaming floor, breaking the groups up into couples, scattering them, sending them spinning . . .

Leila had learned to dance at boarding school. Every Saturday afternoon the boarders were hurried off to a little corrugated iron mission hall where Miss Eccles (of London) held her "select" classes. But the difference between that dusty-smelling hall—with calico texts[5] on the walls, the poor terrified little woman in a brown velvet toque[6] with rabbit's ears thumping the cold piano, Miss Eccles poking the girls' feet with her long white wand—and this was so tremendous that Leila was sure if her partner didn't come and she had to listen to that marvelous music and to watch the others sliding, gliding over the golden floor, she would die at least, or faint, or lift her arms and fly out of one of those dark windows that showed the stars.

---

5. *calico texts:* probably framed religious or moral sayings that were now speckled or spotted like calico cloth.

6. *toque* (tōk): a close-fitting hat without a brim.

"Ours, I think—" Someone bowed, smiled, and offered her his arm; she hadn't to die after all. Someone's hand pressed her waist, and she floated away like a flower that is tossed into a pool.

"Quite a good floor, isn't it?" drawled a faint voice close to her ear.

"I think it's most beautifully slippery," said Leila.

"Pardon!" The faint voice sounded surprised. Leila said it again. And there was a tiny pause before the voice echoed, "Oh, quite!" and she was swung around again.

He steered so beautifully. That was the great difference between dancing with girls and men, Leila decided. Girls banged into each other, and stamped on each other's feet; the girl who was gentleman always clutched you so.

The azaleas were separate flowers no longer; they were pink and white flags streaming by.

"Were you at the Bells' last week?" the voice came again. It sounded tired. Leila wondered whether she ought to ask him if he would like to stop.

"No, this is my first dance," said she.

Her partner gave a little gasping laugh. "Oh, I say," he protested.

"Yes, it is really the first dance I've ever been to." Leila was most fervent. It was such a relief to be able to tell somebody. "You see, I've lived in the country all my life up until now . . ."

At that moment the music stopped, and they went to sit on two chairs against the wall. Leila tucked her pink satin feet under and fanned herself, while she blissfully watched the other couples passing and disappearing through the swing doors.

"Enjoying yourself, Leila?" asked Jose, nodding her golden head.

Laura passed and gave her the faintest little wink; it made Leila wonder for a moment whether she was quite grown up after all. Certainly her partner did not say very much. He coughed, tucked his handkerchief away, pulled down his waistcoat, took a minute thread off his sleeve. But it didn't matter. Almost immediately the band started, and her second partner seemed to spring from the ceiling.

"Floor's not bad," said the new voice. Did one always begin with the floor? And then, "Were you at the Neaves' on Tuesday?" And again Leila explained. Perhaps it was a little strange that her partners were not more interested. For it was thrilling. Her first ball! She was only at the beginning of everything. It seemed to her that she had never known what the night was like before. Up till now it had been dark, silent, beautiful very often—oh, yes—but mournful somehow. Solemn. And now it would never be like that again—it had opened dazzling bright.

"Care for an ice?" said her partner. And they went through the swing doors, down the passage, to the supper room. Her cheeks burned, she was fearfully thirsty. How sweet the ices looked on little glass plates, and how cold the frosted spoon was, iced too! And when they came back to the hall there was the fat man waiting for her by the door. It gave her quite a shock again to see how old he was; he ought to have been on the stage with the fathers and mothers. And when Leila compared him with her other partners he looked shabby. His waistcoat was creased, there was a button off his glove, his coat looked as if it was dusty with French chalk.

"Come along, little lady," said the fat man. He scarcely troubled to clasp her, and they moved away so gently, it was more like walking than dancing. But he said not a word about the floor. "Your first dance, isn't it?" he murmured.

"How *did* you know?"

"Ah," said the fat man, "that's what it is to be old!" He wheezed faintly as he steered her past an awkward couple. "You see, I've been doing this kind of thing for the last thirty years."

"Thirty years?" cried Leila. Twelve years before she was born!

"It hardly bears thinking about, does it?" said the fat man gloomily. Leila looked at his bald head, and she felt quite sorry for him.

"I think it's marvelous to be still going on," she said kindly.

"Kind little lady," said the fat man, and he pressed her a little closer, and hummed a bar of the waltz. "Of course," he said, "you can't hope to last anything like as long as that. No-o," said the fat man, "long before that you'll be sitting up there on the stage, looking on, in your nice black velvet. And these pretty arms will have turned into little short fat ones, and you'll beat time with such a different kind of fan—a black bony one." The fat man seemed to shudder. "And you'll smile away like the poor old dears up there, and point to your daughter, and tell the elderly lady next to you how some dreadful man tried to kiss her at the club ball. And your heart will ache, ache"—the fat man squeezed her closer still, as if he really was sorry for that poor heart—"because no one wants to kiss you now. And you'll say how unpleasant these polished floors are to walk on, how dangerous they are. Eh, Mademoiselle Twinkletoes?" said the fat man softly.

Leila gave a light little laugh, but she did not feel like laughing. Was it—could it all be true? It sounded terribly true. Was this first ball only the beginning of her last ball after all? At that the music seemed to change; it sounded sad, sad; it rose upon a great sigh. Oh, how quickly things changed! Why didn't happiness last forever? Forever wasn't a bit too long.

"I want to stop," she said in a breathless voice. The fat man led her to the door.

"No," she said, "I won't go outside. I won't sit down. I'll just stand here, thank you." She leaned against the wall, tapping with her foot, pulling up her gloves and trying to smile. But deep inside her a little girl threw her pinafore[7] over her head and sobbed. Why had he spoiled it all?

"I say, you know," said the fat man, "you mustn't take me seriously, little lady."

"As if I should!" said Leila, tossing her small dark head and sucking her underlip . . .

Again the couples paraded. The swing doors opened and shut. Now new music was given out by the bandmaster. But Leila didn't want to dance anymore. She wanted to be home, or sitting on the veranda listening to those baby owls. When she looked through the dark windows at the stars, they had long beams like wings . . .

But presently a soft, melting, ravishing tune began, and a young man with curly hair bowed before her. She would have to dance, out of politeness, until she could find Meg. Very stiffly she walked into the middle; very haughtily she put her arm on his sleeve. But in one minute, in one turn, her feet glided, glided. The lights, the azaleas, the dresses, the pink faces, the velvet chairs, all became one beautiful flying wheel. And when her next partner bumped her into the fat man and he said, "Pardon," she smiled at him more radiantly than ever. She didn't even recognize him again.

Responding to the Story

1. Trace the various moods Leila goes through in this story. Given Leila's background, are they all believable? Explain.

2. Did you like Leila? Explain your reaction to her. How did your own background affect your reaction to her? Explain in detail.

---

7. *pinafore:* child's apron.

Exploring the Author's Craft

The first person to dance with Leila, and the fat man, are quite distinct characters. Writers develop a character through describing that character's actions, physical appearance, manner of speaking, and thoughts, and by telling what other characters say or think about a character. How are the two men different from each other, and what techniques did the author use to make them distinct? What do Leila's reactions to the two men tell you about her? What do the men's reactions to Leila tell you about them?

Writing Workshop

Think of a setting in which two people have just met. The setting might be a waiting room, a bus, a store, a park, or any other public place. Then decide what these two people look like and what the two might talk about. Are they friendly? Is one person wary of the other? Are they both antagonistic? Are they both polite? Is one more talkative than the other? Create a dialogue of approximately five hundred words between these two people that captures the separate personalities of the two. Keep the dialogue moving forward as much as possible.

Alternate Media Response

Choose two speakers to read the dialogue you created in the Writing Workshop and record the conversation on an audiocassette. Play the cassette for the class. Discuss how believable and realistic the conversation sounds.

The Bass, the River, and Sheila Mant

W. D. Wetherell

W. D. Wetherell is the author of seven books, including The Man Who Loved Levittown, *a story collection that won the Drue Heinz Literature Prize in 1985;* Chekhov's Sister, *a novel that was selected by the* New York Times *as one of the best dozen novels of 1990; and a collection of essays,* Upland Stream.

Born in 1948 on Long Island, he now lives in rural New Hampshire, the setting for "The Bass, the River, and Sheila Mant." He says that when writing the story, "being the fisherman I am, it was very difficult not to let the boy catch *the bass—not to have him dump the girl out of the boat instead. But the demands of fiction are tougher than the demands of life—the girl must stay, the bass go. What's especially important is to realize that having a heartbreaking crush on a girl isn't a tragedy, far from it; the tragedy would be to go through adolescence and* not *have a crush, a helpless crush, on someone, and learn what painful lessons are there."*

There was a summer in my life when the only creature that seemed lovelier to me than a largemouth bass was Sheila Mant. I was fourteen. The Mants had rented the cottage next to ours on the river; with their parties, their frantic games of softball, their constant comings and goings, they appeared to me denizens[1] of a brilliant existence. "Too

---

1. *denizens* (den ′ ə zənz): inhabitants.

noisy by half," my mother quickly decided, but I would have given anything to be invited to one of their parties, and when my parents went to bed I would sneak through the woods to their hedge and stare enchanted at the candlelit swirl of white dresses and bright, paisley skirts.

Sheila was the middle daughter—at seventeen, all but out of reach. She would spend her days sunbathing on a float my Uncle Siebert had moored in their cove, and before July was over I had learned all her moods. If she lay flat on the diving board with her hand trailing idly in the water, she was pensive, not to be disturbed. On her side, her head propped up by her arm, she was observant, considering those around her with a look that seemed queenly and severe. Sitting up, arms tucked around her long, suntanned legs, she was approachable, but barely, and it was only in those glorious moments when she stretched herself prior to entering the water that her various suitors found the courage to come near.

These were many. The Dartmouth heavyweight crew[2] would scull by her house on their way upriver, and I think all eight of them must have been in love with her at various times during the summer; the coxswain[3] would curse at them through his megaphone, but without effect—there was always a pause in their pace when they passed Sheila's float. I suppose to these jaded twenty-year-olds she seemed the incarnation of innocence and youth, while to me she appeared unutterably suave, the epitome of sophistication. I was on the swim team at school, and to win her attention would do endless laps between my house and the Vermont shore, hoping she would notice the beauty of my flutter kick, the power of my crawl. Finishing, I would boost myself up onto our dock and glance casually over toward her, but she was never watching, and the miraculous day she was, I immediately climbed the diving board and did my best tuck and a half for her, and continued diving until she had left and the sun went down and my longing was like a madness and I couldn't stop.

It was late August by the time I got up the nerve to ask her out. The tortured will-I's, won't-I's, the agonized indecision over what to say, the false starts toward her house and embarrassed retreats—the details of these have been seared from my memory, and the only part

---

2. *Dartmouth . . . crew:* the men from Dartmouth College in New Hampshire rowing in a racing shell, a long, narrow boat.

3. *coxswain* (kok′sən): person who steers a racing shell and gives directions to the crew.

I remember clearly is emerging from the woods toward dusk while they were playing softball on their lawn, as bashful and frighted as a unicorn.

Sheila was stationed halfway between first and second, well outside the infield. She didn't seem surprised to see me—as a matter of fact, she didn't seem to see me at all.

"If you're playing second base, you should move closer," I said.

She turned—I took the full brunt of her long red hair and well-spaced freckles.

"I'm playing outfield," she said, "I don't like the responsibility of having a base."

"Yeah, I can understand that," I said, though I couldn't.

"There's a band in Dixford tomorrow night at nine. Want to go?"

One of her brothers sent the ball sailing over the leftfielder's head; she stood and watched it disappear toward the river.

"You have a car?" she said, without looking up.

I played my master stroke. "We'll go by canoe."

I spent all of the following day polishing it. I turned it upside down on our lawn and rubbed every inch with Brillo, hosing off the dirt, wiping it with chamois until it gleamed as bright as aluminum ever gleamed. About five, I slid it into the water, arranging cushions near the bow so Sheila could lean on them if she was in one of her pensive moods, propping up my father's transistor radio by the middle thwart so we could have music when we came back. Automatically, without thinking about it, I mounted my Mitchell reel on my Pfleuger spinning rod and stuck it in the stern.

I say automatically, because I never went anywhere that summer without a fishing rod. When I wasn't swimming laps to impress Sheila, I was back in our driveway practicing casts, and when I wasn't practicing casts, I was tying the line to Tosca, our springer spaniel, to test the reel's drag, and when I wasn't doing any of those things, I was fishing the river for bass.

Too nervous to sit at home, I got in the canoe early and started paddling in a huge circle that would get me to Sheila's dock around eight. As automatically as I brought along my rod, I tied on a big Rapala plug, let it down into the water, let out some line and immediately forgot all about it.

It was already dark by the time I glided up to the Mants' dock. Even by day the river was quiet, most of the summer people preferring Sunapee or one of the other nearby lakes, and at night it was a solitude difficult to believe, a corridor of hidden life that ran between banks like a tunnel. Even the stars were part of it. They weren't as sharp anywhere else; they seemed to have chosen the river as a guide on their slow wheel toward morning, and in the course of the summer's fishing, I had learned all their names.

I was there ten minutes before Sheila appeared. I heard the slam of their screen door first, then saw her in the spotlight as she came slowly down the path. As beautiful as she was on the float, she was even lovelier now—her white dress went perfectly with her hair, and complimented her figure even more than her swimsuit.

It was her face that bothered me. It had on its delightful fullness a very dubious expression.

"Look," she said. "I can get Dad's car."

"It's faster this way," I lied. "Parking's tense up there. Hey, it's safe. I won't tip it or anything."

She let herself down reluctantly into the bow. I was glad she wasn't facing me. When her eyes were on me, I felt like diving in the river again from agony and joy.

I pried the canoe away from the dock and started paddling upstream. There was an extra paddle in the bow, but Sheila made no move to pick it up. She took her shoes off, and dangled her feet over the side.

Ten minutes went by.

"What kind of band?" she said.

"It's sort of like folk music. You'll like it."

"Eric Caswell's going to be there. He strokes number four."

"No kidding?" I said. I had no idea who she meant.

"What's that sound?" she said, pointing toward shore.

"Bass. That splashing sound?"

"Over there."

"Yeah, bass. They come into the shallows at night to chase frogs and moths and things. Big largemouths. *Micropetrus salmonides*," I added, showing off.

"I think fishing's dumb," she said, making a face. "I mean, it's boring and all. Definitely dumb."

Now I have spent a great deal of time in the years since wondering why Sheila Mant should come down so hard on fishing. Was her father a fisherman? Her antipathy toward fishing nothing more than normal filial rebellion? Had she tried it once? A messy encounter with worms? It doesn't matter. What does, is that at that fragile moment in time I would have given anything not to appear dumb in Sheila's severe and unforgiving eyes.

She hadn't seen my equipment yet. What I *should* have done, of course, was push the canoe in closer to shore and carefully slide the rod into some branches where I could pick it up again in the morning. Failing that, I could have surreptitiously dumped the whole outfit overboard, written off the forty or so dollars as love's tribute. What I actually *did* do was gently lean forward, and slowly, ever so slowly, push the rod back through my legs toward the stern where it would be less conspicuous.

It must have been exactly what the bass was waiting for. Fish will trail a lure sometimes, trying to make up their mind whether or not to attack, and the slight pause in the plug's speed caused by my adjustment was tantalizing enough to overcome the bass's inhibitions. My rod, safely out of sight at last, bent double. The line, tightly coiled, peeled off the spool with the shrill, tearing zip of a high-speed drill.

Four things occurred to me at once. One, that it was a bass. Two, that it was a big bass. Three, that it was the biggest bass I had ever hooked. Four, that Sheila Mant must not know.

"What was that?" she said, turning half around.

"Uh, what was what?"

"That buzzing noise."

"Bats."

She shuddered, quickly drew her feet back into the canoe. Every instinct I had told me to pick up the rod and strike back at the bass, but there was no need to—it was already solidly hooked. Downstream, an awesome distance downstream, it jumped clear of the water, landing with a concussion heavy enough to ripple the entire river. For a moment, I thought it was gone, but then the rod was bending again, the tip dancing into the water. Slowly, not making any motion that might alert Sheila, I reached down to tighten the drag.

While all this was going on, Sheila had begun talking and it was a few minutes before I was able to catch up with her train of thought.

"I went to a party there. These fraternity men. Katherine says I could get in there if I wanted. I'm thinking more of UVM or Bennington. Somewhere I can ski."

The bass was slanting toward the rocks on the New Hampshire side by the ruins of Donaldson's boathouse. It had to be an old bass—a young one probably wouldn't have known the rocks were there. I brought the canoe back out into the middle of the river, hoping to head it off.

"That's neat," I mumbled. "Skiing. Yeah, I can see that."

"Eric said I have the figure to model, but I thought I should get an education first. I mean, it might be a while before I get started and all. I was thinking of getting my hair styled, more swept back? I mean, Ann-Margret? Like hers, only shorter."

She hesitated. "Are we going backwards?"

We were. I had managed to keep the bass in the middle of the river away from the rocks, but it had plenty of room there, and for the first time a chance to exert its full strength. I quickly computed the weight necessary to draw a fully loaded canoe backwards—the thought of it made me feel faint.

"It's just the current," I said hoarsely. "No sweat or anything."

I dug in deeper with my paddle. Reassured, Sheila began talking about something else, but all my attention was taken up now with the fish. I could feel its desperation as the water grew shallower. I could sense the extra strain on the line, the frantic way it cut back and forth in the water. I could visualize what it looked like—the gape of its mouth, the flared gills and thick, vertical tail. The bass couldn't have encountered many forces in its long life that it wasn't capable of handling, and the unrelenting tug at its mouth must have been a source of great puzzlement and mounting panic.

Me, I had problems of my own. To get to Dixford, I had to paddle up a sluggish stream that came into the river beneath a covered bridge. There was a shallow sandbar at the mouth of this stream—weeds on one side, rocks on the other. Without doubt, this is where I would lose the fish.

"I have to be careful with my complexion. I tan, but in segments. I can't figure out if it's even worth it. I wouldn't even do it probably. I saw Jackie Kennedy in Boston and she wasn't tan at all."

Taking a deep breath, I paddled as hard as I could for the middle, deepest part of the bar. I could have threaded the eye of a needle with the canoe, but the pull on the stern threw me off and I overcompensated—the canoe veered left and scraped bottom. I pushed the paddle down and shoved. A moment of hesitation . . . a moment more . . . The canoe shot clear into the deeper water of the stream. I immediately looked down at the rod. It was bent in the same, tight arc—miraculously, the bass was still on.

The moon was out now. It was low and full enough that its beam shone directly on Sheila there ahead of me in the canoe, washing her in a creamy, luminous glow. I could see the lithe, easy shape of her figure. I could see the way her hair curled down off her shoulders, the proud, alert tilt of her head, and all these things were as a tug on my heart. Not just Sheila, but the aura she carried about her of parties and casual touchings and grace. Behind me, I could feel the strain of the bass, steadier now, growing weaker, and this was another tug on my heart, not just the bass but the beat of the river and the slant of the stars and the smell of the night, until finally it seemed I would be torn apart between longings, split in half. Twenty yards ahead of us was the road, and once I pulled the canoe up on shore, the bass would be gone, irretrievably gone. If instead I stood up, grabbed the rod and started pumping, I would have it—as tired as the bass was, there was no chance it could get away. I reached down for the rod, hesitated, looked up to where Sheila was stretching herself lazily toward the sky, her small breasts rising beneath the soft fabric of her dress, and the tug was too much for me, and quicker than it takes to write down, I pulled a penknife from my pocket and cut the line in half.

With a sick, nauseous feeling in my stomach, I saw the rod unbend.

"My legs are sore," Sheila whined. "Are we there yet?"

Through a superhuman effort of self-control, I was able to beach the canoe and help Sheila off. The rest of the night is much foggier. We walked to the fair—there was the smell of popcorn, the sound of guitars. I may have danced once or twice with her, but all I really remember is her coming over to me once the music was done to explain that she would be going home in Eric Caswell's Corvette.

"Okay," I mumbled.

For the first time that night she looked at me, really looked at me. "You're a funny kid, you know that?"

Funny. Different. Dreamy. Odd. How many times was I to hear that in the years to come, all spoken with the same quizzical, half-accusatory tone Sheila used then. Poor Sheila! Before the month was over, the spell she cast over me was gone, but the memory of that lost bass haunted me all summer and haunts me still. There would be other Sheila Mants in my life, other fish, and though I came close once or twice, it was these secret hidden tuggings in the night that claimed me, and I never made the same mistake again.

Responding to the Story

1. How did you like this story? For once, we have an author who sees some humor—not just agony—in the various tensions of adolescence. The big question is, did *you* see humor in the boy's dilemma?

2. Why does Sheila Mant appeal to the narrator?

3. What kind of person is Sheila? Give a portrait of her based entirely on what she says.

Exploring the Author's Craft

Here is a tough analytical question: How does W. D. Wetherell make this story amusing? Start by analyzing the major conflict in the story. You will be analyzing one short story in particular but commenting, really, on the nature of comic writing.

Writing Workshop

It's much easier to see the humor in a painful situation when you're looking back at it from some distance in time. The summer when he was fourteen (assuming this story is at least somewhat autobiographical), the narrator probably saw no humor in that canoe ride.

Tell a story of some aspect of your own "coming of age" that looks amusing to you now. Don't just write that it was amusing; show what made it amusing.

Alternate Media Response

1. Analyze a current situation comedy on television. Is it funny? If it is, where does the humor lie? Are the lines amusing? Is the humor chiefly of the slapstick variety? Is the plot (situation) funny? Report to the class.

2. Study videos or reruns of some famous movie and television comedians of the past, such as the Marx Brothers, Charlie Chaplin, Abbott and Costello, Lucille Ball and Desi Arnaz, and others. If you think these people are funny, tell why in a short paper. If they are not funny to you, analyze why they are not in a short paper.

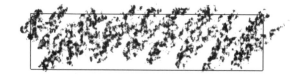

The Osage Orange Tree

William Stafford

William Stafford has had a long and distinguished career as a poet. He was born in 1914 in Hutchinson, Kansas, the oldest of three children. During the Depression in the 1930s, the family moved often within Kansas, and Stafford delivered papers and worked as a field hand and an electrician's assistant to help support the family.

He worked his way through the University of Kansas, and at the start of World War II, registered as a pacifist. During the war he worked in various camps for conscientious objectors. At the end of the war, he married Dorothy Frantz (they have four children), and finished his M.S. degree at the University of Kansas. He received his Ph.D. in 1954 from the University of Iowa.

He began teaching in 1948 at Lewis and Clark College in Portland, Oregon, and remained there until his retirement in 1980. Down in My Heart, *an autobiographical work, was published in 1947 while he worked for a relief agency near San Francisco. Stafford's poetry collections include* West of Your City *(1960);* Traveling Through the Dark *(1962), which won a National Book Award in 1963;* The Rescued Year *(1966);* Allegiances *(1970);* Someday, Maybe *(1973);* Stories That Could Be True: New and Collected Poems *(1977); and* An Oregon Message *(1987).*

In You Must Revise Your Life, *a prose work published in 1986, he wrote, "A person writes by means of that meager and persistent little self he has within him all the time."*

O n that first day of high school in the prairie town where the tree was, I stood in the sun by the flagpole and watched, but pretended not to watch, the others. They stood in groups and talked and knew each other, all except one—a girl though—in a faded blue dress, carrying a sack lunch and standing near the corner looking everywhere but at the crowd.

I might talk to her, I thought. But of course it was out of the question.

That first day was easier when the classes started. Some of the teachers were kind; some were frightening. Some of the students didn't care, but I listened and waited; and at the end of the day I was relieved, less conspicuous from then on.

But that day was not really over. As I hurried to carry my new paper route, I was thinking about how in a strange town, if you are quiet, no one notices, and some may like you, later. I was thinking about this when I reached the north edge of town where the scattering houses dwindle. Beyond them to the north lay just openness, the plains, a big swoop of nothing. There, at the last house, just as I cut across a lot and threw to the last customer, I saw the girl in the blue dress coming along the street, heading on out of town, carrying books. And she saw me.

"Hello."

"Hello."

And because we stopped we were friends. I didn't know how I could stop, but I didn't hurry on. I stood. There was nothing to do but to act as if I were walking on out too. I had three papers left in the bag, and I frantically began to fold them—box them, as we called it—for throwing. We had begun to walk and talk. The girl was timid; I became more bold. Not much, but a little.

"Have you gone to school here before?" I asked.

"Yes, I went here last year."

A long pause. A meadowlark sitting on a fencepost hunched his wings and flew. I kicked through the dust of the road.

I began to look ahead. Where could we possibly be walking to? I couldn't be walking just because I wanted to be with her.

Fortunately, there was one more house, a gray house by a sagging barn, set two hundred yards from the road.

"I thought I'd see if I could get a customer here," I said, waving toward the house.

"That's where I live."

"Oh."

We were at the dusty car tracks that turned off the road to the house. The girl stopped. There was a tree at that corner, a straight but little tree with slim branches and shiny dark leaves.

"I could take a paper tonight to see if my father wants to buy it."

A great relief, this. What could I have said to her parents? I held out a paper, dropped it, picked it up, brushing off the dust. "No, here's a new one"—a great action, putting the dusty paper in the bag over my shoulder and pulling out a fresh one. When she took the paper we stood there a minute. The wind was coming in over the grass. She looked out with a tranquil expression.

She walked away past the tree, and I hurried quickly back toward town. Could anyone in the houses have been watching? I looked back once. The girl was standing on the small bridge halfway in to her house. I hurried on.

The next day at school I didn't ask her whether her father wanted to take the paper. When the others were there I wouldn't say anything. I stood with the boys. In American history the students could choose their seats, and I saw that she was too quiet and plainly dressed for many to notice her. But I crowded in with the boys, pushing one aside, scrambling for a seat by the window.

That night I came to the edge of town. Two papers were left, and I walked on out. The meadowlark was there. By some reeds in a ditch by the road a dragonfly—snake feeders, we called them—glinted. The sun was going down, and the plains were stretched out and lifted, some way, to the horizon. Could I go on up to the house? I didn't think so, but I walked on. Then, by the tree where her road turned off, she was standing. She was holding her books. More confused than ever, I stopped.

"My father will take the paper," she said.

She told me always to leave the paper at the foot of the tree. She insisted on that, saying their house was too far; and it is true that I was far off my route, a long way, a half-mile out of my territory. But I didn't think of that.

And so we were acquainted. What I remember best in that town is those evening walks to the tree. Every night—or almost every night—the girl was there. Evangeline was her name. We didn't say much. On Friday night of the first week she gave me a dime, the cost of the paper. It was a poor newspaper, by the way, cheap, sensational, unreliable. I never went up to her house. We never talked together at school. But all the time we knew each other; we just happened to meet. Every evening.

There was a low place in the meadow by that corner. The fall rains made a pond there, and in the evenings sometimes ducks would be coming in—a long line with set wings down the wind, and then a turn, and a skimming glide to the water. The wind would be blowing and the grass bent down. The evenings got colder and colder. The wind was cold. As winter came on the time at the tree was dimmer, but not dark.

In the winter there was snow. The pond was frozen over; all the plains were white. I had to walk down the ruts of the road and leave the paper in the crotch of the tree, sometimes, when it was cold. The wind made a sound through the black branches. But usually, even on cold evenings, Evangeline was there.

At school we played ball at noon—the boys did. And I got acquainted. I learned that Evangeline's brother was janitor at the school. A big dark boy he was—a man, middle-aged I thought at the time. He didn't ever let on that he knew me. I would see him sweeping the halls, bent down, slow. I would see him and Evangeline take their sack lunches over to the south side of the building. Once I slipped away from the ball game and went over there, but he looked at me so steadily, without moving, that I pretended to be looking for a book, and quickly went back, and got in the game and struck out.

You don't know about those winters, and especially that winter. Those were the dust years. Wheat was away down in price. Everyone was poor—poor in a way that you can't understand. I made two dollars a week, or something like that, on my paper route. I could tell about working for ten cents an hour—and then not getting paid; about families that ate wheat, boiled, for their main food, and burned wheat for fuel. You don't know how it would be. All through that hard winter I carried a paper to the tree by the pond, in the evening, and gave it to Evangeline.

In the cold weather Evangeline wore a heavier dress, a dark, straight, heavy dress, under a thick black coat. Outdoors she wore a knitted cap that fastened under her chin. She was dressed this way when we met and she took the paper. The reeds were broken now. The meadowlark was gone.

And then came the spring. I have forgotten to tell just how Evangeline looked. She was of medium height, and slim. Her face was pale, her forehead high, her eyes blue. Her tranquil face I remember well. I remember her watching the wind come in over the grass. Her dress was long, her feet small. I can remember her by the tree, with her books, or walking on up the road toward her house and stopping on the bridge halfway up there, but she didn't wave, and I couldn't tell whether she was watching me or not. I always looked back as I went over the rise toward town.

And I can remember her in the room at school. She came into American history one spring day, the first really warm day. She had changed from the dark heavy dress to the dull blue one of the last fall; and she had on a new belt, a gray belt, with blue stitching along the edges. As she passed in front of Jane Wright, a girl who sat on the front row, I heard Jane say to the girl beside her, "Why look at Evangeline—that old dress of hers has a new belt!"

"Stop a minute, Evangeline," Jane said, "let me see your new dress."

Evangeline stopped and looked uncertainly at Jane and blushed. "It's just made over," she said, "it's just . . ."

"It's cute, Dear," Jane said; and as Evangeline went on Jane nudged her friend in the ribs and the friend smothered a giggle.

Well, that was a good year. Commencement time came, and—along with the newspaper job—I had the task of preparing for finals and all. One thing, I wasn't a student who took part in the class play or anything like that. I was just one of the boys—twenty-fourth in line to get my diploma.

And graduation was bringing an end to my paper-carrying. My father covered a big territory in our part of the state, selling farm equipment; and we were going to move at once to a town seventy miles south. Only because of my finishing the school year had we stayed till graduation.

I had taught another boy my route, always leaving him at the end and walking on out, by myself, to the tree. I didn't really have to go around with him that last day, the day of graduation, but I was going anyway.

At the graduation exercises, held that May afternoon, I wore my brown Sunday suit. My mother was in the audience. It was a heavy day. The girls had on new dresses. But I didn't see her.

I suppose that I did deserve old man Sutton's "Shhh!" as we lined up to march across the stage, but I for the first time in the year forgot my caution, and asked Jane where Evangeline was. She shrugged, and I could see for myself that she was not there.

We marched across the stage; our diplomas were ours; our parents filed out; to the strains of a march on the school organ we trailed to the hall. I unbuttoned my brown suit coat, stuffed the diploma in my pocket, and sidled out of the group and upstairs.

Evangeline's brother was emptying wastebaskets at the far end of the hall. I sauntered toward him and stopped. I didn't know what I wanted to say. Unexpectedly, he solved my problem. Stopping in his work, holding a partly empty wastebasket over the canvas sack he wore over his shoulder, he stared at me, as if almost to say something.

"I noticed that your sister wasn't here," I said. The noise below was dwindling. The hall was quiet, an echoey place; my voice sounded terribly loud. He emptied the rest of the wastebasket and shifted easily. He was a man, in big overalls. He stared at me.

"Evangeline couldn't come," he said. He stopped, looked at me again, and said, "She stole."

"Stole?" I said. "Stole what?"

He shrugged and went toward the next wastebasket, but I followed him.

"She stole the money from her bank—the money she was to use for her graduation dress," he said. He walked stolidly on, and I stopped. He deliberately turned away as he picked up the next wastebasket. But he said something else, half to himself. "You knew her. You talked to her . . . I know." He walked away.

I hurried downstairs and outside. The new carrier would have the papers almost delivered by now; so I ran up the street toward the north. I took a paper from him at the end of the street and told him to go back. I didn't pay any more attention to him.

No one was at the tree, and I turned, for the first time, up the road to the house. I walked over the bridge and on up the narrow, rutty tracks. The house was gray and lopsided. The ground of the yard was packed; nothing grew there. By the back door, the door to which the road led, there was a grayish-white place on the ground where the dishwater had been thrown. A gaunt shepherd dog trotted out growling.

And the door opened suddenly, as if someone had been watching me come up the track. A woman came out—a woman stern-faced, with a shawl over her head and a dark lumpy dress on—came out on the back porch and shouted, "Go 'way, go 'way! We don't want no papers!" She waved violently with one hand, holding the other on her shawl, at her throat. She coughed so hard that she leaned over and put her hand against one of the uprights of the porch. Her face was red. She glanced toward the barn and leaned toward me. "Go 'way!"

Behind me a meadowlark sang. Over all the plains swooped the sky. The land was drawn up somehow toward the horizon.

I stood there, half-defiant, half-ashamed. The dog continued to growl and to pace around me, stiff-legged, his tail down. The windows of the house were all blank, with blinds drawn. I couldn't say anything.

I stood a long time and then, lowering the newspaper I had held out, I stood longer, waiting, without thinking of what to do. The meadowlark bubbled over again, but I turned and walked away, looking back once or twice. The old woman continued to stand, leaning forward, her head out. She glanced at the barn, but didn't call out any more.

My heels dug into the grayish place where the dishwater had been thrown; the dog skulked along behind.

At the bridge, halfway to the road, I stopped and looked back. The dog was lying down again; the porch was empty; and the door was closed. Turning the other way, I looked toward town. Near me stood our ragged little tree—an Osage orange tree it was. It was feebly coming into leaf, green all over the branches, among the sharp thorns. I hadn't wondered before how it grew there, all alone, in the plains country, neglected. Over our pond some ducks came slicing in.

Standing there on the bridge, still holding the folded-boxed-newspaper, that worthless paper, I could see everything. I looked out along the road to town. From the bridge you would see the road going away, to where it went over the rise.

Glancing around, I flipped that last newspaper under the bridge and then bent far over and looked where it had gone. There they were—a pile of boxed newspapers, thrown in a heap, some new, some worn and weathered, by rain, by snow.

Responding to the Story

1. It's a scene we don't see and can only imagine: What do you think Evangeline might have been thinking and doing when the narrator came up to her house that last time?

2. "In a strange town, if you are quiet, no one notices, and some may like you, later." Do you agree or disagree with this statement? Comment.

Exploring the Author's Craft

1. The term *imagery* refers to the sensory details in a literary work. Find passages that appeal to one or more of the five senses. What would have been lost if these passages had been omitted?

2. Analyze what William Stafford did in this story to make you sympathetic to both the narrator and Evangeline.

Writing Workshop

The setting—"openness, the plains, a big swoop of nothing" and that forlorn house—is as much a character as the people in this

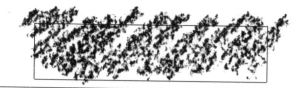

Surprised

Catherine Storr

Catherine Storr is known primarily for her books for children. She was born in London in 1913 and married Anthony Storr in 1942 and Lord Balogh in 1970. She has three daughters by her first marriage.

She was educated at St. Paul's Girls' School, Newham College in Cambridge, and West London Hospital, where she worked as an assistant psychiatrist from 1948–50. She was also an assistant psychiatrist at Middlesex Hospital in London from 1950–62. Since then she has been a full-time writer and has a long list of books to her credit.

Have you ever thought how when you think you know what something's going to be like, it turns out to be quite different? Or if it is anything like you imagined, it's somehow flat, as if you'd had it before. There may be a minute when you say, "It's perfect; it's exactly like I imagined." Then, another minute later, it's disappointing, just because it is how you'd imagined it. Like staying too long at a party, or thinking too much about Christmas before it comes.

My sister Tossie was always disappointed long before the end of Christmas Day. She was the one of us who got most excited about Christmas; she was always awake long before we were supposed to get up on Christmas morning, waking the rest of us up too, poking at our stockings and guessing what was inside them. I remember one Christmas, she can't have been more than ten, because I know I was nearly six; it was the year we'd all had chickenpox. She poked round a sort of long, thin thing in her stocking and said, "It's a watch."

"It couldn't be a *watch*. It's much too expensive," we said.

"It could. It could be a watch. What else would be that shape?"

"A pencil."

"Too flat."

"A bracelet."

"Not in that shaped box."

"A paper knife."

"Mum wouldn't."

We guessed all sorts of things, but Tossie wouldn't listen to any of them. She went off on a sort of dream which she told out loud, about how she'd wear the watch, and how surprised her friends were going to be, and how no one except her in the upper thirds had a watch. How she'd lend it to me for parties—as long as she wasn't going to them herself, of course—and how when she was an old, old lady and died, she'd leave it to her grandchildren, with a message telling them it was the first watch she'd ever had, and she'd been given it the Christmas she was ten.

It turned out to be a pair of compasses, something she'd always wanted before, but of course not like having a proper watch. That was another sad Christmas. Somehow when Tossie was sad it made us all feel as if we'd been disappointed about our presents too. Our Mum used to say she built up such a rigmarole in her head about how marvelous everything was going to be that nothing, not watches or bicycles or diamond rings or the Queen's crown could have come up to what she'd imagined. And it was always like that. She'd come back sad from parties, because each one was going to be the most marvelous party she'd ever been to; then when it turned out to be just being with the same lot of people she'd seen every day at school all term, but wearing different clothes and not having anything special to do, she felt let down and awful. I used to dread Tossie's parties because of her and me sharing the room. I'd be asleep when she came in, but when it had been a bad evening she wouldn't bother about being quiet. She'd drop her shoes, shut the wardrobe door so it slammed as well as squeaked—which you couldn't help—and then lie in bed sighing. Tossie had the biggest sighs I've ever heard; it was like hearing a hippopotamus feeling sad. Sometimes I'd say, "Tossie?"

"What?" she'd say, sounding cross, though she wasn't.

"Was the party fun?"

"No."

"Tell."

"Nothing to tell."

"What happened?"

"Nothing happened."

"Didn't they like your dress?"

"No one said."

"What did you do?"

"Nothing."

"Did you meet any boys?" I knew it was risky asking this, but I generally couldn't stop myself.

"I suppose so."

If I was feeling brave I'd go one step further.

"Did any of them try to kiss you?"

"Go to sleep. It's long past your bedtime."

But I couldn't get to sleep until Tossie had stopped those awful deep sighs, and the restless turning in bed. Even that wasn't the worst, though. The worst was when I heard her sniffing into the pillow. I didn't feel better about this until one morning when I heard Tossie tell Mum that she'd cried till her pillow was wet with tears. So at least one of Tossie's imaginings had been made to come true.

When Tossie started going with boys, I mean really, not just seeing them gooping at the parties, but having them call for her and taking her out to coffee bars, I knew we had a bad time coming. When I said this to Mum she said not to be a something or other.

"What's that?"

"Jeremiah.[1] Sad sort of chap, always saw bad things coming."

"Am I? I mean, do I?"

"Not more than most, I daresay. Still, you and Tossie, you are a pair."

"I see things the way they are. Tossie sees them how she wants them to be."

Mum said, "Well, I don't know." She often said that, but I thought she knew quite a lot, really.

As it turned out, Tossie's love affairs weren't so much awful as wearing. That isn't quite true, because the first few were awful. Then I got used to the way they happened. In fact I got so used, I could almost tell when the next stage was due. They went like this. First of all Tossie would go very quiet and mysterious. If you said anything to her, she'd sort of come back to earth with a start, as if she'd been miles away. If you asked, she'd say no, she wasn't thinking about anything in particular, smiling all the time, a secret smile that meant just the opposite of what she said. This was while she and the boy were sort of eyeing each other; they hadn't said anything yet. Then when he'd come out with saying he was crazy about her, or whatever it was, and they'd

---

1. *Jeremiah:* Biblical prophet.

kissed a bit, Tossie couldn't talk about anything else. As far as I can remember, with the first one or two, or perhaps three, I really did think, "This is it. Tossie's going to marry John (or perhaps it was Martin or David or Joe), she'll be a bride at sixteen, I'll be an aunt before I take my 'O' levels."[2] It would be a marvelous time—it got boring later—with Tossie on top of the world, telling us how tremendous John (or Martin or David) was, and how she'd never felt like this before; how it was all that love was written up to be, and better. She'd keep me awake late into the night, talking about whichever it was; how she loved him, how he loved her, how clever he was, how they must have been meant for each other, the lot. Of course when she got on to the later ones there'd be a lot of comparing: How John had really been too changeable, she could see that now, and how she'd wondered at the time if Martin was a strong enough character for her, and how David had been slow in the uptake, but how now Joe . . .

Then there'd come the time that was like opening the stocking and finding it wasn't a watch after all. First of all, she'd be home evenings when we'd thought she'd be out, sometimes explaining, sometimes not. Then she'd be very touchy; you couldn't say anything without having your head bitten off. After a bit of this, there'd be a night when she'd keep me awake gulping and sighing, even groaning sometimes, saying things in between like, "Don't ever fall in love, Barb," or "I know now, everything they say about not trusting men is true." After a week or so of this, with Tossie going around looking like Ophelia and The Lady of the Camellias[3] rolled into one (a lot of eyeshadow, and I swear that even Mum got worried once or twice about the cough she used to get at these times), she'd begin to recover. First of all she'd be a brave little woman who was going to bury herself in her work (it was a tremendous piece of luck that she had a month just before her "A" levels in between Sammy and Dan) and then, sometimes gradually, sometimes suddenly, it would begin all over again. She'd forget her career and it would be all romance. She had a bottom drawer she put things into when she got something new and pretty. The trouble was it went through off-seasons like Tossie's love life, and when she was going to be a career woman she'd take out the new nylon nightie she'd

---

2. "O" levels: in the British school system, ordinary level examinations. "A" levels are advanced level examinations.

3. Ophelia and The Lady of the Camellias: two tragic fictional characters. In Shakespeare's Hamlet, Ophelia is driven mad and drowns. In Alexandre Dumas's The Lady of the Camellias, Camille dies of tuberculosis soon after being reunited with her lover.

put there for her wedding to John/Martin/David/Joe, etc. and she'd wear it, enjoying herself, in a way, doing it and suffering. She talked a lot about suffering during this time. She'd get me worried sometimes, thinking that whatever happened to Tossie was, of course, going to happen to me as soon as I was old enough. For me, you see, it was almost like having a crystal ball showing me what my life would be like in a year or so, and though I wanted this business of being in love and going out with boys and everything, I didn't want to suffer. Or at least, not like Tossie did.

I think I'm sounding rather callous about Tossie and her sufferings, but this really isn't fair. She certainly did suffer. The trouble is that when you share a room with someone who suffers such a lot you sort of get used to it. You even get a bit bored.

I can't remember now how long Tossie went on like that. It was probably quite a time, because I know that I'd got to that sort of stage myself, where I was wondering all the time when some boy would want to take me out, and feeling sure none of them ever would. So perhaps I didn't notice so much about Tossie: or it may have been that if something goes on long enough, you don't notice all at once if it stops. Like a headache. You suddenly realize you haven't been noticing it for the last quarter of an hour, which means that it's gone. I suddenly noticed about Tossie that way. Not that she'd gone, but that she was different.

I said before how at the beginning of a new boy she'd go quiet; but it never lasted. What I realized this time was that she'd been quiet for ever so long.

I would have said it wasn't natural, only that she didn't feel unnatural. She was kind of peaceful, and yet it wasn't peaceful like being asleep. It was more like waiting. Even that's not quite right, because it wasn't like waiting for something you're worried about, not like that feeling that you *can't* wait it's so exciting, like a birthday or a party or a match. More like waiting for something to grow, like mustard and cress on a flannel in a saucer, where you notice each leaf as it comes out, and it almost doesn't matter when you eat it, because the growing it's been exciting too.

But it wasn't like Tossie. It wasn't like her to wait that way. It wasn't like her not to have to talk about it. I could see she wasn't unhappy, either. Every night she was out, and every night she'd come in so quietly I never woke up. There wasn't any sighing and groaning. I couldn't understand it. It was funny. Different.

At last I said to her, "Tossie. What's going on?"

"What's going on?" she said back.

"It isn't Jamie, is it?" I knew it wasn't really. Jamie had been weeks back.

"Jamie and I broke up seven weeks and two days ago."

I saw then what a long time I'd taken to catch on. And I was interested she'd got it so exact too, Tossie being apt to exaggerate a lot.

"What's up, then, Toss?"

She said, "I don't really know."

Now that was the first time I'd heard my sister Tossie admit she didn't know what was up.

"Is it Barry, Tossie?" Barry was the fellow she'd been going out with lately.

"Course it's Barry."

"Is he crazy about you?"

"I don't know," she said again.

"Are you in love with him?"

This time, when she said, "I don't know," again, she really shook me. I'd been a bit drowsy before, but that really woke me up with a jolt.

"But Tossie, you must know. You've been in love before."

"I'm not sure I have," she said.

I thought about this.

"What does it feel like, then?" I asked.

She said, "Barb, it's different."

"Well, do you love him?" I asked.

"He's not the sort of boy I generally go for," she said.

"Go on."

"I sort of can't help liking him. You know. I like him being around. I feel sort of . . ."

"Sort of what?"

"Comfortable. When he's there."

"Not in love, then?" I said, disappointed.

"I don't know."

Tossie seemed to me, by this time, so experienced I couldn't understand how it was she didn't know if she was in love or not. I said, "Well, what then?"

She said, slowly, "Perhaps I am. P'raps this is what it's really like. Not like anything you thought it would be."

"What then?" I asked again wanting to know, so I'd be able to tell when it happened to me.

Tossie said, "Surprised. All the time I don't feel like what I thought I would. I'm always being surprised."

Responding to the Story

1. Is Tossie a recognizable character? Have her feelings and behavior been demonstrated, at least in part, by anyone you know?

2. Are Tossie's feelings common to both boys and girls? Explain.

3. In one of the rare moments in this story when something is dramatized rather than summarized, Tossie says, "Jamie and I broke up seven weeks and two days ago." What does she reveal about herself here?

4. According to the narrator's portrait of Tossie, what are the steps involved in falling in (and out) of love?

Exploring the Author's Craft

Of the three main components of a short story—plot, setting, and character—which is the least important to "Surprised"? Which is the most important? What is the main conflict in this story?

Writing Workshop

Many country-and-western songs deal with different aspects of love. With a group, try writing the words to a country song based on the events in this story. Title the song "Surprised."

Alternate Media Response

Create a TV talk show. Choose an interviewer who should prepare questions directed toward audience members (the class). The subject is "What It's Like to Be in Love." For those courageous enough to talk about this all-important and sensitive subject, start with Catherine Storr's chronicle of being in love, and then modify it based on your own thoughts and observations.

I Go Along

Richard Peck

One of the most popular young adult novelists, Peck has written over twenty books, including adult novels. He was born in Decatur, Illinois, in 1934 and attended the University of Exeter in 1954–55, received his B.A. degree from DePauw in 1956, and his M.A. degree from Southern Illinois University in 1959. He has been a college instructor in English, a high school English teacher, a textbook editor, and, since 1971, a full-time writer.

His books for younger readers include Dreamland Lake, Blossom Culp and the Sleep of Death, Don't Look and It Won't Hurt, *and* The Dreadful Future of Blossom Culp.

Some of Peck's most popular books for older readers include Secrets of the Shopping Mall, Remembering the Good Times, Those Summer Girls I Never Met, Through a Brief Darkness, *and* Unfinished Portrait of Jessica.

Many of his books have won awards from the American Library Association. Are You in the House Alone? *and* Father Figure *were made-for-TV movies.*

Peck has also written poetry and short stories and frequently visits schools, libraries, and teachers' organizations to speak with young adults and teachers. His novels deal with the serious problems of growing up, but also offer humorous situations and witty dialogue.

Anyway, Mrs. Tibbetts comes into the room for second period, so we all see she's still in school. This is the spring she's pregnant, and there are some people making some bets about when she's due. The smart money says she'll make it to Easter, and after that we'll have a sub teaching us. Not that we're too particular about who's up there at the front of the room, not in this class.

Being juniors, we also figure we know all there is to know about sex. We know things about sex no adult ever heard of. Still, the sight of a pregnant English teacher slows us down some. But she's married to Roy Tibbets, a plumber who was in the service and went to jump school, so that's okay. We see him around town in his truck.

And right away Darla Craig's hand is up. It's up a lot. She doesn't know any more English than the rest of us, but she likes to talk.

"Hey, Mrs. Tibbets, how come they get to go and we don't?"

She's talking about the first-period people, the Advanced English class. Mrs. Tibbetts looks like Darla's caught her off base. We never hear what a teacher tells us, but we know this. At least Darla does.

"I hadn't thought," Mrs. Tibbetts says, rubbing her hand down the small of her back, which may have something to do with being pregnant. So now we're listening, even here in the back row. "For the benefit of those of you who haven't heard," she says, "I'm taking some members of the—other English class over to the college tonight, for a program."

The college in this case is Bascomb College at Bascomb, a thirty-mile trip over an undivided highway.

"We're going to hear a poet read from his works."

Somebody halfway back in the room says, "Is he living?" And we all get a big bang out of this.

But Mrs. Tibbets just smiles. "Oh, yes," she says, "he's very much alive." She reaches for her attendance book, but this sudden thought strikes her. "Would anyone in this class like to go too?" She looks up at us, and you see she's being fair, and nice.

Since it's only the second period of the day, we're all feeling pretty good. Also it's a Tuesday, a terrible TV night. Everybody in the class puts up their hands. I mean everybody. Even Marty Crawshaw, who's already married. And Pink Hohenfield, who's in class today for the first time this month. I put up mine. I go along.

Mrs. Tibbetts looks amazed. She's never seen this many hands up in our class. She's never seen anybody's hand except Darla's. Her eyes get wide. Mrs. Tibbetts has really great eyes, and she doesn't put anything on them. Which is something Darla could learn from.

But then she sees we have to be putting her on. So she just says, "Anyone who would like to go, be in the parking lot at five-thirty. And eat first. No eating on the bus."

Mrs. Tibbetts can drive the school bus. Whenever she's taking the advanced class anywhere, she can go to the principal for the keys. She can use the bus anytime she wants to, unless the coach needs it.

Then she opens her attendance book, and we tune out. And at

five-thirty that night I'm in the parking lot. I have no idea why. Needless to say, I'm the only one here from second period. Marty Crawshaw and Pink Hohenfield will be out on the access highway about now, at 7-Eleven, sitting on their hoods. Darla couldn't make it either. Right offhand I can't think of anybody who wants to ride a school bus thirty miles to see a poet. Including me.

The advanced-English juniors are milling around behind school. I'm still in my car, and it's almost dark, so nobody sees me.

Then Mrs. Tibbetts wheels the school bus in. She's got the amber fogs flashing, and you can see the black letters along the yellow side: CONSOLIDATED SCHOOL DIST. She swings in and hits the brakes, and the doors fly open. The advanced class starts to climb aboard. They're more orderly than us, but they've got their groups too. And a couple of smokers. I'm settling behind my dashboard. The last kid climbs in the bus.

And I seem to be sprinting across the asphalt. I'm on the bus, and the door's hissing shut behind me. When I swing past the driver's seat, I don't look at Mrs. Tibbetts, and she doesn't say anything. I wonder where I'm supposed to sit.

They're still milling around in the aisle, but there are plenty of seats. I find an empty double and settle by the window, pulling my ball cap down in front. It doesn't take us long to get out of town, not this town. When we go past 7-Eleven, I'm way down in the seat with my hand shielding my face on the window side. Right about then, somebody sits down next to me. I flinch.

"Okay?" she says, and I look up, and it's Sharon Willis.

I've got my knee jammed up on the back of the seat ahead of me. I'm bent double, and my hand's over half my face. I'm cool, and it's Sharon Willis.

"Whatever," I say.

"How are you doing, Gene?"

I'm trying to be invisible, and she's calling me by name.

"How do you know me?" I ask her.

She shifts around. "I'm a junior, you're a junior. There are about fifty-three people in our whole year. How could I not?"

Easy, I think, but don't say it. She's got a notebook on her lap. Everybody seems to, except me.

"Do you have to take notes?" I say, because I feel like I'm getting into something here.

"Not really," Sharon says, "but we have to write about it in class tomorrow. Our impressions."

I'm glad I'm not in her class, because I'm not going to have any impressions. Here I am riding the school bus for the gifted on a Tuesday night with the major goddess girl in school, who knows my name. I'm going to be clean out of impressions because my circuits are starting to fail.

Sharon and I don't turn this into anything. When the bus gets out on the route and Mrs. Tibbetts puts the pedal to the metal, we settle back. Sharon's more or less in with a group of the top girls around school. They're not even cheerleaders. They're a notch above that. The rest of them are up and down the aisle, but she stays put. Michelle Burkholder sticks her face down by Sharon's ear and says, "We've got a seat for you back here. Are you coming?"

But Sharon just says, "I'll stay here with Gene." Like it happens every day.

I look out the window a lot. There's still some patchy snow out in the fields, glowing gray. When we get close to the campus of Bascomb college, I think about staying on the bus.

"Do you want to sit together," Sharon says, "at the program?"

I clear my throat. "You go ahead and sit with your people."

"I sit with them all day long," she says.

At Bascomb College we're up on bleachers in a curtained-off part of the gym. Mrs. Tibbetts says we can sit anywhere we want to, so we get very groupy. I look up, and here I am sitting in these bleachers, like we've gone to State in the play-offs. And I'm just naturally here with Sharon Willis.

We're surrounded mainly by college students. The dean of Bascomb college gets up to tell us about the grant they got to fund their poetry program. Sharon has her notebook flipped open. I figure it's going to be like a class, so I'm tuning out when the poet comes in.

First of all, he's only in his twenties. Not even a beard, and he's not dressed like a poet. In fact, he's dressed like me: Levi's and Levi's jacket. Big heavy-duty belt buckle. Boots, even. A tall guy, about a hundred and eighty pounds. It's weird, like there could be poets around and you wouldn't realize they were there.

But he's got something. Every girl leans forward. College girls, even. Michelle Burkholder bobs up to zap him with her flash camera. He's got a few loose-leaf pages in front of him. But he just begins.

"I've written a poem for my wife," he says, "about her."

Then he tells us this poem. I'm waiting for the rhyme, but it's more like talking, about how he wakes up and the sun's bright on the bed and his wife's still asleep. He watches her.

"Alone," he says, "I watch you sleep
Before the morning steals you from me,
Before you stir and disappear
Into the day and leave me here
To turn and kiss the warm space
You leave beside me."

He looks up and people clap. I thought what he said was a little too personal, but I could follow it. Next to me Sharon's made a note. I look down at her page and see it's just an exclamation point.

He tells us a lot of poems, one after another. I mean, he's got poems on everything. He even has one about his truck:

"Old buck-toothed, slow-to-start mama,"

something like that. People laugh, which I guess is okay. He just keeps at it, and he really jerks us around with his poems. I mean, you don't know what the next one's going to be about. At one point they bring him a glass of water, and he takes a break. But mainly he keeps going.

He ends up with one called "High School."

"On my worst nights," he says, "I dream myself back.
I'm the hostage in the row by the radiator, boxed in,
Zit-blasted, and they're popping quizzes at me.
I'm locked in there, looking for words
To talk myself out of being this young
While every girl in the galaxy
Is looking over my head, spotting for a senior.
On my really worst nights it's last period
On a Friday and somebody's fixed the bell
So it won't ring:
  And I've been cut from the team,
  And I've forgotten my locker combination,
  And I'm waiting for something damn it to hell
  To happen."

And the crowd goes wild, especially the college people. The poet just gives us a wave and walks over to sit down on the bottom bleacher. People swarm down to get him to sign their programs. Except Sharon and I stay where we are.

"That last one wasn't a poem," I tell her. "The others were, but not that one."

She turns to me and smiles. I've never been this close to her before, so I've never seen the color of her eyes.

"Then write a better one," she says.

We sit together again on the ride home.

"No, I'm serious," I say. "You can't write poems about zits and your locker combination."

"Maybe nobody told the poet that," Sharon says.

"So what are you going to write about him tomorrow?" I'm really curious about this.

"I don't know," she says. "I've never heard a poet reading before, not in person. Mrs. Tibbetts shows us tapes of poets reading."

"She doesn't show them to our class."

"What would you do if she did?" Sharon asks.

"Laugh a lot."

The bus settles down on the return trip. I picture all these people going home to do algebra homework, or whatever. When Sharon speaks again, I almost don't hear her.

"You ought to be in this class," she says.

I pull my ball cap down to my nose and lace my fingers behind my head and kick back in the seat. Which should be answer enough.

"You're as bright as anybody on this bus. Brighter than some."

We're rolling on through the night, and I can't believe I'm hearing this. Since it's dark, I take a chance and glance at her. Just the outline of her nose and her chin, maybe a little stubborn.

"How do you know I am?"

"How do you know you're not?" she says. "How will you ever know?"

But then we're quiet because what else is there to say? And anyway, the evening's over. Mrs. Tibbetts is braking for the turnoff, and we're about to get back to normal. And I get this quick flash of tomorrow, in second period with Marty and Pink and Darla, and frankly it doesn't look that good.

Responding to the Story

1. Is this story appropriately placed in a section called "Falling in Love"? Explain.

2. What do you think the narrator means by the last line?

Exploring the Author's Craft

In some short stories, the main character wrestles with physical challenges, but in others, like this one, the main character simply gains new insight or changes in some way. Does the author provide sufficient motivation for Gene's new insight in your opinion? Discuss.

Writing Workshop

1. Write about the next day in the narrator's life from Gene's point of view.

2. In a paragraph or two, fill in some additional details of Gene's life based on what you know about him. What kind of car does he drive? Does he now have, or has he had, a girlfriend? If so, what is, or was, she like? Does he have a part-time job? If so, where? What kind of parents does he have? Will he graduate? What will he do when he's out of high school? Compare your character sketch with those written by others in your class.

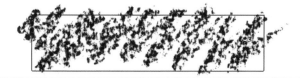

Broken Chain

Gary Soto

Gary Soto was born in Fresno in 1952. He graduated magna cum laude from California State University in 1974 and earned an M.F.A. degree in creative writing in 1976. He married Carolyn Oda in 1975.

In 1977 he began teaching at the University of California in Berkeley in the English and Chicano Studies Department. He won an Academy of American Poets prize in 1975, Poetry *magazine's Bess Hokin Prize in 1977, and a Guggenheim Fellowship in 1979.* Living Up the Street: Narrative Recollections *received an American Book Award in 1985.*

Soto's other books include Small Faces *(1986);* Lesser Evils: Ten Quartets *(1988);* Baseball in April and Other Stories *(1990);* The Shirt *(1992), a children's book; and* A Summer Life *(1990).*

Known primarily as a poet and writer for young adults, Soto writes about the streets and neighborhoods of urban California with directness and clarity.

A lfonso sat on the porch trying to push his crooked teeth to where he thought they belonged. He hated the way he looked. Last week he did fifty sit-ups a day, thinking that he would burn those already apparent ripples on his stomach to even deeper ripples, dark ones, so when he went swimming at the canal next summer, girls in cut-offs would notice. And the guys would think he was tough, someone who could take a punch and give it back. He wanted "cuts" like those he had seen on a calendar on an Aztec warrior standing on a pyramid with a woman in his arms. (Even she had cuts he could see beneath her thin dress.) The calendar hung above the cash register at La Plaza. Orsua, the owner, said Alfonso could have the calendar at the end of the year if the waitress, Yolanda, didn't take it first.

Alfonso studied the magazine pictures of rock stars for a hairstyle. He liked the way Prince looked—and the bass player from Los Lobos. Alfonso thought he would look cool with his hair razored into a V in the back and streaked purple. But he knew his mother wouldn't go for it. And his father, who was *puro Mexicano*, would sit in his chair after work, sullen as a toad, and call him "sissy."

Alfonso didn't dare color his hair. But one day he had had it butched on the top, like in the magazines. His father had come home that evening from a softball game, happy that his team had drilled four homers in a thirteen-to-five bashing of Color Tile. He'd swaggered into the living room, but had stopped cold when he saw Alfonso and asked, not joking but with real concern, "Did you hurt your head at school? *Qué pasó?*"[1]

Alfonso had pretended not to hear his father and had gone to his room, where he studied his hair from all angles in the mirror. He liked what he saw until he smiled and realized for the first time that his teeth were crooked, like a pile of wrecked cars. He grew depressed and turned away from the mirror. He sat on his bed and leafed through the rock magazine until he came to the rock star with the butched top. His mouth was closed, but Alfonso was sure his teeth weren't crooked.

Alfonso didn't want to be the handsomest kid at school, but he was determined to be better looking than average. The next day he spent his lawn-mowing money on a new shirt, and, with a pocketknife, scooped the moons of dirt from under his fingernails.

He spent hours in front of the mirror trying to herd his teeth into place with his thumb. He asked his mother if he could have braces, like Frankie Molina, her godson, but he asked at the wrong time. She was at the kitchen table licking the envelope to the house payment. She glared up at him. "Do you think money grows on trees?"

His mother clipped coupons from magazines and newspapers, kept a vegetable garden in the summer, and shopped at Penney's and K-Mart. Their family ate a lot of frijoles, which was OK because nothing else tasted so good, though one time Alfonso had had Chinese pot stickers and thought they were the next best food in the world.

He didn't ask his mother for braces again, even when she was in a better mood. He decided to fix his teeth by pushing on them with his thumbs. After breakfast that Saturday he went to his room, closed the

---

1. *Qué pasó?* (kā pa sō′): What happened? [Spanish].

door quietly, turned the radio on, and pushed for three hours straight.

He pushed for ten minutes, rested for five, and every half hour, during a radio commercial, checked to see if his smile had improved. It hadn't.

Eventually he grew bored and went outside with an old gym sock to wipe down his bike, a ten-speed from Montgomery Ward. His thumbs were tired and wrinkled and pink, the way they got when he stayed in the bathtub too long.

Alfonso's older brother, Ernie, rode up on *his* Montgomery Ward bicycle looking depressed. He parked his bike against the peach tree and sat on the back steps, keeping his head down and stepping on ants that came too close.

Alfonso knew better than to say anything when Ernie looked mad. He turned his bike over, balancing it on the handlebars and seat, and flossed the spokes with the sock. When he was finished, he pressed a knuckle to his teeth until they tingled.

Ernie groaned and said, "Ah, man."

Alfonso waited a few minutes before asking, "What's the matter?" He pretended not to be too interested. He picked up a wad of steel wool and continued cleaning the spokes.

Ernie hesitated, not sure if Alfonso would laugh. But it came out. "Those girls didn't show up. And you better not laugh."

"What girls?"

Then Alfonso remembered his brother bragging about how he and Frostie met two girls from Kings Canyon Junior High last week on Halloween night. They were dressed as gypsies, the costume for all poor Chicanas—they just had to borrow scarves and gaudy red lipstick from their *abuelitas*.[2]

Alfonso walked over to his brother. He compared their two bikes: his gleamed like a handful of dimes, while Ernie's looked dirty.

"They said we were supposed to wait at the corner. But they didn't show up. Me and Frostie waited and waited like *pendejos*.[3] They were playing games with us."

Alfonso thought that was a pretty dirty trick but sort of funny too. He would have to try that some day.

"Were they cute?" Alfonso asked.

"I guess so."

"Do you think you could recognize them?"

---

2. *abuelitas* (a bwā lē′ tas): little grandmothers [Spanish].

3. *pendejos* (pen dā′ hōs): silly, stupid ones [Spanish].

"If they were wearing red lipstick, maybe."

Alfonso sat with his brother in silence, both of them smearing ants with their floppy high tops. Girls could sure act weird, especially the ones you meet on Halloween.

Later that day, Alfonso sat on the porch pressing on his teeth. Press, relax; press, relax. His portable radio was on, but not loud enough to make Mr. Rojas come down the steps and wave his cane at him.

Alfonso's father drove up. Alfonso could tell by the way he sat in his truck, a Datsun with a different-colored front fender, that his team had lost their softball game. Alfonso got off the porch in a hurry because he knew his father would be in a bad mood. He went to the backyard, where he unlocked his bike, sat on it with the kickstand down, and pressed on his teeth. He punched himself in the stomach, and growled, "Cuts." Then he patted his butch and whispered, "Fresh."

After a while Alfonso pedaled up the street, hands in his pockets, toward Foster's Freeze, where he was chased by a ratlike Chihuahua. At his old school, John Burroughs Elementary, he found a kid hanging upside down on the top of a barbed-wire fence with a girl looking up at him. Alfonso skidded to a stop and helped the kid untangle his pants from the barbed wire. The kid was grateful. He had been afraid he would have to stay up there all night. His sister, who was Alfonso's age, was also grateful. If she had to go home and tell her mother that Frankie was stuck on a fence and couldn't get down, she would get scolded.

"Thanks," she said. "What's your name?"

Alfonso remembered her from his school and noticed that she was kind of cute, with ponytails and straight teeth. "Alfonso. You go to my school, huh?"

"Yeah. I've seen you around. You live nearby?"

"Over on Madison."

"My uncle used to live on that street, but he moved to Stockton."

"Stockton's near Sacramento, isn't it?"

"You been there?"

"No." Alfonso looked down at his shoes. He wanted to say something clever the way people do on TV. But the only thing he could think to say was that the governor lived in Sacramento. As soon as he shared this observation, he winced inside.

Alfonso walked with the girl and the boy as they started for home. They didn't talk much. Every few steps, the girl, whose name was Sandra, would look at him out of the corner of her eye, and Alfonso would look away. He learned that she was in seventh grade, just like him, and that she had a pet terrier named Queenie. Her father was a mechanic at Rudy's Speedy Repair, and her mother was a teacher's aide at Jefferson Elementary.

When they came to the street, Alfonso and Sandra stopped at her corner, but her brother ran home. Alfonso watched him stop in the front yard to talk to a lady he guessed was their mother. She was raking leaves into a pile.

"I live over there," she said, pointing.

Alfonso looked over her shoulder for a long time, trying to muster enough nerve to ask her if she'd like to go bike riding tomorrow.

Shyly, he asked, "You wanna go bike riding?"

"Maybe." She played with a ponytail and crossed one leg in front of the other. "But my bike has a flat."

"I can get my brother's bike. He won't mind."

She thought a moment before she said, "OK. But not tomorrow. I have to go to my aunt's."

"How about after school on Monday?"

"I have to take care of my brother until my mom comes home from work. How 'bout four-thirty?"

"OK," he said. "Four-thirty." Instead of parting immediately, they talked for a while, asking questions like, "Who's your favorite group?" "Have you ever been on the Big Dipper at Santa Cruz?" and "Have you ever tasted pot stickers?" But the question-and-answer period ended when Sandra's mother called her home.

Alfonso took off as fast as he could on his bike, jumped the curb, and, cool as he could be, raced away with his hands stuffed in his pockets. But when he looked back over his shoulder, the wind raking through his butch, Sandra wasn't even looking. She was already on her lawn, heading for the porch.

That night he took a bath, pampered his hair into place, and did more than his usual set of exercises. In bed, in between the push-and-rest on his teeth, he pestered his brother to let him borrow his bike.

"Come on, Ernie," he whined. "Just for an hour."

"*Chale*, I might want to use it."

"Come on, man, I'll let you have my trick-or-treat candy."

"What you got?"

"Three baby Milky Ways and some Skittles."

"Who's going to use it?"

Alfonso hesitated, then risked the truth. "I met this girl. She doesn't live too far."

Ernie rolled over on his stomach and stared at the outline of his brother, whose head was resting on his elbow. "*You* got a girlfriend?"

"She ain't my girlfriend, just a girl."

"What does she look like?"

"Like a girl."

"Come on, what does she look like?"

"She's got ponytails and a little brother."

"Ponytails! Those girls who messed with Frostie and me had ponytails. Is she cool?"

"I think so."

Ernie sat up in bed. "I bet you that's her."

Alfonso felt his stomach knot up. "She's going to be my girlfriend, not yours!"

"I'm going to get even with her!"

"You better not touch her," Alfonso snarled, throwing a wadded Kleenex at him. "I'll run you over with my bike."

For the next hour, until their mother threatened them from the living room to be quiet or else, they argued whether it was the same girl who had stood Ernie up. Alfonso said over and over that she was too nice to pull a stunt like that. But Ernie argued that she lived only two blocks from where those girls had told them to wait, that she was in the same grade, and, the clincher, that she had ponytails. Secretly, however, Ernie was jealous that his brother, two years younger than himself, might have found a girlfriend.

Sunday morning, Ernie and Alfonso stayed away from each other, though over breakfast they fought over the last tortilla. Their mother, sewing at the kitchen table, warned them to knock it off. At church they made faces at one another when the priest, Father Jerry, wasn't looking. Ernie punched Alfonso in the arm, and Alfonso, his eyes wide with anger, punched back.

Monday morning they hurried to school on their bikes, neither saying a word, though they rode side by side. In first period, Alfonso worried himself sick. How would he borrow a bike for her? He considered asking his best friend, Raul, for his bike. But Alfonso knew Raul, a paper boy with dollar signs in his eyes, would charge him, and he had less than sixty cents, counting the soda bottles he could cash.

Between history and math, Alfonso saw Sandra and her girlfriend huddling at their lockers. He hurried by without being seen.

During lunch Alfonso hid in metal shop so he wouldn't run into Sandra. What would he say to her? If he weren't mad at his brother, he could ask Ernie what girls and guys talk about. But he *was* mad, and anyway, Ernie was pitching nickels with his friends.

Alfonso hurried home after school. He did the morning dishes as his mother had asked and raked the leaves. After finishing his chores, he did a hundred sit-ups, pushed on his teeth until they hurt, showered, and combed his hair into a perfect butch. He then stepped out to the patio to clean his bike. On an impulse, he removed the chain to wipe off the gritty oil. But while he was unhooking it from the back sprocket, it snapped. The chain lay in his hand like a dead snake.

Alfonso couldn't believe his luck. Now, not only did he not have an extra bike for Sandra, he had no bike for himself. Frustrated, and on the verge of tears, he flung the chain as far as he could. It landed with a hard slap against the back fence and spooked his sleeping cat, Benny. Benny looked around, blinking his soft gray eyes, and went back to sleep.

Alfonso retrieved the chain, which was hopelessly broken. He cursed himself for being stupid, yelled at his bike for being cheap, and slammed the chain onto the cement. The chain snapped in another place and hit him when it popped up, slicing his hand like a snake's fang.

"Ow!" he cried, his mouth immediately going to his hand to suck on the wound.

After a dab of iodine, which only made his cut hurt more, and a lot of thought, he went to the bedroom to plead with Ernie, who was changing to his after-school clothes.

"Come on, man, let me use it," Alfonso pleaded. "Please, Ernie, I'll do anything."

Although Ernie could see Alfonso's desperation, he had plans with his friend Raymundo. They were going to catch frogs at the Mayfair canal. He felt sorry for his brother, and gave him a stick of gum to make him feel better, but there was nothing he could do. The canal was three miles away, and the frogs were waiting.

Alfonso took the stick of gum, placed it in his shirt pocket, and left the bedroom with his head down. He went outside, slamming the screen door behind him, and sat in the alley behind his house. A sparrow landed in the weeds, and when it tried to come close, Alfonso screamed for it to scram. The sparrow responded with a squeaky chirp and flew away.

At four he decided to get it over with and started walking to Sandra's house, trudging slowly, as if he were waist-deep in water. Shame colored his face. How could he disappoint his first date? She would probably laugh. She might even call him *menso*.[4]

He stopped at the corner where they were supposed to meet and

---

4. *menso* (men′ sō): stupid [Spanish].

watched her house. But there was no one outside, only a rake leaning against the steps.

Why did he have to take the chain off? he scolded himself. He always messed things up when he tried to take them apart, like the time he tried to repad his baseball mitt. He had unlaced the mitt and filled the pocket with cotton balls. But when he tried to put it back together, he had forgotten how it laced up. Everything became tangled like kite string. When he showed the mess to his mother, who was at the stove cooking dinner, she scolded him but put it back together and didn't tell his father what a dumb thing he had done.

Now he had to face Sandra and say, "I broke my bike, and my stingy brother took off on his."

He waited at the corner a few minutes, hiding behind a hedge for what seemed like forever. Just as he was starting to think about going home, he heard footsteps and knew it was too late. His hands, moist from worry, hung at his sides, and a thread of sweat raced down his armpit.

He peeked through the hedge. She was wearing a sweater with a checkerboard pattern. A red purse was slung over her shoulder. He could see her looking for him, standing on tiptoe to see if he was coming around the corner.

What have I done? Alfonso thought. He bit his lip, called himself *menso*, and pounded his palm against his forehead. Someone slapped the back of his head. He turned around and saw Ernie.

"We got the frogs, Alfonso," he said, holding up a wiggling plastic bag. "I'll show you later."

Ernie looked through the hedge, with one eye closed, at the girl. "She's not the one who messed with Frostie and me," he said finally. "You still wanna borrow my bike?"

Alfonso couldn't believe his luck. What a brother! What a pal! He promised to take Ernie's turn next time it was his turn to do the dishes. Ernie hopped on Raymundo's handlebars and said he would remember that promise. Then he was gone as they took off without looking back.

Free of worry now that his brother had come through, Alfonso emerged from behind the hedge with Ernie's bike, which was mud-splashed but better than nothing. Sandra waved.

"Hi," she said.

"Hi," he said back.

She looked cheerful. Alfonso told her his bike was broken and asked if she wanted to ride with him.

"Sounds good," she said, and jumped on the crossbar.

It took all of Alfonso's strength to steady the bike. He started off slowly, gritting his teeth, because she was heavier than he thought. But once he got going, it got easier. He pedaled smoothly, sometimes with only one hand on the handlebars, as they sped up one street and down another. Whenever he ran over a pothole, which was often, she screamed with delight, and once, when it looked like they were going to crash, she placed her hand over his, and it felt like love.

Responding to the Story

1. Does Gary Soto have it right about being in seventh grade and being in love, which is what it "felt like" at this story's end? List all of Alfonso's behaviors that strike you as accurate about being in seventh grade and infatuated, or in love.

2. What other aspects of being in seventh grade does the author understand? List them and explain why you think Gary Soto portrayed them correctly. Is there anything in the story that doesn't ring true? Explain.

Exploring the Author's Craft

This story is filled with the "stuff" of daily life, including references to performers who were popular at the time the story was written. What kind of world does Gary Soto evoke?

Writing Workshop

In Gary Soto's California, Alfonso "liked the way Prince looked— and the bass player from Los Lobos." Alfonso's mother shopped at Penney's and K-Mart. Write about daily life for a character in a contemporary setting that you are familiar with. Write several hundred words. You can get a plot started, but you don't have to finish it; the main thing is to create your atmosphere—alive with contemporary energy and action. What kind of notes will you make before starting to write?

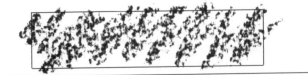

And Summer Is Gone

Susie Kretschmer

Student-written story

Susie Kretschmer was a senior at Talawanda High School in Oxford, Ohio, when her story won a Scholastic Writing Award in 1986.

W e're both sophomores in high school now. I'm fifteen; she'll be sixteen in a week. I know when her birthday is, of course, just as she knows mine. Birthdays don't change.

Almost sixteen, yeah, but I can still see her the summer I turned twelve; the day we first met, the day I moved into the newly built house at the end of her street. I was standing half-asleep in the sunlight, looking in despair at the expanse of bare dirt that purported to be our lawn. And suddenly she was there in front of me, all buck teeth and gangling legs and tumbling, tangled blond-brown hair, tall as I was and unafraid to claim every inch of it.

"Hi, I'm Amy," she said, jumping agilely over the exposed water meter and looking right into my face.

"I'm David," I mumbled, but I couldn't help smiling, answering her frankly appraising stare with my own.

Two hours later we were covered with mud, in the midst of a great canal-digging project in the bare gravelly dirt of my "lawn." She landscaped it with wildflowers from the drainage ditch behind our houses and asked if I'd ever been to the creek. I said no, and she showed it to me.

We were friends from then on, best friends that summer. She lived three houses down from me: If I knelt on the edge of the sink in the upstairs bathroom and craned my neck, I could see the lights of her house. I knew how far it was exactly, because with two tin cans and three balls of string we had once run a message line from her house to mine.

The phones hadn't worked, of course, and the irate lady who lived in the house in between ordered it dismantled at once—pieces of it are still probably tangled in the weeds of the drainage ditch—but I remember how it felt to have that line stretching between us, connecting us even though we were apart, for that was how I always felt with her.

She showed me the creek and we spent most of our summers there, wading in the current, catching crawdads and minnows with my parents' abducted spaghetti colander, building dams and then pushing out the one stone that would send the water flooding through. We dug up creek clay and made pots, and painted ourselves wildly with its blue streaks, pretending to be Indians, Aztecs, or Mayas. I remember her standing in the algae-green water that first summer, her long, tanned legs half wet and shiny, half dry with the cracking clay stripes and dots of an Aztec king.

We took out every book in the library on Aztecs and Mayas. I was an artist, always had been, and I would paint in their style—in reds, oranges and rusts, on the rocks by the creek—geometric designs and the Nine Lords of the Night. Amy would build little pyramids of clay. My tempera always washed away with the next rain, and Amy's pyramids would dissolve when the water rose, but we were content to make them new each time.

And sometimes we would just sit by the creek in the sun. When she grinned, her newly acquired braces would gleam; she'd sit patiently with her mouth open while I peered into it with clinical interest, and we'd shoot her rubber bands at each other. In the summer, she was mine alone, and I was hers.

But she hardly spoke to me at school, ever. I thought a million times that I understood why. Her female friends were the sort that are almost popular, those who get invited to every party but never give any, those who carry gossip but never provoke it, extras surrounding the popular ones for atmosphere and dramatic staging. All of them had names that ended in -*i*, and they all dotted their *i*'s with circles: Kelli, Lori, Shelli, Tammi, Lani, Terri—and Ami. Though Amy wore cutoffs and grungy T-shirts in the summer, during the school year her clothes were the same as theirs.

She moved differently, when she came back to me that summer between seventh and eighth grade. She'd always been more agile than I was, scrambling up on the bluffs far ahead of me, but the way she moved was different now. No buck-toothed, lanky colt-girl now, but curvy and lithe, proportioned as a woman, not a child. And it disturbed me, upset my world—and I liked it. So I would follow her on the bluffs despite my paralyzing fear of heights, and when she took my hand to pull me up over the edge I liked her touch. It was no longer merely the pleasant, reassuring touch of a friend, but something electric as well.

Yet as her body changed, she herself changed. No longer would she wade with me, or wrestle on the couch, and she refused to play pretend games any more. She got rid of her dress-up clothes some time in seventh grade, and by this, the third summer, they were gone. Well, I hid mine, too—my Dracula capes and Arabian turbans; and I hid away my wooden swords since she'd no longer duel with me. She stopped eating around me, too. We had both been famous for the amount of food we could consume and had demolished entire bags of chocolate chips and monstrous salads together. But now she complained she was fat and affected to eat little. She didn't look fat to me, but she said she was. Increasingly, the popular names crept into her conversation. She always wanted to talk about the people in our grade, but only the ones she knew—and I hardly knew any of them. She stopped listening to her Simon and Garfunkel records, replacing them with Duran Duran.

So we lay on her living room floor and watched old movies, and I learned to curb my satirical remarks, for what she would once have laughed at had become serious to her now. We went less and less often to the creek.

I spent more time on my art, alone, and didn't show it to her, for she didn't want to see it anymore. And in August she went away to camp. She came back the day before school started and never did call me. And I was alone.

I'd always been alone at school, with a few acquaintances good enough to talk to between classes, or to get assignments from. But for friendship, I had looked to her. And I saw that she had not spoken to me at school, or dared to associate with me in public. I thought, that eighth-grade year, that it was because Amy had grown up, had left behind childhood while I was still immature.

So the first Christmas went by that I didn't give her a present, and soon after, her fourteenth birthday went by, too. I lived in the worlds that I drew.

Amy's grades slipped. We had both been bright, straight-A's, but now she was getting B's and C's. I didn't keep close track, for I never saw her except when we passed on the way to school in the morning. I'd see her leave her house every evening—there seemed no night when she didn't go out. After a while, I stopped watching.

The less said about the summer before high school, the better. I was alone. But when it was over, we went to high school, Amy and I. She joined the flag corps—I joined the newspaper. She was in my top-level English class but dropped down after a week, and I never had her in a class again. I hung around with some guys from the swim team—I'd joined my freshman year—and went through the motions of studying, dreaming of college.

So we lived, separate. I didn't date at all—she dated ten guys a month. I hid alone—she went to every party, every football game, every prestigious event at school. I was pretty surprised to see her, then, sophomore year, at the local art exhibit where I'd won for the second year in a row. Masquerading as a museum, the local library was filled with people milling about with juice and cookies at the reception for the winners.

Why she was there, I don't really know. I think perhaps some friends of hers had gotten an honorable mention, and they had stopped by to pick her up. But she was there, and she was with her friends.

I was standing next to Danny, otherwise known as fourth honorable mention for his loving depiction of a souped-up red Maserati, when she came to my picture. I had painted a great Aztec pyramid under oily black storm clouds, with nine masque-hideous faces upon it, one face for each tier. The lighting was angry and hellish and red, and an uneasy orange fire burned in each masque-face's eyes. The picture was called "The Nine Lords of the Night."

Amy saw it. One slender hand to her feathered blond hair, the nails polished in coral, a boy's class ring on one finger, she saw it. As she turned around, I met her blue eyes with a level calm stare. Electric our glance, for she knew. She remembered. I had not thought she would forget. And I saw in her eyes that she knew that I saw.

We held it but a moment, for her friend broke in with a mocking harsh laugh. "What a *gay* picture. But everyone knows that all artists are gay anyway."

"Yeah," replied the other one, bored, "and the more they win, the gayer they are."

Amy turned her back on me, but not before I heard her assenting. "Yeah, I know." And they left laughing.

And I stood in silence, and I knew I had lost her. She had been more truly mine than I had ever known, for the person she'd been for me had not existed for anyone else. I watched her go, and I cried within, for I understood that it was I who had grown up and she who had gotten lost. For I have kept who I am, and it is what I always will be. And Amy is gone.

Responding to the Story

1. Is it believable that a boy and girl at age twelve could be as good friends as Amy and David were? Discuss.

2. Did you sympathize with the narrator's plight? Why or why not?

Exploring the Author's Craft

Identify two places in the story where you feel the author should have dramatized a scene rather than told us that it had occurred. What would be gained by having these scenes dramatized—that is, having us see the characters in action?

Writing Workshop

1. "All of them had names that ended in -i, and they all . . ." This sentence appears in a particularly telling paragraph; here the author captures, with examples, behavioral customs of the teenage world. Now you do the same. In one simple paragraph, describe the behavioral customs of the teenagers you know.

2. Author Susie Kretschmer created a male first-person narrator. Take on that same challenging task; create the voice of someone of the opposite sex. Do the start, or more, of a narrative. Write four or five paragraphs in that voice. Brainstorm with a small group to come up with a topic for your paragraphs.

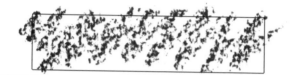

Responding to

Part Three

1. "Her First Ball" was written over seventy years ago. Discuss whether it has relevance to today's readers.

2. *Suspense* is the condition of being uncertain about how a story will end. In your opinion, which story in this part contained the most suspense?

3. *Style* refers to the way an author uses language. Style may involve word choice (diction), sentence length, use of figurative language, and other devices that make a story distinctive. Readers familiar with these stories and their writers would know immediately that Gary Soto did not write "The Osage Orange Tree" and that Richard Peck did not write "Her First Ball." But how would they know if the authors' names had not appeared? Choose two stories in this part and compare *or* contrast the style of each in an oral presentation or in a short paper.

Out in the World

A visit to a nursing home. The first death of one's life. A boy who gets expelled from his school. A girl's attempt to be initiated into a sorority.

These are just a few of the subjects explored in this section of the book as young people learn about the world beyond their homes and families and friends. As most students would readily acknowledge, our learning about life occurs in far more places than just the school classroom. In these stories we meet characters who are out in the classroom of daily living and learning about what life has to offer—learning about themselves. Of course, that is what we hope has been happening all along for you with this book.

A Visit of Charity

Eudora Welty

Born in 1909 in Jackson, Mississippi, Eudora Welty began her working life as a publicity agent for the State Office of the Works Progress Administration (WPA) in 1933. She attended Mississippi State College for women from 1925 to 1927 and received her B.A. degree in 1929 from the University of Wisconsin. She also attended Columbia University.

One Writer's Beginnings (1984) is an autobiographical work that describes incidents in Welty's life that influenced her writing. She received the National Medal of Arts in 1986 and an award from the National Endowment for the Arts in 1989.

Known primarily as a short story writer and novelist, her first collection of stories, A Curtain of Green, *was published in 1941. This was followed by* The Wide Net *(1943),* The Golden Apples *(1949), and* The Bride of Innisfallen *(1955). The title story of* A Curtain of Green *won the O. Henry Memorial Award.*

Her novels include Delta Wedding *(1946),* The Ponder Heart *(1954),* Losing Battles *(1970), and* The Optimist's Daughter *(1972), which won a Pulitzer Prize.*

Though Welty's stories and novels are set in the South, they depict a wide spectrum of individuals, often portrayed humorously, who struggle to accommodate their lives and beliefs to a world that often seems puzzling and indifferent.

I t was mid-morning—a very cold, bright day. Holding a potted plant before her, a girl of fourteen jumped off the bus in front of the Old Ladies' Home, on the outskirts of town. She wore a red coat, and her straight yellow hair was hanging down loose from the pointed white cap all the little girls were wearing that year. She stopped for a moment beside one of the prickly dark shrubs with which the city had beautified the Home, and then proceeded slowly toward the building, which was of whitewashed brick and reflected the winter sunlight like a block of ice. As she walked vaguely up the steps she shifted the small pot from hand to hand; then she had to set it down and remove her mittens before she could open the heavy door.

"I'm a Campfire Girl. . . . I have to pay a visit to some old lady," she told the nurse at the desk. This was a woman in a white uniform who looked as if she were cold; she had close-cut hair which stood up on the very top of her head exactly like a sea wave. Marian, the little girl, did not tell her that this visit would give her a minimum of only three points in her score.

"Acquainted with any of our residents?" asked the nurse. She lifted one eyebrow and spoke like a man.

"With any old ladies? No—but—that is, any of them will do," Marian stammered. With her free hand she pushed her hair behind her ears, as she did when it was time to study Science.

The nurse shrugged and rose. "You have a nice *multiflora cineraria*[1] there," she remarked as she walked ahead down the hall of closed doors to pick out an old lady.

There was loose, bulging linoleum on the floor. Marian felt as if she were walking on the waves, but the nurse paid no attention to it. There was a smell in the hall like the interior of a clock. Everything was silent until, behind one of the doors, an old lady of some kind cleared her throat like a sheep bleating. This decided the nurse. Stopping in her tracks, she first extended her arm, bent her elbow, and leaned forward from the hips—all to examine the watch strapped to her wrist; then she gave a loud double-rap on the door.

"There are two in each room," the nurse remarked over her shoulder.

"Two what?" asked Marian without thinking. The sound like a sheep's bleating almost made her turn around and run back.

One old woman was pulling the door open in short, gradual jerks, and when she saw the nurse a strange smile forced her old face dangerously awry. Marian, suddenly propelled by the strong, impatient arm of the nurse, saw next the side-face of another old woman, even older,

---

1. *multiflora cineraria* (mul''ti flôr'ə sin ə rer' ē ə): plant with clusters of white, red, or purple flowers and heart-shaped leaves.

who was lying flat in bed with a cap on and a counterpane[2] drawn up to her chin.

"Visitor," said the nurse, and after one more shove she was off up the hall.

Marian stood tongue-tied; both hands held the potted plant. The old woman, still with that terrible, square smile (which was a smile of welcome) stamped on her bony face, was waiting. . . . Perhaps she said something. The old woman in bed said nothing at all, and she did not look around.

Suddenly Marian saw a hand, quick as a bird claw, reach up in the air and pluck the white cap off her head. At the same time, another claw to match drew her all the way into the room, and the next moment the door closed behind her.

"My, my, my," said the old lady at her side.

Marian stood enclosed by a bed, a washstand and a chair; the tiny room had altogether too much furniture. Everything smelled wet—even the bare floor. She held onto the back of the chair, which was wicker and felt soft and damp. Her heart beat more and more slowly, her hands got colder and colder, and she could not hear whether the old women were saying anything or not. She could not see them very clearly. How dark it was! The window shade was down, and the only door was shut. Marian looked at the ceiling. . . . It was like being caught in a robbers' cave, just before one was murdered.

"Did you come to be our little girl for a while?" the first robber asked.

Then something was snatched from Marian's hand—the little potted plant.

"Flowers!" screamed the old woman. She stood holding the pot in an undecided way. "Pretty flowers," she added.

Then the old woman in bed cleared her throat and spoke. "They are not pretty," she said, still without looking around, but very distinctly.

Marian suddenly pitched against the chair and sat down in it.

"Pretty flowers," the first old woman insisted. "Pretty—pretty . . ."

Marian wished she had the little pot back for just a moment—she had forgotten to look at the plant herself before giving it away. What did it look like?

"Stinkweeds," said the other old woman sharply. She had a bunchy white forehead and red eyes like a sheep. Now she turned them toward

---

2. *counterpane:* bedspread.

Marian. The fogginess seemed to rise in her throat again, and she bleated, "Who—are—you?"

To her surprise, Marian could not remember her name. "I'm a Campfire Girl," she said finally.

"Watch out for the germs," said the old woman like a sheep, not addressing anyone.

"One came out last month to see us," said the first old woman.

A sheep or a germ? wondered Marian dreamily, holding onto the chair.

"Did not!" cried the other old woman.

"Did so! Read to us out of the Bible, and we enjoyed it!" screamed the first.

"Who enjoyed it!" said the woman in bed. Her mouth was unexpectedly small and sorrowful, like a pet's.

"We enjoyed it," insisted the other. "You enjoyed it—I enjoyed it."

"We all enjoyed it," said Marian, without realizing that she had said a word.

The first old woman had just finished putting the potted plant high, high on the top of the wardrobe, where it could hardly be seen from below. Marian wondered how she had ever succeeded in placing it there, how she could ever have reached so high.

"You mustn't pay any attention to old Addie," she now said to the little girl. "She's ailing today."

"Will you shut your mouth?" said the woman in bed. "I am not."

"You're a story."

"I can't stay but a minute—really, I can't," said Marian suddenly. She looked down at the wet floor and thought that if she were sick in here they would have to let her go.

With much to-do the first old woman sat down in a rocking chair— still another piece of furniture!—and began to rock. With the fingers of one hand she touched a very dirty cameo pin on her chest. "What do you do at school?" she asked.

"I don't know . . ." said Marian. She tried to think but she could not.

"Oh, but the flowers are beautiful," the old woman whispered. She seemed to rock faster and faster; Marian did not see how anyone could rock so fast.

"Ugly," said the woman in bed.

"If we bring flowers—" Marian began, and then fell silent. She had almost said that if Campfire Girls brought flowers to the Old Ladies'

Home, the visit would count one extra point, and if they took a Bible with them on the bus and read it to the old ladies, it counted double. But the old woman had not listened, anyway; she was rocking and watching the other one, who watched back from the bed.

"Poor Addie is ailing. She has to take medicine—see?" she said, pointing a horny finger at a row of bottles on the table, and rocking so high that her black comfort shoes lifted off the floor like a little child's.

"I am no more sick than you are," said the woman in bed.

"Oh, yes you are!"

"I just got more sense than you have, that's all," said the other old woman, nodding her head.

"That's only the contrary way she talks when *you all* come," said the first old lady with sudden intimacy. She stopped the rocker with a neat pat of her feet and leaned toward Marian. Her hand reached over—it felt like a petunia leaf, clinging and just a little sticky.

"Will you hush! Will you hush!" cried the other one.

Marian leaned back rigidly in her chair.

"When I was a little girl like you, I went to school and all," said the old woman in the same intimate, menacing voice. "Not here—another town. . . ."

"Hush!" said the sick woman. "You never went to school. You never came and you never went. You never were anything—only here. You never were born! You don't know anything. Your head is empty, your heart and hands and your old black purse are all empty, even that little old box that you brought with you you brought empty—you showed it to me. And yet you talk, talk, talk, talk, talk all the time until I think I'm losing my mind! Who are you? You're a stranger—a perfect stranger! Don't you know you're a stranger? Is it possible that they have actually done a thing like this to anyone—sent them in a stranger to talk, and rock, and tell away her whole long rigmarole? Do they seriously suppose that I'll be able to keep it up, day in, day out, night in, night out, living in the same room with a terrible old woman—forever?"

Marian saw the old woman's eyes grow bright and turn toward her. This old woman was looking at her with despair and calculation in her face. Her small lips suddenly dropped apart, and exposed a half circle of false teeth with tan gums.

"Come here, I want to tell you something," she whispered. "Come here!"

Marian was trembling, and her heart nearly stopped beating altogether for a moment.

"Now, now, Addie," said the first woman. "That's not polite. Do you know what's really the matter with old Addie today?" She, too, looked at Marian; one of her eyelids drooped low.

"The matter?" the child repeated stupidly. "What's the matter with her?"

"Why, she's mad because it's her birthday!" said the first old woman, beginning to rock again and giving a little crow as though she had answered her own riddle.

"It is not, it is not!" screamed the old woman in bed. "It is not my birthday, no one knows when that is but myself, and will you please be quiet and say nothing more, or I'll go straight out of my mind!" She turned her eyes toward Marian again, and presently she said in the soft, foggy voice, "When the worst comes to the worst, I ring this bell, and the nurse comes." One of her hands was drawn out from under the patched counterpane—a thin little hand with enormous black freckles. With a finger which would not hold still she pointed to a little bell on the table among the bottles.

"How old are you?" Marian breathed. Now she could see the old woman in bed very closely and plainly, and very abruptly, from all sides, as in dreams. She wondered about her—she wondered for a moment as though there was nothing else in the world to wonder about. It was the first time such a thing had happened to Marian.

"I won't tell!"

The old face on the pillow, where Marian was bending over it, slowly gathered and collapsed. Soft whimpers came out of the small open mouth. It was a sheep that she sounded like—a little lamb. Marian's face drew very close, the yellow hair hung forward.

"She's crying!" She turned a bright, burning face up to the first old woman.

"That's Addie for you," the old woman said spitefully.

Marian jumped up and moved toward the door. For the second time, the claw almost touched her hair, but it was not quick enough. The little girl put her cap on.

"Well, it was a real visit," said the old woman, following Marian through the doorway and all the way out into the hall. Then from behind she suddenly clutched the child with her sharp little fingers. In an affected, high-pitched whine she cried, "Oh, little girl, have you a penny to spare for a poor old woman that's not got anything of her own? We don't have a thing in the world—not a penny for candy—not a thing! Little girl, just a nickel—a penny——"

Marian pulled violently against the old hands for a moment before she was free. Then she ran down the hall, without looking behind her and without looking at the nurse, who was reading *Field and Stream* at her desk. The nurse, after another triple motion to consult her wrist watch, asked automatically the question put to visitors in all institutions: "Won't you stay and have dinner with *us*?"

Marian never replied. She pushed the heavy door open into the cold air and ran down the steps.

Under the prickly shrub she stooped and quickly, without being seen, retrieved a red apple she had hidden there.

Her yellow hair under the white cap, her scarlet coat, her bare knees all flashed in the sunlight as she ran to meet the big bus rocketing through the street.

"Wait for me!" she shouted. As though at an imperial command, the bus ground to a stop.

She jumped on and took a big bite out of the apple.

Responding to the Story

1. " 'How old are you?' Marian breathed. Now she could see the old woman in bed very closely and plainly, and very abruptly, from all sides, as in dreams. She wondered about her—she wondered for a moment as though there was nothing else in the world to wonder about. It was the first time such a thing had happened to Marian." What exactly has happened to Marian? Does it relate to the idea of "coming of age"? Explain.

2. Before Marian has spoken more than three full sentences the writer has conveyed certain information about her. What has been conveyed?

3. Why do you suppose the author ends the story as she does?

Exploring the Author's Craft

"A Visit of Charity" is told from the *third-person point of view*. Unlike many of the stories in this book, the narrator is not a character in the story but stands at some distance from the events. Sometimes a third-person narrator writes from an omniscient point of view and knows the thoughts and feelings of all the characters, but in this story the narrator tells the story from a limited point of view. Although we know what other people say, we have no insight into their thoughts; the point of view is limited to what Marian thinks and feels and observes. Although the point of view is limited to what Marian reacts to, the reader tends to understand more than Marian does.

1. What does the hallway of the Home feel and smell like to Marian?

2. What does the detail of the nurse's reading *Field and Stream* convey to the reader? Does Marian do more than notice this detail?

3. What is the author's purpose in having the two old women in constant disagreement with each other? What might the reader understand about them that Marian fails to grasp?

Writing Workshop

Write a journal entry as Marian might have written it after her visit to the Old Ladies' Home.

A Veil of Water

Amy Boesky

Student-written story

"A Veil of Water" won a Scholastic Writing Award in 1977 when Boesky was a senior at Seaholm Senior High School in Birmingham, Michigan. As Boesky explains, "I have always loved reading and writing, but I preferred to do both on my own—I was frustrated with school assignments, and writing fiction became an important outlet for me during high school. The feelings which inspired this story (feelings of sorrow and loss) were both real and personal, but the tragedy at the center of the story was imagined. Though I was hesitant at first about sending stories and poems to magazines, I found the idea of an 'audience' encouraged me to write. I published a short story in Seventeen Magazine *before I graduated from high school but in college began to concentrate on poetry."*

Boesky published individual poems and a book in verse for children while in college. She went on to graduate school in Renaissance English literature, first at the Oxford University in England and then at Harvard. After completing her doctorate she taught at Georgetown University, and is currently teaching English at Boston College.

I t is cold out. We are standing outside on the lawn, which is stiff and crunching under our boots. My aunt is crying. No one asks why. My aunt is a big woman, and the tears seem silly. It is as solemn and inappropriate as if a man were crying. My brother is tired, there are circles under his eyes, and the circles look artificial—like dark makeup on his thin face. I am reminded of Halloween. Last year I was a ballerina. My aunt says it is time to come inside, out of the cold.

We sit down at the kitchen table. My aunt's house is smaller than ours, and noisier. She has three sons, my cousins. We can hear them making odd sounds in the other rooms, the other rooms of their house. The heat makes my fingers tingle. My cousins are named Jamie, Bob, and Eddie. None of them is kind to me. On other days they have tormented me, pulling my hair, making mean jokes about my dress. (Usually I wear blue jeans, like my brother, but when we come to visit, my mother tells me to wear a dress.) There is lace on the collar and it is scratching my neck. Today we sit alone at the table, my aunt, my brother, myself. My aunt makes hot chocolate and pours it into plastic cups. She forgets to put marshmallows in it. Joshua, who is my brother and older than me, drinks his. I don't.

My aunt leans back in her chair, and the chair sways back with her. She looks huge and somehow blurred. She stretches her arms out to me, offering me something. I stare at her and wait for something to become clear. I am tired. I can feel the floor moving uncertainly beneath my feet. My uncle comes in the room. He is a huge man, his stomach shakes when he walks. He puts his arms around me and I am entirely hidden, a part of nothing. "We're going to sleep now, princess," he says to me, into my ear. His voice is too strong to hear all at once. Then I am up in the air, floundering, the floor is a million miles away. "Just hold on!" my uncle booms. I clutch at his shirt with hysterical fingers. I can smell pipe tobacco on him, on his neck and collar. My legs grab at the empty air, kicking for support. We bump our way up the short stairway. He lays me down on a bed that is too big for me, and I squirm away into the wide expanse of blankets. He does not undress me. He turns the lights out, and he closes the door behind him. A minute later he pushes the door open a little. The light from the hall slips fuzzily through the crack. I sleep. I am dreaming about a bird, a big black bird that is somehow familiar to me, and somehow terrible. In my sleep I am exhausted and not frightened. Then a door opens, and a light turns on, and I wake in terror to see my aunt leaning over me, unfastening the buttons on my dress. I cry out, jerking away from her. Her hands are cold. She reaches for me again, and I scream at her. I can feel the rush of wings near me. She moves away, and the light is gone, and I am alone in the darkness.

When I wake again I am utterly drained, as if I had walked for hours in my sleep. I am lying in a tangle of rumpled sheets, still in my navy dress. My tights have slid down low on my legs. My shoes are gone. I feel stiff and bleary-eyed, as if I had cried in my sleep. I have no clear idea where I am, or what I am doing here. Joshua is next to me in bed, asleep, breathing hard through his mouth.

There is spittle on his cheek. He is wearing pajamas, but they are not his. The pajamas are light blue with little brown footballs on them. I decide they are Eddie's, and I inch away from him, feeling betrayed. I'm not certain where I am. I don't remember anything that happened yesterday, or before that.

I help my aunt with the breakfast dishes. She has red blotches on her face. "All my life I've wanted a daughter," she says. Her voice sounds the way Joshua's does when he has done something very bad. She does not look at me. We are alone in the kitchen and the heat of the water rises up at us, eager for escape. My aunt says she is worried about me. She wants me to see the doctor. She says she is afraid I am sick, but I can tell from the way she says it that she doesn't really believe it. I nod at her anyway. I know there is nothing wrong with me.

My aunt talks to me about school. She says that she has called my teacher, and she understands that it will take me a while to adjust. She waits for me to say something but I don't. I listen to her talk and I wipe the steaming dishes with a yellow towel.

After breakfast I sit on the couch and watch TV. There are two cartoons, Bugs Bunny and another one I don't recognize. In the cartoons the animals and people are always getting hurt, but in the next scene they are better again. After the cartoons there are game shows. Sometimes the dog comes and rubs slowly against the sides of my legs. My mother never wanted a dog. She told Joshua they make muddy messes.

My aunt comes in and sits down next to me. "I want to talk to you about what happened," she says. There is something in her voice that I don't like.

"What happened? Nothing happened," I say stubbornly. I don't know what she's talking about.

My uncle comes home from work in the middle of the day. "We're going out," he says to me. I nod at him. My head feels light and funny, like a helium balloon bobbing at the end of a piece of limp yarn. He takes me by the hand and we walk together. It is snowing, and the motion of the whiteness is so fast and constant it is as if the sky were turning inside out. Inside my mittens my fingers are numbed with cold.

We take the bus. My boots leak snow, and two small puddles form under my feet. I read the ads over my head, and my uncle smokes a pipe. When the bus stops we get off again. I trip a little on the second step, but my uncle catches me. We walk for a long time. The snow is in my face. When I breathe the air dragons out of my mouth in a pale white fume, like pipe smoke. My uncle holds my hand so tightly it hurts. "Am I walking too fast?" he asks me, and his voice is high up and lost in the whiteness. "I'm not used to holding hands with a girl."

We are inside a building now, and we are wet and tired of walking. My uncle shakes the snow from his gloves and takes some loose coins from his pocket. He hands them to the lady behind the desk and she gives him two paper tickets, one pink and one yellow.

We are in the aquarium. I have been here before. My uncle leads me by the hand and we walk slowly from glass to glass. Inside the tiny aqua squares the fish are swimming awkwardly, their bubble faces pushing out at us.

My uncle stoops, putting his face against the glass. He blows his face out at the fish, and they dart away, terrified. "I used to come here," he says. His voice is low. "When I was growing up, your father used to take me here almost every Sunday. There was something magic here, some magic that was only here when he was."

We keep walking. There is something aching at the back of my throat.

"I remember how our parents used to tease him," he says. He looks down at me. Then he laughs. His voice is not happy, but the laughter is in it, and the sadness too. "I never knew a man with that much color inside of him."

I blink. The air is alive, pushing me back. "Sometimes he would say stories . . ." I say brokenly. My uncle looks down at me, waiting.

"Sometimes he would make stories," I say lamely. "He would make stories up about the fish—which one was the father, and which one was his little girl. Sometimes . . ."

A week ago, or two weeks ago, or more, my father had stood here next to me, and I had pressed my nose to the glass while he laughed. I used to think the fish could hear his voice. "Look, they're dancing for you now," my father would say, and when I looked I could see that he was right. I want to tell my uncle this now, but there is something else he is waiting to hear. I stare at him, and now he looks different; I am seeing him through a veil of water, he bubbles before me brokenly, like a fish. I am crying. He holds me, holds me with both his arms. I am not crying very hard, but I am crying.

We leave soon. There is no reason to stay. We walk outside awkwardly, bumping into each other and into other people, and my eyes are blinded with my tears. The world looks different suddenly. I am seeing it through water, and it will never look the same again.

Responding to the Story

1. What has happened to the characters in this story? Once you have determined that, do you believe that the narrator's behavior and reactions are understandable? Explain.
2. What clues are there about the ages of the narrator and her brother?

Exploring the Author's Craft

1. Another story with a bird as a symbol! What does the "big black bird" symbolize? How are the cartoons the narrator watches symbolic?
2. A *motif* (mō̄ tēf') is an idea, element, incident, or object that recurs in a literary work. What is the motif in "A Veil of Water"? Is it appropriate to the story? Discuss.

Writing Workshop

Amy Boesky, who wrote this story as a senior in high school, hadn't experienced a death close to her when she wrote "A Veil of Water." Your job now as a budding writer is to create a similarly believable and compelling first-person narrative. Imagine your circumstances exactly ten years from now. Write a diary entry that conveys where you are and what you have done on that day.

Alternate Media Response

In any medium you wish, illustrate a moment in this story that you find especially gripping or dramatic.

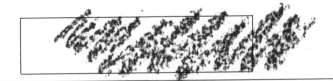

Teenage Wasteland

Anne Tyler

Although Anne Tyler was born in 1941 in Minneapolis, she has spent most of her life in the South. She grew up in Raleigh, North Carolina, and now lives in Baltimore with her husband, a psychiatrist and novelist. They have two grown daughters.

Tyler received her B.A. degree from Duke University in 1961 and studied Russian at Columbia University. She worked as a librarian at Duke and at McGill University in Montreal.

She has had stories published in Harper's, Southern Review, Redbook, McCall's, *and the* New Yorker. *Her twelfth novel,* Saint Maybe, *was published in 1992 and was named a Notable Book of the Year by the* New York Times. *Previous novels include* Dinner at the Homesick Restaurant *(1982);* The Accidental Tourist *(1985), which was filmed; and* Breathing Lessons *(1988), which received a Pulitzer Prize.*

Edward Hoagland, writing in the New York Times, *said that Anne Tyler "might be described as a domestic novelist, one of that great line descending from Jane Austen."*

He used to have very blond hair—almost white—cut shorter than other children's so that on his crown a little cowlick always stood up to catch the light. But this was when he was small. As he grew older, his hair grew darker, and he wore it longer—past his collar even. It hung in lank, taffy-colored ropes around his face, which was still an endearing face, fine-featured, the eyes an unusual aqua blue. But his cheeks, of course, were no longer round, and a sharp new Adam's apple jogged in his throat when he talked.

In October, they called from the private school he attended to request a conference with his parents. Daisy went alone; her husband was at work. Clutching her purse, she sat on the principal's couch and learned that Donny was noisy, lazy, and disruptive; always fooling around with his friends, and he wouldn't respond in class.

In the past, before her children were born, Daisy had been a fourth-grade teacher. It shamed her now to sit before this principal as a parent, a delinquent parent, a parent who struck Mr. Lanham, no doubt, as unseeing or uncaring. "It isn't that we're not concerned," she said. "Both of us are. And we've done what we could, whatever we could think of. We don't let him watch TV on school nights. We don't let him talk on the phone till he's finished his homework. But he tells us he doesn't *have* any homework or he did it all in study hall. How are we to know what to believe?"

From early October through November, at Mr. Lanham's suggestion, Daisy checked Donny's assignments every day. She sat next to him as he worked, trying to be encouraging, sagging inwardly as she saw the poor quality of everything he did—the sloppy mistakes in math, the illogical leaps in his English themes, the history questions left blank if they required any research.

Daisy was often late starting supper, and she couldn't give as much attention to Donny's younger sister. "You'll never guess what happened at . . ." Amanda would begin, and Daisy would have to tell her, "Not now, honey."

By the time her husband, Matt, came home, she'd be snappish. She would recite the day's hardships—the fuzzy instructions in English, the botched history map, the morass of unsolvable algebra equations. Matt would look surprised and confused, and Daisy would gradually wind down. There was no way, really, to convey how exhausting all this was.

In December, the school called again. This time, they wanted Matt to come as well. She and Matt had to sit on Mr. Lanham's couch like two bad children and listen to the news: Donny had improved only slightly, raising a *D* in history to a *C*, and a *C* in algebra to a *B*-minus. What was worse, he had developed new problems. He had cut classes on at least three occasions. Smoked in the furnace room. Helped Sonny Barnett break into a freshman's locker. And last week, during athletics, he and three friends had been seen off the school grounds; when they returned, the coach had smelled beer on their breath.

Daisy and Matt sat silent, shocked. Matt rubbed his forehead with his fingertips. Imagine, Daisy thought, how they must look to Mr. Lanham: an overweight housewife in a cotton dress and a too-tall, too-thin insurance agent in a baggy, frayed suit. Failures, both of them—

the kind of people who are always hurrying to catch up, missing the point of things that everyone else grasps at once. She wished she'd worn nylons instead of knee socks.

It was arranged that Donny would visit a psychologist for testing. Mr. Lanham knew just the person. He would set this boy straight, he said.

When they stood to leave, Daisy held her stomach in and gave Mr. Lanham a firm, responsible handshake.

Donny said the psychologist was a jackass and the tests were really dumb; but he kept all three of his appointments, and when it was time for the follow-up conference with the psychologist and both parents, Donny combed his hair and seemed unusually sober and subdued. The psychologist said Donny had no serious emotional problems. He was merely going through a difficult period in his life. He required some academic help and a better sense of self-worth. For this reason, he was suggesting a man named Calvin Beadle, a tutor with considerable psychological training.

In the car going home, Donny said he'd be damned if he'd let them drag him to some stupid tutor. His father told him to watch his language in front of his mother.

That night, Daisy lay awake pondering the term "self-worth." She had always been free with her praise. She had always told Donny he had talent, was smart, was good with his hands. She had made a big to-do over every little gift he gave her. In fact, maybe she had gone too far, although, Lord knows, she had meant every word. Was that his trouble?

She remembered when Amanda was born. Donny had acted lost and bewildered. Daisy had been alert to that, of course, but still, a new baby keeps you so busy. Had she really done all she could have? She longed—she ached—for a time machine. Given one more chance, she'd do it perfectly—hug him more, praise him more, or perhaps praise him less. Oh, who can say . . .

The tutor told Donny to call him Cal. All his kids did, he said. Daisy thought for a second that he meant his own children, then realized her mistake. He seemed too young, anyhow, to be a family man. He wore a heavy brown handlebar mustache. His hair was as long and stringy as Donny's, and his jeans as faded. Wire-rimmed spectacles slid down his nose. He lounged in a canvas director's chair with his fingers laced across his chest, and he casually, amiably questioned Donny, who sat upright and glaring in an armchair.

"So they're getting on your back at school," said Cal. "Making a big deal about anything you do wrong."

"Right," said Donny.

"Any idea why that would be?"

"Oh, well, you know, stuff like homework and all," Donny said.

"You don't do your homework?"

"Oh, well, I might do it sometimes but not just exactly like they want it." Donny sat forward and said, "It's like a prison there, you know? You've got to go to every class, you can never step off the school grounds."

"You cut classes sometimes?"

"Sometimes," Donny said, with a glance at his parents.

Cal didn't seem perturbed. "Well," he said, "I'll tell you what. Let's you and me try working together three nights a week. Think you could handle that? We'll see if we can show that school of yours a thing or two. Give it a month; then if you don't like it, we'll stop. If *I* don't like it, we'll stop. I mean, sometimes people just don't get along, right? What do you say to that?"

"Okay," Donny said. He seemed pleased.

"Make it seven o'clock till eight, Monday, Wednesday, and Friday," Cal told Matt and Daisy. They nodded. Cal shambled to his feet, gave them a little salute, and showed them to the door.

This was where he lived as well as worked, evidently. The interview had taken place in the dining room, which had been transformed into a kind of office. Passing the living room, Daisy winced at the rock music she had been hearing, without registering it, ever since she had entered the house. She looked in and saw a boy about Donny's age lying on a sofa with a book. Another boy and a girl were playing Ping-Pong in front of the fireplace. "You have several here together?" Daisy asked Cal.

"Oh, sometimes they stay on after their sessions, just to rap. They're a pretty sociable group, all in all. Plenty of goof-offs like young Donny here."

He cuffed Donny's shoulder playfully. Donny flushed and grinned.

Climbing into the car, Daisy asked Donny, "Well? What did you think?"

But Donny had returned to his old evasive self. He jerked his chin toward the garage. "Look," he said. "He's got a basketball net."

Now on Mondays, Wednesdays, and Fridays, they had supper early—the instant Matt came home. Sometimes, they had to leave before they were really finished. Amanda would still be eating her dessert. "Bye, honey. Sorry," Daisy would tell her.

Cal's first bill sent a flutter of panic through Daisy's chest, but it was worth it, of course. Just look at Donny's face when they picked him up: alight and full of interest. The principal telephoned Daisy to tell her how Donny had improved. "Of course, it hasn't shown up in his grades yet, but several of the teachers have noticed how his attitude's changed. Yes, sir, I think we're onto something here."

At home, Donny didn't act much different. He still seemed to have a low opinion of his parents. But Daisy supposed that was unavoidable—part of being fifteen. He said his parents were too "controlling"—a word that made Daisy give him a sudden look. He said they acted like wardens. On weekends, they enforced a curfew. And any time he went to a party, they always telephoned first to see if adults would be supervising. "For God's sake!" he said. "Don't you trust me?"

"It isn't a matter of trust, honey . . ." But there was no explaining to him.

His tutor called one afternoon. "I get the sense," he said, "that this kid's feeling . . . underestimated, you know? Like you folks expect the worst of him. I'm thinking we ought to give him more rope."

"But see, he's still so suggestible," Daisy said. "When his friends suggest some mischief—smoking or drinking or such—why, he just finds it hard not to go along with them."

"Mrs. Coble," the tutor said, "I think this kid is hurting. You know? Here's a serious, sensitive kid, telling you he'd like to take on some grown-up challenges, and you're giving him the message that he can't be trusted. Don't you understand how that hurts?"

"Oh," said Daisy.

"It undermines his self-esteem—don't you realize that?"

"Well, I guess you're right," said Daisy. She saw Donny suddenly from a whole new angle: his pathetically poor posture, that slouch so forlorn that his shoulders seemed about to meet his chin . . . oh, wasn't it awful being young? She'd had a miserable adolescence herself and had always sworn no child of hers would ever be that unhappy.

They let Donny stay out later, they didn't call ahead to see if the parties were supervised, and they were careful not to grill him about his evening. The tutor had set down so many rules! They were not allowed any questions at all about any aspect of school, nor were they to speak with his teachers. If a teacher had some complaint, she should phone Cal. Only one teacher disobeyed—the history teacher, Miss Evans. She called one morning in February. "I'm a little concerned about Donny, Mrs. Coble."

"Oh, I'm sorry, Miss Evans, but Donny's tutor handles these things now . . ."

"I always deal directly with the parents. You are the parent," Miss Evans said, speaking very slowly and distinctly. "Now, here is the problem. Back when you were helping Donny with his homework, his grades rose from a D to a C, but now they've slipped back, and they're closer to an F."

"They are?"

"I think you should start overseeing his homework again."

"But Donny's tutor says . . ."

"It's nice that Donny has a tutor, but you should still be in charge of his homework. With you, he learned it. Then he passed his tests. With the tutor, well, it seems the tutor is more of a crutch. 'Donny,' I say, 'a quiz is coming up on Friday. Hadn't you better be listening instead of talking?' 'That's okay, Miss Evans,' he says. 'I have a tutor now.' Like a *talisman!*[1] I really think you ought to take over, Mrs. Coble."

"I see," said Daisy. "Well, I'll think about that. Thank you for calling."

Hanging up, she felt a rush of anger at Donny. A talisman! For a talisman, she'd given up all luxuries, all that time with her daughter, her evenings at home!

She dialed Cal's number. He sounded muzzy. "I'm sorry if I woke you," she told him, "but Donny's history teacher just called. She says he isn't doing well."

"She should have dealt with me."

"She wants me to start supervising his homework again. His grades are slipping."

"Yes," said the tutor, "but you and I both know there's more to it than mere grades, don't we? I care about the *whole* child—his happiness, his self-esteem. The grades will come. Just give them time."

When she hung up, it was Miss Evans she was angry at. What a narrow woman!

It was Cal this, Cal that, Cal says this, Cal and I did that. Cal lent Donny an album by the Who. He took Donny and two other pupils to a rock concert. In March, when Donny began to talk endlessly on the phone with a girl named Miriam, Cal even let Miriam come to one of the tutoring sessions. Daisy was touched that Cal would grow so involved in Donny's life, but she was also a little hurt, because she had offered to have Miriam to dinner and Donny had refused. Now he asked them to drive her to Cal's house without a qualm.

This Miriam was an unappealing girl with blurry lipstick and masses of rough red hair. She wore a short, bulky jacket that would not have been out of place on a motorcycle. During the trip to Cal's she was

---

1. *talisman* (tal′i smən): something thought to have magical powers.

silent, but coming back, she was more talkative. "What a neat guy, and what a house! All those kids hanging out, like a club. And the stereo playing rock . . . gosh, he's not like grown-up at all! Married and divorced and everything, but you'd think he was our own age."

"Mr. Beadle was married?" Daisy asked.

"Yeah, to this really controlling lady. She didn't understand him a bit."

"No, I guess not," Daisy said.

Spring came, and the students who hung around at Cal's drifted out to the basketball net above the garage. Sometimes, when Daisy and Matt arrived to pick up Donny, they'd find him there with the others—spiky and excited, jittering on his toes beneath the backboard. It was staying light much longer now, and the neighboring fence cast narrow bars across the bright grass. Loud music would be spilling from Cal's windows. Once it was the Who, which Daisy recognized from the time that Donny had borrowed the album. "Teenage Wasteland," she said aloud, identifying the song, and Matt gave a short, dry laugh. "It certainly is," he said. He'd misunderstood; he thought she was commenting on the scene spread before them. In fact, she might have been. The players looked like hoodlums, even her son. Why, one of Cal's students had recently been knifed in a tavern. One had been shipped off to boarding school in midterm; two had been withdrawn by their parents. On the other hand, Donny had mentioned someone who'd been studying with Cal for five years. "Five years!" said Daisy. "Doesn't anyone ever stop needing him?"

Donny looked at her. Lately, whatever she said about Cal was read as criticism. "You're just feeling competitive," he said. "And controlling."

She bit her lip and said no more.

In April, the principal called to tell her that Donny had been expelled. There had been a locker check, and in Donny's locker they found five cans of beer and half a pack of cigarettes. With Donny's previous record, this offense meant expulsion.

Daisy gripped the receiver tightly and said, "Well, where is he now?"

"We've sent him home," said Mr. Lanham. "He's packed up all his belongings, and he's coming home on foot."

Daisy wondered what she would say to him. She felt him looming closer and closer, bringing this brand-new situation that no one had prepared her to handle. What other place would take him? Could they enter him in public school? What were the rules? She stood at the living room window, waiting for him to show up. Gradually, she realized that he was taking too long. She checked the clock. She stared up the street again.

When an hour had passed, she phoned the school. Mr. Lanham's secretary answered and told her in a grave, sympathetic voice that yes, Donny Coble had most definitely gone home. Daisy called her husband. He was out of the office. She went back to the window and thought awhile, and then she called Donny's tutor.

"Donny's been expelled from school," she said, "and now I don't know where he's gone. I wonder if you've heard from him?"

There was a long silence. "Donny's with me, Mrs. Coble," he finally said.

"With you? How'd he get there?"

"He hailed a cab, and I paid the driver."

"Could I speak to him, please?"

There was another silence. "Maybe it'd be better if we had a conference," Cal said.

"I don't *want* a conference. I've been standing at the window picturing him dead or kidnapped or something, and now you tell me you want a—"

"Donny is very, very upset. Understandably so," said Cal. "Believe me, Mrs. Coble, this is not what it seems. Have you asked Donny's side of the story?"

"Well, of course not, how could I? He went running off to you instead."

"Because he didn't feel he'd be listened to."

"But I haven't even—"

"Why don't you come out and talk? The three of us," said Cal, "will try to get this thing in perspective."

"Well, all right," Daisy said. But she wasn't as reluctant as she sounded. Already, she felt soothed by the calm way Cal was taking this.

Cal answered the doorbell at once. He said, "Hi, there," and led her into the dining room. Donny sat slumped in a chair, chewing the knuckle of one thumb. "Hello, Donny," Daisy said. He flicked his eyes in her direction.

"Sit here, Mrs. Coble," said Cal, placing her opposite Donny. He himself remained standing, restlessly pacing. "So," he said.

Daisy stole a look at Donny. His lips were swollen, as if he'd been crying.

"You know," Cal told Daisy, "I kind of expected something like this. That's a very punitive school you've got him in—you realize that. And any half-decent lawyer will tell you they've violated his civil rights. Locker checks! Where's their search warrant?"

"But if the rule is—" Daisy said.

"Well, anyhow, let him tell you his side."

She looked at Donny. He said, "It wasn't my fault. I promise."

"They said your locker was full of beer."

"It was a put-up job! See, there's this guy that doesn't like me. He put all these beers in my locker and started a rumor going, so Mr. Lanham ordered a locker check."

"What was the boy's name?" Daisy asked.

"Huh?"

"Mrs. Coble, take my word, the situation is not so unusual," Cal said. "You can't imagine how vindictive kids can be sometimes."

"What was the boy's *name*," said Daisy, "so that I can ask Mr. Lanham if that's who suggested he run a locker check."

"You don't believe me," Donny said.

"And how'd this boy get your combination in the first place?"

"Frankly," said Cal, "I wouldn't be surprised to learn the school was in on it. Any kid that marches to a different drummer, why, they'd just love an excuse to get rid of him. The school is where I lay the blame."

"Doesn't *Donny* ever get blamed?"

"Now, Mrs. Coble, you heard what he—"

"Forget it," Donny told Cal. "You can see she doesn't trust me."

Daisy drew in a breath to say that of course she trusted him—a reflex. But she knew that bold-faced, wide-eyed look of Donny's. He had worn that look when he was small, denying some petty misdeed with the evidence plain as day all around him. Still, it was hard for her to accuse him outright. She temporized[2] and said, "The only thing I'm sure of is that they've kicked you out of school, and now I don't know what we're going to do."

"We'll fight it," said Cal.

"We can't. Even you must see we can't."

"I could apply to Brantly," Donny said.

Cal stopped his pacing to beam down at him. "Brantly! Yes. They're really onto where a kid is coming from, at Brantly. Why, *I* could get you into Brantly. I work with a lot of their students."

Daisy had never heard of Brantly, but already she didn't like it. And she didn't like Cal's smile, which struck her now as feverish and avid— a smile of hunger.

On the fifteenth of April, they entered Donny in a public school,

---

2. *temporized:* evaded the matter to avoid trouble.

and they stopped his tutoring sessions. Donny fought both decisions bitterly. Cal, surprisingly enough, did not object. He admitted he'd made no headway with Donny and said it was because Donny was emotionally disturbed.

Donny went to his new school every morning, plodding off alone with his head down. He did his assignments, and he earned average grades, but he gathered no friends, joined no clubs. There was something exhausted and defeated about him.

The first week in June, during final exams, Donny vanished. He simply didn't come home one afternoon, and no one at school remembered seeing him. The police were reassuring, and for the first few days, they worked hard. They combed Donny's sad, messy room for clues; they visited Miriam and Cal. But then they started talking about the number of kids who ran away every year. Hundreds, just in this city. "He'll show up, if he wants to," they said. "If he doesn't, he won't."

Evidently, Donny didn't want to.

It's been three months now and still no word. Matt and Daisy still look for him in every crowd of awkward, heartbreaking teenage boys. Every time the phone rings, they imagine it might be Donny. Both parents have aged. Donny's sister seems to be staying away from home as much as possible.

At night, Daisy lies awake and goes over Donny's life. She is trying to figure out what went wrong, where they made their first mistake. Often, she finds herself blaming Cal, although she knows he didn't begin it. Then at other times she excuses him, for without him, Donny might have left earlier. Who really knows? In the end, she can only sigh and search for a cooler spot on the pillow. As she falls asleep, she occasionally glimpses something in the corner of her vision. It's something fleet and round, a ball—a basketball. It flies up, it sinks through the hoop, descends, lands in a yard littered with last year's leaves and striped with bars of sunlight as white as bones, bleached and parched and cleanly picked.

Responding to the Story

1. How did you respond to this story? Are you sympathetic toward Donny? Are you irritated—even angry—with him? Write several paragraphs of personal response.

2. Why do you think you responded as you did? Has anything in your life made you respond this way?

3. Why do you think the author titled this story "Teenage Wasteland"?

Exploring the Author's Craft

What is the author's attitude toward her subject, her tone? Write several paragraphs justifying one of the following positions:

a. The author of "Teenage Wasteland" sympathizes with the parents.

b. The author of "Teenage Wasteland" sympathizes with the son.

c. The author of "Teenage Wasteland" sympathizes with both the parents and the son.

d. The author of "Teenage Wasteland" presents an unbiased, neutral portrait of this family.

Writing Workshop

Try to imagine a different ending for this story, perhaps one in which Donny returns home. Write your alternate ending and compare it with the alternate endings written by others in your class.

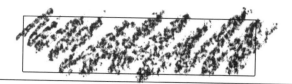

Initiation

Sylvia Plath

Sylvia Plath is known primarily as a poet, with most of her work published after her death by suicide in 1963. She was born in Boston in 1932, and after the death of her father in 1940, the family moved to Wellesley. The following short story was written when Plath was a teenager and was published in Seventeen *just before she entered Smith College in 1950. After a suicide attempt in 1953, Plath returned to Smith and graduated* summa cum laude *in 1955. Her academic excellence enabled her to win a Fulbright scholarship for study at Cambridge in England. There she met English poet Ted Hughes, and they were married in 1956. She taught English at Smith during the 1957–58 year, but in 1959, she and her husband returned to England and lived in London and Devon. They had two children and were separated in 1962.*

Plath's first book of poems, The Colossus, *was published in 1960. Other collections are titled* Ariel *(1965),* Crossing the Water *(1971), and* Winter Trees *(1972). Her only novel* The Bell Jar *appeared in 1963 under the pseudonym Victoria Lucas but was republished under her own name.* Letters Home *edited by her mother appeared in 1975, and* Collected Poems *edited by Ted Hughes was published in 1981.*

The basement room was dark and warm, like the inside of a sealed jar, Millicent thought, her eyes getting used to the strange dimness. The silence was soft with cobwebs, and from the small, rectangular window set high in the stone wall there sifted a faint bluish light that must be coming from the full October moon. She could see now that what she was sitting on was a woodpile next to the furnace.

Millicent brushed back a strand of hair. It was stiff and sticky from the egg that they had broken on her head as she knelt blindfolded at the sorority altar a short while before. There had been a silence, a slight crunching sound, and then she had felt the cold, slimy egg-white flattening and spreading on her head and sliding down her neck. She had heard someone smothering a laugh. It was all part of the ceremony.

Then the girls had led her here, blindfolded still, through the corridors of Betsy Johnson's house and shut her in the cellar. It would be an hour before they came to get her, but then Rat Court would be all over and she would say what she had to say and go home.

For tonight was the grand finale, the trial by fire. There really was no doubt now that she would get in. She could not think of anyone who had ever been invited into the high school sorority and failed to get through initiation time. But even so, her case would be quite different. She would see to that. She could not exactly say what had decided her revolt, but it definitely had something to do with Tracy and something to do with the heather birds.

What girl at Lansing High would not want to be in her place now? Millicent thought, amused. What girl would not want to be one of the elect,[1] no matter if it did mean five days of initiation before and after school, ending in the climax of Rat Court on Friday night when they made the new girls members? Even Tracy had been wistful when she heard that Millicent had been one of the five girls to receive an invitation.

"It won't be any different with us, Tracy," Millicent had told her. "We'll still go around together like we always have, and next year you'll surely get in."

"I know, but even so," Tracy had said quietly, "you'll change, whether you think you will or not. Nothing ever stays the same."

And nothing does, Millicent had thought. How horrible it would be if one never changed . . . if she were condemned to be the plain, shy Millicent of a few years back for the rest of her life. Fortunately there was always the changing, the growing, the going on.

It would come to Tracy, too. She would tell Tracy the silly things the girls had said, and Tracy would change also, entering eventually into the magic circle. She would grow to know the special ritual as Millicent had started to last week.

"First of all," Betsy Johnson, the vivacious blonde secretary of the sorority, had told the five new candidates over sandwiches in the school cafeteria last Monday, "first of all, each of you has a big sister. She's the one who bosses you around, and you just do what she tells you."

"Remember the part about talking back and smiling," Louise Ful-

---

1. *the elect:* people who belong to an exclusive group.

lerton had put in, laughing. She was another celebrity in high school, pretty and dark and vice-president of the student council. "You can't say anything unless your big sister asks you something or tells you to talk to someone. And you can't smile, no matter how you're dying to." The girls had laughed a little nervously, and then the bell had rung for the beginning of afternoon classes.

It would be rather fun for a change, Millicent mused, getting her books out of her locker in the hall, rather exciting to be part of a closely knit group, the exclusive set at Lansing High. Of course, it wasn't a school organization. In fact, the principal, Mr. Cranton, wanted to do away with initiation week altogether, because he thought it was undemocratic and disturbed the routine of school work. But there wasn't really anything he could do about it. Sure, the girls had to come to school for five days without any lipstick on and without curling their hair, and of course everybody noticed them, but what could the teachers do?

Millicent sat down at her desk in the big study hall. Tomorrow she would come to school, proudly, laughingly, without lipstick, with her brown hair straight and shoulder length, and then everybody would know, even the boys would know, that she was one of the elect. Teachers would smile helplessly, thinking perhaps: So now they've picked Millicent Arnold. I never would have guessed it.

A year or two ago, not many people would have guessed it. Millicent had waited a long time for acceptance, longer than most. It was as if she had been sitting for years in a pavilion outside a dance floor, looking in through the windows at the golden interior, with the lights clear and the air like honey, wistfully watching the couples waltzing to the never-ending music, laughing in pairs and groups together, no one alone.

But now at last, amid a week of fanfare and merriment, she would answer her invitation to enter the ballroom through the main entrance marked "Initiation." She would gather up her velvet skirts, her silken train, or whatever the disinherited princesses wore in the story books, and come into her rightful kingdom. . . . The bell rang to end study hall.

"Millicent, wait up!" It was Louise Fullerton behind her, Louise who had always before been very nice, very polite, friendlier than the rest, even long ago, before the invitation had come.

"Listen," Louise walked down the hall with her to Latin, their next class, "are you busy right after school today? Because I'd like to talk to you about tomorrow."

"Sure. I've got lots of time."

"Well, meet me in the hall after homeroom then, and we'll go down to the drugstore or something."

Walking beside Louise on the way to the drugstore, Millicent felt a surge of pride. For all anyone could see, she and Louise were the best of friends.

"You know, I was so glad when they voted you in," Louise said.

Millicent smiled. "I was really thrilled to get the invitation," she said frankly, "but kind of sorry that Tracy didn't get in, too."

Tracy, she thought. If there is such a thing as a best friend, Tracy has been just that this last year.

"Yes, Tracy," Louise was saying, "she's a nice girl, and they put her up on the slate, but . . . well, she had three blackballs against her."

"Blackballs? What are they?"

"Well, we're not supposed to tell anybody outside the club, but seeing as you'll be in at the end of the week I don't suppose it hurts." They were at the drugstore now.

"You see," Louise began explaining in a low voice after they were seated in the privacy of the booth, "once a year the sorority puts up all the likely girls that are suggested for membership. . . ."

Millicent sipped her cold, sweet drink slowly, saving the ice cream to spoon up last. She listened carefully to Louise who was going on, ". . . and then there's a big meeting, and all the girls' names are read off and each girl is discussed."

"Oh?" Millicent asked mechanically, her voice sounding strange.

"Oh, I know what you're thinking," Louise laughed. "But it's really not as bad as all that. They keep it down to a minimum of catting.[2] They just talk over each girl and why or why not they think she'd be good for the club. And then they vote. Three blackballs eliminate a girl."

"Do you mind if I ask you what happened to Tracy?" Millicent said.

Louise laughed a little uneasily. "Well, you know how girls are. They notice little things. I mean, some of them thought Tracy was just a bit *too* different. Maybe you could suggest a few things to her."

"Like what?"

"Oh, like maybe not wearing knee socks to school, or carrying that old bookbag. I know it doesn't sound like much, but well, it's things like that which set someone apart. I mean, you know that no girl at

---

2. *catting:* making mean or spiteful remarks.

Lansing would be seen dead wearing knee socks, no matter how cold it gets, and it's kiddish and kind of green[3] to carry a bookbag."

"I guess so," Millicent said.

"About tomorrow," Louise went on. "You've drawn Beverly Mitchell for a big sister. I wanted to warn you that she's the toughest, but if you get through all right it'll be all the more credit for you."

"Thanks, Lou," Millicent said gratefully, thinking, this is beginning to sound serious. Worse than a loyalty test, this grilling over the coals. What's it supposed to prove anyway? That I can take orders without flinching? Or does it just make them feel good to see us run around at their beck and call?

"All you have to do really," Louise said, spooning up the last of her sundae, "is be very meek and obedient when you're with Bev and do just what she tells you. Don't laugh or talk back or try to be funny, or she'll just make it harder for you, and believe me, she's a great one for doing that. Be at her house at seven-thirty."

And she was. She rang the bell and sat down on the steps to wait for Bev. After a few minutes the front door opened and Bev was standing there, her face serious.

"Get up, gopher," Bev ordered.

There was something about her tone that annoyed Millicent. It was almost malicious. And there was an unpleasant anonymity about the label "gopher," even if that was what they always called the girls being initiated. It was degrading, like being given a number. It was a denial of individuality.

Rebellion flooded through her.

"I said get up. Are you deaf?"

Millicent got up, standing there.

"Into the house, gopher. There's a bed to be made and a room to be cleaned at the top of the stairs."

Millicent went up the stairs mutely. She found Bev's room and started making the bed. Smiling to herself, she was thinking: How absurdly funny, me taking orders from this girl like a servant.

Bev was suddenly there in the doorway. "Wipe that smile off your face," she commanded.

There seemed something about this relationship that was not all fun. In Bev's eyes, Millicent was sure of it, there was a hard, bright spark of exultation.

---

3. *green:* naive, unsophisticated.

On the way to school, Millicent had to walk behind Bev at a distance of ten paces, carrying her books. They came up to the drugstore where there already was a crowd of boys and girls from Lansing High waiting for the show.

The other girls being initiated were there, so Millicent felt relieved. It would not be so bad now, being part of the group.

"What'll we have them do?" Betsy Johnson asked Bev. That morning Betsy had made her "gopher" carry an old colored parasol through the square and sing "I'm Always Chasing Rainbows."

"I know," Herb Dalton, the good-looking basketball captain, said.

A remarkable change came over Bev. She was all at once very soft and coquettish.

"You can't tell them what to do," Bev said sweetly. "Men have nothing to say about this little deal."

"All right, all right," Herb laughed, stepping back and pretending to fend off a blow.

"It's getting late," Louise had come up. "Almost eight-thirty. We'd better get them marching on to school."

The "gophers" had to do a Charleston[4] step all the way to school, and each one had her own song to sing, trying to drown out the other four. During school, of course, you couldn't fool around, but even then, there was a rule that you mustn't talk to boys outside of class or at lunchtime . . . or any time at all after school. So the sorority girls would get the most popular boys to go up to the "gophers" and ask them out, or try to start them talking, and sometimes a "gopher" was taken by surprise and began to say something before she could catch herself. And then the boy reported her and she got a black mark.

Herb Dalton approached Millicent as she was getting an ice cream at the lunch counter that noon. She saw him coming before he spoke to her, and looked down quickly, thinking: He is too princely, too dark and smiling. And I am much too vulnerable. Why must he be the one I have to be careful of?

I won't say anything, she thought, I'll just smile very sweetly.

She smiled up at Herb very sweetly and mutely. His return grin was rather miraculous. It was surely more than was called for in the line of duty.

"I know you can't talk to me," he said, very low. "But you're doing fine, the girls say. I even like your hair straight and all."

---

4. *Charleston:* lively dance popular in the 1920s.

Bev was coming toward them, then, her red mouth set in a bright, calculating smile. She ignored Millicent and sailed up to Herb.

"Why waste your time with gophers?" she caroled gaily. "Their tongues are tied, but completely."

Herb managed a parting shot. "But that one keeps *such* an attractive silence."

Millicent smiled as she ate her sundae at the counter with Tracy. Generally, the girls who were outsiders now, as Millicent had been, scoffed at the initiation antics as childish and absurd to hide their secret envy. But Tracy was understanding, as ever.

"Tonight's the worst, I guess, Tracy," Millicent told her. "I hear that the girls are taking us on a bus over to Lewiston and going to have us performing in the square."

"Just keep a poker face outside," Tracy advised. "But keep laughing like mad inside."

Millicent and Bev took a bus ahead of the rest of the girls; they had to stand up on the way to Lewiston Square. Bev seemed very cross about something. Finally she said, "You were talking with Herb Dalton at lunch today."

"No," said Millicent honestly.

"Well, I *saw* you smile at him. That's practically as bad as talking. Remember not to do it again."

Millicent kept silent.

"It's fifteen minutes before the bus gets into town," Bev was saying then. "I want you to go up and down the bus asking people what they eat for breakfast. Remember, you can't tell them you're being initiated."

Millicent looked down the aisle of the crowded bus and felt suddenly quite sick. She thought: How will I ever do it, going up to all those stony-faced people who are staring coldly out of the window. . . .

"You heard me, gopher."

"Excuse me, madam," Millicent said politely to the lady in the first seat of the bus, "but I'm taking a survey. Could you please tell me what you eat for breakfast?"

"Why . . . er . . . just orange juice, toast, and coffee," she said.

"Thank you very much." Millicent went on to the next person, a young business man. He ate eggs sunny side up, toast and coffee.

By the time Millicent got to the back of the bus, most of the people were smiling at her. They obviously know, she thought, that I'm being initiated into something.

Finally, there was only one man left in the corner of the back seat.

He was small and jolly, with a ruddy, wrinkled face that spread into a beaming smile as Millicent approached. In his brown suit with the forest-green tie he looked something like a gnome or a cheerful leprechaun.

"Excuse me, sir," Millicent smiled, "but I'm taking a survey. What do you eat for breakfast?"

"Heather birds' eyebrows on toast," the little man rattled off.

"*What?*" Millicent exclaimed.

"Heather birds' eyebrows," the little man explained. "Heather birds live on the mythological moors and fly about all day long, singing wild and sweet in the sun. They're bright purple and have *very* tasty eyebrows."

Millicent broke out into spontaneous laughter. Why, this was wonderful, the way she felt a sudden comradeship with a stranger.

"Are you mythological, too?"

"Not exactly," he replied, "but I certainly hope to be someday. Being mythological does wonders for one's ego."

The bus was swinging into the station now; Millicent hated to leave the little man. She wanted to ask him more about the birds.

And from that time on, initiations didn't bother Millicent at all. She went gaily about Lewiston Square from store to store asking for broken crackers and mangoes, and she just laughed inside when people stared and then brightened, answering her crazy questions as if she were quite serious and really a person of consequence. So many people were shut up tight inside themselves like boxes, yet they would open up, unfolding quite wonderfully, if only you were interested in them. And really, you didn't have to belong to a club to feel related to other human beings.

One afternoon Millicent had started talking with Liane Morris, another of the girls being initiated, about what it would be like when they were finally in the sorority.

"Oh, I know pretty much what it'll be like," Liane had said. "My sister belonged before she graduated from high school two years ago."

"Well, just what *do* they do as a club?" Millicent wanted to know.

"Why, they have a meeting once a week . . . each girl takes turns entertaining at her house. . . ."

"You mean it's just a sort of exclusive social group. . . ."

"I guess so . . . though that's a funny way of putting it. But it sure gives a girl prestige value. My sister started going steady with the captain of the football team after she got in. Not bad, I say."

No, it wasn't bad, Millicent had thought, lying in bed on the morning of Rat Court and listening to the sparrows chirping in the gutters. She thought of Herb. Would he ever have been so friendly if she were without the sorority label? Would he ask her out (if he ever did) just for herself, no strings attached?

Then there was another thing that bothered her. Leaving Tracy on the outskirts. Because that is the way it would be; Millicent had seen it happen before.

Outside, the sparrows were still chirping, and as she lay in bed Millicent visualized them, pale gray-brown birds in a flock, one like the other, all exactly alike.

And then, for some reason, Millicent thought of the heather birds. Swooping carefree over the moors, they would go singing and crying out across the great spaces of air, dipping and darting, strong and proud in their freedom and their sometime loneliness. It was then that she made her decision.

Seated now on the woodpile in Betsy Johnson's cellar, Millicent knew that she had come triumphant through the trial of fire, the searing period of the ego which could end in two kinds of victory for her. The easiest of which would be her coronation as a princess, labeling her conclusively as one of the select flock.

The other victory would be much harder, but she knew that it was what she wanted. It was not that she was being noble or anything. It was just that she had learned there were other ways of getting into the great hall, blazing with lights, of people and of life.

It would be hard to explain to the girls tonight, of course, but she could tell Louise later just how it was. How she had proved something to herself by going through everything, even Rat Court, and then deciding not to join the sorority after all. And how she could still be friends with everybody. Sisters with everybody. Tracy, too.

The door behind her opened and a ray of light sliced across the soft gloom of the basement room.

"Hey Millicent, come on out now. This is it." There were some of the girls outside.

"I'm coming," she said, getting up and moving out of the soft darkness into the glare of light, thinking: This is it, all right. The worst part, the hardest part, the part of initiation that I figured out myself.

But just then, from somewhere far off, Millicent was sure of it, there came a melodic fluting, quite wild and sweet, and she knew that it must be the song of the heather birds as they went wheeling and gliding against wide blue horizons through vast spaces of air, their wings flashing quick and purple in the bright sun.

Within Millicent another melody soared, strong and exuberant, a triumphant answer to the music of the darting heather birds that sang so clear and lilting over the far lands. And she knew that her own private initiation had just begun.

Responding to the Story

1. Why was the "part of initiation that I figured out myself" the "worst part, the hardest part" for Millicent?

2. How do you interpret the story's last line?

3. Do you agree with Millicent's decision not to join the sorority? Explain your response.

Exploring the Author's Craft

A *flashback* is an interruption in a chronological narrative that shows something that happened before that point in the story. A flashback provides background information on characters or events that helps explain a character's motivations and reactions. A flashback is not just reminiscence but an actual shift in time to show past events.

1. Where does the flashback in "Initiation" begin and end?

2. What does the flashback in this story accomplish?

Writing Workshop

1. Create a one- or two-paragraph response in narrative form from the following people after they learn of Millicent's decision. Write from the first-person point of view.

    a. Beverly Mitchell

    b. sorority secretary Betsy Johnson

    c. Herb Dalton

    d. Millicent's friend Tracy

2. Author Sylvia Plath used two similes in this story to reflect Millicent's emotions: "The basement room was dark and warm, like the inside of a sealed jar . . ." and "It was as if she had been sitting for years in a pavilion outside a dance floor, looking in through the windows at the golden interior, with the lights clear and the air like honey, wistfully watching the couples waltzing to the never-ending music, laughing in pairs and groups together, no one alone."

Choose a moment in the story—or maybe one that you envision just after Millicent reveals her decision not to join the sorority—and express it in terms of an appropriate simile. Use the third-person point of view.

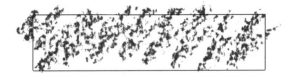

Betty

Margaret Atwood

Margaret Atwood has written poems, novels, short stories, children's books, and plays. In addition, she is a cartoonist and illustrator.

She was born in 1939 in Ottawa, Ontario, the second of three children, and spent summers in the north woods with her parents. She received her B.A. degree from the University of Toronto in 1961, her Master's degree from Radcliffe College in 1962, and was enrolled for graduate study at Harvard in 1962 and 1965. She has taught English and was editor and a member of the board of directors for the House of Anansi Press in Toronto from 1971 to 1973.

Atwood has published over thirty books, among them Blue-beard's Egg *(1983), a story collection;* The Handmaid's Tale *(1985), a novel which won a Governor General's Award;* Cat's Eye *(1989), also a novel; and* Wilderness Trips *(1991), a book of poetry. She also compiled* The New Oxford Book of Canadian Verse in English *(1983).*

W hen I was seven we moved again, to a tiny wooden cottage on the Saint Mary's River, upstream from Sault Sainte Marie.[1] We were only renting the cottage for the summer, but for the time being it was our house, since we had no other. It was dim and mousy smelling and very cramped, stuffed with all the things from the place before that were not in storage. My sister and I preferred to spend most of our time outside it.

---

1. *Sault Sainte Marie* (sü sänt mə rē′): rapids in the St. Mary's River between Michigan and Ontario; city in Ontario near the rapids. (*Sault* is French for "rapids.")

There was a short beach, behind which the cottages, with their contrasting trim—green against white, maroon against robin's-egg blue, brown against yellow—were lined up like little shoe boxes, each with its matching outhouse at an unsanitary distance behind. But we were forbidden to swim in the water, because of the strong current. There were stories of children who had been swept away, down toward the rapids and the locks and the Algoma Steel fires of the Soo[2] which we could sometimes see from our bedroom window on overcast nights, glowing dull red against the clouds. We were allowed to wade, though, no further than the knee, and we would stand in the water, strands of loose weed tangling against our ankles, and wave at the lake freighters as they slid past, so close we could see not only the flags and sea gulls at their sterns but the hands of the sailors and the ovals of their faces as they waved back to us. Then the waves would come, washing over our thighs up to the waist of our bloomered and skirted seersucker bathing suits[3], and we would scream with delight.

Our mother, who was usually on the shore, reading or talking to someone but not quite watching us, would sometimes mistake the screams for drowning. Or she would say later, "You've been in over your knees," but my sister would explain that it was only the boat waves. My mother would look at me to see if this was the truth. Unlike my sister, I was a clumsy liar.

The freighters were huge, cumbersome, with rust staining the holes for their anchor chains and enormous chimneys from which the smoke spurted in gray burps. When they blew their horns, as they always did when approaching the locks, the windows in our cottage rattled. For us they were magical. Sometimes things would drop or be thrown from them, and we would watch these floating objects eagerly, running along the beach to be there when they landed, wading out to fish them in. Usually these treasures turned out to be only empty cardboard boxes or punctured oil cans, oozing dark brown grease and good for nothing. Several times we got orange crates, which we used as cupboards or stools in our hideouts.

We liked the cottage partly because we had places to make these hideouts. There had never been room before, since we had always lived in cities. Just before this it was Ottawa, the ground floor of an old three-tiered red-brick apartment building. On the floor above us lived

---

2. *Soo*: canals on the rapids on the St. Mary's River between Lakes Superior and Huron.

3. *bloomered and skirted . . . bathing suits:* bathing suits with skirts and loose trousers (bloomers) that came to the knee.

a newly married couple, the wife English and Protestant, the husband French and Catholic. He was in the air force and was away a lot, but when he came back on leave he used to beat up his wife. It was always about eleven o'clock at night. She would flee downstairs to my mother for protection, and they would sit in the kitchen with cups of tea. The wife would cry, though quietly, so as not to wake us—my mother insisted on that, being a believer in twelve hours of sleep for children—display her bruised eye or cheek, and whisper about his drinking. After an hour or so there would be a discreet knock on the door, and the airman, in full uniform, would ask my mother politely if he could have his wife back upstairs where she belonged. It was a religious dispute, he would say. Besides, he'd given her fifteen dollars to spend on food and she had served him fried Kam. After being away a month, a man expected a good roast, pork or beef, didn't my mother agree? "I kept my mouth shut and my eyes open," my mother would say. He never seemed that drunk to her, but with the polite kind you couldn't tell what they would do.

I wasn't supposed to know about any of this. I was considered either too young or too good; but my sister, who was four years older, was given hints, which she passed along to me with whatever she thought fit to add. I saw the wife a number of times, going up or down the stairs outside our door, and once she did have a black eye. I never saw the man, but by the time we left Ottawa I was convinced he was a murderer.

This might have explained my father's warning when my mother told him she had met the young couple who lived in the right-hand cottage. "Don't get too involved," he said. "I don't want her running over here at all hours of the night." He had little patience with my mother's talents as a sympathetic listener, even when she teased him by saying, "But I listen to *you*, dear." She attracted people like sponges.

He didn't seem to have anything to worry about. This couple was very different from the other one. Fred and Betty insisted on being called Fred and Betty, right away. My sister and I, who had been drilled to call people Mr. and Mrs., had to call them Fred and Betty also, and we could go over to their house whenever we wanted to. "I don't want you to take that at face value," our mother said. Times were hard, but our mother had been properly brought up, and we were going to be, too. Nevertheless, at first we went to Fred and Betty's as often as we could.

Their cottage was exactly the same as ours, but since there was less furniture in it, it seemed bigger. Ours had Ten-Test walls between the rooms, painted lime green, with lighter squares on the paint where other people had once hung pictures. Betty had replaced her walls with real plywood and painted the inside bright yellow, and she'd made yellow-and-white curtains for the kitchen, a print of chickens coming out of eggshells. She'd sewed herself a matching apron from the leftover material. They owned their cottage rather than renting it; as my mother said, you didn't mind doing the work then. Betty called the tiny kitchen a kitchenette. There was a round ironwork table tucked into one corner, with two scrolled ironwork chairs painted white, one for Betty and one for Fred. Betty called this corner the breakfast nook.

There was more to do at Fred and Betty's than at our house. They had a bird made of hollow colored glass that perched on the edge of a tumbler of water, teetering back and forth until it would finally dip its head into the water and take a drink. They had a front-door knocker in the shape of a woodpecker: you pulled a string and the woodpecker pecked at the door. They also had a whistle in the shape of a bird that you could fill with water and blow into and it would warble, "like a canary," Betty said. And they took the Sunday colored funnies. Our parents didn't. They didn't like us reading trash, as they called it. But Fred and Betty were so friendly and kind to us, what, as my mother said, could they do?

Beyond all these attractions there was Fred. We both fell in love with Fred. My sister would climb into his lap and announce that he was her boyfriend and she was going to marry him when she grew up. She would then make him read the funnies to her and tease him by trying to take the pipe out of his mouth or by tying his shoelaces together. I felt the same way, but I knew it was no good saying so. My sister had staked her claim: when she said she was going to do a thing she usually did it. And she hated my being what she called a copycat. So I would sit in the breakfast nook on one of the scrolled ironwork chairs while Betty made coffee, watching my sister and Fred on the living-room couch.

There was something about Fred that attracted people. My mother, who was not a flirtatious woman—she went in for wisdom, instead—was livelier when he was around. Even my father liked him and would sometimes have a beer with him when he got back from the city. They would sit on the porch of Fred's cottage in Betty's yellow wicker chairs, swatting at the sand flies and discussing baseball scores. They seldom mentioned their jobs. I'm not sure what Fred did, but it was in an office. My father was "in wallpaper," my mother said, but I was never clear about what that meant. It was more exciting when they talked about the war. My father's bad back had kept him out of it, much to his disgust, but Fred had been in the navy. He never said too much about it, though my father was always prompting him; but we knew from Betty that they were engaged just before Fred left and married right after he came back. Betty had written letters to him every single night and mailed them once a week. She did not say how often Fred had written to her. My father didn't like many people, but he said that Fred wasn't a fool.

Fred didn't seem to make any efforts to be nice to people. I don't think he was even especially handsome. The difficulty is that though I can remember Betty down to the last hair and freckle, I can't remember what Fred looked like. He had dark hair and a pipe, and he used to sing to us if we pestered him enough. "Sioux City Sue," he would sing, "your hair is red, your eyes are blue, I'd swap my horse and dog for you. . . ." Or he would sing "Beautiful Brown Eyes" to my sister, whose eyes were brown, as compared with my own watery blue. This hurt my feelings, as the song contained the line "I'll never love blue eyes again." It seemed so final, a whole lifetime of being unloved by Fred. Once I cried, which was made worse by the fact that I couldn't explain to anyone what was wrong; and I had to undergo the humiliation of Fred's jocular concern and my sister's scorn, and the worse humiliation of being comforted by Betty in the kitchenette. It was a humiliation because it was obvious even to me that Betty didn't grasp things very well. "Don't pay any attention to *him*," she said, having guessed that my tears had something to do with Fred. But that was the one piece of advice I couldn't take.

Fred, like a cat, wouldn't go two steps out of his way for you really, as my mother said later. So it was unfair that everyone was in love with Fred, but no one, despite her kindness, was in love with Betty. It was Betty who always greeted us at the door, asked us in, and talked to us while Fred slouched on the couch reading the paper. She fed us cookies and milk shakes and let us lick out the bowls when she was baking. Betty was such a nice person; everyone said so, but no one would have called Fred exactly that. Fred, for instance, did not laugh much, and he only smiled when he was making rude remarks, mostly to my sister. "Stuffing your face, again?" he would say. "Hey, baggy-pants." Whereas Betty never said things like that, and she was always either smiling or laughing.

She laughed a lot when Fred called her Betty Grable, which he did at least once a day. I couldn't see why she laughed. It was supposed to be a compliment, I thought. Betty Grable was a famous movie star; there was a picture of her thumbtacked to the wall in Fred and Betty's outhouse. Both my sister and I preferred Fred and Betty's outhouse to our own. Theirs had curtains on the window, unlike ours, and it had a little wooden box and a matching wooden scoop for the lye. We only had a cardboard box and an old trowel.

Betty didn't really look like Betty Grable, who was blond and not as plump as our Betty. Still, they were both beautiful, I thought. I didn't realize until much later that the remark was cruel, for Betty Grable was renowned for her legs, whereas our Betty had legs that started at her waist and continued downward without a curve or a pause until they reached her feet. At the time they seemed like ordinary legs. Sitting in the kitchenette, I saw a lot of Betty's legs, for she wore halter tops and shorts, with her yellow apron over them. Somehow Betty could never get her legs to tan, despite the hours she spent crocheting in her wicker chair, the top part of her in the shade of the porch but her legs sticking out into the sun.

My father said that Betty had no sense of humor. I couldn't understand this at all. If you told her a joke she would always laugh, even if you got it mixed up.

My father also said that Betty had no sex appeal. This didn't seem to bother my mother in the least. "She's a very nice girl," she would answer complacently, or, "She has very nice coloring." My mother and Betty were soon collaborating on a scheme for making the preserving easier. Most people still had Victory Gardens, though the war was over, and the months of July and August were supposed to be spent putting up as many jars of fruit and vegetables as you could. My mother's garden was half-hearted, like most of her housekeeping efforts. It was a small patch beside the outhouse where squash vines rambled over a thicket of overgrown tomato plants and a few uneven lines of dwarfed carrots and beets. My mother's talent, we had heard her say, was for people. Betty and Fred didn't have a garden at all. Fred wouldn't have worked in it, and when I think of Betty now I realize that a garden would have been too uncontained for her. But she had Fred buy dozens of six-quart baskets of strawberries, peaches, beans, tomatoes , and Concord grapes on his trips into the city, and she persuaded my mother to give up on her own garden and join her in her mammoth canning sessions.

My mother's wood stove was unbearably hot for such an operation, and Betty's little electric range was too small, so Betty got "the boys," as she called Fred and my father, to set up the derelict woodstove that until then had been rusting behind Betty's outhouse. They put it in our backyard, and my mother and Betty would sit at our kitchen table, which had been carried outside, peeling, slicing, and talking, Betty with her round pincushion cheeks flushed redder than usual by the heat and my mother with an old bandana wrapped around her head, making her look like a gypsy. Behind them the canning kettles bubbled and steamed, and on one side of the table the growing ranks of Crown jars, inverted on layers of newspaper, cooled and sometimes leaked or cracked. My sister and I hung around the edges, not wanting to be obvious enough to be put to work, but coveting the empty six-quart baskets. We could use them in our hideout, we felt; we were never sure what for, but they fitted neatly into the orange crates.

I learned a lot about Fred during Betty's canning sessions: how he liked his eggs, what size socks he took (Betty was a knitter), how well he was doing at the office, what he refused to eat for dinner. Fred was a picky eater, Betty said joyfully. Betty had almost nothing else to talk about, and even my mother, veteran of many confidences, began to talk less and smoke more than usual when Betty was around. It was easier to listen to disasters than to Betty's inexhaustible and trivial cheer. I began to think that I might not want to be married to Fred after all. He unrolled from Betty's mouth like a long ribbon of soggy newspaper printed from end to end with nothing but the weather. Neither my sister nor I was interested in sock sizes, and Betty's random, unexciting details diminished Fred in our eyes. We began to spend less of our playtime at Fred and Betty's and more in our hideout, which was in a patch of scrubby oak on a vacant lot along the shore. There we played complicated games of Mandrake the Magician[4] and his faithful servant Lothar, with our dolls as easily hypnotized villains. My sister was always Mandrake. When we tired of this, we would put on our bathing suits and go wading along the shore, watching for freighters and throwing acorns into the river to see how quickly they would be carried away by the current.

It was on one of these wading expeditions that we met Nan. She lived ten lots down, in a white cottage with red trim. Unlike many of the other cottages, Nan's had a real dock, built out into the river and anchored around the posts with piles of rocks. She was sitting on this dock when we first saw her, chewing gum and flipping through a stack of airplane cards from Wings cigarettes. Everyone knew that only boys collected these. Her hair and her face were light brown, and she had a sleek plump sheen, like caramel pudding.

"What're you doing with *those*?" were my sister's first words. Nan only smiled.

That same afternoon Nan was allowed into our hideout, and after a cursory game of Mandrake, during which I was demoted to the lowly

---

4. *Mandrake the Magician:* once popular comic strip.

position of Narda, the two of them sat on our orange crates and exchanged what seemed to me to be languid and pointless comments.

"You ever go to the store?" Nan asked. We never did. Nan smiled some more. She was twelve; my sister was only eleven and three quarters.

"There's cute boys at the store," Nan said. She was wearing a peasant blouse with a frill and an elastic top that she could slide down over her shoulders if she wanted to. She stuck her airplane cards into her shorts pocket and we went to ask my mother if we could walk to the store. After that, my sister and Nan went there almost every afternoon.

The store was a mile and a half from our cottage, a hot walk along the shore past the fronts of other cottages where fat mothers basked in the sun and other, possibly hostile, children paddled in the water; past rowboats hauled up on the sand, along cement breakwaters, through patches of beach grass that cut your ankles if you ran through it and beach peas that were hard and bitter tasting. In some places we could smell the outhouses. Just before the store, there was an open space with poison ivy, which we had to wade around.

The store had no name. It was just "the store," the only store for the cottagers, since it was the only one they could walk to. I was allowed to go with my sister and Nan, or rather my mother insisted that I go. Although I hadn't said anything to her about it, she could sense my misery. It wasn't so much my sister's desertion that hurt, but her blithe unconsciousness of it. She was quite willing to play with me when Nan wasn't around.

Sometimes, when the sight of my sister and Nan conspiring twenty paces ahead of me made me too unhappy, I would double back and go to Fred and Betty's. There I would sit facing backward on one of Betty's kitchen chairs, my two hands rigid in the air, holding a skein of sky-blue wool while Betty wound it into balls. Or, under Betty's direction, I crocheted sweaty, uneven little pink and yellow dolls' dresses for the dolls my sister was, suddenly, too old to play with.

On better days I would make it as far as the store. It was not beautiful or even clean, but we were so used to wartime drabness and grime that we didn't notice. It was a two-story building of unpainted wood which had weathered gray. Parts of it were patched with tar paper, and it had colored metal signs nailed around the front screen door and windows: Coca-Cola, 7-Up, Salada Tea. Inside, it had the sugary, mournful smell of old general stores, a mixture of the cones for the ice-cream cones, the packages of Oreo cookies, the open boxes of jawbreakers and licorice whips that lined the counter, and that other smell, musky and sharp, part dry rot and part sweat. The bottles of pop were kept in a metal cooler with a heavy lid, filled with cold water and chunks of ice melted to the smoothness of the sand-scoured pieces of glass we sometimes found on the beach.

The owner of the store and his wife lived on the second floor, but we almost never saw them. The store was run by their two daughters, who took turns behind the counter. They were both dark and they both wore shorts and polka-dot halter tops, but one was friendly and the other one, the thinner, younger one, was not. She would take our pennies and ring them into the cash register without saying a word, staring over our heads out the front window with its dangling raisin-covered flypapers as if she were completely detached from the activity her hands were performing. She didn't dislike us; she just didn't see us. She wore her hair long and done in a sort of roll at the front, and her lipstick was purplish.

The first time we went to the store we found out why Nan collected airplane cards. There were two boys there, sitting on the gray, splintery front steps, their arms crossed over their knees. I had been told by my sister that the right thing to do with boys was to ignore them; otherwise they would pester you. But these boys knew Nan, and they spoke to her, not with the usual taunts but with respect.

"You got anything new?" one of them said.

Nan smiled, brushed back her hair, and wiggled her shoulders a little inside her peasant blouse. Then she slid her airplane cards slowly out of her shorts pocket and began riffling through them.

"You got any?" the other boy said to my sister. For once she was humbled. After that, she got my mother to switch brands and built up her own pack. I saw her in front of the mirror about a week later, practicing that tantalizing slide, the cards coming out of her pocket like a magician's snake.

When I went to the store I always had to bring back a loaf of wax-papered bread for my mother, and sometimes a package of Jiffy Pie Crust, if they had any. My sister never had to: she had already discovered the advantages of being unreliable. As payment, and, I'm sure, as compensation for my unhappiness, my mother gave me a penny a trip, and when I had saved five of these pennies I bought my first Popsicle. Our mother had always refused to buy them for us, although she permitted ice-cream cones. She said there was something about Popsicles that was bad for you, and as I sat on the front steps of the store, licking down to the wooden stick, I kept looking for this thing. I visualized it as a sort of core, like the white fingernail-shaped part in a kernel of corn, but I couldn't find anything.

My sister and Nan were sitting beside me on the front steps. There were no boys at the store that day, so they had nothing else to do. It was even hotter than usual, and airless; there was a shimmer over the river, and the freighters wavered as they passed through it. My Popsicle was melting almost before I could eat it. I had given my sister half of it, which she had taken without the gratitude I had hoped for. She was sharing it with Nan.

Fred came around the corner of the building and headed toward the front door. This was no surprise, as we had seen him at the store several times before.

"Hi, beautiful," he said to my sister. We moved our rumps along the step to let him in the door.

After quite a long time he came out, carrying a loaf of bread. He asked us if we wanted a lift with him in his car: he was just coming back from the city, he said. Of course we said yes. There was nothing unusual about any of this, except that the daughter, the thinner, purple one, stepped outside the door and stood on the steps as we were driving off. She folded her arms across her chest in that slump-shouldered pose of women idling in doorways. She wasn't smiling. I thought she had come out to watch the Canada Steamship Lines freighter that was going past, but then I saw that she was staring at Fred. She looked as if she wanted to kill him.

Fred didn't seem to notice. He sang all the way home. "Katie, oh, beautiful Katie," he sang, winking at my sister, whom he sometimes called Katie since her name was Catherine. He had the windows open, and dust from the rutted gravel road poured over us, whitening our eyebrows and turning Fred's hair gray. At every jolt my sister and Nan screamed gleefully, and after a while I forgot my feelings of exclusion and screamed too.

It seemed as if we had lived in the cottage for a long time, though it was only summer. By August I could hardly remember the apartment in Ottawa and the man who used to beat up his wife. That had happened in a remote life; and, despite the sunshine, the water, the open space, a happier one. Before, our frequent moves and the insecurities of new schools had forced my sister to value me: I was four years younger, but I was loyal and always there. Now those years were a canyon between us, an empty stretch like a beach along which I could see her disappearing ahead of me. I longed to be just like her, but I could no longer tell what she was like.

In the third week of August the leaves started to turn, not all at once, just a single red one here and there, like a warning. That meant it would soon be time for school and another move. We didn't even know where we would be moving to this time, and when Nan asked us what school we went to, we were evasive.

"I've been to eight different schools," my sister said proudly. Because I was so much younger, I had only been to two. Nan, who had been to the same one all her life, slipped the edge of her peasant blouse over her shoulders and down to her elbows to show us that her breasts were growing. The rings around her nipples had softened and started to puff out; otherwise she was as flat as my sister.

"So what," said my sister, rolling up her jersey. This was a competition I couldn't be part of. It was about change, and, increasingly, change frightened me. I walked back along the beach to Betty's house, where my latest piece of grubby crocheting was waiting for me and where everything was always the same.

I knocked on the screen door and opened it. I meant to say, "Can I come in?" the way we always did, but I didn't say it. Betty was sitting by herself at the iron table of the breakfast nook. She had on her shorts and a striped sailor top, navy blue and white with a little anchor pin, and the apron with the yellow chickens coming out of their eggs. For once she wasn't doing anything, and there was no cup of coffee in front of her. Her face was white and uncomprehending, as if someone had just hit her for no reason.

She saw me, but she didn't smile or ask me in. "What am I going to do?" she said.

I looked around the kitchen. Everything was in its place: the percolator gleamed from the stove, the glass bird was teetering slowly down, there were no broken dishes, no water on the floor. What had happened?

"Are you sick?" I said.

"There's nothing I can do," Betty said.

She looked so strange that I was frightened. I ran out of the kitchen and across the hillocky grass to get to my mother, who always knew what should be done.

"There's something wrong with Betty," I said.

My mother was mixing something in a bowl. She rubbed her hands together to get the dough off, then wiped them on her apron. She didn't look surprised or ask me what it was. "You stay here," she said. She picked up her package of cigarettes and went out the door.

That evening we had to go to bed early because my mother wanted to talk to my father. We listened, of course; it was easy through the Ten-Test walls.

"I saw it coming," my mother said. "A mile away."

"Who is it?" my father said.

"She doesn't know," said my mother. "Some girl from town."

"Betty's a fool," my father said. "She always was." Later, when husbands and wives leaving each other became more common, he often said this, but no matter which one had left it was always the woman he called the fool. His highest compliment to my mother was that she was no fool.

"That may be," said my mother. "But you'd never want to meet a nicer girl. He was her whole life."

My sister and I whispered together. My sister's theory was that Fred had run away from Betty with another woman. I couldn't believe this; I had never heard of such a thing happening. I was so upset I couldn't sleep, and for a long time after that I was anxious whenever my father was away overnight, as he frequently was. What if he never came back?

We didn't see Betty after that. We knew she was in her cottage, because every day my mother carried over samples of her tough and lumpy baking, almost as if someone had died. But we were given strict orders to stay away, and not to go peering in the windows as our mother must have known we longed to do. "She's having a nervous breakdown," our mother said, which for me called up an image of Betty lying disjointed on the floor like a car at the garage.

We didn't even see her on the day we got into my father's second-hand Studebaker, the back seat packed to the window tops with only a little oblong space for me to crouch in, and drove out to the main highway to begin the six-hundred-mile journey south to Toronto. My father had changed jobs again; he was now in building materials, and he was sure, since the country was having a boom, that this was finally the right change. We spent September and part of October in a motel while my father looked for a house. I had my eighth birthday and my sister turned twelve. I almost forgot about Betty.

But a month after I had turned twelve myself, Betty was suddenly there one night for dinner. We had people for dinner a lot more than we used to, and sometimes the dinners were so important that my sister and I ate first. My sister didn't care, as she had boyfriends at that time. I was still in public school and had to wear lisle stockings instead of the seamed nylons my sister was permitted. Also, I had braces. My sister had had braces at that age too, but she had somehow managed to make them seem rakish and daring, so that I longed for a mouthful of flashing silver teeth like hers. But she no longer had them, and my own mouth in its shackles felt clumsy and muffled.

"You remember Betty," my mother said.

"Elizabeth," Betty said.

"Oh, yes, of course," said my mother.

Betty had changed a lot. Before, she had been a little plump; now she was buxom. Her cheeks were as round and florid as two tomatoes, and I thought she was using too much rouge until I saw that the red was caused by masses of tiny veins under her skin. She was wearing a long black pleated skirt, a white short-sleeved angora sweater with a string of black beads, and open-toed black velvet pumps with high heels. She smelled strongly of lily of the valley. She had a job, my mother told my father later, a very good job. She was an executive secretary and now called herself Miss instead of Mrs.

"She's doing very well," my mother said, "considering what happened. She's pulled herself together."

"I hope you don't start inviting her to dinner all the time," said my father, who still found Betty irritating in spite of her new look. She laughed more than ever now and crossed her legs frequently.

"I feel I'm the only real friend she has," said my mother. She didn't say Betty was the only real friend she had, though when my father said "your friend" everyone knew who he meant. My mother had a lot of friends, and her talent for wise listening was now a business asset for my father.

"She says she'll never marry again," said my mother.

"She's a fool," my father said.

"If I ever saw anyone cut out for marriage, it was her," said my mother. This remark increased my anxiety about my own future. If all Betty's accomplishments had not been enough for Fred, what hope was there for me? I did not have my sister's natural flair, but I had thought there would be some tricks I could learn, dutifully, painstakingly. We were taking home economics at school and the teacher kept saying that the way to a man's heart was through his stomach. I knew this wasn't true—my mother was still a slapdash cook, and when she gave the best dinners she had a woman in to help—but I labored over my blanc-mange and Harvard beets as if I believed it.

My mother started inviting Betty to dinner with men who were not married. Betty smiled and laughed and several men seemed interested, but nothing came of it.

"After the way she was hurt, I'm not surprised," my mother said. I was now old enough to be told things, and besides, my sister was never around. "I heard it was a secretary at his company he ran off with. They even got married, after the divorce." There was something else about Betty, she told me, although I must never mention it, as Betty found it very distressing. Fred's brother, who was a dentist, had killed his wife because he got involved—my mother said "involved" richly, as if it were a kind of dessert—with his dental technician. He had put his wife into the car and ran a tube in from the exhaust pipe, and then tried to pretend it was suicide. The police had found out, though, and he was in jail.

This made Betty much more interesting in my eyes. It was in Fred's blood, then, this tendency toward involvement. In fact, it could just as easily have been Betty herself who had been murdered. I now came to see Betty's laugh as the mask of a stricken and martyred[5] woman. She was not just a wife who had been deserted. Even I could see that this was not a tragic position, it was a ridiculous and humiliating one. She was much more than that: she was a woman who had narrowly escaped death. That Betty herself saw it this way I soon had no doubt. There was something smug and even pious about the way she kept mother's single men at a polite distance, something faintly nunlike. A lurid aura of sacrificial blood surrounded her. Betty had been there, she had passed through it, she had come out alive, and now she was dedicating herself to, well, to something else.

But it was hard for me to sustain this version of Betty for long. My mother soon ran out of single men, and Betty, when she came to dinner, came alone. She talked as incessantly about the details surrounding the other women at her office as she had about Fred. We soon knew how they all took their coffee, which ones lived with their mothers, where they had their hair done, and what their apartments looked like. Betty herself had a darling apartment on Avenue Road, and she had redone it all herself and even made the slipcovers. Betty was as devoted to her boss as she had once been to Fred. She did all his Christmas shopping, and each year we heard what he had given to his employees, what to his wife and children, and what each item had cost. Betty seemed, in a way, quite happy.

We saw a lot of Betty around Christmas; my mother said she felt sorry for her because she had no family. Betty was in the habit of giving us Christmas presents that made it obvious she thought we were younger than we were. She favored Parchesi sets and angora mittens a size too small. I lost interest in her. Even her unending cheerfulness came to seem like a perversion, or a defect almost like idiocy. I was fifteen now and in the throes of adolescent depression. My sister was away at Queen's; sometimes she gave me clothes she no longer wanted. She was not exactly beautiful—both her eyes and her mouth were too large—but everyone called her vivacious. They called me nice. My braces had come off, and it didn't seem to make any difference. What right had Betty

---

5. *martyred* (mär′ tərd): suffering great pain.

to be cheerful? When she came to dinner, I excused myself early and went to my room.

One afternoon, in the spring of grade eleven, I came home from school to find my mother sitting at the dining-room table. She was crying, which was so rare that my immediate fear was that something had happened to my father. I didn't think he had left her; that particular anxiety was past. But perhaps he had been killed in a car crash.

"Mum, what is it?" I said.

"Bring me a glass of water," she said. She drank some of it and pushed back her hair. "I'm all right now," she said. "I just had a call from Betty. It was very upsetting; she said horrible things to me."

"Why?" I said. "What did you do?"

"She accused me of . . . horrible things." My mother swabbed at her eyes. "She was screaming. I've never heard Betty scream in my life before. After all that time I spent with her. She said she never wanted to speak to me again. Where would she get such an idea?"

"What idea?" I said. I was just as mystified as my mother was. My mother was a bad cook, but she was a good woman. I could not imagine her doing anything that would make anyone want to scream at her.

My mother held back slightly. "Things about Fred," she said. "She must be crazy. I hadn't seen her for a couple of months, and then suddenly, just like that."

"There must be something wrong with her," my father said at dinner that night. Of course he was right. Betty had an undetected brain tumor, which was discovered when her strange behavior was noticed at the office. She died in the hospital two months later, but my mother didn't hear about it till afterward. She was contrite; she felt she should have visited her friend in the hospital, despite the abusive phone call.

"I ought to have known it was something like that," she said. "Personality change, that's one of the clues." In the course of her listening, my mother had picked up a great deal of information about terminal illnesses.

But for me, this explanation wasn't good enough. For years after that, Betty followed me around, waiting for me to finish her off in some way more satisfactory to both of us. When I first heard about her death I felt doomed. This, then, was the punishment for being devoted and obliging, this was what happened to girls such as (I felt) myself. When I opened the high school yearbook and my own face, in page-boy haircut and tentative, appeasing smile, stared back at me, it was Betty's eyes I superimposed on mine. She had been kind to me when I was a child, and with the callousness of children toward those who are kind but not enchanting I had preferred Fred. In my future I saw myself being abandoned by a succession of Freds who were running down the beach after a crowd of vivacious girls, all of whom looked remarkably like my sister. As for Betty's final screams of hatred and rage, they were screams of protest against the unfairness of life. That anger, I knew, was my own, the dark side of that terrible and deforming niceness that had marked Betty like the aftermath of some crippling disease.

People change, though, especially after they are dead. As I passed beyond the age of melodrama I came to see that if I did not want to be Betty, I would have to be someone else. Furthermore, I was already quite different from Betty. In a way, she had absolved me from making the demanded choices by having made them so thoroughly herself. People stopped calling me a nice girl and started calling me a clever one, and after a while I enjoyed this. Betty herself, baking oatmeal cookies in the ephemeral sunlight of fifteen years before, slid back into three dimensions. She was an ordinary woman who died too young of an incurable disease. Was that it, was that all?

From time to time I would like to have Betty back, if only for an hour's conversation. I would like her to forgive me for my rejection of her angora mittens, for my secret betrayals of her, for my adolescent contempt. I would like to show her this story I have told about her and ask her if any of it is true. But I can think of nothing I want to ask her that I could phrase in a way that she would care to understand. She would only laugh in her accepting, uncomprehending way and offer me something, a chocolate brownie, a ball of wool.

Fred, on the other hand, no longer intrigues me. The Freds of this world make themselves explicit by what they do and choose. It is the Bettys that are mysterious.

Responding to the Story

We learn every day, not just from textbooks in school, but from what is around us. This story is about a lot of learning that the narrator did over several years of her adolescence; she's still thinking about some of those events and people as she writes the story some time later.

1. Write a statement explaining what the narrator learned. Don't limit yourself to the encounters with Betty; the narrator was learning from other experiences and other people, too.

2. Explain what you think the author means by the last paragraph.

Exploring the Author's Craft

In this story we come to know a number of people, each of whom stands out as an individual. Pick any three persons from the story and compile a list of the details that characterize each person. Include what other characters say about them as well as details about their physical appearance and actions.

How does the author make even minor characters memorable?

Writing Workshop

1. Tell about the learning you have done outside of school, maybe from a part-time job you have had or from the people around you. In essence you will be telling about yourself "out in the world." You may write this in a narrative essay or as fiction, creating a character to represent you.

2. Betty seems a very ordinary person; yet she is the title character of the story. Discuss Betty in a short paper. Consider the following questions before you write: What did her topics of conversation reveal about her? Did she have insight into herself? Why did Fred marry her? Why did she marry Fred? What were her purposes in life? Did she deserve pity? You will have to make some inferences based on what the author reveals about her.

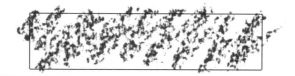

On the Late Bus

Susan Engberg

Born Johanna Susan Herr in 1940 in Dubuque, Iowa, Susan Engberg married architect Charles Engberg in 1963. They have two children and live in Milwaukee.

She graduated from Lawrence University in Appleton, Wisconsin, and did graduate study at the University of Iowa from 1972 to 1974. She worked in the Department of Publications at the Metropolitan Museum of Modern Art, as a fiction reader for the Iowa Review, *and was a teacher at the Iowa Writer's Workshop in 1978.*

In 1983 she received a fiction award from the Society of Midland Authors and the Banta Award from the Wisconsin Library Association. In 1987 she received a Creative Writing Fellowship from the National Endowment for the Arts.

Engberg has had short stories included in Prize Stories: the O. Henry Awards *in 1969, 1977, and 1978 and in* Pushcart Prize VI: Best of the Small Presses, *1982. Her three collections of stories are* Pastorale *(1982),* A Stay by the River *(1985), and* Sarah's Laughter and Other Stories *(1991). Reviewer Russell Banks wrote of Engberg's first collection: ''[These] stories are so good they could change your life.''*

O ther people always stirred things up. Here was a fat man asking in a wheezy voice if the seat was taken, sweetheart, when Alison had barely gotten the sound of her stepmother's *Sorry it didn't work out* simmered down in her head, and so she had to cram her duffle under her feet on the filthy bus floor and allow this monstrous body to stuff itself down next to her, so close, just inches away. There was something wrong with the way buses were made. His breaths eddied around her.

She heard him sucking, on a hard candy maybe. She was empty herself, no food. Going far? he wanted to know. What was *far*? Not speaking, she tilted her face toward the window and pressed her knees together, angled away from him. At least she had the window.

She was fifteen years old and nobody's sweetheart. The window was what she'd had for the last hour, and she'd used it to put golden aspens and red maples and dark green pines in the place of the people in her head, the ones who stirred things up the most—a father and stepmother in the place she was going from and a mother and her boyfriend in the place she was going toward. Sorry it didn't work out, said the woman in one place. Who do you think you are! said her mother, the one who was supposed to know who her own daughter was, in the other place. Don't listen too much to your mother, said her father, she's what you might called disturbed. Cool it, said her mother's boyfriend. The evening light in the aspens was like a cloud of gold. Last night in bed—actually, a mattress on the floor of her father's small house—she had heard geese flying high overhead, the same direction her bus was going now, south, but for her that didn't make much difference because she was still riding straight into winter. The geese had sounded like geese and also like someone rubbing on window glass, far away.

The man had stopped sucking and was now peeling off the top of a package of gum. His arm poked out in front of her, too close, as he offered her a piece. She shook her head, no. She felt light-headed with hunger. Don't talk much, do you? said the man. He was unspeakable. She ducked her face. Fat people were disgusting to start with, and then when they did and said disgusting things, it could make you gag to be around them. She should vomit in his lap—that would cause a stir. She could be just as good a troublemaker as anyone else.

But the trouble was, she didn't have anything to throw up. She had refused her stepmother's cold cereal this morning and her sandwiches this noon—she wasn't going to take any more food from a woman who didn't even want her around. Finicky, she had been called, so all right finicky was what she was really, really going to be. Her stepmother had two new children, one a baby guzzling breast milk. Every time Alison turned around out came the bare breast again and there was another baldheaded half-brother getting exactly what he wanted and slurping while he was about it, too. The expression on her father's face as he watched was so silly it made Alison want to put a cooking pot or a grocery bag down over his head. The other kid always wanted her to get down on the floor and play with him, and the first few visits she had, until she finally figured out that this was just what her father and her stepmother wanted, to get her down on the floor and out of the way, and so this time she stayed stubbornly on their level, at the table, on the couch, her arms folded over her chest. Anyway, it was impossible for her to play like a kid, getting interested in whether or not the blocks were going to fall over, making the sounds of a truck—there was no way she was ever going to have that again.

What she did have was her eyes, good eyes, better than twenty-twenty, the doctor said. She wished she could go back to that doctor once a week and have him look at her and tell her about her eyes. Right now she could see so far into the trees that she could probably be a wild animal if she needed to. She could get off the bus and streak into the woods as her eyes were doing and never have to go back to one house or the other. Wild animal mothers sometimes took care of human babies. But she was too old for that. Anyway, what wild animal mother would want a child like her, an upright stick of a girl with ringworm on her left thigh and a coil of black feeling in her heart? She'd have to learn to *be* the wild animal, tough and wily, all on her own. Trouble was, in the woods she'd run out of that vile ointment she had to rub on the raised, scaly circle of the worm and then pretty soon her whole body would become one gigantic parasite. She'd be eaten up. Then she'd start infecting the whole forest. The other animals would run her out.

She caused trouble no matter where she was, even when she was absolutely still, her arms over her chest, just existing. Every time she came into a room where there were other people, in one house or the other, she could tell that she was stirring things up. No one knew what to do with her, even when she was doing nothing but breathing. One day her mother had fallen and torn a tendon in her ankle while Alison was walking right beside her, and just before her mother fell Alison had seen the split in the sidewalk—the concrete square was like a hardened country, she had thought swiftly, with something wrong in its middle—probably in time to warn her mother, clicking along beside her in her stupid high heels, and probably her mother knew that—that her daughter was to blame for the cast and the crutches and the difficulties every day in getting to work and making her way home and trying to stand up to cook dinner. Alison tried to help, but her mother didn't like her messing up the kitchen. Then, when she wandered into the living room to sit with her mother's boyfriend, her mother shouted at her for watching television when there was so much to be done. She was sent up to her father's so that at least the house would be quiet for the weekend.

At her father's she caused more trouble than she ever had before. Anyone could see that with the new baby there wasn't room for her now. This time they had put down a mattress for her behind a tacked-up sheet at the end of the bedroom hallway, under a tiny window. Well, at least she had had the window and heard the far-away, matter-of-fact music of the geese and seen the full moon, with its gigantic eyes looking back at her. *Sorry it didn't work out*. What did *it* mean? There was something wrong with the way sentences were put together.

It's going to get dark now, said the fat man, leaning toward her slightly and peering out the glass. Gets dark early now.

Oh boy, what a genius this guy was, a regular Sherlock Holmes. That's what her stepfather had called her the other day when she had said that college would probably cost too much. You're a regular Sherlock Holmes, Alison.

You goin' home or goin' away from home? asked the fat man.

Neither one, she couldn't stop herself from saying. Oh god, you open your mouth once and then there's no telling what will rush back to you.

Neither one? he said, breathing hard. Now that's a situation peculiar like mine. Me, I'm goin' from one daughter to t'other. Neither one wants their old pa. I bet you wouldn't do that to your old pa, would you? You're a nice, smooth-like girl. My girls, they've got pricklers all over them. He shook his head sadly. He sounded as if he talked to himself a lot.

What a creep! She wished she could give him her ringworm, that itchy, creeping circle that made her feel so dirty. She'd have to slide down her jeans and press her palm on the discolored patch and then find someplace to transfer it to him when he wasn't paying attention. She'd show him how smooth she was!

Her teachers used to think she was a good girl, before she started crossing her arms and not saying anything. She knew most of the answers, but what good did it do anymore to let people hear her? Besides, knowing an answer and keeping it to herself gave her a kind of invisible arrow that she could send out through her eyes toward the teacher, or anybody else she needed power against. The secret to being able to send the arrow, she was discovering, was not saying anything. She cast a sideways glance at the fat man, just with her eyes, and saw that his chin was lowered to his chest. Mr. No-neck. She'd save her arrow for when she really needed it.

Outside there were fewer pine trees, more coppery oaks, dying colors. And there were more signs of people and the messes they made. When she got back to the city, she'd be drinking softened water again and sleeping in the room right next to the giant legs of the electrical transformer tower. The water up north at her father's tasted like rocks.

Her mother's boyfriend called the ice cubes in his whiskey glass rocks. He'd probably be the one to meet her bus, practically at midnight, and he'd be mad because her father hadn't come out of the woods with his chain saw in time to get her on the early bus. Her mother would be at home with her foot up, or maybe already asleep. The cast went nearly to her knee, and her toes sticking out of it were discolored.

The fall, the bad injury, the cast, the days and nights even more messed up than before—everything had happened so fast. One minute Alison had been walking beside her mother, being scolded and criticized by her and at the same time sort of daydreaming about the broken sidewalk just ahead, and the next minute her mother was down on the ground, crying, Oh, my foot, my foot, and then every minute in their lives got more difficult. Like that, just like that mothers and fathers divorced—one day in the same house, the next day not. Earthquake, crack down the middle, fast.

And fast was how her best friend Lois had died last year, inside her white cast, from a greenstick fracture. Well, of course it hurts, you've broken it, just let it heal now, her parents kept saying, but Lois couldn't stop talking about how much her arm hurt. They took her back to the hospital too late. Alison had sat stiffly on the couch at her own house and heard her mother saying the words *gangrene* and *shock*. In the coffin at the funeral home Lois's honey-colored hair had been clipped back neatly with two barrettes, just the way she had always worn it to school. Don't get hysterical now, her mother had whispered behind her, but Alison wasn't about to let anything out her own lips. It was only in her room, with the door locked, that she would take out Lois's picture, prop it on the stem of her desk light, and let her own face crack open as she looked and looked at the smooth hair, the serene heavy brows, the sweet mouth that were now flat underground, facing up beneath the lid of the coffin. Fast, unfair—what could possibly be said? Lois was the last person she had laughed with, the real kind of laughter.

The trouble was with the people who were supposed to be parents. There was something so wrong about the parents that you couldn't even talk about it. Fast was how they wanted you out of their house, before their lives were worn out, before they had to admit the mistake they had made in having you. She had one other friend, Joann, who had been given exactly three more years to live at home. Graduation, and she had to be out the door, out, and that meant no more money, no food, no bed, no nothing, so she was supposed to start thinking now about what she could do ahead. Her mother had a new baby, too, and a new husband. Joann told Alison that having a high-school-age daughter around must remind her mother of how old she was. I could really give her gray hair if I wanted to, said Joann, but she's not worth it, I'm saving my energy.

The fat man was right: it was getting nearly dark. She should say to him, Hey, genius, look at that, you were right, it got dark. Pretty soon there wouldn't be much at all to see out the window. A wild animal at night, unless it was the night kind, crawled into its home with a full belly and went to sleep until daylight. Human beings didn't live like that. They traveled all night if they wanted to. They played around with what was normal. They turned everything inside out and upside down, they broke things in half, in thousands of pieces.

Close beside her the fat man took out a soiled handkerchief and blew his nose, loud enough to blow up the bus. Honk, blast. Alison closed her eyes. She felt faint with disgust, or was it just hunger? Her mouth tasted awful. She had never gone a whole day without a single thing to eat. Suddenly she thought, I don't know anything about life, I don't know any of the answers.

Are you one tired girl? The man's voice made her open her eyes. He didn't even wait for an answer—he had caught on to her fast—he just kept on talking. I'll tell you, I'm one tired old man. I don't have much left, and that's the truth. I don't know how it got to be this way, but it sure has.

There was that *it* again! Words sounded so queer to her tonight. Everything seemed put together in the strangest way, without enough reason. Maybe that's what happened to your head when you didn't eat. She thought about her duffle bag under the seat, no food in it, just her flannel pajamas and some extra jeans and her American history book. She saw that the fat man's hands were shaking a little as he clumsily folded his handkerchief and stuffed it back in the jacket of his cheap-looking suit coat. But he couldn't be shaking from hunger—oh no, he was too fat to be hungry.

Most people around the world didn't have much, she knew that now. But for as long as she could remember her father had talked about wanting to be rich, the head of a big family—a sprawl of horses, dogs, buildings, pastures, children. Even these days he had schemes for getting the life he wanted, and he usually talked about someone or other who was going to help him. What he actually had now was a small house near a small woodlot, a chain saw, a stack of firewood, a job in a cannery, and a different family. If her father had been the one to offer her the sandwich at lunch, she might have taken it. But he hadn't even been in the house most of the day—he had been out in the lot making his saw scream through wood.

There was an acid-tasting heat in her throat. She wasn't going to cry! Not in this repulsive place!

I'd say we're going to have ourselves another moon tonight, like last night, said the man.

Well, what did he expect! That's what she could say to him—Hey, genius, what did you expect, it's like twenty-four hours later than the moon last night.

Then he leaned slightly toward her to peer out the window, and she was forced to see the side of his creased face, his jowls, his whiskers, his nose hair, his sad, red-rimmed, drooping eyes. He was a lot older than she had thought at first. Yes sir, it can be real pretty when it comes up like that, he said, wheezing, pursing his lips. For a while I thought maybe those clouds would keep it from us.

That's what he had meant, clouds. She hadn't understood him. She was sorry that she hadn't understood him. She looked as he pointed. The orange moon had just cleared the horizon. She didn't think she had ever seen it so close and so big. Last night she had had the moon whole, and tonight right here she had it again, even better. And so had this old man beside her, the one whose daughters didn't like him anymore. What could he have done to them? she wondered. Would she ever be like that some day—not wanting her father to visit? And where was this place she was going to live in, when she was old enough to have a father visiting her? And what was the way she was going to live, how was she going to be?

This tells me it's time to eat, said the man. He brought to his lap the vinyl bag that had been wedged between his feet. Mind if I do? he asked as he flipped on the little light over their seats. Now what do we have here? Well, ha, I ought to know, I packed it myself. Peanut butter and more peanut butter. Belle—she's the one daughter—didn't have much else to pick from. I would've liked a turkey sandwich, I could get my teeth into that. Now, what do you like, little miss? Are you going to help me eat these peanut butter sandwiches? I've got four. I thought, well, even if that's all she's got, I'd better take plenty. I learned a long time ago not to pass up a meal.

He lowered the bag to the floor, balancing the wrapped pile of sandwiches on his lap. Now, he said, do you want number one, two, three, or four?

None, she was going to say, I'm finicky, see, I don't eat much, though she would restrain herself from adding that she was especially finicky about whom she took food *from*, but at that very moment she was aghast to see her own hand snaking out like an animal's to grasp the top square package. Thank you, her voice said. It was what he had said about getting his teeth into a turkey sandwich that had gotten her own mouth so crazy for anything to put in it, she didn't care what kind of bread, or what was between it. And her stomach had grown hands that were grabbing and clawing for something to fill them.

That's better, said the man. It wouldn't do any good to have me sitting here eating in front of you. Though I've done that plenty, I'll have to say. Oh, he sighed as he bit into his own bread. It's not too bad. It'll do. You can turn that light off now, honey. You don't have to see to fill your mouth with what you've already got in your hands. Isn't that so? Oh, lordy, I always feel better when I'm eating.

She turned out the light and unwrapped her own sandwich. There was moonlight on her hands. She bit in. She had the moon to look at while she chewed, the watchful moon. Last night, tonight, this feeling of being seen was something new. She had a new secret, the strength of the moon, looking at her.

I'm not what you might think I am, said the old grandfather beside her. I've just been through some hard times. She turned and nodded at him.

This business about trouble, she thought. Everybody caused trouble or had troubles. And everyone lived off other people, in one way or another. She went back to chewing and staring at the cavernous eyes of the moon. There was something she was trying to get right in her head, a thought that had just appeared out of nowhere at the moment she had first bitten into the sandwich, something else about trouble, people stirring things up. Here it came again, from she didn't know where: if people could turn on the trouble, they could make other things happen, too, besides trouble. Was that what she had thought? Was that what could be called an idea of her own?

Responding to the Story

1. Explain how the life situation of the girl in this story has contributed to her mood. Be specific.

2. Although the girl resents the man who is with her on the bus, how are their life situations similar?

3. Is the ending of the story optimistic or pessimistic? Explain.

4. Why do you think the author ends the story stressing the girl's having "an idea of her own"? Explain your answer.

Exploring the Author's Craft

How does the moon function as a symbol here? Trace its use in the story.

Writing Workshop

"Other people always stirred things up." In this story we learn about a number of people, all of whom have "stirred things up" in the girl's life. In a short sketch of about 750 words, create a character and show his or her life being influenced by one person who "stirs things up." Show incidents that reveal the stirring up; don't just summarize someone's actions.

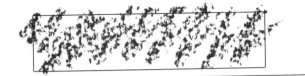

A Walk to the Jetty

Jamaica Kincaid

Jamaica Kincaid won the Morton Dauwen Zabel Award from the American Academy and Institute of Arts and Letters for her story collection At the Bottom of the River *published in 1983.* Annie John, *also a collection of stories, was published in 1985. Both collections were about life on the island of Antigua where Kincaid was born in 1949.*

She emigrated to the U.S. and married Allen Shawn, and they have a daughter. She lives in New York City and became a staff writer for the New Yorker *in 1976. A third book,* A Small Place, *was published in 1988 and is about Antigua, its colonial history, and the aftermath of that history.*

"My name is Annie John." These were the first words that came into my mind as I woke up on the morning of the last day I spent in Antigua,[1] and they stayed there, lined up one behind the other, marching up and down, for I don't know how long. At noon on that day, a ship on which I was to be a passenger would sail to Barbados,[2] and there I would board another ship, which would sail to England, where I would study to become a nurse. My name was the last thing I saw the night before, just as I was falling asleep; it was written in big, black letters all over my trunk, sometimes followed by my address in Antigua, sometimes followed by my address as it would be in England. I did not want to go to England, I did not want to be a nurse, but I would have

---

1. *Antigua:* (an tē′ gwa): island in the West Indies, a chain of islands between Florida and South America.
2. *Barbados:* (bär bā′ doz): island in the West Indies.

chosen going off to live in a cavern and keeping house for seven unruly men rather than go on with my life as it stood. I never wanted to lie in this bed again, my legs hanging out way past the foot of it, tossing and turning on my mattress, with its cotton stuffing all lumped just where it wasn't a good place to be lumped. I never wanted to lie in my bed again and hear Mr. Ephraim driving his sheep to pasture—a signal to my mother that she should get up to prepare my father's and my bath and breakfast. I never wanted to lie in bed and hear her get dressed, washing her face, brushing her teeth, and gargling. I especially never wanted to lie in my bed and hear my mother gargling again.

Lying there in the half-dark of my room, I could see my shelf, with my books—some of them prizes I had won in school, some of them gifts from my mother—and with photographs of people I was supposed to love forever no matter what, and with my old thermos, which was given to me for my eighth birthday, and some shells I had gathered at different times I spent at the sea. In one corner stood my washstand and its beautiful basin of white enamel with blooming red hibiscus painted at the bottom and an urn that matched. In another corner were my old school shoes and my Sunday shoes. In still another corner, a bureau held my old clothes. I knew everything in this room, inside out and outside in. I had lived in this room for thirteen of my seventeen years. I could see in my mind's eye even the day my father was adding it onto the rest of the house. Everywhere I looked stood something that had meant a lot to me, that had given me pleasure at some point, or could remind me of a time that was a happy time. But as I was lying there my heart could have burst open with joy at the thought of never having to see any of it again.

If someone had asked me for a little summing up of my life at that moment as I lay in bed, I would have said, "My name is Annie John. I was born on the fifteenth of September, seventeen years ago, at Holberton Hospital, at five o'clock in the morning. At the time I was born, the moon was going down at one end of the sky and the sun was coming up at the other. My mother's name is Annie also. My father's name is Alexander, and he is thirty-five years older than my mother. Two of his children are four and six years older than she is. Looking at how sickly he has become and looking at the way my mother now has to run up and down for him, gathering the herbs and barks that he boils in water, which he drinks instead of the medicine the doctor has ordered for him, I plan not only never to marry an old man but certainly never to marry at all. The house we live in my father built with his own hands. The bed I am lying in my father built with his own hands. If I get up and sit on a chair, it is a chair my father built with his own hands. When my mother uses a large wooden spoon to stir the porridge we sometimes eat as part of our breakfast, it will be a spoon that my father has carved with his own hands. The sheets on my bed my mother made with her own hands. The curtains hanging at my window my mother made with her own hands. The nightie I am wearing, with scalloped neck and hem and sleeves, my mother made with her own hands. When I look at things in a certain way, I suppose I should say that the two of them made me with their own hands. For most of my life, when the three of us went anywhere together I stood between the two of them or sat between the two of them. But then I got too big, and there I was, shoulder to shoulder with them more or less, and it became not very comfortable to walk down the street together. And so now there they are together and here I am apart. I don't see them now the way I used to, and I don't love them now the way I used to. The bitter thing about it is that they are just the same and it is I who have changed, so all the things I used to be and all the things I used to feel are as false as the teeth in my father's head. Why, I wonder, didn't I see the hypocrite in my mother when, over the years, she said that she loved me and could hardly live without me, while at the same time proposing and arranging separation after separation, including this one, which, unbeknownst to her, *I* have arranged to be permanent? So now I, too, have hypocrisy, and breasts (small ones), and hair growing in the appropriate places, and sharp eyes, and I have made a vow never to be fooled again."

Lying in my bed for the last time, I thought, This is what I add up to. At that, I felt as if someone had placed me in a hole and was forcing me first down and then up against the pressure of gravity. I shook myself and prepared to get up. I said to myself, "I am getting up out of this bed for the last time." Everything I would do that morning until I got on the ship that would take me to England I would be doing for the last time, for I had made up my mind that, come what may, the road for me now went only in one direction: away from my home, away from my mother, away from my father, away from the everlasting blue sky, away from the everlasting hot sun, away from people who said to me, "This happened during the time your mother was carrying you." If I had been asked to put into words why I felt this way, if I had been given years to reflect and come up with the words of why I felt this way, I would not have been able to come up with so much as the letter "A." I only knew that I felt the way I did, and that this feeling was the strongest thing in my life.

The Anglican church bell struck seven. My father had already bathed and dressed and was in his workshop puttering around. As if the day of my leaving were something to celebrate, they were treating it as a holiday, and nothing in the usual way would take place. My father would not go to work at all. When I got up, my mother greeted me with a big, bright "Good morning"—so big and bright that I shrank before it. I bathed quickly in some warm bark water that my mother had prepared for me. I put on my underclothes—all of them white and all of them smelling funny. Along with my earrings, my neck chain, and my bracelets, all made of gold from British Guiana,[3] my underclothes had been sent to my mother's obeah woman[4], and whatever she had done to my jewelry and underclothes would help protect me from evil spirits and every kind of misfortune. The things I never wanted to see or hear or do again now made up at least three weeks' worth of grocery lists. I placed a mark against obeah women, jewelry, and white underclothes. Over my underclothes, I put on an around-the-yard dress of my mother's. The clothes I would wear for my voyage were a dark-blue pleated skirt and a blue-and-white checked blouse (the blue in the blouse matched exactly the blue of my skirt) with a large sailor collar and with a tie made from the same material as the skirt—a blouse that came down a long way past my waist, over my skirt. They were lying on a chair, freshly ironed by my mother. Putting on my clothes was the last thing I would do just before leaving the house. Miss Cornelia came and pressed my hair and then shaped it into what felt like a hundred corkscrews, all lying flat against my head so that my hat would fit properly.

At breakfast, I was seated in my usual spot, with my mother at one end of the table, my father at the other, and me in the middle, so that as they talked to me or to each other I would shift my head to the left or to the right and get a good look at them. We were having a Sunday breakfast, a breakfast as if we had just come back from Sunday-morning services: salt fish and antroba and souse and hard-boiled eggs, and even special Sunday bread from Mr. Daniel, our baker. On Sundays, we ate this big breakfast at eleven o'clock and then we didn't eat again until four o'clock, when we had our big Sunday dinner. It was the best breakfast we ate, and the only breakfast better than that was the one we ate on Christmas morning. My parents were in a festive mood, saying what a wonderful time I would have in my new life, what a wonderful opportunity this was for me, and what a lucky person I was. They were eating away as they talked, my father's false teeth making that clop-clop sound like a horse on a walk as he talked, my mother's mouth going

---

3. *British Guiana:* (gē an′ ə): now Guyana, a country on the northeast coast of South America.

4. *obeah woman:* (ō′ bē ə): woman who practices sorcery and magic.

up and down like a donkey's as she chewed each mouthful thirty-two times. (I had long ago counted, because it was something she made me do also, and I was trying to see if this was just one of her rules that applied only to me.) I was looking at them with a smile on my face but disgust in my heart when my mother said, "Of course, you are a young lady now, and we won't be surprised if in due time you write to say that one day soon you are to be married."

Without thinking, I said, with bad feeling that I didn't hide very well, "How absurd!"

My parents immediately stopped eating and looked at me as if they had not seen me before. My father was the first to go back to his food. My mother continued to look. I don't know what went through her mind, but I could see her using her tongue to dislodge food stuck in the far corners of her mouth.

Many of my mother's friends now came to say goodbye to me, and to wish me God's blessings. I thanked them and showed the proper amount of joy at the glorious things they pointed out to me that my future held and showed the proper amount of sorrow at how much my parents and everyone else who loved me would miss me. My body ached a little at all this false going back and forth, at all this taking in of people gazing at me with heads tilted, love and pity on their smiling faces. I could have left without saying any goodbyes to them and I wouldn't have missed it. There was only one person I felt I should say goodbye to, and that was my former friend Gwen. We had long ago drifted apart, and when I saw her now my heart nearly split in two with embarrassment at the feelings I used to have for her and things I had shared with her. She had now degenerated into complete silliness, hardly able to complete a sentence without putting in a few giggles. Along with the giggles, she had developed some other schoolgirl traits that she did not have when she was actually a schoolgirl, so beneath her were such things then. When we were saying our goodbyes, it was all I could do not to say cruelly, "Why are you behaving like such a monkey?" Instead, I put everything on a friendly plain, wishing her well and the best in the future. It was then that she told me that she was more or less engaged to a boy she had known while growing up early on in Nevis,[5] and that soon, in a year or so, they would be married. My reply to her was "Good luck," and she thought I meant her well, so she grabbed me and said, "Thank you. I knew you would be happy about it." But to me it was as if she had shown me a high point from which she was going to jump

---

5. *Nevis:* (nev ′is): island in the British West Indies in the Leeward Islands.

and hoped to land in one piece on her feet. We parted, and when I turned away I didn't look back.

My mother had arranged with a stevedore to take my trunk to the jetty ahead of me. At ten o'clock on the dot, I was dressed, and we set off for the jetty. An hour after that, I would board a launch that would take me out to sea, where I then would board the ship. Starting out, as if for old time's sake and without giving it a thought, we lined up in the old way: I walking between my mother and my father. I loomed way above my father and could see the top of his head. We must have made a strange sight: a grown girl all dressed up in the middle of a morning, in the middle of the week, walking in step in the middle between her two parents, for people we didn't know stared at us. It was all of half an hour's walk from our house to the jetty, but I was passing through most of the years of my life. We passed by the house where Miss Dulcie, the seamstress that I had been apprenticed to for a time, lived, and just as I was passing by, a wave of bad feeling for her came over me, because I suddenly remembered that in the months I spent with her all she had me do was sweep the floor, which was always full of threads and pins and needles, and I never seemed to sweep it clean enough to please her. Then she would send me to the store to buy buttons or thread, though I was only allowed to do this if I was given a sample of the button or thread, and then she would find fault even though they were an exact match of the samples she had given me. And all the while she said to me, "A girl like you will never learn to sew properly, you know." At the time, I don't suppose I minded it, because it was customary to treat the first-year apprentice with such scorn, but now I placed on the dustheap of my life Miss Dulcie and everything that I had had to do with her.

We were soon on the road that I had taken to school, to church, to Sunday school, to choir practice, to Brownie meetings, to Girl Guide meetings, to meet a friend. I was five years old when I first walked on this road unaccompanied by someone to hold my hand. My mother had placed three pennies in my little basket, which was a duplicate of her bigger basket, and sent me to the chemist's shop to buy a pennyworth of senna leaves, a pennyworth of eucalyptus leaves, and a pennyworth of camphor. She then instructed me on what side of the road to walk, where to make a turn, where to cross, how to look carefully before I crossed, and if I met anyone that I knew to politely pass greetings and keep on my way. I was wearing a freshly ironed yellow dress that had printed on it scenes of acrobats flying through the air and swinging on a trapeze. I had just had a bath, and after it, instead of powdering me with my baby-smelling talcum powder, my mother had, as a special favor, let me use her own talcum powder, which smelled quite perfumy and came in a can that had painted on it people going out to dinner in nineteenth-century London and was called Mazie. How it pleased me to walk out the door and bend my head down to sniff at myself and see that I smelled just like my mother. I went to the chemist's shop, and he had to come from behind the counter and bend down to hear what it was that I wanted to buy, my voice was so little and timid then. I went back just the way I had come, and when I walked into the yard and presented my basket with its three packages to my mother, her eyes filled with tears and she swooped me up and held me high in the air and said that I was wonderful and good and that there would never be anybody better. If I had just conquered Persia, she couldn't have been more proud of me.

We passed by our church—the church in which I had been christened and received and had sung in the junior choir. We passed by a house in which a girl I used to like and was sure I couldn't live without had lived. Once, when she had mumps, I went to visit her against my mother's wishes, and we sat on her bed and ate the cure of roasted, buttered sweet potatoes that had been placed on her swollen jaws, held there by a piece of white cloth. I don't know how, but my mother found out about it, and I don't know how, but she put an end to our friendship. Shortly after, the girl moved with her family across the sea to somewhere else. We passed the doll store, where I would go with my mother when I was little and point out the doll I wanted that year for Christmas. We passed the store where I bought the much-fought-over shoes I wore to church to be received in. We passed the bank. On my sixth birthday, I was given, among other things, the present of a sixpence.[6] My mother and I then went to this bank, and with the sixpence I opened my own savings account. I was given a little gray book with my name in big letters on it, and in the balance column it said "6d." Every Saturday morning after that, I was given a sixpence— later a shilling,[7] and later a two-and-sixpence piece—and I would take it to the bank for deposit. I had never been allowed to withdraw even a farthing from my bank account until just a few weeks before I was to

---

6. *sixpence:* former British unit of money. The symbol for pence is "d."

7. *shilling:* former British unit of money equal to twelve pence. The farthing, mentioned later, is equal to one-fourth of a penny. A pound is a unit of money in several countries.

leave; then the whole account was closed out, and I received from the bank the sum of six pounds ten shillings and two and a half pence.

We passed the office of the doctor who told my mother three times that I did not need glasses, that if my eyes were feeling weak a glass of carrot juice a day would make them strong again. This happened when I was eight. And so every day at recess I would run to my school gate and meet my mother, who was waiting for me with a glass of juice from carrots she had just grated and then squeezed, and I would drink it and then run back to meet my chums. I knew there was nothing at all wrong with my eyes, but I had recently read a story in *The Schoolgirl's Own Annual* in which the heroine, a girl a few years older than I was then, cut such a figure to my mind with the way she was always adjusting her small, round, horn-rimmed glasses that I felt I must have a pair exactly like them. When it became clear that I didn't need glasses, I began to complain about the glare of the sun being too much for my eyes, and I walked around with my hands shielding them—especially in my mother's presence. My mother then bought for me a pair of sunglasses with the exact horn-rimmed frames I wanted, and how I enjoyed the gestures of blowing on the lenses, wiping them with the hem of my uniform, adjusting the glasses when they slipped down my nose, and just removing them from their case and putting them on. In three weeks, I grew tired of them and they found a nice resting place in a drawer, along with some other things that at one time or another I couldn't live without.

We passed the store that sold only grooming aids, all imported from England. This store had in it a large porcelain dog—white, with black spots all over and a red ribbon of satin tied around its neck. The dog sat in front of a white porcelain bowl that was always filled with fresh water, and it sat in such a way that it looked as if it had just taken a long drink. When I was a small child, I would ask my mother, if ever we were near this store, to please take me to see the dog, and I would stand in front of it, bent over slightly, my hands resting on my knees, and stare at it and stare at it. I thought this dog more beautiful and more real than any actual dog I had ever seen or any actual dog I would ever see. I must have outgrown my interest in the dog, for when it disappeared I never asked what became of it. We passed the library, and if there was anything on this walk that I might have wept over leaving, this most surely would have been the thing. My mother had been a member of the library long before I was born. And since she took me everywhere with her when I was quite little, when she went to the library she took me along there, too. I would sit in her lap very quietly as she read books that she did not want to take home with her. I could not read the words yet, but just the way they looked on the page was interesting to me. Once, a book she was reading had a large picture of a man in it, and when I asked her who he was she told me that he was Louis Pasteur and that the book was about his life. It stuck in my mind, because she said it was because of him that she boiled my milk to purify it before I was allowed to drink it, that it was his idea, and that that was why the process was called pasteurizaton. One of the things I had put away in my mother's old trunk in which she kept all my childhood things was my library card. At that moment, I owed sevenpence in overdue fees.

As I passed by all these places, it was as if I were in a dream, for I didn't notice the people coming and going in and out of them, I didn't feel my feet touch ground, I didn't even feel my own body—I just saw these places as if they were hanging in the air, not having top or bottom, and as if I had gone in and out of them all in the same moment. The sun was bright; the sky was blue and just above my head. We then arrived at the jetty.

My heart now beat fast, and no matter how hard I tried, I couldn't keep my mouth from falling open and my nostrils from spreading to the ends of my face. My old fear of slipping between the boards of the jetty and falling into the dark-green water where the dark-green eels lived came over me. When my father's stomach started to go bad, the doctor had recommended a walk every evening right after he ate his dinner. Sometimes he would take me with him. When he took me with him, we usually went to the jetty, and there he would sit and talk to the night watchman about cricket or some other thing that didn't interest me, because it was not personal; they didn't talk about their wives, or their children, or their parents, or about any of their likes and dislikes. They talked about things in such a strange way, and I didn't see what they found funny, but sometimes they made each other laugh so much that their guffaws would bound out to sea and send back an echo. I was always sorry when we got to the jetty and saw that the night watchman on duty was the one he enjoyed speaking to; it was like being locked up in a book filled with numbers and diagrams and what-ifs. For the thing about not being able to understand and enjoy what they were saying was I had nothing to take my mind off my fear of slipping in between the boards of the jetty.

Now, too, I had nothing to take my mind off what was happening to me. My mother and my father—I was leaving them forever. My home on an island—I was leaving it forever. What to make of everything? I felt a familiar hollow space inside. I felt I was being held down against my will. I felt I was burning up from head to toe. I felt that someone was tearing me up into little pieces and soon I would be able to see all the little pieces as they floated out into nothing in the deep blue sea. I didn't know whether to laugh or cry. I could see that it would be better not to think too clearly about any one thing. The launch was being made ready to take me, along with some other passengers, out to the ship that was anchored in the sea. My father paid our fares, and we joined a line of people waiting to board. My mother checked my bag to make sure that I had my passport, the money she had given me, and a sheet of paper placed between some pages in my Bible on which were written the names of the relatives—people I had not known existed—with whom I would live in England. Across from the jetty was a wharf, and some stevedores were loading and unloading barges. I don't know why seeing that struck me so, but suddenly a wave of strong feeling came over me, and my heart swelled with a great gladness as the words ''I shall never see this again'' spilled out inside me. But then, just as quickly, my heart shriveled up and the words ''I shall never see this again'' stabbed at me. I don't know what stopped me from falling in a heap at my parents' feet.

When we were all on board, the launch headed out to sea. Away from the jetty, the water became the customary blue, and the launch left a wide path in it that looked like a road. I passed by sounds and smells that were so familiar that I had long ago stopped paying any attention to them. But now here they were, and the ever-present ''I shall never see this again'' bobbed up and down inside me. There was the sound of the seagull diving down into the water and coming up with something silverish in its mouth. There was the smell of the sea and the sight of small pieces of rubbish floating around in it. There were boats filled with fishermen coming in early. There was the sound of their voices as they shouted greetings to each other. There was the hot sun, there was the blue sea, there was the blue sky. Not very far away, there was the white sand of the shore, with the run-down houses all crowded in next to each other, for in some places only poor people lived near the shore. I was seated in the launch between my parents, and when I realized that I was gripping their hands tightly I glanced quickly to see if they were looking at me with scorn, for I felt sure that they must have known of my never-see-this-again feelings. But instead my father kissed me on the forehead and my mother kissed me on the mouth, and they both gave over their hands to me, so that I could grip them as much as I wanted. I was on the verge of feeling that it had all been a mistake, but I remembered that I wasn't a child anymore, and that now when I made up my mind about something I had to see it through. At that moment, we came to the ship, and that was that.

The good-byes had to be quick, the captain said. My mother introduced herself to him and then introduced me. She told him to keep an eye on me, for I had never gone this far away from home on my own. She gave him a letter to pass on to the captain of the next ship that I would board in Barbados. They walked me to my cabin, a small space that I would share with someone else—a woman I did not know. I had never before slept in a room with someone I did not know. My father kissed me goodbye and told me to be good and to write home often. After he said this, he looked at me, then looked at the floor and swung his left foot, then looked at me again. I could see that he wanted to say something else, something that he had never said to me before, but then he just turned and walked away. My mother said, "Well," and then she threw her arms around me. Big tears streamed down her face, and it must have been that—for I could not bear to see my mother cry— which started me crying, too. She then tightened her arms around me and held me to her close, so that I felt that I couldn't breathe. With that, my tears dried up and I was suddenly on my guard. "What does she want now?" I said to myself. Still holding me close to her, she said, in a voice that raked across my skin, "It doesn't matter what you do or where you go, I'll always be your mother and this will always be your home."

I dragged myself away from her and backed off a little, and then I shook myself, as if to wake myself out of a stupor. We looked at each other for a long time with smiles on our faces, but I know the opposite of that was in my heart. As if responding to some invisible cue, we both said, at the very same moment, "Well." Then my mother turned around and walked out the cabin door. I stood there for I don't know how long, and then I remembered that it was customary to stand on deck and wave to your relatives who were returning to shore. From the deck, I could not see my father, but I could see my mother facing the ship, her eyes searching to pick me out. I removed from my bag a red cotton handkerchief that she had earlier given me for this purpose, and I waved it wildly in the air. Recognizing me immediately, she waved just as wildly, and we continued to do this until she became just a dot in the matchbox-size launch swallowed up in the big blue sea.

I went back to my cabin and lay down on my berth. Everything trembled as if it had a spring at its very center. I could hear the small waves lap-lapping around the ship. They made an unexpected sound, as if a vessel filled with liquid had been placed on its side and now was slowly emptying out.

Responding to the Story

It is difficult to read Jamaica Kincaid's story without thinking of separations in one's own life. "I shall never see this again," she thinks, both joyfully and sadly. Describe the recollections you had reading this story or just the feelings the story brought you. If you want to put the feelings in a poem or, perhaps, a drawing, go ahead.

Exploring the Author's Craft

Sometimes being a good writer is just having the willingness and patience to recall and write everything down in a clear manner. And sometimes being a good writer is just being honest; it's a great start, in any case.

Without looking at "A Walk to the Jetty" again, write two or three paragraphs spelling out the sense impressions, the details, the ideas, and the varied feelings that stood out to you from this piece. The more you can recall from the writing, the more of a tribute it is to the author's craft.

Writing Workshop

The narrator of this story describes her room, the only room she had ever lived in, in exquisite detail. "Everywhere I looked stood something that had meant a lot to me, that had given me pleasure at some point, or could remind me of a time that was a happy time," she writes. And she names specific things. She goes on to see that she was also glad she was leaving this place, but let's leave that aside for a moment.

Name the specifics—and describe them—of a place you know intimately. It may be your own room, or another room in your home.

Alternate Media Response

This story should have evoked many feelings. It's a tribute to the author that one might never have seen any place like Antigua, in the West Indies, but one can still "feel" this story. Here's your chance to show that feeling in your own art form—a drawing, a dance, a drama, a short film. Let yourself go.

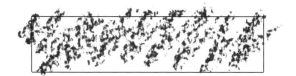

Responding to
Part Four

1. Being out in the world involves contacts with persons outside of one's familiar circle of family and friends, contacts that may be exhilarating, puzzling, frightening, or painful, but always challenging. What challenges do Marian in "A Visit of Charity" and the narrator in "Initiation" meet and how well do they meet them, in your opinion?

2. Leaving one's childhood home is a necessary part of growing up, but those who leave and those who are left behind have varying emotions. Compare and contrast the emotions of parent and child in "Teenage Wasteland" and "A Walk to the Jetty."

3. The mood or atmosphere of "On the Late Bus" is quite different from the mood of "A Walk to the Jetty," or is it? Try to think of a single word that could describe the mood of each story. Do you come up with a different word for each one?

4. Which author in Part Four would you most like to meet and talk with and why?

Acknowledgments

"Betty" from *Dancing Girls* by Margaret Atwood. Copyright © 1977, 1982 by O. W. Toad Ltd. Reprinted by permission of Simon & Schuster, Inc., and by McClelland & Stewart, Inc.

"Raymond's Run" from *Gorilla, My Love* by Toni Cade Bambara. Copyright © 1972 by Toni Cade Bambara. Reprinted by permission of Random House, Inc.

"A Veil of Water" by Amy Boesky. Reprinted by permission of the author.

"A Christmas Memory" from *Breakfast at Tiffany's* by Truman Capote. Copyright © 1956 by Truman Capote. Reprinted by permission of Random House, Inc.

"The Man in the Casket" by Beth Cassavell. Reprinted by permission of the author.

"Eleven" from *Woman Hollering Creek*. Copyright © 1991 by Sandra Cisneros. Published in the United States by Vintage Books, a division of Random House, Inc., New York, and simultaneously in Canada by Random House of Canada Ltd., Toronto. Originally published in hardcover by Random House, Inc., New York, in 1991. Reprinted by permission of Susan Bergholz Literary Services, New York.

"Marigolds" by Eugenia Collier. Originally published in the *Negro Digest*, November 1969. Reprinted by permission of the author.

"Guess What? I Almost Kissed My Father Good Night" by Robert Cormier from *Eight Plus One*, © 1980 Robert Cormier. Published by Pantheon Books, reprinted by permission of Random House, Inc.

Excerpt from page 11 of *An American Childhood* by Annie Dillard. Copyright © 1987 by Annie Dillard. Reprinted by permission of HarperCollins Publishers Inc.

"On the Late Bus" from *Sarah's Laughter and Other Stories* by Susan Engberg. Copyright © 1991 by Sarah Engberg. Reprinted by permission of Alfred A. Knopf, Inc.

"A Private Talk with Holly" by Henry G. Felsen. Originally published in *Seventeen®* magazine, September 1981.

"The Scarlet Ibis" by James Hurst from *The Atlantic Monthly*, July 1960. Copyright 1988 by James Hurst. Reprinted by permission of the author.

"Louisa, Please Come Home" copyright © 1960 by Shirley Jackson. From *Come Along with Me* by Shirley Jackson. Used by permission of Viking Penguin, a division of Penguin Books USA Inc.

"A Walk to the Jetty" from *Annie John* by Jamaica Kincaid. Copyright © 1984, 1985 by Jamaica Kincaid. Reprinted by permission of Farrar, Straus & Giroux, Inc.

"And Summer Is Gone" by Susie Kretschmer. Originally published in *Literary Cavalcade*. Reprinted by permission of the author.

Index of Authors and Titles

"Adjö Means Good-bye," 71
"And Summer Is Gone," 206
"Asphalt," 147
Atwood, Margaret, 250

Bambara, Toni Cade, 23
"Bass, the River, and Sheila Mant, The," 167
"Betty," 250
Boesky, Amy, 223
"Broken Chain," 197

Capote, Truman, 76
Cassavell, Beth, 62
"Christmas Memory, A," 76
Cisneros, Sandra, 3
Collier, Eugenia, 137
Cormier, Robert, 125

"Eleven," 3
Engberg, Susan, 267

Felsen, Henry Gregor, 113
"Guess What? I Almost Kissed My Father Goodnight," 125

"Her First Ball," 159
Hurst, James, 89

"I Go Along," 190
"Initiation," 239

Jackson, Shirley, 45
Kincaid, Jamaica, 276
Kretschmer, Susie, 206

"Louisa, Please Come Home," 45

"Man in the Casket, The," 62
Mansfield, Katherine, 159
"Marigolds," 137
McCullers, Carson, 102
"Mother in Mannville, A," 14

Norris, Leslie, 117

"On the Late Bus," 267
"Osage Orange Tree, The," 175

Peck, Richard, 190
Plath, Sylvia, 239
Pollack, Frederick, 147
"Private Talk with Holly, A," 113

Rawlings, Marjorie Kinnan, 14
"Raymond's Run," 23
Ríos, Alberto Alvaro, 7

"Scarlet Ibis, The," 89
"Secret Lion, The," 7
"Shaving," 117
Soto, Gary, 197
Stafford, William, 175
Storr, Catherine, 183

"Sucker," 102
"Surprised," 183

Tan, Amy, 32
"Teenage Wasteland," 228
"Two Kinds," 32
Tyler, Anne, 228

"Veil of Water, A," 223
"Visit of Charity, A," 215

"Walk to the Jetty, A," 276
Welty, Eudora, 215
Wetherell, W. D., 167

Young, Carrie A., 71